MW00654409

DENYING THE ALPHA

EVERNIGHT PUBLISHING ®

www.evernightpublishing.com

Copyright© 2019

Evernight Publishing

Editor: Audrey Bobak

Cover Art: Jay Aheer

ISBN: 978-1-77339-934-8

ALL RIGHTS RESERVED

DENYING THE ALPHA

DENYING THE ALPHA

Caleb by Loralynne Summers

Crossing Boundaries by Rose Wulf

Guarding What's Hers by Kait Gamble

The Librarian and Her Dragon by Doris O'Connor

Eagle's Seduction by Elyzabeth M. VaLey

Make Her Purr by Sam Crescent and Stacey Espino

Claiming the Coyote by Roberta Winchester

My Very Soul by Tesla Storm

Bearly Caught by Sarah Marsh

DENYING THE ALPHA

Loralynne Summers

Chapter One

"You can't do this!"

"Are you crazy?"

"What would your father say?"

Caleb held his hand up, hoping to silence the room without resorting to using his Alpha dominance. That last comment stung a bit, but he had expected backlash from the den, especially the older members.

"Look, we all know that the mountain is becoming too dense. This was always in the long-term maintenance plan for the forest that our ancestors initiated when they banded together and settled here." He said the last with a pointed look toward the elder who'd spoken out last. "We need to clear out some trees, make more room for cabins. The den is growing beyond the handful of families we started with years ago. And we need money. This kills two birds with one stone. We get a percentage of the logging sales, which will offset the costs of building, and we can expand the tourist lodging, increasing our bottom-line revenue. Unless some of you want to move off the mountain and get jobs in the city?"

A few of the younger members laughed lightly. Caleb gave a heavy sigh.

"Listen. This has to happen. It's going to happen. Anyone who wishes to permanently relocate higher up the mountain, I'll help you build your new cabin with none of the power or running water or communication that you all have come to enjoy. But you can't stop the inevitable. Developments are slowly being built closer and closer to the mountain. Either we keep the humans where we want them, or we run out of room and places to shift. And keeping them at bay requires money."

There were grumbles, but nobody decided to talk back to him this time.

"You all had a chance to help me with this, you knew it was coming. After some research conducted by Ryan and myself, I've been in negotiations with Connors Logging. They'll be here in two weeks to start. I'll be marking areas for clear-cutting and thinning. You're all being given a map that shows these areas so there will be no confusion. Anyone caught in bear form within a hundred yards of the work zones is in for serious shit with me. Shifting is restricted to the top half of the mountain while the loggers are here."

He moved for the door and grabbed the handful of maps from Ryan, who served as his right-hand man. Caleb was personally going to make sure that each family received one, so nobody could try to feign ignorance later on. The elders didn't shift as often anymore but were rather set in their ways, and there were a few that could potentially cause trouble and try to give the loggers a scare, despite his decree.

What he didn't tell the den was that he'd selected this company specifically because of their relationship with shifters—the owner, and at least some of the employees, were aware of shifters or even shifters themselves. They'd been recommended from another den in a neighboring county. Likely as not, any antics his bears might get up to would not have the effect they'd hope for.

"Well, that went about as expected," Ryan commented as the last member left the lobby of the visitor's center. It was the only room large enough to hold them all now. One of the buildings that Caleb intended to add was a meeting hall, which could also serve as a place to hold small weddings to increase income.

"Tell me about it," he grumbled. "The elders hate change. They're used to being more solitary. It's how they grew up. Having so many bears in a relatively small territory is still new to them, even if it's been several decades. We grew up with it, but we're still ironing out the kinks. The world is shrinking. If we don't find a way to keep our woods, we won't have any."

Ryan grasped his shoulder. "My grandfather and the others are stubborn, but everyone knows the mountain needs maintenance. And they *did* agree to follow you when your father died and you showed the same dominant power, instead of voting for a different leader. I know it feels weird to use the terms that wolves do, but you *are* our Alpha. They'll come around. You'll see."

****

"I'm looking for George," Caleb said to a man climbing down from a truck.

"At the front," he said, jerking his head.

"Thanks." Caleb worked his way among the men and the equipment being unloaded along the access road. He was rather impressed. George's email had said they'd be here to start at seven-thirty AM and Caleb hadn't expected the crew to arrive at seven. Apparently, he intended to have his crew actually in the trucks and on the trees at seven-thirty.

As he reached the lead flatbed, he saw a decidedly feminine silhouette and paused. Though dressed in work boots, heavy jeans, and a yellow vest over her sweatshirt, there was no way that ass was a man's. The pink—*pink!*—work gloves hanging out of a back pocket were also a bit of a dead giveaway. He wondered briefly if she was an inspector, here to double- and triple-check the paperwork that he'd already checked a hundred times over.

"God damn it, Peterson, if I have to fucking climb up there and unhook that fucking skidder for you I'm going to fucking beat your skinny little ass with your own prick. What's the fucking holdup?"

Caleb blinked at the slew of profanity spewing forth from her and nearly choked on his coffee.

A young man poked his head out of the window of the vehicle, a grin on his face.

"Sorry, George. I forgot to release one of the tie-downs. Coming down now."

Caleb's brows drew together as the woman laughed.

"I know I dragged you from your beauty sleep, little brother, but seriously, thanks for jumping in to help out at the last minute."

The guy in the cab—Peterson—flashed a thumbs-up as the engine roared to life and he expertly backed the large machine down off the flatbed in the blink of an eye, though he looked barely old enough to shave.

Caleb cleared his throat, and the woman turned around.

"Oh! Hey, sorry, didn't see you there. How can I help you?"

"I'm Caleb Michonne. I'm looking for George."

"Well, you found her."

"You're … George … Connors?" The words came out slowly in his confusion.

"The one and only," she answered, a defiant look in her eyes.

"And thank God for that. Her name really is Georgia, by the way, but she won't answer to it," Peterson said as he walked by.

She spun, throwing a playful jab at her brother, who had already dodged out of reach.

"Pete, I swear to Christ I'm going to leave you on this mountain to get eaten by a bear!"

"Oooh, you promise? You know I love me a big hairy Daddy bear."

Pete winked at Caleb before heading off to join the rest of the men donning work gloves and safety gear. Flustered, Caleb returned his attention to George, who stood with her hands on her hips and a look of silent challenge on her face.

"I've been climbing trees and running this equipment since I was tall enough—" she began, but he held his hand up and shook his head. Her eyes narrowed, but she stopped talking.

"There's no need for explanations. If you're the person I've been emailing the past few days, that's all I need to know. In this business, you wouldn't be in your position if you weren't capable."

She held his gaze a moment before taking a deep breath and giving a slight nod.

"Good. Now let's go over the map. I know you walked the property with my dad and I meant to come out here in person sooner, but with him getting laid up last week, my brothers and I have been running around like crazy. I do apologize for that."

Her demeanor quickly became professional as they reconfirmed which areas would be cleared and which thinned. They walked toward the small motorhome that served as a mobile office. One of her emails had explained the necessity of needing room for it. Due to the location and terrain, the equipment she traveled with provided her up-to-the-minute weather and satellite information, allowing them to wring every minute of work possible out of the day in the event of a questionable forecast.

As George powered up the laptop on the counter, he studied her, trying to figure her out. She still projected an air of combativeness, her stance one of tension, as if she were permanently in the "fight" mode of "fight or flight."

Of course she is, he thought to himself. *She's a young woman in a field dominated by men. How many clients have dismissed her simply because of what's between her legs? Would they treat her the same if she wasn't so fucking gorgeous?* While she may not meet the guidelines of runway model looks, George was magnificent as far as Caleb was concerned. Golden-brown hair was pinned neatly in some sort of fancy twist thing on the back of her head. He didn't know what to call it but it looked oddly elegant in contrast to her chosen profession. He'd have expected her to have short hair. Her height rivaled his own—the top of her head was nearly at his nose, and he stood six-foot-four. Though clad in work clothes and a loose sweatshirt, she had a clearly muscular build and broad shoulders.

Now that they were inside, away from all the other crew members and machinery, her scent hit him like a sledgehammer. His pulse quickened as he inhaled deeply, the smell of earth and pine and fresh air mixed with a musky undertone and a hint of strawberry—

shampoo perhaps?—to make one delicious and tantalizing smell that was all her.

And it told him that she was *his*.

The one he'd been looking for.

His mate.

"Can I help you with something?" she snapped, glaring at him.

Crap. He'd been caught staring. He swallowed, brain scrambling to backpedal and be polite, be human, not an animal that was only interested in one thing at the moment.

"Apologies. I was only trying to figure out why you look the way you do."

"I wear makeup and do my hair in ways that won't offend men's sensitive egos and upset them," she said with a sigh.

"I ... what?" That wasn't what he'd meant at all, though he was, in fact, curious about those things as well.

"Men expect women to look and act a certain way. I may only be twenty-nine, but I learned quickly that no amount of knowledge or skill outweighs placating men's egos. Contract negotiations and meetings always go better when I look more ... acceptable."

Caleb scoffed. "Well, that's a load of shit. Anyone who spends five minutes listening to you would see the stupidity behind that mindset. And I meant your ... stature. Your build and your scent are ... but your brother is ... so small." He didn't normally trip over his words like this, but seeing as she was already on the defensive, he was afraid of upsetting her and getting things off to a very bad start.

Her expression softened slightly.

"Thank you for that. Most people only talk, they don't listen. My mother's side of the family carries the shifter gene, but I lost out on that particular gift. I'm just built like a brick wall without the extra benefits. Pete is my half-brother. There's no extra genes in that pool. He's just a skinny little Irishman."

"I'm sorry to hear that. I bet your bear would be every bit as beautiful as you." It was a cheesy line, he knew it the moment the words left his mouth. Regardless, her breath caught and their gazes locked.

"You actually mean that, don't you?" she whispered.

"Yes," he replied softly.

"Most people are just being polite when they say things like that."

"I never say anything I don't believe is true."

"I believe that."

What he really believed was that she lied about not being a shifter. He didn't understand how all the signs could be there, yet she implied that she'd never shifted, and as far as she was concerned, she was human.

She didn't smell human.

His bear didn't give a damn what she thought she was, as long as she was his.

They stood side by side, staring at each other in silence as tension grew until a knock on the door made her jump. Pete stuck his head in.

"Umm, guys? Mr. Michonne? I don't know what's going on, but a couple of the guys are acting weird. They're saying you're doing it…" He trailed off, gaze darting back and forth between Caleb and George.

Caleb cleared his throat, his gaze returning to George. "My apologies. I shall reassure them momentarily. Ask them to wait nearby, please?" With a conscious effort, he reined in his bear. The beast was going wild inside him, wanting to claim Georgia and make her his, and making sure every bear in the vicinity knew it by sending out ridiculous amounts of dominant power. Thankfully, most of his own den was either still sleeping or too far up the mountain to be affected.

"And apologies to you, Ms. Connors. I was out of line. I shall leave you and your crew to get to work. You have my contact information should you need anything."

He turned and headed out the door. He needed to haul ass to the top of the mountain and away from her before he did something he'd regret.

****

Georgia blew out a heavy breath the moment the door clicked behind Caleb.

She'd been doing fine ignoring him—she was used to men checking her out, after all—until she realized he didn't look at her like she was a curiosity. He looked at her like a man dying of thirst might eye a glass of water. That, she didn't know how to handle.

"Sis? You okay?" Pete hadn't moved far from the door, as if he were afraid to come near her.

"Yeah, I'm good. He just threw me off, that's all."

"Can't say as I blame you. He's an especially scrumptious specimen. I'm willing to bet he could crack a walnut with his ass."

"Believe me, I noticed." She laughed.

"And his arms are like, twice the size of my head," Pete continued.

"Your *mom's* arms are twice the size of your head, twig-boy." Her brother laughed but still didn't move from the wall he leaned against. Georgia cocked her head. "What's wrong?"

"I'm just waiting for you to be normal again."

"Umm, I *am* normal? My cousins won that roulette spin, remember?"

"Then why are your eyes glowing?"

"Huh?"

She went to the bathroom and sure enough, her usually dark-brown eyes were lighter, flecked with gold, and nearly radiant. Other than being a bit flushed, the rest of her face seemed to be the same.

"What the hell is that shit? I feel fine." Georgia washed her face, cooling her heated cheeks. Checking her reflection again, she headed out to the crew while fixing her hair into a braid instead of a French twist that would never fit comfortably under her hardhat. It was time to get to work. The sooner they started, the sooner she'd be done having to deal with Mr. Off-limits-sexypants-client.

Muscle-bound, dominant, and wanna-be-alpha men surrounded her day in and day out at work. She considered herself immune to them all at this point. Unfortunately, she needed to remind her hormones of that because she wanted to be all over him like white on rice. No matter what kind of vibes he'd been sending out, Caleb was a client. End of story.

Georgia hadn't gotten the full complement of special abilities, but by all accounts—and based on her own experiences and observations—minus the actual gift of shifting, she had many of the other traits. She could *feel* the power coming from Caleb, but knew not one bit of it had been directed toward her, as if he didn't dare try to influence her. It felt more like he was warning others away, a territorial display.

She'd seen it happen before with the few shifters she employed. They'd finished early one day due to weather, and had stopped at a diner. One of the men caught the scent of a woman in the building and immediately his disposition toward his workmates changed. He hadn't been an Alpha, so no surge of power even remotely close to the levels Caleb had thrown out, but the idea was the same.

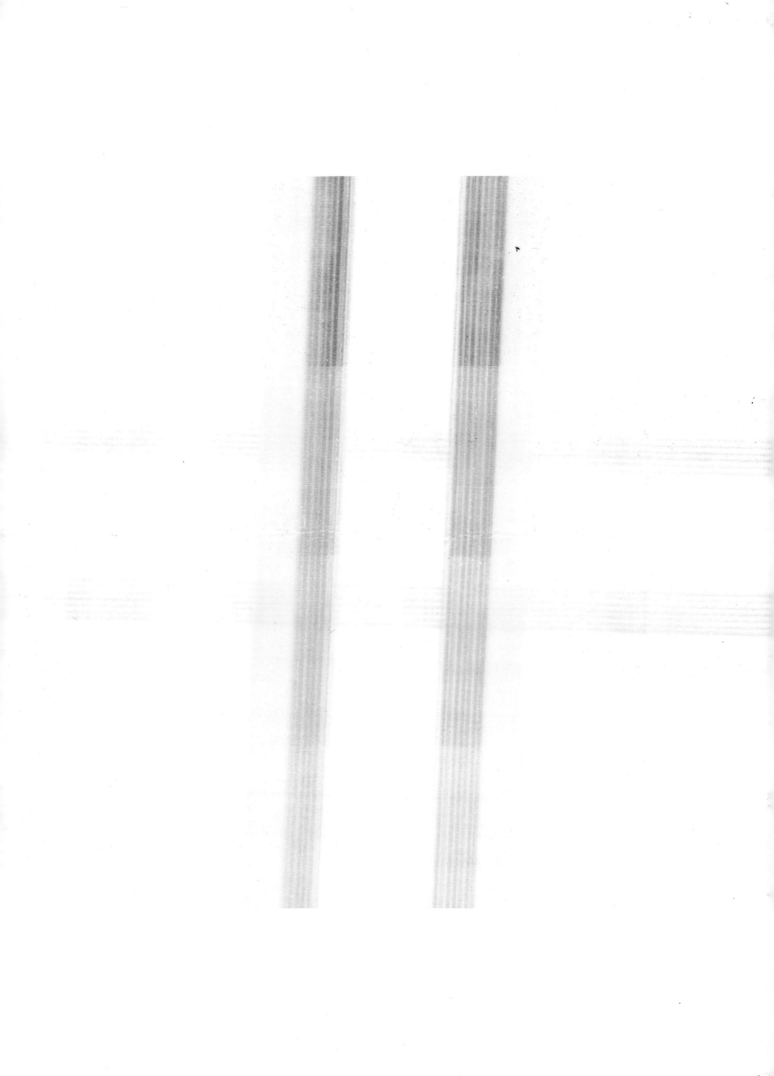

Whatever Caleb's reason may have been, Georgia wasn't interested.

That was her story and she'd stick to it.

****

Georgia sat at the table in the small motorhome she called her office and watched through the open door as the sun completed its slide below the horizon. After sending everyone home for the day, she'd made sure she was parked on level ground, dropped the stabilizers, and extended out the sides, opening up the interior and giving her more room. Peterson had ridden back with some of the crew, leaving her pickup here for whenever she got around to going home.

The first day of work was complete, and she was reviewing progress made versus the projected timeline, adjusting the plan for tomorrow. The den kept the access roads well-maintained, so they hadn't needed to do much work there. Add Caleb's clear and thorough marking of the trees, and they were ahead of where she'd expected to be on day one. Several dozen trees had already been felled, de-limbed, cut to length, and stacked. She'd need to have tractor trailers here sooner than expected to start hauling the wood away.

The storage space above the driving cab was outfitted with several screens, and she glanced up to them, trying to decide when to bring the trucks in. One screen showed a constant radar sweep, one was the local news (also for the weather) and one had the stock market, giving up-to-date lumber pricing.

In the back of the motorhome, the closet and the queen-sized bed were piled with boxes of gear. Hydraulic fluid, chainsaw blades, cleats, gloves, you name it, she had it. It was a long drive back to their actual office, and lost time meant lost money. Their company was the best for a reason. She'd tried to plan for every eventuality and they'd shelled out a lot of money to purchase a few motorhomes and equip them with satellite and everything else they added, but they'd paid for themselves in the long run with the increased productivity. Hers was the newest and most comfortable—she was the only one with a bed, but with no family to go home to in her tiny studio apartment, she sometimes crashed on-site. When the time had come to upgrade hers, she'd opted for an actual bed instead of the fold-down.

The sound of an all-terrain vehicle approaching caught her attention. She knew before his face appeared in the doorway that it would be Caleb.

"Come on in, Mr. Michonne. What can I help you with?" She didn't miss the way he swallowed hard at her words.

"I thought I'd see how much you were able to get done today and was surprised to see a truck here and lights on. So I stopped to make sure everything was okay." He looked around the inside of the motorhome and she saw his nostrils flare as he scented the air. "You shouldn't be here by yourself so late."

"Everything is fine, and the day went well. And I can take care of myself. But thank you, Mr. Michonne, for your concern."

He narrowed his eyes slightly. "I'd feel better if you called me Caleb."

"Which is why I won't."

"Excuse me?"

He clearly wasn't used to not getting his way. Georgia sighed as she closed her laptop.

"I'm not here to make you feel better. I'm here to do a job. We don't need to be friends for that to happen."

A low growl rumbled from him, but he remained where he stood inside the door, leaning against the sink for the small kitchenette. She stood, squaring her shoulders. His eyes raked her body and she held her ground. She'd ditched her sweatshirt hours ago and had taken off the sports bra she wore over her regular bra when she'd changed from her dirty clothes into a pair of sweatpants and a simple tank top. With the sun down, the air would cool quickly, but she was plenty warm in the light clothing.

"I don't care about the professionalism of it." He took a step closer, arms crossed. In the narrow space, he didn't have to go far to get to her. "Don't tell me you don't feel it too." Georgia was used to being the same height or, more often than not, taller than the men around her. To have this hulking bear looming over her gave her butterflies in the best of ways. Still, she refused to back down.

"That doesn't matter. Testicles aren't little balls of special that give you carte blanche to do whatever the fuck you want."

Caleb took a deep breath. He wore a muscle shirt—*of course,* she thought. A tribal pattern tattoo covered his left shoulder, and his biceps flexed as he dropped his arms and caged her against the table behind her. His body pressed up against hers and she felt the rock-hard evidence of his erection between them.

"God damn it, Georgia," he ground out between clenched teeth.

She took deep breaths, trying to steady her racing heart.

"Don't call me that," she whispered, eyes zeroed in on his lips.

"Stop me," he replied. The bastard grinned at her. He fucking grinned. When he said nothing further and didn't move, she lifted her eyes to his. They were a gorgeous light-brown, though at the moment they'd darkened considerably, either from lust or from the rise of his bear. Or probably a combination of both.

"Stop fighting it, Georgia," he whispered.

"Shut up," she breathed.

He quirked an eyebrow. *Christ, he's fucking sexy.* Despite their positions, and how heavily muscled he was, she didn't feel the slightest bit threatened. She noted the errant silver hairs dotting the black hair along his temples and dabbled throughout his neatly trimmed short beard. *What could he possibly want with me? He's easily ten years my senior. And why is he still single at his age? That probably says something.* Amusement lines crinkled the corners of his eyes and he dipped his head, sniffing at her neck. *Damned traitorous hormones.*

"Is there a problem, *Georgia*?"

"I said shut up!" she roared, shoving him backward. He grabbed her by the waist as he went and they crashed against the sink, knocking empty water bottles from the counter to the floor.

"There you are," he said softly, eyes filled with wonder. A large hand cupped her face, his calloused thumb stroking her cheek. Georgia's head swam. She felt dizzy, her ears rang, and her skin burned beneath Caleb's touch. She could see his lips moving but was incapable of processing the words. His head inched closer to hers, and their mouths collided.

Every reason why this was wrong fled from her brain. Georgia buried her hands in his thick hair and leaned into Caleb, plastering her body to his as her tongue delved into his mouth. With a groan, he slid a hand down her back and grabbed her ass, squeezing almost painfully tight. She hissed and bit his lower lip. He dropped his hand from her face and grabbed the other side of her ass, lifting her, and she wrapped herself around him. He took one long stride forward and with one arm swept the table clear. Her laptop and paperwork fell into a jumbled mess on the bench seating before he deposited her onto the surface.

Caleb leaned forward, forcing her down onto her back. Georgia rolled her hips, grinding against him, seeking relief from the need pulsing throughout her body. Warm hands made their way under her tank, kneading her breasts and teasing at her nipples through her bra.

"Caleb," she exhaled, arching into the caress.

He kissed a path along her jaw and then worked his way down her stomach, pushing her tank up. She lifted her shoulders and pulled it off while he unhooked her bra. His beard tickled her, raising goosebumps on her heated flesh as he trailed his tongue around a nipple, teasing the stiff bud.

"So perfect," he whispered, kissing her navel. She almost didn't hear him, didn't know if he'd even meant to say it aloud. His fingers toyed with the waistband of her pants and he lifted his head. The lust in his gaze made her breath catch.

"May I?"

It surprised her that he'd stopped to ask. She held his gaze, thinking about it. Maybe if they just got whatever this was out of their systems they'd be fine. Nobody would even need to know. Wham, bam, thank you ma'am, one-and-done and be on their merry ways. After all, she'd never been with a shifter, but according to her brother, they had ridiculous stamina. There was a first time for everything, right?

Chapter Two

Caleb thought he'd die if Georgia said no. He held his breath, frozen in place, the scent of her arousal so close and yet so far away, driving him mad.

"Yes," she said after what seemed like an eternity. He was unable to contain the growl that rumbled through him as he made quick work of her sweats and panties. When he'd caught sight of her without all that heavy clothing hiding her luscious curves, all logical thought had fled from him. It had been hard enough keeping his hands to himself this morning with all the crew around, but finding her here by herself, knowing that she reacted to him as well, he lost the will to fight.

One leg at a time, he kissed her from her ankles to the apex of her thighs. They were gorgeous legs, so long and toned, strong legs that he wanted to wrap around him and squeeze him tight as she screamed his name. His cock hardened further at the thought, painfully constricted by his jeans. Georgia squirmed under his ministrations, the evidence of her need coating her folds and beckoning to him. Caleb dropped to his knees. He leaned in and inhaled deeply, rumbling his pleasure as her scent enveloped him.

"Please," she gasped.

With a grin, he drove his tongue into her and then up to circle her clit. Her moan was nearly his undoing. He slipped one finger, and then another into her, working her, driving her higher. She draped her legs over his shoulders, pulling him closer, panting, whimpering as he held her at the edge.

"Damn it, Caleb!"

He hummed, sucking her clit and hooking his

fingers, finding the magic bundle of nerves that sent her skyrocketing. She shrieked, her thighs clamping around his head as her hips lifted from the edge of the table.

Caleb worked her through the orgasm as her breathing returned to normal.

"Thought you weren't going to call me that?" he smirked as he rose.

"Shut up." Her grin took any anger out of the words. She sat up, reaching for him, tugging at his shirt. He covered her hands with his own, stilling her. She cocked her head to the side, brows twitching in confusion—and he thought he saw a twinge of hurt in her eyes.

"I don't have anything with me. I hadn't expected … this."

Her eyes nearly glittered, and a decidedly wicked smile split her face.

"Then get on the table, cowboy."

Caleb laughed as she stood before him, completely perfect in all her naked glory. She spun them around, and the back of his legs bumped the table. Georgia popped the button on his jeans, dragging her fingers along his shaft as she pulled down the zipper with torturous slowness.

"Commando?" There was an unasked question in her voice.

"Makes it easier for shifting. And saves money on clothing to replace when I have to shift without the benefit of undressing first." The last word ended as a hiss when Georgia's hand wrapped around him. She gave him a nudge, and he settled on the edge of the table.

"Down." Her free hand was firm against his chest.

He fell back, and she worked his jeans down over his hips. In one swift move, Georgia's mouth encased his cock, taking him deep. She worked her hand at the base of his cock as she sucked, pulling back to drag her teeth over the sensitive edge of his head. He grabbed onto the edges of the table, groaning as he fought for control, wanting this to last. She withdrew, licking and teasing along the slit, collecting the pre-cum escaping him.

"Get a hold on him," she said, and he knew she referred to his bear. "If you fuck my place up, I'll fuck you up." Her hand squeezed. "And not in any way that you'd like."

She didn't wait for a response before resuming, tormenting him again with her teeth before pulling him even deeper into her mouth, flattening her tongue along the underside of his cock.

"Christ, Geor—" He couldn't finish her name, couldn't warn her as he exploded, his cum shooting down her throat. She took all he had to offer, maintaining the vacuum-like suction she had on him, drawing out his orgasm and milking every drop from him.

Caleb shuddered.

"Better now?"

Georgia stood and retrieved her clothing. In the blink of an eye, her demeanor changed. Gone was the warm, welcoming body. What was left was brusque, cold, and instantly doused any lingering hopes he might have had about getting her into his cabin tonight. Caleb sighed as he tucked himself back into his jeans. He'd seen a flickering of the bear he just knew must be hiding inside her, and he'd hoped the sudden, unplanned, and frenetic intimacy would help awaken her, trigger that call of the mate bond. Instead, she appeared to regret their actions.

"George," he said softly. He intentionally used her preferred nickname, trying to put her at ease. She turned to face him, and the distance in her eyes nearly killed him. He swallowed hard. "Do I owe you an apology?" *Fuck, did I completely misread the situation?*

Her shoulders dropped.

"No, Caleb." Georgia rubbed her face with her hands. "I agreed. I knew what I was doing." Her eyes remained downcast. "That was very unlike me. I shouldn't have let it happen. I ... I don't know what came over me. You're a client. I'll see if someone else can take over running this contract."

Like hell, he thought.

"There is no need for that. On my mother's grave, I swear to keep my distance. I apologize for any impropriety on my part. I did not think through my actions and how they might affect you."

"Most guys don't," she snapped, the fire back in her eyes as she glared at him. "And you never get punished for it. I'm under a fucking microscope every minute of my life because I've got tits and a cunt instead of a dick. Everything I do is judged by others in this business. Every. Fucking. Thing. Do you know how hard it was to get some of these guys to listen to me? It has taken me years to build my crew. I will *not* let you ruin this for me."

By the time she was finished, she was only inches from him. Her anger was beautiful to behold, and he knew she was the perfect mate for him. He needed her more than his next breath. But he wouldn't push her again, for fear of driving her away for good.

"On my life, I will never touch you again without your permission."

"Remember that vow."

Georgia grabbed the sides of Caleb's head and kissed him fiercely until they both were breathless. He groaned, rock-hard again despite the amazing blowjob she'd just given him.

"Now get the hell out of my trailer."
****

Georgia remained rooted in place until she could no longer hear the drone of Caleb's ATV. Finally, she took a deep breath and sat down, her entire body shaking from a combination of adrenaline, need, and some unknown feeling she couldn't quite put her finger on. What just happened between them could not happen again. She was kicking herself for allowing it to happen in the first place. The fire Caleb ignited within her was beyond anything she'd ever experienced with previous lovers. But she needed to keep him off-limits, at least until the contract was completed. And even then, for a good amount of time afterward still, for appearances' sake.

Christ, what is wrong with me? While the orgasm he'd given her had been phenomenal, the ache in her core hadn't dissipated. If anything, her need grew with each tick of the clock. She wanted to feel that magnificent, huge cock of his inside her, filling her. A moan escaped her at the visual that thought conjured, and she slipped a hand inside her pants. It only took a few flicks of her fingers over her clit to bring herself off again, as wound up as she was. The relief was slight, but enough for now. *This is not normal. What the fuck?*

She locked up the motorhome and hurried to her truck, taking off at a decidedly unsafe speed.
****

The dream was the same one she'd been having off and on since puberty. In the beginning, she'd had it whenever she spent time with her birth mother's family. As she'd grown older, it happened more when she was under extra stress, usually work-related and because of stupid ignorant men. It was the only time her dreams became lucid.

Her dream started the way it always did: she was running through the woods, searching, always searching, looking for someone or something, she didn't know what. All she knew was a sense of urgency, a *need* to find this elusive thing, a feeling of being lost and incomplete.

Tonight, someone ran beside her.

She could hear the crashing, the heavy footfalls, could almost feel the body heat, but couldn't see who it was.

Georgia spun, turning this way and that, and stopped suddenly, anything she could think of to try to catch a glimpse of who or what was next to her. Each time she did, she failed. It felt as though the being was right behind her, part of her shadow, right on her heels every time she strayed from forward.

"Show yourself!" she screamed in frustration. "Who are you? What do you want?"

Her own voice echoed back at her. Anger drove her to slam her fist into a tree. It shattered into millions of tiny splinters, spraying outward in slow-motion.

An incessant buzzing began, ringing in her ears as if a swarm of mosquitoes had taken up residence inside her head. She clapped her hands over her ears, and the buzzing was accompanied by banging. Finally, she heard a voice through the din.

"Georgia Leah Connors! I swear to God I'm going to bust this door down if you don't open it!"

Confused, she looked around for her brother. The forest disappeared, and she found herself on the floor of her bedroom, tangled in the sheet.

Now fully awake, Georgia blinked, dropping her hands. The buzzing was her doorbell. She craned her head to see the clock on the nightstand behind her and groaned. It was well past eight. No wonder he was here.

Where the hell was her phone? She had an alarm set on that, though she never slept past six AM, even in the winter slow season.

Extricating herself from the sheet, she started down the stairs. She could hear her middle brother Sean clearly, on the phone, anxiety in his voice.

"Pete, she's not answering. I'm gonna kick down the door in a second." He resumed his pounding.

"You break my door and I break your face!" she yelled. While Peterson, the youngest of the three of them, was tiny, Sean was at least closer to Georgia's build, and between logging and hours in the gym, he was plenty strong enough to kick the door in.

"What the fuck, George?" he bellowed.

"I'm coming," she grumbled. Georgia opened the door and grabbed the phone from Sean's hand. "Pete, I'm sorry. I don't know where my phone is, my alarm didn't—"

"It's here in the motorhome, I tried calling you like five hundred times, but then I heard it ringing inside. Which freaked me the hell out, because your truck isn't here, and since I've got a key I went in to check… What the fuck, George?" He echoed their brother's sentiment, and she heard the barely contained panic.

"I'm sorry. I'm okay. I didn't realize I left my phone. I overslept. I'll be there as soon as I can."

"I'm kicking your ass when you get here."

"You can try." She laughed.

"This isn't funny, George." Sean glared at her with his arms crossed.

"Oh my God, I'm late one fucking time and you two freak the hell out."

"Yeah, exactly. You're never late. We're your brothers. We worry about you." Sean eyed her up and down.

"Nothing is wrong, Sean. I just overslept. It happens occasionally to everyone. Stop with the chick flick moment."

With an exaggerated sigh, he pushed past her into the house.

"I'll start the coffee and food. Get your ass dressed. You're standing in the doorway showing the world your underwear."

"Well, I am now that you moved your big ass out of the way."

He eyed her again as she shut the door.

"Why are you looking at me like that?"

"Pete said there was some weird dominance power play between you and the client yesterday. Said he's a bear and it was affecting some of the guys."

"So? I've dealt with shifters before. He's no different."

"Yeah, but your eyes never turned gold before, either."

She threw her hands up in exasperation. "I don't shift!"

"Not yet," he muttered before going to the kitchen. "Just get ready."

Thirty minutes later, she was on her way to the site, coffee mug in hand. She lived on the outskirts of town, so her drive wasn't too long, but it was still nearly ten o'clock by the time she arrived.

Caleb stood talking with Pete outside the motorhome.

Great. Just who I didn't want to deal with today.

"Morning, Mr. Michonne." She gave him a curt nod. "Pete, how's it looking so far?"

Pete looked back and forth between her and Caleb and cleared his throat.

"Good," he said. "They guys are making good

progress on the lots to be cleared. We'll probably need trucks here tomorrow before we run out of room."

"Great, I'll let Dad know." She glanced at Caleb. "I'll be there in a minute, Pete. Just need to grab my gear and check my messages. Sorry I was late."

"Sure, see you in a bit." With a last look between the two of them, Pete left her and Caleb and jumped in his truck. She heard him key the CB radio to update the crew as he pulled away.

Without a second look at Caleb, she entered the motorhome. Pete had plugged in her phone, bless him, and she could see all the missed calls, emails, and texts from him, clients, and even her father. She powered up the laptop so she could quickly reply to the emails.

"I wasn't sure I'd see you again," Caleb said softly. She glanced in the direction of his voice. He remained on the ground, outside the motorhome, speaking into the open door. She felt her body flush at the memory of last night.

"Pete's never run a contract this big before. Sean's wife is going to pop out their first kid any second now, so he needs to be closer to home. Didn't have much choice, really," she said, returning her attention to the screen of her computer. His presence irritated her. She hated how her body reacted to him and wanted him as far away as possible, as quickly as possible, even though as the landowner and contract holder he had every right to be there.

"Well, I'm glad to see you again." He started to walk away, then abruptly turned back and leaned into the opening. "And for the record, I like this look much better," he said, pointing toward her head and wiggling his finger in a circle.

Georgia opened and closed her mouth a few times, imitating a fish out of water as she floundered for words. With a self-satisfied smirk, Caleb turned and stalked off.

"It wasn't for you!" she finally shouted after him. He lifted an arm and waved, never breaking stride.

She huffed, too flustered to focus on the email she'd been trying to read. Instead, she went into the tiny bathroom and yanked out her ponytail, using her fingers to comb her hair and quickly put it into a loose braid. She couldn't wear the pony under her hardhat anyway, but in her hurry to leave the house she'd pulled it back to get it out of her face—which was free of makeup today, also thanks to her rush.

Pete often teased her about the length of her hair, asking why she kept it so long. In part, it was for the same reasons she'd given Caleb about wearing makeup. But also, she just didn't look good with short hair. Some women looked awesome with pixie cuts or bobs. She looked like a man in a horrible drag outfit. She'd tried it once, while she'd been taking business classes at college part-time and working for her dad full-time. It was an experiment she'd never repeat. Her face was too wide, her jaw too square for it to look good.

"Who the hell does he think he is?" she grumbled as she quickly worked the strands back and forth through her fingers. "It's not like he has a say about my appearance. I'm not his."

A shudder ran through her at the thought. A fling with him would be just fine, but she got the distinct impression that he was interested in much more than that. Georgia had no interest in being tied down. She certainly wasn't about to fall on her back and be a good little wife and den mother. That life was a death sentence to her. She'd never quit her job, and highly doubted he'd want his woman running all over creation with a bunch of other guys from sunup 'til sundown half the year.

"I'm pretty sure he has a different opinion about that."

Georgia jumped.

"Fuck's sake, Kyle, knock or something!"

"Where's the fun in that? Besides, I figured you smelled my approach."

"Why the hell would I have done that? We all smell like earth and fresh-cut timber and exhaust and oil. How would I have noticed anything different from how the inside of this trailer smells?"

"Because we have the same grandfather. And your mother was a shifter."

"I'm not a shifter."

He stared at her pointedly.

"Why the hell do you all keep looking at me like I'm about to shoot out claws and fur?"

"George, you may have never shifted, but I'm telling you, you *are* a shifter. It's there, in you. Everyone on this side of the family can sense it when you're around. The guys on the crew can sense it. But for some reason, your bear hasn't decided to come out yet. I have a feeling that's going to change soon. And after the client's power display yesterday, frankly, I'm amazed that you didn't drop then." He held up a hand when she opened her mouth. "As your *family*, and not just as your crew, I'm telling you to steer clear of Ike and Tom. Your pheromones are off the chart. You want this guy bad, and every bear on the mountain can smell you."

She felt her cheeks immediately flame with embarrassment.

"Nothing to be ashamed of, 'cuz. Our kind knows their mates when they meet. You can't control it. Better not to fight it."

"I'm not interested in a mate. And I'm not your kind. But I *am* your boss, and I say get your ass back to work. There's talk of storms coming in next week."

Kyle smiled knowingly at her.

"Sure thing, *boss.*"

Chapter Three

Caleb watched from a safe distance each night as the crew left for the day. After that first night, Georgia never lingered long, heading out herself before the dust from the last truck had settled. He had no idea how early she arrived, but for a week straight he had yet to beat her to the worksite in the morning.

He watched her emerge from the mobile office. The sun barely edged over the top of the mountain, leaving much of the valley below still in shadow. She turned and looked up the slope, walking directly toward him. In just a few minutes she'd closed much of the distance.

"I know you're there, Caleb," she called out. "I can feel you watching me."

She drew closer, her pace slowing as she looked around for him.

"I don't need a chaperone, you know. I'm quite safe on my own."

He huffed, and she paused mid-step. *Time to push her again*, he thought. Digging into the trunk with his front claws, he pulled himself up from the branch he sat on and swung his back legs down.

"Oh!"

With ease, Caleb quickly backed down the tree and faced Georgia. She'd retreated a few paces and now stood braced against a tree.

"Caleb?" Her voice was breathy, his name barely more than a whisper. He nodded his head, all the while smiling internally.

Hesitantly, she moved forward.

"I've only ever seen my cousins as bears, and

only a few times. My mother died when I was very young. I can hardly even remember her."

Caleb held still as she reached a hand toward him. There was no fear in her scent, which pleased him greatly.

"Will you shift so I can talk with you?"

He shook his head.

"Why?"

Gently, he nipped at the sleeve of her sweatshirt as she stroked the fur on his shoulders, hoping she'd understand.

She laughed. "Not like I haven't already seen it."

A low growl escaped him at the shift in her scent. She sucked in a breath, her arousal increasing. *Fuck, if I don't shift now, I'll never be able to control him with her smelling like that.*

Caleb shook her hand off and took a few steps away. He briefly considered going behind the tree, so that the process would be mostly hidden from her view, before deciding against it. She'd asked him to shift, so she'd get what she got.

A thought occurred to him: perhaps she *wanted* to see the process? He was dying to know what kept her from shifting for so long. Most shifters experienced their first transformation shortly after puberty, yet for some reason, her bear had never made itself known. There was very little documentation about shifters raised in human families, as they nearly always stayed exclusively within the shifter community.

She watched him, her face a mixture of awe and fascination, as fur receded, muscles shrank, and bones relocated, until he stood before her, once again a man. As used to the process as he was from shifting for nearly thirty years, he didn't make any noises or cries of pain. Even if he'd felt compelled to cry out, he'd have kept silent, so as not to scare her. Her eyes roamed his body as he rolled his neck and stretched his arms. The same gold shimmer that he'd seen the first day reappeared, her eyes glimmering in the growing light.

"That's amazing," she said before her gaze fell to his cock. "Really?" she asked, amusement coloring her voice at his salute.

"You're aroused. I can smell it. If I hadn't shifted, I'd have had to run away. My bear wants to claim you … as my mate."

"So I've been told." She sounded rather unimpressed by that idea.

"It's why I've been watching you. I can't help it. I leave my cabin to head down to the visitor's lodge, and I find myself here instead. I sleep, only to dream of you. You're like an unattainable drug, a fabled high that I'm desperate to have. So I get what little fix I can manage."

Georgia swallowed hard.

"Maybe I need a fix too."

His cock jumped at the thought.

"Georgia…" His arm lifted, reaching for her, but then he remembered his promise to her and quickly dropped it to his side.

Breathing fast and shallow, she stepped closer to him.

"Tell me," he said, nearly begging her for permission.

"No touching." The grin on her face was wicked as she placed a hand on his chest.

"Not fair," he groaned. *Christ, when did I lose the ability to speak in full sentences? What the hell does she do to me?* He let her push him until his back encountered rough bark.

"Stay."

Caleb narrowed his eyes.

"I'm a bear, not a fucking dog," he rumbled.

"I'm aware," she purred, running her fingers through the hair in the valley between his pecs.

He desperately wanted to shred her clothing from her and stop this teasing. She closed the remaining distance and leaned into him.

"What is it about you that makes me want to break every one of my rules?"

He moved to kiss her and she quickly retreated.

"I said no touching."

"You also said you want to break all your rules." He buried a hand in her silken hair, holding the back of her head. Her nostrils flared and she glared at him. "Don't forget, sweetheart, I can *smell* how much you want me. But you go ahead and feign anger and indifference if that's your kink."

Caleb slammed his mouth to hers. She gasped, and he used the opportunity to drive his tongue through her parted lips. A moan escaped her and she ground her hips against him, wrapping her arms around his shoulders and clinging to him until they were both left breathless.

"Cocky old bastard, aren't you?" she panted, their foreheads pressed together.

"Say the word and I'll show you just how old I am, little girl. Or is that what's holding you back?"

It was the first time either of them had commented on the age gap. Though he was a dozen years her senior, it didn't faze him in the least. She was everything he could have hoped for in a mate: independent, strong-willed, and intelligent. Gorgeous was just the icing on the cake. Age meant nothing to him.

"I'm quite certain I can teach you a thing or two that the boys you're used to haven't bothered to figure out yet."

Georgia's breath did that little hitch again, the

one she got when aroused, and the one that made his cock ache to fill her.

"I don't care how old you are," she said at last.

"Then what's the hold-up here, Georgia?" He pulled back to meet her eyes. "Because something keeps making you say no when your body screams yes."

"I'm not interested in being tied down."

"Well, that's a shame. I'd love to tie you up and drive you out of your mind with pleasure."

Twin spots of color flamed in her cheeks before she answered.

"That's not what I meant."

He sighed and released her, turning away. Now more than ever, he'd love it if her bear would make an appearance and help him out.

"I know what you fucking meant. But this isn't something I can just turn off, Georgia. You are the only woman I will want for the rest of my life."

"I know," she said softly, and he could hear the regret in her voice. "And I'm sorry to have done this to you."

He raked his fingers through his hair, trying not to let his frustration get the better of him.

"What is it that you fear so much about commitment? I wouldn't ask you to change who you are. I wouldn't take you from what you love, from what drives you."

"You say that now. But the long hours and endless string of days without a break will wear on you one day as well. So it's better if we stop this before it gets harder for you to walk away."

"You're the one who came to me this morning!" he yelled. "Christ, Georgia! What the fuck do you want from me? I'll always be here waiting for you, don't you get that? I can't just 'walk away' from you!" Agitation had him dangerously close to shifting or doing something he'd regret.

"Don't you fucking put this on me, asshole! What makes you think I like knowing I'm being fucking watched all the time while I'm here? Of course I came up here to confront you about it!"

"I'm protecting you!"

"From *what*?" She nearly screamed the last word.

"I don't fucking know!" he shot back.

His words threw her. Her head cocked to the side, bewilderment drawing her brows together.

Caleb released an exasperated sigh. That was the kicker—he really had no clue what it was that he worried about. She wasn't some tiny, frail, meek little thing.

"All I know," he said quietly, stepping in front of her, "is that I worry about you constantly. I have this drive, this need, to make sure you are safe when you are here alone. It's a bit better when you're not on the mountain and I can't just come down and see you, but I still am concerned about you at all times." He tucked a section of hair behind her ear and then took her hands in his. She didn't fight him, and he took that as a small win. "When a shifter mates, they bond with their partner. You know about this, yes?"

"A little bit."

He held her gaze. "They form a kind of psychic connection, a mental bond. It's how we can communicate with each other when we shift. We can sense the other one, and 'talk' to them telepathically if desired or needed. Without having that bond with you, I worry constantly. That is why I watch you. You are the one thing that matters most to me in the world now. Not the mountain, not the work we're doing, not the den members. Nothing. Only you, until we are mated."

"Stop saying that! I'm not mating anybody! Not

even you!" She jerked her hands free and began pacing angrily.

"What do I have to do to convince you that this is not a death knell? That it's not a punishment of some sort?"

"There's nothing to be done for it. I'm sorry, but that's how it is."

With an angry roar, Caleb shifted and took off through the woods.

"Caleb! *Caleb!* Are you fucking kidding me with this?" He could hear her yelling after him, outraged that he'd left in such a manner. But if he kept arguing with Georgia, things would not end well.

How do things keep going to shit between us just when I think we're getting somewhere?

****

"You know, blood-soaked wood doesn't exactly burn well."

Caleb blindly hurled the piece of wood he'd just split behind him in Ryan's general direction.

With a sigh, he dropped the ax and pulled his shirt off. Tearing strips of material from it, he wrapped his cracked and blistered hands, then wiped the handle with the remains of his shirt. He wasn't worried about his hands; they'd be healed by the time the sun set in a few hours.

Ryan cleared his throat as he slowly came to Caleb's side and held out a bottle of water.

"Thanks," Caleb said roughly, his throat like sandpaper from hours of nonstop exertion.

"Georgia?"

Caleb grunted.

"You need to just claim her and be done with it."

"Not going to force her."

"Yeah, I figured that part out about five cords of

wood ago. I'm pretty sure all the cabins are set for next winter now. And then some."

Every scrap piece of wood that had been cut or trimmed in the last week had been collected in one large pile near the main visitor's lodge. Only leaves, needles, and bits of bark remained. He'd split and stacked a dozen cords of wood to add to the constant supply they maintained for the rental cabins. His flesh was caked with dirt, sweat, and blood, but he didn't give a damn.

"I did a drive-through on the four-wheeler. They're just about done. She'll be out of here soon. Probably only another week as they finish clearing the last few new roads and building lots, and then the cleanup."

"That won't help, but thanks for the update."

The cleanup process was one of the things that made Connors Logging stand out from some of the other companies he'd looked at. On large jobs such as this, the amount of debris left behind in the form of wood chips, scattered limbs and branches, and stumps, plus ruts and ground and road damage from the machines could leave quite a headache for the landowner. Connors would bring in graders and rollers to level back out any major ruts. He was paying for them to clear out the stumps in the building lots, and the unsaleable wood was left to the owner's discretion. Caleb had chosen to keep it for firewood, but if he'd asked, they'd have taken it away, either to mulch it or put it to some other use. They had a very low percentage of actual waste, and it had been a major influencing factor when he'd picked their company, despite not being the cheapest bid.

"I know, man. I know." Ryan's voice was steady, but the pain in his eyes reflected Caleb's own torment. Ryan had caught a scent one day while hiking near the coast on vacation and recognized her as his mate immediately. He'd followed the trail until he'd found her. Unfortunately for him, her car was wrapped around a tree, with her still inside it. Ryan mourned a love he'd never even known or had.

Caleb hadn't been looking for a mate, though lately, he'd grown restless thinking about getting older and not having a family, worried about the future of the den with no strong Alpha line to take over when he eventually became unable to lead. Yet now that he'd met Georgia, the idea of having a mate consumed his every thought.

"Fuck, Ryan, I don't want to end up like you. But I'm at a loss here. She has no interest in being mated, or 'tied down,' as she puts it."

Ryan grasped Caleb's shoulder. As he was about to speak, his gaze shifted to a point off in the distance, confusion spreading across his face.

"They weren't going to be burning anything on the mountain, right?"

Caleb whipped his head around, and his chest tightened at the sight below them.

"That smoke is too dark to be brush," he said, already running for the shed nearby that housed the four-wheelers and carts used for transportation of supplies and people among the lodge guests. He hopped on the first one and flipped the key, jamming his thumb down onto the start button. The engine kicked on and he tore down the narrow hiking path that wound all throughout the lower forest, taking turns at breakneck speed, nearly rolling the all-terrain vehicle more than once.

After what felt like an eternity, Caleb broke through the tree line to find men yelling and shouting, trying to put out the fire with the extinguishers they kept on their vehicles.

"Goddamn it, somebody get her the fuck away

from here!" someone yelled.

That was all Caleb needed to hear to make a mad dash for the machine currently still billowing smoke and flame.

"Pete!" Georgia cried her brother's name as she broke free of the men holding her back and scrambled for the harvester that lay on its side.

Caleb tackled her around the waist, the two of them slamming into the ground just as the fuel tank exploded.

She screamed, clawing at Caleb's arms in an effort to escape his hold. He pulled her tight against him, her back to his chest, offering her silent strength as she watched the futile efforts to save her brother from the inferno. Eventually, she sank into him, sobs wracking her body.

Caleb surveyed the scene. The heat buffeting them abated as the fuel reserves burned off, though the large Douglas fir tree that pinned the harvester machine down was still aflame. The vehicle had a hydraulic arm that extended out, with a grappling mechanism at the end that held a large saw blade. It appeared that a line had ruptured, causing hydraulic fluid to ignite when it sprayed on the super-heated engine. The broken line had caused the tree to fall backward and throw the balance of the machine off, tipping it and pinning it—with Pete inside—to the ground.

Though it was hell on his back after all the wood splitting he'd done today, and his legs had pretty much fallen asleep, he didn't try to move Georgia from their spot. The crew seemed to understand and worked around them in silence, tears streaking almost every face. Caleb could hear the sirens in the distance as emergency vehicles made their way to the mountain, and he bitterly wondered why they bothered with the sirens at all, knowing full well there was nobody to be saved once they reached their location.

Despite the ever-retreating sun slipping below the horizon, the area remained well-lit. Spotlights, and vehicle headlights—a mix of Connors crew trucks and police and fire apparatus—cast a harsh light on the burnt wreckage. At some point, her father had arrived, navigating the area as best he could on crutches, his wife at his side. People came to speak with Georgia, but she refused to move from Caleb's lap.

Officers took preliminary statements from everyone on site, and Caleb's theory about what had happened to the harvester proved correct. Medical personnel tried to check them both, but she just waved them away.

"Why are your hands bandaged? And where is your shirt?"

Caleb pressed a kiss to the top of her head, happy to hear her voice, no matter how trivial of a matter she chose to focus on at the moment. Her fingers toyed absently with the hair on his chest, something he decided he rather liked.

"My shirt is, well, wrapped around my hands, but I'm sure they're fine by now. I spent the entire day splitting all that wood piled by the visitor's center, and they blistered and cracked."

"All of it? That was a huge pile."

"Yep. Ended up with nearly a dozen cords."

"By yourself?"

"Yeah. I had a lot of … energy … to burn off."

She sniffed, snuggling further into his embrace. "Sorry 'bout that."

"Don't be. It's my problem to deal with, not yours. Never was."

Georgia's fingers traced over the handful of even

scratches lining Caleb's forearms.

"From the wood splitting?"

Caleb cleared his throat, shifting his position slightly. "Not exactly."

"What happened? They're still a bit fresh, they're obviously from today. They're barely healed."

"They're … from you," he said softly.

Georgia immediately inspected the tips of her fingers, undoubtedly noticing the shortness of her nails and how incapable she'd be of doing such a thing.

"That's not possible."

Caleb stifled a sigh. He didn't want to argue with her about this. Especially not right now.

"Don't worry about it, sweetheart."

He focused on staying calm, on providing her with the strength she needed at the moment. The issue of his arms could wait until she was ready to accept her true nature and what she'd just done to him.

Chapter Four

Georgia didn't want to leave the comfort of Caleb's arms. He sat on the ground with her for hours, never once complaining as he held her, watching the horrifying scene play out. Pete's body had been removed a while ago. Caleb stiffened slightly when the crews had loaded him, as if expecting her to take off. But the lull of Caleb's warmth, his steady breathing, and the rhythm of his heartbeat beneath her cheek kept her calm.

Police officers came to her, along with medical personnel, and even her father and stepmother, and she answered them all in a daze, reliving the awful moment each time. Darkness crept in as vehicles slowly began to leave. Her father appeared in front of her once more.

"George," he said softly, his voice cracking. "It's time to leave, sweetie." He held a hand out, as if to help her stand. She stared at it, for probably longer than she should have, before deciding.

"Caleb will help me."

Her father cocked an eyebrow and lifted his gaze to Caleb, whose heartbeat had started a jackhammer pace.

"Now, Georgia. You're in no shape to drive yourself."

She sighed and pressed herself further into Caleb's embrace. Caleb cleared his throat as if to say something and her father narrowed his eyes. As he began to speak, Kyle appeared and silenced her father with a hand on his arm. With a pointed look at Caleb's arms intertwined with hers, Kyle whispered something into her father's ear. She watched her father's eyes go wide.

"Okay," he said, nodding his head and looking

between her and Caleb. He took a deep breath. "Okay," he repeated.

She didn't know what Kyle had told her father and couldn't bring herself to care, either. Numbness was taking over, dulling her ability to feel anything. But the thought of being separated from Caleb's unwavering strength terrified her, and she was grateful for whatever Kyle had said to change her father's mind so quickly.

Georgia was fully aware that she was being selfish. Knowing how he felt about her, she knew Caleb wouldn't refuse her request. Taking advantage of his emotions right now probably made her a terrible person. Yet she was also aware enough of her mental state to be worried about what might happen to her when she was alone. She knew that Caleb was keeping her grounded right now, in more ways than one.

Chills raced along her arms as Caleb stood, taking his body heat with him. Before she could rise, she found herself in the air, in his arms, as he lifted her as though she weighed nothing. He and her father exchanged a long look before her father stepped closer to press a kiss to her forehead.

"I love you, baby. Always and no matter what."

"I love you too, Dad."

With a nod to Caleb, her father made his way back to his vehicle. Caleb carried her to his four-wheeler and set her on it before climbing on himself.

She didn't question it when he took a turn on the path that led them further up the mountain instead of to her truck. Leaving the mountain would make everything real, would mean facing the truth of Pete's death. At least for now, she could not deal with it for just a little while longer.

Eventually, she found herself standing behind Caleb's cabin, the faint light from within illuminating the woods surrounding them. The darkness was inviting. She wanted to run, enter that darkness and disappear, lose herself among the dense trees. Caleb stepped out onto the porch, blotting out some of the light, and she turned to him. The clothing he carried in one hand fell to the wooden steps as he joined her, naked, in the grass.

"Going for a stroll?"

"Yes. And so are you. I suggest you take your shoes off unless you want to ruin them."

"Excuse me? I'm not going into the woods barefoot."

"You won't be. Take your shoes off. And anything else you don't want to rip to shreds."

She sighed, seeing where this was going.

"Caleb, I can't fucking shift. I'm like one of those people from *Harry Potter*, the ones who are born from magical parents but can't do magic. I can't believe you're pulling this shit right now."

"Last chance," he growled.

"Caleb! Enough!"

She glared at him, nails digging into her palms as she clenched her fists.

Belatedly, the action and the associated pain registered in her brain. Opening her hands, she stared in shock at the spots of blood that her lengthened nails—*claws,* she thought, *let's be honest here, I have claws right now*—had left in her broken skin.

She stared in disbelief, watching as her fingers returned to normal.

"Moments of extreme emotional duress can trigger a shift in someone with dormant genes. Because you were raised in a human family, with limited interaction with your shifter family, your bear went dormant. Think of it as she was hibernating. But she's very much awake now." Caleb lifted his arm, brandishing his scarred skin in front of her face. "And she wants out. I can help you with this, or I can force it. Either way, I suggest you strip. Because if you don't do this now, and come to an understanding with her, she'll force her way out and you won't have a say in where or when it happens."

She looked again at her fingers. They ached and tingled.

"Will it hurt?"

"Like a motherfucker."

She looked up at him in surprise, remembering his transformation in the woods—was it just that morning?—and how he'd not made a sound.

"I won't lie to you, Georgia. It's going to hurt a whole freaking lot in the beginning." He stepped closer and cupped her face. "Over time, as you grow accustomed to it, your shifts will be faster and less painful. I promise."

"I'm scared," she whispered.

"I know, sweetheart." Caleb kissed her, soft and gentle. "It's all overwhelming. But trust me. Please?"

Georgia let out a shaky breath. She thought of all the dreams she'd had over the years, and how they'd intensified, the urgency of them having grown since meeting Caleb. Things started to make sense, despite her not wanting to believe it.

"Okay." She nodded. "Okay."

Caleb held her eyes. "I'll be right here. No matter what."

He gave her another gentle kiss, and it left her wanting more. *Am I that fucked up in the head? I just watched my brother die and now I'm up here playing in the woods at night, preparing to shift, and I want to climb Caleb like a tree.*

He stepped back, folding his arms across his

impressive chest.

"Go ahead."

"What the fuck do you mean? I don't know what I'm supposed to—" She gasped as strange feeling overtook her. It wasn't so much the rise of an *other* inside her, though she was aware of the presence of her bear, a presence that had always been there but remained silent except in her dreams.

What she felt was a lack of Caleb's influence.

She hadn't realized that he'd been exerting so much power over her throughout the day, holding her back. Moments of extreme emotional duress, indeed.

Spasms rocked through her body, and she hurried to get her workboots off. She had clothes in her truck and the motorhome, but not more boots. Caleb helped her strip, and just as her legs were freed, she fell to the ground, the cool earth and damp grass a welcomed feeling against her super-heated skin. She writhed and screamed as joints dislocated, muscles stretched, and bones broke and reset in rapid succession.

Her scream turned to a roar as the pain subsided.

Georgia looked around as she caught her breath. The world seemed strange from this height, the ground too close. Smells were intensified—the damp earth beneath her, the late season flowers, the sap in the trees, she could smell it all. And Caleb. She hadn't noticed it before, that he had his own specific scent, but she recognized it immediately and associated it with him. It was woodsy, fresh, and comforting. Swinging her head around, she found him. He stood a few paces away, still a man, chest heaving as he watched her.

She was pleased to note that she retained her consciousness, her awareness of what she was doing. It was a fear she'd been afraid to voice, the fear of losing all control of herself and her actions. Without thinking too much about how to do it, she took a few small steps toward him. Caleb dropped to his knees and reached a hand out to stroke down her back. The sensation was odd, raising goosebumps along her skin, but it felt good.

"Christ, you're gorgeous."

She nudged at his chest, wanting him to shift as well. She certainly wasn't about to go wander off in the woods at night without him, despite being able to see better.

"I'm changing too, sweetheart. Don't worry."

She watched him shift once again, fluid and quick, with no cries of pain. He sniffed all along her sides, nuzzling her before heading off down a path. She followed, marveling at the sensory overload. At a clearing near a stream, Caleb made her shift back.

"How do you feel?" he asked, concern etched on his face.

"Like my skin is on fire."

He nodded. "It'll get better in time. I want you to shift again, on your own. You need to learn how to call your bear, and how to hold her back when needed. That one was all her."

"Please, not now." She rubbed her arms, trying to relieve the aches and tingles. This high up the mountain, and this late in the year, the water would be frigid, but she waded in anyway, to splash some over her limbs. The cold was wonderfully refreshing and surprisingly deep, coming up to her waist.

"It gets deeper by those rocks over there," Caleb said, pointing off to the left. She hadn't heard him enter the water. He pressed a kiss to her shoulder before moving away, taking a few steps and then falling onto his back, floating just out of reach. The cold water did nothing to diminish the erection he sported, and the sight of it sent heat through her core. Georgia slipped through the water after him.

"Over the years I've managed to carve out a nice little pool over here. I even made a seat of sorts with rocks. It's gorgeous in the middle of summer, when everything is green and in bloom."

She caught up to him, sliding right into his arms. Her knees bumped the rocks he sat on, his legs rubbing along the outsides of hers.

"I thought the cold water might help with the after-effects," he said softly.

"It does," she murmured. The nearly-full moon sat fat and bright in the sky above them. She watched a sparkling droplet of water slide down Caleb's hair and fall to his shoulder. Georgia leaned forward and kissed it away. Caleb groaned, his hands tightening around her waist.

She buried her face in his neck, inhaling deeply.

"Why do you smell so fucking good?"

He fisted a hand in her hair and yanked her head back when she licked him. Keeping her eyes locked on his, she lifted her legs, placing her knees to either side of his hips.

"Georgia," he whispered, cupping her cheek with his other hand. "This isn't—"

"Shh."

She rubbed against him, Caleb's thick shaft sliding between her folds and teasing along her clit. His head dropped back against the bank of the stream as she continued to rock her hips. Soon they were both panting, on the cusp of release.

"Caleb," she breathed, and he brought his head up. "Kiss me."

He slammed his mouth to hers, devouring her. Georgia lifted herself slightly and impaled herself on his cock, taking him fully in one swift motion. Caleb cried out, going still. She felt his heartbeat racing beneath her palms as she held his neck. Inside her, his cock pulsed.

In one quick movement, he stood. She wrapped her legs around him, keeping them locked together as he moved to where the water wasn't as high, and he could brace her against the side of the little pond he'd created. Cool mud and soft grasses pressed against her back, while firm muscles and hot flesh filled her arms. He held her waist firmly and began pistoning in and out of her.

Georgia buried her hands in Caleb's hair, trying to get as close to him as possible, get him as deep inside her as possible. A rumble reverberated through his chest and he wrapped his arms around her, holding her tight against his chest.

"Yes," she gasped. "More. Harder." Caleb filled her completely, hitting all the right spots with every thrust. But it wasn't enough. She didn't know what she needed, only that something was missing, keeping her from flying over the edge.

"More," she begged, tugging at his hair and biting his bottom lip.

Caleb grabbed her hair and yanked her head back, nostrils flaring.

"Tell me you're mine," he ground out, his voice low and rough.

"Yes."

"Mine," he repeated, his teeth grazing along her shoulder.

She shuddered, that simple action driving her even higher.

"Yours," she agreed, breathless, staring up at the stars. Georgia knew what would come next but was unwilling to fight it any longer.

Caleb lifted his head back and roared, the sound of it setting her blood on fire. Pain knifed through her as his mouth locked over the top of her shoulder and his teeth—*no, his fangs,* she corrected herself—pierced her skin. She shrieked as her orgasm hit, overwhelming her senses. Her skin burned. Her ears rang. Her eyes became unfocused. Everything felt far away, as if her brain was floating above the scene, observing it and recording details.

She *felt* Caleb's euphoria. It felt as though her heart would explode from joy. She turned this sensation over in her brain, examining it, trying to figure out where she ended and Caleb began.

"*Shh,*" Caleb said, and she heard him in her head as well as felt his lips moving against hers. "Turn off your brain, sweetheart." He peppered kisses along her jaw, working his way to where he'd just marked her. She hissed when he hit the sensitive wound. "Sorry," he murmured, feathering his lips over the same spot.

"It's not that it hurts," she said, squirming as another jolt of electricity shot from beneath his lips straight to her clit.

Caleb chuckled. "Hmm, that's going to come in handy."

She shoved at him playfully, splashing cold water at him.

His expression turned serious.

"We didn't use any protection."

"Well, I haven't had sex in about two years, and I was clean when I got tested after my last breakup. Though according to my cousin, shifters rarely catch any illnesses or diseases."

"That is true." He nodded. "Since I took over the den about five years ago I haven't dated, either. Too much to do. But there's still the other concern…" He trailed off, as though unsure of what to say.

She smiled. "Implant." His brows drew together

in confusion. "Good Lord, it's like you live on a mountain," she scoffed. He tried to maintain a straight face, but his lips quirked. "They make these things called IUDs—intrauterine devices—that are implanted and prevent pregnancy. Mainly I got it because it also stops monthly periods, and I don't exactly have time on a job site to be running to the bathroom to change out a tampon every few hours for five days a month."

"Oh." He looked uncomfortable, and Georgia laughed.

"I'm scheduled to have it removed in a year. We can discuss a family then. But for now, can we get out of the water?"

****

Caleb lay on his side, watching Georgia sleep. Or try to sleep, at any rate. She should have been exhausted enough to sleep for days, yet he knew she was awake despite her closed eyes. He tucked a strand of golden hair behind her ear—her bear also was blonde, a gorgeous honey-brown that complemented his near-black nicely—and snugged the blanket up over her shoulder.

"Caleb," she said softly with a smile. "Stop fretting. I can feel your anxiety, you know."

He cleared his throat. After exiting the stream, they'd shifted again for the walk home. Georgia had managed to call her bear all on her own doing and without any influence by him. Once back inside and in minimal clothing—her skin had been ultra-sensitive, so she'd chosen one of his t-shirts and nothing else—he'd gotten her to eat something. Now they lay together, both wrapped up in their own heads, trying in vain to fall asleep.

She rolled onto her back and looked up at him.

"You didn't push me into this." Her hand cupped his cheek and he grabbed it, kissing her palm as she gave voice to his biggest worry. "I've been denying my true nature for years, not wanting to accept it. I was afraid that once I embraced that side of me, I'd be forced to find a mate and have kids, because of my lineage." His grip on her hand tightened. "Never in my wildest dreams did I think I'd find someone like you," she continued. "You saw *me*, not some girl trying to do what men do. *Me*, not a girl who got her job just because it's her daddy's company. *Me*, for my brain, not just my body. Even if you did decide I was your mate the first time you met me, you let me come to the decision myself."

"But did I? Are you sure it's not just because…" He didn't want to bring up Pete's death, but he wasn't completely stupid. It was a very normal psychological response to death to seek out the comfort of another's touch and the connection of sex.

Georgia closed her eyes and swallowed. She kept the pain from her face, but he could feel her anguish.

"No," she said finally. "I know we were arguing in the morning, but honestly I was pushing you. Every time I try to knock you down, you come back swinging with the right answer. And then this afternoon…" She took a deep breath before continuing. "You just sat there and held me. Didn't try to calm me or placate me with meaningless and stupid bullshit. You let me just sit there and cry and scream, and you calmed my bear. You didn't try to make me move before I was ready to."

Caleb wanted to sweep her into his arms, to take away the pain in her eyes, but he knew only time could soften that.

Gently, she pushed against his chest. He fell back onto the mattress and she rose up to straddle him.

"Before the accident, I had already decided to find you again once the crew left for the day."

His cock came to life at her words. She rubbed

herself along his hardening shaft, speeding up the process significantly.

"I was going to ask you to help me with my bear."

Caleb slid his hands up her sides to cup her breasts. He rolled her nipples between his fingers, enjoying the way her eyelids fluttered when he did so.

"And maybe even ride this magnificent cock of yours."

He groaned, thrusting his hips into hers. In response, she raked her nails down his chest.

"Maybe see what kind of tricks this old dog might still know." The twinkling in her eyes gave her away, and in a flash, he flipped her onto her back and pinned her hands above her head.

"Bear," he growled, thrusting into her slick heat.

Georgia's head tipped back, a smile on her lips.

"*Mmm,* yes, bear." Her eyes opened, darkened with lust. "*My* bear."

He dropped his head to suck a nipple into his mouth and she writhed beneath him.

"Yours." The words were whispered against her lips before he thrust his tongue past them, delving into her mouth and twining with hers. He began a slow rolling of his hips, languid and gentle, knowing it would drive her crazy because she wanted it rough.

"Damn it, Caleb," she growled at last, ripping her mouth from his.

"Not so old now, am I?" he asked, grinning. She bucked beneath him. "Easy, sweetheart," he murmured, kissing along her shoulder. The skin where he'd marked her had healed from shifting, but the scars remained tender and receptive to his touch. Georgia shuddered.

"I wonder, could I make you come just from this?" Caleb trailed his tongue across the scars and she gasped, her pussy tightening around his cock. He smiled, enjoying her reaction. When he hummed, she began panting and rocked her hips in an effort to get him to move.

"Please," she begged.

Caleb nipped gently at sensitive skin and she shrieked. He alternated between licks and bites, and in no time she came undone. Her body trembled beneath him as the orgasm overtook her. With a few well-angled thrusts, he was able to push her right back over. Those perfect legs hooked around the backs of his thighs, pulling him in, holding him tight against her as her cream coated his cock.

Caleb groaned, needing to come himself before his balls exploded from holding back.

"Fucking hell that's crazy," Georgia said at last, with a long, contented sigh.

He chuckled. "What's that, sweetheart?"

"No way you can do that to me if I can't torture you in the same manner. I'm definitely marking you." He cleared his throat and she canted her head to the side. "What?"

"Well, actually … you already *have* marked me." Her eyes followed his gaze, to the scars crisscrossing his forearms, left by her claws.

"I don't understand. You shifted. Twice. Why do you have scars from superficial wounds?"

"You drew my blood in a heightened emotional state while partially shifted. We are true mates. Even though I hadn't claimed you yet, and though you hadn't undergone your first full shift, it still counts."

The confusion left her eyes, replaced by mischief.

"So, what you're saying is, if I do this—" She turned her head and trailed the tip of her tongue along one of the scars. Caleb moaned, his sac drawing up tight as electricity zinged through his spine. "Hah!" Georgia exclaimed triumphantly, a devilish grin on her face. "Oh, you're in trouble now."

Somehow, she managed to work his cock with her hips while driving him insane, licking, kissing, and nipping at the scars on each arm until he ached with the need to come. Caleb's arms shook as he struggled to keep his elbows locked so that he didn't collapse onto her. Georgia lifted her legs higher up, locking them around his waist and seating him fully inside her.

"Christ, woman," he ground out.

"Give it to me, old man." She turned and bit down hard where several scars intersected.

Caleb shouted as his orgasm powered through him, the base of his spine on fire as his seed erupted from him. His chest heaved when he finally remembered to breathe again.

"Jesus." He rested his forehead against hers, utterly spent.

"Told you so." She tipped her chin up to kiss him, a smile on her lips.

He shifted his weight and dropped his forearms down to rest alongside hers, interlocking their fingers.

"I'm glad you came to my mountain, Georgia Connors." He punctuated his words with kisses. He knew she wasn't ready to hear him say how he truly felt, but damn it, he'd show her somehow.

"Connors-Michonne," she corrected him.

Caleb faltered, meeting her gaze.

"Eventually we'll make it official. Because of the company, I won't completely change my name. But I'll hyphenate it for you."

Amazed, Caleb kissed her again, sure his heart couldn't hold any more happiness. Not even twenty-four hours ago he'd thought they'd never get to this point, as steadfast as she'd been in her resolve to not enter into a relationship with him. Then with the events of the afternoon, he'd been preparing himself for the worst, that she'd leave the mountain and never come back. No one had been more surprised than Caleb when she'd refused her father's hand and instead remained with him.

As the first tentative hints of dawn lit the morning sky, he lay holding her tucked into his side, listening to her steady breathing, still unable to turn his brain off and go to sleep. They had a tough road ahead of them. All too soon she'd have to face the reality of her brother's death. There would be much to figure out regarding work and living situations, among other things. But none of that existed until she left his arms. He pulled her closer, as if he could keep her there forever.

"I love you, Georgia," he whispered, pressing a kiss to her temple.

"Love you too," she mumbled, surprising him. "Now go to sleep, old man."

The End

CROSSING BOUNDARIES

Rose Wulf

Chapter One

Two Years Ago

"I've never fucked a dog before."

Those had been her words, right before she'd flattened her slender palm over Maddox's chest and pushed him to the ground. The Alpha in him rose at the challenge, but the male in him held back, curious to see what the sexy cougar-shifter would do. They were both nude, a result of having shifted to their human forms in the interest of communication, and the scent of her arousal on the wind did nothing for his own immediate—and aching—hard-on. Maybe she was in heat, or maybe she just liked what she saw. Maddox didn't fucking care.

She knelt to the ground, straddling him with her lithe body. Miles of creamy, perfectly tanned skin beneath her long, jet-black hair. Full, rounded breasts begging to be sucked. Mischief and lust lit her amber eyes as she licked her lips and trailed a finger down his chest. "Do you think you know where everything goes?"

Maddox choked on a snort, caught her hand by the wrist, and flashed her his best wicked grin. "Oh, I know where it goes." He released her wrist, latched his hands onto her hips, and pulled her down as he drove himself up. Sinking his aching dick deep into her slick, tight heat. She felt so good he wanted to roar, his primal instincts nearly driving him to flip her over and literally fuck her like a dog. He hadn't seen her ass yet. It was probably divine.

Instead, he held her in place, surging up repeatedly as she arched and rolled over him, creating something of an erotically beautiful dance. Her nails dug into his chest and arm as she began grinding her hips over his, moaning each time he filled her. "Harder," she pleaded, beginning a faster, bouncier, rhythm. "C'mon, Wolf, *harder*!"

She wanted to egg him on, did she? He could play that game. For as much as he was enjoying his view— and even the feel of her bouncing up and down on his dick—he knew exactly how to give her *harder*.

Maddox caught a fistful of her flying hair in one hand, tugging her down as he surged up, catching one of her breasts in the other. He locked his lips over hers with a wet, feverish kiss as he thumbed her nipple. She made a semblance of a mewling sound against his lips, arching into his chest. In the next moment, Maddox flipped them over, landing her on her back on the grass, and broke from the kiss in order to properly balance himself above her.

"Missionary?" she asked, her breathing unsteady as he took control of their pace. The question and arched brow indicated her lack of excitement with the standard and traditional position.

Making a point to thrust into her with increased force, Maddox responded, "So I can suck on your tits while I fuck you."

Her lips lifted at the corners and she added a teasing hip-roll that had them both groaning. "I like a man with a plan."

Oh, he had a plan. He was going to take her so hard she screamed her ecstasy to the skies. Already her core was beginning to pulsate around his cock, as if begging for release. But he wasn't done. He didn't know if he'd ever see this vixen again. He needed to at least make it last. So Maddox bowed his head and pressed his tongue to her neck, earning a soft moan from his lover. She tasted sweet beneath the salt of the beginnings of sweat. Not cloyingly so, but subtly. He slid his tongue slowly down her skin, swirling it over her collarbone, all the while pumping swiftly in and out of her body.

Her hips were lifting to meet his by the time he finally closed his mouth around one of her nipples. He stroked his tongue over it, applying a bit of pressure, and a long, throaty moan escaped her as she buried her hands in his hair. Maddox growled around her areola when her nails scraped his scalp, his hips snapping forward with extra force. She gasped and squirmed as if trying to get closer. Wanting more.

Focusing his attention on the tight little peak of her nipple, Maddox licked and sucked as he let loose, nearing his breaking point. He slammed into her repeatedly, driving his dick as deep as it would go and grinding hard for good measure. She obviously enjoyed it, the way she continuously mewled and gasped, until he finally hit the spot that earned him an outcry. He nearly came right then, but it wasn't enough. So he switched to her neglected breast with renewed vigor and repeated the sharp, grinding thrusts with his hips, filling her core with his cock until his balls were tucked tight against her folds. A little adjustment of the hips on the next thrust and—

There it was. The unnamed vixen beneath him convulsed as an unmistakable cry of ecstasy sang through the trees, her walls clamping around him and triggering his own hard release. Her breast popped from his mouth as the roar poured from his throat, his body taking over to sneak in a couple more hard and fast thrusts before finally bursting. It was all he could do not to collapse on top of her.

Maddox couldn't remember the last time he'd come that hard.

Chapter Two

Present Day

Aniya gave herself a reflexive shake before shifting out of her fur in the enclosed entryway. As always, her body tingled, an effect of going from four-legged, feline, and furry, to two-legged, human, and fleshy. It felt like trying to walk on limbs that weren't quite awake, though the sensation faded almost immediately. She moved to the long, narrow table along the far wall and lifted the appropriate terrycloth robe that was always left out for whomever came to visit without their own change of clothing. There were several robes of varying sizes available—her mother was thoughtful like that.

Properly robed, Aniya pulled her long, straight black hair free from confinement and entered the heart of the building, in search of her father. It struck her, as it always did, how unchanged everything around her felt as she walked down the hall. She'd grown up in this house, as her father had before her, and in all her life it had looked almost exactly the same. The paint would fade and be touched up, but always the same color. The furniture would wear down and need replacing, but always with something similar and in exactly the same places as the old. *They're such traditionalists.*

"We like what we like," her mother would always say. It wasn't a statement Aniya could argue with when the evidence was so strong.

But Aniya was different. She craved excitement. She loved experiencing new things. Sure, sometimes they went poorly, but sometimes … sometimes they went *so well*. She had to suppress the shiver at the flash of a memory, quickly shoving it down before her body could awaken to it. That was definitely at the top of the list of worthwhile risks. Just the memory of that wolf, whose name she'd deliberately failed to get, had brought her to orgasm several times since that day. *Damn him, anyway. Why couldn't he be one of us?* Like it was his fault for being born the wrong species. Probably, there was something wrong with her for ever having lusted after a wolf in the first place.

That, however, was a reflection for another day. It wouldn't do for her to be reminiscing about her brief affair when she met up with her father, Regis. She'd gone two years without him finding out—she intended to go the rest of her life.

She found him in the sunroom, which he used as an office, leaning back in his fancy office chair and gazing out the window. Though terming it a window was putting it lightly. It was floor-to-ceiling, wall-to-wall, and in the center was a custom-built pair of French doors. The window wall faced westward, allowing for maximum sunlight despite the respectable natural shading of forest trees outside. Aniya understood why her father had claimed this as his office space. It was the most beautiful room in the house.

"Aniya," her father called, turning his attention to her with a calm smile. His eyes crinkled at the corners, accentuating his age. Shifters lived for a significantly longer time than humans, it was true, but they did still grow old over time. Her father had ruled over their clan of werecougars for nearly two centuries, and he'd been an adult when he'd taken command.

"Hi, Dad," Aniya said, smiling warmly at him and stepping up to give him a quick hug. He looked tired, a thought she had far too often these days. She tamped it firmly down, however, and answered his question before he could voice it. "I'm heading into the city. With the twins' birthdays coming up, I thought I'd see what kind of obnoxious gift I could find to send to them."

His eyes flickered with amusement even as his lips dipped in a frown. "Aniya," he said again. "You go into town too much as it is. Just mail them something from here."

Aniya rolled her eyes. "You're so paranoid, Dad. It's just a place. Places aren't bad. Besides, I came here specifically to offer to pick up anything you or Mom might want while I'm out." She flashed him her best sweet smile. It was manipulative, yes, but so much easier than an actual argument. She didn't want to rile her father, and she wanted even less to rile her Alpha, who could technically command her to stay whenever he wanted. Not that he ever had.

Her father sighed and turned his gaze briefly toward the doorway. "I know what you're doing," he warned.

Aniya moved and lifted an old photograph he kept on his desk, of her and her twin baby brothers when they were younger. All three of them had been rambunctious, but when it came to her brothers, their behavior had been written off as that which was to be expected of future Alphas. In her case, though, it had always earned her heavy sighs and exasperating arguments. Apparently, only boys were allowed to live freely and play by their own rules. A subject which she suspected she would always bristle over.

Instead, she turned the picture around and held in front of her father patiently. "Dad," she said. "I'm not a child anymore. Just because I haven't moved away to another clan doesn't mean I'm still young and naïve. You don't need to worry so much." Honestly, if exposing herself in a moment of raw, thoughtless passion to a wolf hadn't killed her, the city would be a cakewalk. It wasn't as if she hadn't gone before.

"Fine," Regis said at length. "But check with your mother in case she wants anything first. And don't do anything reckless."

****

"I don't think I can ever understand you," Ty declared as he stepped up beside Maddox, already shaking his head. "I mean, there's no harm in *tasting* sometimes."

Maddox rolled his eyes. Ty, his Beta and longtime friend, was, again, referring to his utter disinterest in any of the pack's females. In truth, it was unfortunate. Maddox was in the prime of his life and, as Alpha, he had a certain responsibility to provide a future for the pack. Since the majority of Alphas were sired by Alphas themselves, it was commonly expected for the reigning Alpha to take a mate young and start a family fairly quickly. Maddox, though, had been sitting at the top of the pack for a little over six years already and not once shown enough interest in a pack female to claim her for his own.

If I could look outside *the pack...* But he couldn't, not when the woman he really wanted wasn't a wolf at all. Or at least human—which would have been problematic enough.

Ty released an audible sigh, heavy with dramatized exhaustion. "Okay, what was wrong with this one?"

Knowing his friend would only continue pressing, Maddox knocked him upside the head. "What would Mimi say if she heard you talking like this? Aren't mated men supposed to immediately forget about the existence of other females?"

Ty laughed easily. "Mimi's not so insecure," he said. "She knows I'm only looking on your behalf. *My eyes are for her.*"

Maddox gagged and turned, striding toward the edge of their naturally sheltered territory. Maddox's grandfather had settled this piece of the forest in his youth, with a larger and heavily male pack, as Maddox understood it. Though they ventured out for food and play, of course, their real territory remained tucked in a natural crevice where two mountains met. The sloping hillsides and towering trees provided solid cover from prying eyes, and the canopy of trees helped filter out the summer's direct heat or the winter's cold rains. Sometime since settling there, Maddox's family and pack had dug out several crevices they called caves into the sides of the mountains. With the additional convenience of a large creek that ran past on one side of the settlement, as well as the accumulated boulders and shrubbery over the generations, they had all they needed for a good, simple life.

Except, in the modern world, it wasn't safe to live blindly in the forest. Maddox understood that, and as Alpha, it was his job to occasionally trek into the nearest city and touch base. Sometimes he made Ty do it, but with Ty newly mated, he suspected his well-meaning Beta would become distracted.

"I need to go into town," Maddox declared. "Make sure there aren't rumors floating around about people turning into wolves in the woods. Redirect any predator-based hunting parties. The usual."

"Always fun," Ty said from half a step behind him. "But don't think I'm so easily dissuaded. When was the last time you got laid?"

A simple question was all it took for the memory to rush back. Maddox ground his teeth in an effort to keep from physically reacting to it. He knew exactly how long it'd been since he'd last made love to a woman. That luscious werecougar who'd made no bones about seducing him after their chance encounter on a hunt. With the adrenaline already coursing through his system, and the sight of her delectable body, it had never once occurred to him to stop her. Even two years later, the only thing he regretted was never catching her name.

"Tell me your name," he'd murmured against her skin, his lips at her throat, as he came down from the high of an explosive orgasm.

She moaned and arched a little into him as if she were stretching, reminding him of her feline nature, and angled her head until her teeth and tongue teased his ear. "Shh. Don't ruin it. The anonymity is part of the fun."

He'd agreed, in a twisted way, but he should have insisted. Or followed her scent later.

It had been two years and he hadn't felt the least bit compelled to touch another woman. He hadn't seen his cougar since that afternoon, hadn't caught her scent, and though he was pretty sure he knew where to find her, he knew hunting her down would raise all kinds of hell.

That was the other problem.

She was a cougar. He was a wolf. More to the point, he was *Alpha*.

For longer than he even knew, their packs had been teetering on the brink of war. It stemmed from some old rivalry that he prayed ran deeper than 'cats versus dogs,' and for the most part, the two species did their best to avoid contact. Maddox had heard stories, most of which had been tales even during his father's tenure, but he had yet to have a problem with the felines. An encounter, however—well, he'd certainly had one of those.

Exasperated, Maddox raked a hand through his hair. "Do you ever think about things besides sex anymore?"

Ty barked out a laugh and clapped him on the back. "I'm newly mated, Alpha. So, no, not really."

Kudos for honesty, I guess. Maddox came to a stop at the invisible territory line. "Just try to clear your head long enough to keep everything running while I'm out, got it? Don't make me be an ass about it."

Ty grinned and tucked his hands into his pockets. "Relax, Alpha. The pack's important to me too. I'll keep watch for you."

"Good answer," Maddox said, inclining his head in acknowledgment. He stepped back a couple of feet, stripped, handed off his clothes for safekeeping, and shifted to his wolf form. All he had to do was unlock the cage in his mind, releasing the more primal part of himself, and the change took over from there. His muscles rippled in waves, a disorienting kind of numbness taking hold of his pain receptors, and then he'd settled on four sturdy paws, sporting a healthy coat of dark-gray and white fur. The picture of a large, not-so-ordinary wolf.

"Safe travels!" Ty called after him as Maddox turned and trotted into the neutral part of the forest.

He appreciated the sentiment, but he wasn't particularly worried. Around here, *he* was the primary predator.

Chapter Three

"I swear this city gets bigger every time I see it," Aniya declared as she and Liv made their way to the UPS store.

Beside her, Olivia, or Liv, as Aniya called her, laughed easily. "You know that's not really true. You're just not very used to it, so you forget what it's like."

Aniya shrugged, acknowledging that her friend was *probably* right.

She had run into Liv on a sojourn into the city several years past, in a bar, and the two had hit it off. Aniya had been in a particularly rebellious state, so had crashed on Liv's couch for over a week before reluctantly turning tail and heading home. In that time they'd come to know each other incredibly well, and so whenever Aniya visited the city, she made a point to drag her human friend along on her adventures. Liv had yet to complain, even though this time her new fiancé seemed to find Aniya's unannounced arrival off-putting.

"Well," Aniya said, lifting the chilled, sweet coffee concoction she held in one hand, "I'm sure this place wasn't there before. I'd remember."

Liv grinned. "Please don't tell me caffeine is the were-cat equivalent of catnip."

Aniya narrowed her eyes. "Don't make me hurt you."

Laughing now, Liv waved a hand at her. "You're so easy! No, no, that place went up about four or five months ago. Probably less than a month after your last visit, actually."

Popping the straw back into her mouth, Aniya said, "Glad you haven't been holding out on me, then."

The drink really was divine. Liv swore the larger cities had at least a dozen of those shops in them and Aniya could only imagine how dangerous that would be. Her father would *fillet* her if she traveled down into the valley to visit a main city—again—but sometimes she was so tempted. It'd been well over a decade since her last time, after all. And it was hard to stay up on current events in the world by just keeping tabs on one city from time to time.

"Now are you sure you're not getting them anything else?" Liv asked as they neared the shipping store. "I know you said birthdays aren't a huge celebration, but it seems like you've gone out of your way for a small thing…"

Reflexively glancing down at the shopping bag in her other hand, Aniya grinned. "I'm sure. They're easy to goad, it's enough." She bumped into Liv with her arm, adding, "Besides, the shopping was an excuse. Once this is done, I have all day."

"I have so missed you," Liv said, smiling as she opened the door.

They filed into the small shipping store, where Liv held Aniya's drink while Aniya went about sending off the joke gifts she'd found for her brothers and the letters her mother had sent with her. The male working the counter helped her easily enough, though it didn't escape her notice that he was interested. It wafted off him. But his youthful baby face didn't appeal to her in the slightest, so she kept her smile small and casual, pretending to remain oblivious.

"Too young for you?" Liv asked after they'd stepped back onto the street.

Aniya sucked on her straw, an image of her nameless wolf watching her with lust in his hazel-green eyes as she rode him popped up in her mind. She barely tasted the swallow of her drink. "Among other things." Not wanting to get distracted while she was out with her friend, Aniya turned the conversation around. "So, you're getting married? That was unexpected. Five months ago you were on the fence about him."

Liv shrugged. "I know," she said. "We were in a rough patch. But what can I say? We made up. The truth is I thought about dumping him and it broke my heart just to think the words. So instead we argued about it for a couple of weeks, and that was horrible, but we got better. He only popped the question about three weeks ago." She turned a bright smile to Aniya. "I know you might not be able to answer me yet, but, I'd really love it if you could come to the wedding."

Tears stung Aniya's eyes at the offer. They were good friends, but she'd always felt guilty, because at the end of the day she had to keep their bond a secret. Her old-fashioned father would likely not approve of her being friends with a human. He would definitely not approve of that human knowing that Aniya was a were. So to have the woman who, really, was her best friend, invite her to *her* most intimate and personal affair was touching. A gift Aniya didn't know if she'd ever be able to reciprocate.

Despite that, her answer was easy. "I would be honored."

Liv came to a stop and pulled Aniya into a hug. "Thank you! Next time I see you, we'll have a date. I promise."

Aniya returned the embrace as best she could with one free hand. "Deal."

She was so caught up in the moment she nearly failed to process the tingling sense of danger behind her. In the city, there were so many pairs of footfalls it became a headache trying to isolate them all, so she'd missed the fact that one pair was too close. Until it was close enough to come with the indescribable vibrations of a threat that made her inner feline want to turn and flee.

Aniya pulled back from the hug and turned in time to find a large man, maybe six-foot or six-foot-two, looming over them with a scowl. He was muscular, in a tries-too-hard kind of way, and despite the fairly clean clothes and overlaying scent of soap, she smelled something else too. *Violence. Old blood.* Whether he intended to harm them, she couldn't be sure, but the proclivity didn't seem to ever be out of the question if the scent was so strong. However it was the blood that concerned her.

That blood was coyote blood.

Clinging to his skin after at least one wash, it couldn't have been more than a day old. *This man, he's a poacher!*

"Ah," Liv said awkwardly, "you can go around, you know. There's room."

He narrowed his eyes at Liv, shifted his focus back to Aniya, and Aniya heard his teeth grind. Was he going to say something? Could he somehow possibly know what she was?

"Move," he finally said.

No, Aniya realized, he didn't know what she was. He was simply an asshole. She had no patience for assholes. Returning his glare, Aniya said, "*You* move."

"Aniya," Liv whispered, her scent spiking with nerves.

"What did you say, woman?" The disdain in his voice was galling.

Gesturing with her drink to the open area of the sidewalk, Aniya repeated, "You move. Like she said, there's room."

His arm shot out and her drink went flying into the road, the remnants spilling everywhere as the lid popped off. Her wrist stung a little, but mostly she was struck with shock. She hadn't honestly expected him to strike her.

Liv made a startled sound and took half a step backward, likely on reflex. The scent of her spiking fear only made Aniya angrier.

"Next time it's you," the poacher warned. "*Move.*"

"Touch me and I'll rip your arm off," Aniya said, silently daring him to try. Someone had honked at the sight of the flying cup but otherwise, no one around seemed to be interested in their confrontation. That suited her fine. Bastard deserved to have his arms ripped off, anyway, for what he chose to do with his time.

She could tell by his scent, and the darkening of his eyes, that her challenge tipped him over the edge. Apparently, he didn't like women who weren't afraid of him. He clenched his hand at his side and raised his arm, as if he actually intended to punch her right there on the sidewalk. But she saw him think better of it, only to instead dip his hand into his pocket and extract a switchblade. An actual blade. "I'll cut out that tongue and hang it on my wall, whore," he spat as he swung.

The forward momentum of his arm ceased when another large, male hand wrapped around his forearm and squeezed.

"Drop the knife or lose your head."

Aniya's heart skipped a beat and her adrenaline spiked. She may never have heard the tone before, but she knew that voice. She knew that hand, and the strong arm extending from it. She remembered well what other wonderful things that hand could do. Her mouth went dry as heat pooled low in her belly and she dared to drag her gaze from her would-be assailant to the wolf who'd just stepped between them.

What a mistake that was.

Either he'd grown sexier in the two years since their encounter or her memory hadn't actually done him justice. He towered over her respectable five feet, eight inches by nearly a foot, had strong, broad shoulders and a chiseled jawline the likes of which sculptures aspired for. His reddish-brown hair was just as long as before, hanging past his ears on either side of his devastatingly handsome face and accentuating the green in his hazel eyes. Even as he leveled an angry glare at someone else, Aniya couldn't suppress the surge of desire in her blood.

This was exactly how it had happened before. Minus the poacher, the clothes, and change the setting. Was it any wonder she'd been unable to control herself?

The poacher released a sound of disgust, jerked his arm free—likely assuming they couldn't tell he was in pain—and turned, walking away. His arm would be sore for days with the grip her wolf had had on it.

My wolf? Well, it wasn't like she knew his name. She officially had to refer to him somehow.

The full force of those green-hued hazel eyes settled on Aniya and she had to fight to keep from running away like a startled housecat. But what was she supposed to do? Did she say something? Should she pretend they'd never met? What was the protocol here? *What if he's not alone?* She couldn't smell another wolf nearby, but her nose seemed pretty focused on him at the moment so she could certainly have missed one or two. *Why does he smell so good...?*

"What were you thinking," he began after a moment of intense silence, "squaring off with a poacher in broad daylight?"

Well. *That* certainly wasn't a contender on her list

of probable first-conversation topics.

Aniya drew as deep a breath as she dared, despite knowing the danger, and forced herself to keep his gaze. The way he held her stare … it was almost as if… *Oh, God!* There was no way. Could he be— Could she have—?

"Um," Liv said, her tone cautious but significantly less frightened. Her renewed presence at Aniya's side did a decent job of distracting Aniya from her building panic. "Did you say 'poacher'?"

The nameless wolf Aniya prayed to any listening deity wasn't an Alpha inclined his head with a brief glance in Liv's direction. Then it slid right back to her and Aniya swallowed before she even realized one was building. How had she missed it before? This man standing before her was *all* Alpha. Now if only she could decide whether that was more frightening or exciting.

A slow, sexy smirk tipped his lips. "What's the matter, cat got your tongue?"

That snapped her out of it. Aniya frowned and planted her hands on her hips. "Hilarious." Checking herself, partially in light of their current location and partially in recognition of the fact that he'd willingly assisted her, Aniya eased her stance and added, "Thank you, though. Not that I needed the help, but I appreciate the gesture."

"You're welcome." Damn, his voice was deep and smooth at the same time. It sent chills down her spine.

Liv cleared her throat. "So now that I've taken a breath. Obviously you two know each other." She extended her hand toward Aniya's mystery wolf. "I'm Liv."

Aniya's eyes widened. *No!*

His expression softened to simple and friendly

and his hand lifted, reaching for Liv's. "I'm—"

"Late!" Aniya exclaimed loudly, grabbing Liv's outstretched arm by the elbow and tugging gently. "So sorry, but we're running late! Happy hunting and all that!"

"What? Wait, An—!"

"Don't dawdle!" Aniya called as she practically dragged her poor, baffled friend back the way they'd come. Away from the wolf whose name she was suddenly terrified to learn.

Chapter Four

Maddox watched, stupefied, as his favorite cat panicked and ran away. At the prospect of learning his name. Or had it been the idea of him touching her friend's hand? He doubted that. Though the idea was kind of amusing.

He shook his head and turned, looking down the sidewalk in the direction the damned poacher had run off in.

Poachers. Of all the fucking things. It was good he'd chosen now to come and check in, he supposed. Running into poachers in the woods never went well. *Then again...* The memory of spotting *her* of all people across the street, in a stare down with a poacher, popped up in his mind. How he'd kept from just ripping the man's head off right there and then, he actually had no idea. When that knife had come out of the poacher's pocket, Maddox's first instinct had been to shift and sink his fangs into the bastard's throat. But that kind of behavior wasn't permitted in the city.

Still, what *had* she been thinking? She never had answered him. Something he wouldn't have let a pack member get away with. Was that a good enough reason to track her down this time? Maybe, but not when there was an angry poacher on the loose. Maddox had a responsibility to his pack that took priority over his raging lust. He'd have to take the poacher off the board before he found his cougar—whether he liked it or not.

It didn't take Maddox long to track the scent to a cheap motel on the outskirts of town. The motel seemed to be where the monster was staying, though he hadn't lingered for long this time. What concerned Maddox, however, was the additional scent around the door. Apparently this particular poacher didn't fly solo. That was a problem.

Two poachers were harder to lure to their 'accidental' deaths. Especially while maintaining his secret. He would have to be careful.

So would his unnamed cougar.

****

"Aniya!" Liv exclaimed when they settled on an old bench. It was one of Aniya's favorite spots, on the edge of the city, overlooking the wide creek. That was probably why she'd dragged them there.

Aniya sagged back against the bench, absently humming her inquiry. Her mind was still reeling and her body was still sizzling. How, after two years, had she not gotten him out of her system? He was a wolf! An Alpha, no less! She only wished she could tell herself that knowledge might have stopped her last time. But she knew better.

"Don't 'hmm?' me!" Liv pushed, poking Aniya's shoulder. "What the heck was that? Possibly the sexiest man alive saves us from an asshole—who was apparently a poacher—and you go running in the other direction?"

"What happened to your fiancé?"

Liv's cheeks flushed. "I think if he saw that guy even he'd feel things."

Aniya laughed in wholehearted sympathy.

"Okay, but, seriously," Liv said after a moment, "what was up with that?"

Looking around to be sure no one was eavesdropping, despite that she *knew* they were alone, Aniya finally glanced over to her friend and confided, "That was him."

Liv gave her a blank stare.

Not wanting to say it all out loud in the open,

Aniya emphasized, "*Him*."

Recognition lit Liv's eyes and her mouth fell open. "Oh. My. God." She looked behind them, in the direction they'd come from, before returning her gaze to Aniya. "Wow. Girl, no wonder you jumped him! I'd jump him if I were single!"

"Not so loud!" Aniya said with a hiss. "Anyway, it's not like I was ever expecting to run into him again, you know? Random, anonymous encounter. One-time thing."

"Ani," Liv said, using her silly nickname for Aniya, "you might not have been expecting to see him again, but you did." A mischievous grin spread across her face and Aniya knew the next words from her friend's lips were going to be dangerous. "You're here for the day, he's in town … could be a prime opportunity."

Aniya groaned and dropped her head into her hands. Yep. Dangerous.

****

Maddox was searching for the second poacher, wanting to get a good look at him, when he bumped into her again. Except this time she seemed to have been looking for him, and she was alone. He stared into her amber eyes for a moment, and when she didn't back down, he took a step forward and invaded her personal space. "Looking for me?"

Her chest rose with a deep inhale. "Guilty," she said with a small grin. She lifted one hand and danced her fingertips lightly up his chest until they covered his heart. "You're a hard man to forget, Wolf."

Her touch shot sparks through him and his cock twitched, hardening quickly.

"Glad to know I left an impression," Maddox said, his voice low and gruff. He caught her wrist and tugged her up against him fully, unashamed at letting her feel his erection. Catching her other wrist as well, Maddox wrapped his arms around her waist, effectively pinning her arms behind her back. He lowered his head, running his nose over her hair until his lips found her ear, and he smirked when she shivered. "I'm surprised you came looking for me."

"What can I say," she whispered, her lips teasing his throat, "I'm a glutton for punishment." She tested his grip and made a half-whimper sound that had him fighting the urge to spin them around and take her against the side of the building next to them. "Is it really necessary for you to restrain me?" He could hear the pout in her voice and he couldn't help but press his lips to the skin beneath her ear. She moaned low, leaning in to him, and he knew he wasn't the only one fighting his baser urges.

"You have a history of fleeing," he replied. "And we need to talk."

"Do we?" she asked, not seeming to find it necessary to argue the first comment. At least she knew herself, then. "Talking's not exactly high on my agenda right now."

His dick throbbed as she followed her teasing promise with a sensual lick over his pulse point.

"Baby," Maddox began, his voice little more than a carnal growl, "do that again and I'm gonna fuck you right here in the heart of town."

She tested his grip again and found it solid. Instead, she pushed up on her tiptoes in order to brush her own lips over his ear. "Promises, promises."

Oh, he was tempted. He might have even caved if not for the almost immediate sound of semi-distant gunfire.

Both lifted their heads, temporarily forgetting

their lustful banter, and looked in the direction of the sound. A single shot. Maddox waited, holding perfectly still, but no urgent sense of panic filled him. He released a breath.

"Maybe it wasn't even the poacher," the woman still in his arms whispered, her tone somewhere between doubtful and hopeful.

He sympathized. But it was a good reminder of why he couldn't just fall on her the way he wanted to. Instead, he adjusted his grip, releasing one arm and taking her other hand in his, and began walking. He held tight enough that she would have to comply, because he couldn't let her disappear again. He was still telling himself it was because of the poacher threat, but a voice in the back of his head whispered it was more than that. His biggest regret of the past two years wasn't bedding a cougar—it was not chasing after her when she ran off once they were done. Not at least getting her name.

Before his venture into the city was through, he was going to know her name. He was going to find out just why he hadn't been able to shake her from his mind—or his hormones—for the past two years. And if it meant what he suspected it did, then he'd deal with that, too. Even if she was a werecougar. Even if their packs—or clans, or whatever her people called them—were at war. If she was his, if she was meant to be his, no stupid, old political feud would keep him from her.

Chapter Five

They'd only been a few blocks from the small house Maddox's pack kept on the edge of town, so he took her there. It was the safest place to talk outside of pack territory. Once they were inside, he let go of her hand, at that point fairly confident she wouldn't leap out a window, and took a moment to lock the door behind him.

She stepped a couple of feet forward, into the sitting room, surprise coloring her scent. "You have a house here? I always thought the wolves' territory was in the heart of the forest?"

Maddox watched her for a moment as her gaze traveled from the sitting room to the partially separated kitchen area. The house wasn't elaborate by any means, but it sufficed. "You're right on both accounts," he said. He strode up next to her, looped his arm around her waist, and hauled her up to him. They needed to have a conversation about the poachers. But first, he needed a taste of her.

She started but offered no resistance when he sealed his mouth over hers. Instead, she leaned into the kiss, grabbing hold of his head with both hands and challenging him for control. Their tongues fought in sensuous combat from mouth to mouth as Maddox held her locked against him, a growl vibrating up his chest.

He was ready to lay her over the counter and have his way with her by the time he managed to break the kiss.

Judging from her scent, she wouldn't have complained.

"Is it possible you missed me?" she teased against

his lips, her voice breathless and ragged.

He scoffed, angled his head to nip at the edge of her shoulder where her shirt collar opened, and rumbled, "I'll let you figure that you on your own."

She hummed, the sound almost a purr, and he found himself smiling in satisfaction. He recalled earning a similar sound from her before. It felt oddly congratulatory.

Knowing the limits of his restraint, Maddox lifted his head and loosened his arms until he could look into her warm amber eyes again. "I was serious before, though. We do need to talk."

She arched a brow at him. "About what?"

He guided her to the single sofa and tugged her down beside him, angled so he could face her while keeping her in arm's reach. "That poacher earlier," he said.

She huffed in frustration and rolled her eyes. "He was an ass. I could have handled it. I'm not some frail kitten."

Maddox couldn't help but smirk. Oh, he had no doubt this woman could handle herself. The way she manipulated him with so little effort was convincing enough. "That isn't what I was getting at," he said. "I'd have loved to watch you put him on his ass." *I'd also have loved to rip his head off.* Neither were really publicly appropriate by human standards.

The eyebrow arch returned. "Then what?"

"There are two."

A couple of seconds ticked by before her eyes widened. "Two? Two poachers? *Here*?"

Maddox nodded.

She shook her head in disbelief. "What is there even to poach around here? Rabbits? The occasional bear?"

"Us."

She paled as horror spiked in her scent. That obviously hadn't occurred to her. It wasn't a thought he liked, either. He'd simply had no choice but to acknowledge the truth of what she had just been pondering. They didn't have reliable game to poach in their area. Mostly because the more desirable predators tended to give a wide berth to their shifter cousins. From a poacher's perspective, however, a wolf—or a cougar—was still just a wolf. All it would have taken was a solid rumor and a hungry hunter.

"You can't be serious," she mumbled.

"It's a high possibility," he said.

She clenched her hands into fists in her lap and he could tell she was trying to control her instinctive fear. It was a natural reaction to be afraid of a threat like this. Especially when she was alone and exposed, so far from her pack.

Maddox scowled at the thought. Without considering his actions, he scooped her into his lap and tucked her head beneath his chin. She stiffened for a moment before relaxing against him. "Just be careful while you're in town," he said quietly, his fingers threading her long, dark hair. "I'll deal with them."

She adjusted in his lap until her nose pressed against his throat. "By yourself?"

"Obviously."

"Don't be ridiculous," she lectured. "You're outnumbered."

He grinned and gave her thigh a squeeze. "I'm an Alpha, baby. They don't stand a chance."

Her hands twisted in his shirt and the fear formerly lingering in her scent gave way to a new wave of arousal. "Damn you, wolf," she muttered. "I can't get close enough to smell you without wanting to rub myself all over you. It's driving me crazy."

"You say that like it's a bad thing," he replied, visualizing her doing exactly what she'd described.

"I mean, it sort of *is*," she said. "We're supposed to hate each other, remember?"

Maddox snorted and rolled her beneath him on the sofa, angling so that his face landed in the hollow of her throat. He took a deep breath of her intoxicating scent as one of his hands stroked down the side of her body. She shivered and moaned. "The only thing I hate about you," he murmured as he dropped a kiss to her collarbone, "are your clothes."

"Then take them off," she said. "Yours too. I want that big dick I remember inside me again."

Well. No man in his right mind would argue with that.

****

Aniya gasped and dug her fingers into the cushions of the sofa when her lover slipped two long fingers inside her. They'd stripped in a flurry of desire, barely climbing up from the couch, and then he'd seated her on it properly before pulling her hips to the edge. The sight of that large, powerful man dropping to his knees before her and pressing his face between her thighs was startlingly erotic. Now he was fucking her with his fingers, hard and fast, while he licked at her folds and worked his way to where she really needed him. There was no way she would last long like this, and she suspected he knew that.

He stroked her spot with his tongue, gently at first, making her writhe desperately. The angle of his hand shifted and then he flattened his tongue on her clit. She cried out, so close she might have been able to will herself over if she tried hard enough. Her wolf plunged his fingers into her at an accelerated rate and sucked without warning or preamble, and she came. Just like that.

His fingers slipped from her and she watched, still breathless and lightheaded, as he licked them clean. Slowly.

Then he scooped her up and carried her down the short hall, past the kitchen, to the bedroom she hadn't been able to see before. It was just as large as the living room, but she didn't pay much attention to the décor as he playfully tossed her onto the large bed. He crawled on after her and she pouted, having recovered enough now to regain her composure.

"Come on, wolf," she started, intending to tease him about having done it missionary-style before. The truth was she'd always *thought* that position was boring—until she'd experienced it with him. So if he wanted to repeat history, she was willing to play along. She just didn't want to tell him that.

He had other ideas, however.

"*Maddox*," he said, his voice thick and nearly growling.

She cut herself off, her eyes widening. He trapped her in a stare that wasn't at all threatening, but instead ignited a new level of fire in her blood. A challenge not to her life, but possibly to her sanity.

Then he grabbed her by the hip and flipped her onto her stomach before leaning over her, his chest on her back, and brought his lips to her ear. "My name is Maddox," he said. "And after tonight, every time you think my name, your body will crave mine. You're not leaving this bed until the walls echo with my name and your orgasm."

Liquid heat rushed to her nether regions and Aniya swallowed hard. She had no doubt he could fulfill that promise. She *wanted* him to fulfill that promise. "If you manage that," she whispered, "I'll tell you my name."

He growled over her ear in acceptance of her challenge and another thrill shot through her. Oh, she was pretty sure he'd know her name by sunrise. But he still had to earn it. His hands took hold of her hips and tugged them up. She complied and spread her legs, knowing exactly what he wanted. He wanted her ass in the air so he could sink his beautiful cock into her sopping wet pussy and ride her hard.

She wanted it too.

Maddox leaned over her and dragged kisses and nips down her spine before reaching around and running his fingers over her folds. She moaned at the teasing touch. "Fuck," he said. "You're ready to go, huh? That's good, baby." He used his fingers to open her again as she felt him settle behind her, his erection brushing her ass.

She wondered if he had lube stashed away in the house somewhere for them to try that position later too.

The thought fled her mind, though, when Maddox snapped his hips forward and buried himself deep inside her pussy. In fact, *all* thought fled her mind. He felt so much bigger, and stronger, than she remembered. It was amazing.

Maddox grunted over her and began driving himself in and out of her body with a barely controlled rhythm. The wildness spurned her on and she rocked her ass backward to take him as deep as physically possible. She clutched fistfuls of the comforter beneath her, her forehead pressed to the bed, and shamelessly moaned and gasped each time he slammed home. She loved his fervor. The way his lust took hold and compelled him to fuck her like a man starved.

She gasped his name when he angled his hips on the next thrust, hitting something new that felt so good, her body jerked against him. He must have liked that, because he did it again, harder, and this time he reached around and caught one of her breasts in his hand.

Aniya nearly lost it when he pinched her nipple. Dots of white popped in her vision and her attempt at maintaining rhythm faltered. "Maddox," she gasped, "Maddox, *please.*"

He withdrew, flipped her over, lifted her legs to his shoulders, and sank his cock to the hilt inside her with one sharp thrust. Aniya cried his name to the ceiling, to the gods, to whomever, arching her hips, desperate to keep herself united with him. To keep that glorious dick seated entirely inside her hungry, pulsating core. Instead of completely withdrawing, he slid back and rocked his hips as he plunged forward, several times repeatedly in sharp, short movements.

His cock filled her again and she finally burst, her vision exploding in sparkling white, his name tearing from her throat as her body rocked with his without her control. Her orgasm ripped through her, shattering and burning and euphoric, and just when she thought she couldn't get enough, she felt him slam home one more time as his release hit too. The walls echoed with his roar as his body quivered above her.

He'd definitely earned her name.

Chapter Six

Aniya stretched when she woke from her cat nap, her body sore in all the best ways, and rolled onto her side only to find the bed empty. A strange pang of disappointment hit her and she frowned. This was *his* house, surely Maddox hadn't—

"You're awake," Maddox's deep, delicious voice declared from the doorway, drawing her attention.

The disappointment fled and she chose not to dwell on it, instead sitting up, pulling the top sheet of the blanket with her. She drank in the sight of her werewolf lover, leaning against the doorframe in nothing but a worn-in pair of jeans that hung dangerously low on his hips. A thin smattering of chest hair covered his pecs and trailed down to a point aimed at what he hid behind the denim.

"Aniya," he said, her name rolling like a caress off his tongue, "keep looking at me like that and you're never leaving that bed."

She couldn't deny the flicker of excitement that stole through her at the promise. Her lips lifted in a coy smile. "Was that supposed to dissuade me?"

A growl rumbled up his chest, just barely reaching her ears, and her skin heated. She remembered clearly what that growl felt like pressed against her body, vibrating her chest and rolling over his tongue as he kissed her.

"You're trouble," Maddox said, shaking his head. "You're definitely trouble."

Her smile widened. "I am." She took a deep breath and finally registered the smell of coffee from the kitchen. Coffee, and food. Her stomach growled so she slid to her feet, letting go of the sheet. It wasn't like he hadn't seen and thoroughly explored her naked body at this point, and in truth, she wasn't *that* modest. "Please tell me you're not going to make me watch you eat."

He chuckled, the sound warm and surprisingly appealing, and moved to the closet. "I actually came to wake you. The fridge was a little bare, but I found enough to make do." He extracted a large men's t-shirt, black, and held it out for her. Judging from the size, it was probably his. "Here."

Aniya looked at the shirt for a moment. If she wore it, she'd literally be wrapping herself in his scent. She laughed at herself. *Because I haven't done that in spades already.* Taking the shirt, Aniya grinned up at him and tugged it over her head. His scent hit her like a changing breeze as it fell into place over her shoulders, and her toes curled. *Actually* curled. When she'd considered what wrapping herself in his scent would mean, she'd been thinking of the consequences if the scent lingered by the time she returned home. It hadn't crossed her mind what it would mean for her. But the shirt, and his presence, brought the strangest sense of peace to her. It was wonderful, to be sure, but she didn't understand it.

"You coming?"

Startling, Aniya gathered herself and turned to face him, finding him smirking at her in the doorway. Damn. He'd definitely noticed. What was worse, she found that proud smirk annoyingly sexy.

He led the way to the kitchen bar, the outcropping which served to separate it from the living room, and she finally noticed the cushioned barstools. Though there was space for probably four, there were only two. It made eating more comfortable, even though really, when Maddox took his seat beside her, she realized there probably *wasn't* space for four.

"Mm, coffee," she said with a delighted moan as she took her first sip. He'd doctored it exactly the way she'd directed him. It was perfect. "I wish we had coffee at home."

His shoulders shook with an almost silent chuckle. "Too rustic?" he asked, lifting his own mug to his lips.

Aniya shook her head. "Not really. We have a house. My family just…" Her voice trailed and she shrugged, not sure how to explain it. Was there a valid reason? Her parents weren't entirely anti-modernism. They adopted it where it fit their needs. Her mother *loved* Facebook, as odd as it was. Though she only used it to keep in touch with Aniya's brothers and extended family. They had a fair assortment of kitchen appliances, never too out of date.

"What?" Maddox asked, his tone curious, as he bit into his thick sausage link.

Aniya smiled with silent laughter. "I just realized. I think my parents don't like coffee."

Maddox laughed. "And yet you clearly love it," he said. Amusement flashed in his eyes.

Thoughtlessly, Aniya blurted, "So help me, *one* catnip joke and no sex for a week, you got that?"

She froze when she realized what she'd said. Or, more specifically, what she'd implied. All of a sudden she was behaving as if they were an item. She *felt* like she was with him. But she wasn't. Not really. Except she'd just gone and made a very relationship-oriented statement. A statement which heavily implied continued personal interaction for—well, for a while, at least. She swallowed a lump that had suddenly formed in her throat.

Maddox lowered his coffee to the counter. "Then

it's a deal. No catnip jokes."

Oh, man. What did she do with that?

She knew what she *wanted* to do with that. All of a sudden it was clear as day. This—this bizarre, playful, sexy, whatever it was—she liked it. A lot. She didn't want to let it go.

"Aniya," Maddox said. He reached over and covered her nearest hand with his own. "What's with the panic?"

Jerking herself out of her jumbled thoughts, Aniya looked up at him. He was frowning with concern at her and her heart melted a little. Was this more than just sex for him? Or was that her newly-discovered voice of hope projecting her desires? She wasn't sure she'd ever know. "Ah, sorry. Nothing."

He looked decidedly less than convinced. She couldn't blame him.

She reached for the coffee to buy herself more time to sort out her chaotic thoughts when a flash of urgency and the burning need to go home shot through her. She sucked in a sharp breath, her entire body tensing up at the unexpected and entirely uncharacteristic summons.

"Aniya?"

"I"—she drew a shaky breath and met his gaze—"I have to go home. Right now."

Recognition dawned and he nodded, releasing her hand. Of course he would understand. He was an Alpha. How could she forget he was an Alpha, again? But this wasn't the time to wonder how in the world she could hope to pursue something with the reigning Alpha of the werewolves. Something was wrong at home. It had to be. There was just no other reason her father would actually summon her.

****

Maddox watched from his backyard as Aniya, in her feline form, raced into the forest in answer to the Alpha summons she'd received minutes earlier. His heart clenched and he ground his teeth. He'd seen the fear in her eyes, smelled it in her scent. Whatever the typical conditions were for her Alpha to summon his people, it seemed enough to bring her true worry. And the moment that worry had gripped her, Maddox found himself having to resist the need to go with her. If something was wrong, if there was some kind of danger ... he couldn't stomach the thought of not being there to protect her. Or at least support her.

But it wasn't his place. Not when it involved her pack. Especially not with him being Alpha of their informal enemies.

He snorted and turned to go back inside.

Enemies. Please.

Even as a pup he'd questioned the legitimacy, and the necessity, of their feud. Now, as a man on the verge of some very dangerous, very serious emotions, he knew without a doubt those rivalries were ridiculous. There wasn't a single reason they couldn't coexist. They had far more in common than they did separate. But how would he be able to get that across to everyone else? If he wanted half a chance with Aniya, he needed to smooth over ages-old grudges on both sides. He couldn't just order his pack to accept his choice, because though they'd have no alternative, they would also have resentment.

Maddox dragged a hand down his face and moved to the bathroom, in need of a shower before he resumed his work. He couldn't focus on building new alliances with the cougars until the threat of the poachers was dealt with. And somewhere in between, he needed to find a way to check on Aniya. The knot in his stomach wasn't going to ease until he knew for himself she was okay.

First things first.

Maddox showered quickly, changed, and exited the house. He made a mental note to remember to call the maid company he usually hired after his visits to come and clean up again too. But that was better left for once he was sure he was done.

He set off into town, navigating easily to the more populous areas in hopes of catching a trail on his way to the motel he'd found earlier. He struck out and continued on. It was always possible they'd taken whatever they might have shot before back to their motel, or left altogether, even. But he doubted he had that kind of luck.

He was right. The poacher's vehicle remained exactly where it had been before. In fact, Maddox suspected it hadn't been moved at all. But the scents—both the one of the man he'd met and the other—were fresher. They'd been back, but they'd also left again. This time, though, they'd left together, and armed. Maddox frowned and adjusted course to follow the trail. Armed was bad.

His bad feeling didn't ease when the trail quickly led him to the forest line and past the trees. Veering away from his own territory, which was good, but too uncomfortably similar in direction to the way Aniya had run earlier. And they were still a couple of hours ahead of him.

Maddox grit his teeth, glanced around, and ducked behind a tree to shed his clothes. As soon as he was free, he broke into a run, shifting as he moved. He'd catch them faster with four legs.

****

Aniya's heart was pumping so loud in her ears by

the time she made it home she almost didn't hear the first yowls of pain. She skidded to a stop a few yards from the building in the heart of their territory—her family's home—as the next thing registered. Out-of-place scents. Two of them. Human. Maybe a couple of hours old at the most and, worst of all, one of them seemed familiar. It was that man from before.

The poachers!

It didn't make sense. None of it made sense. But at the moment, none of it mattered, either. There was actually a guard posted outside the front door, for the first time since her brothers were cubs, and Aniya could barely breathe. It was impossible to tell which of the surrounding, echoing cries were of sympathy and which from the ones in actual pain. *Or worse...*

She brought herself to the door and paused again, glancing around, her tail swishing slow and hesitant. *"What's going on?"*

The guard looked away. *"Just get inside."*

Aniya couldn't remember a time she'd been as afraid of what awaited her as she was the moment she eased the door open with her front paw. The doors were designed to be easily opened in their feline forms since so many of their clan preferred to stay feline. A fact that had never seemed problematic to her until the scent of blood slipped past the door and up to her nose.

Blood...? In the house?

She took a cautious step inside, not wanting to breathe the scent in any further. Not wanting to identify its source, even though she needed to know. Her gut told her she wasn't going to find an eviscerated poacher in their living room. Once she was fully in the entryway, her nose told her the blood wasn't human at all. No, this was her nightmare.

The blood was her father's.

Chapter Seven

Aniya raced through the house, still pulling on the robe she'd grabbed when she'd shifted, following a combination of her nose and the visual trail of blood. The trail, for better or worse, was inconsistent. It had pooled too much just beyond the entryway but thinned to just a handful of droplets forming a vague line at this point. There was a handprint in the blood on the wall of the doorway leading into the bedroom, and a larger gathering of droplets. Still glistening on the floor.

"Dad!" Aniya cried, tears in her eyes, when she spotted her parents on the floor beside their bed.

Her mother sat with her back against the mattress, tears rolling steadily down unnaturally pale cheeks, with Regis held in her lap. His head was propped on her chest. He was still breathing, but his breathing was ragged and shallow. Blood dribbled from his lips and colored the carpet beneath his torso—beneath his wife's knees.

Florence looked up, meeting Aniya's gaze, agony shining back at her. "Aniya," she said, her own voice weak. Aniya couldn't smell a drop of her mother's blood. The only physical pain her mother suffered was the breaking of her heart, but it was enough. More than enough. It would kill her all the same.

Aniya hit her knees beside them as her own tears fell. "What," she said, choking on her words, her hands trembling as she reached for her father's. "What happened?" Her father's hands were colder than she'd ever felt them. Caked in blood.

He wheezed, as if trying to speak, and for the first time Aniya caught a whiff of the silver. *Silver...?* The poachers ... had brought silver weapons? But that would mean they'd known…

"Shh, Regis," Florence whispered brokenly, running her fingers through his thinning hair. Again she lifted her eyes to Aniya. "Humans came. Poachers." She swallowed. "They shot a deer a little ways off, and one of ours went to claim it."

Aniya's stomach hit the floor. *The gunshot.* The gunshot she'd heard while she'd been on the street with Maddox.

"He came back wounded," her mother said, oblivious to Aniya's realization. "He said he'd chased the men away. Not to worry." She drew a sharp, unsteady breath as Regis coughed. Both women's hands found somewhere to rub gentle, soothing circles over him. Florence continued. "In the early morning, your father startled awake. Said he thought he'd sensed a scuffle, some sort of problem." She pressed her lips to his head. "By the time we made it to the doorway, even I could hear the commotion. I begged him not to open the door. But in the end, it didn't matter, because one of those poachers … he let himself in."

And her father had done what any male would do to protect his mate. It didn't need to be said.

"How?" Aniya asked around the lump in her throat as she gave her father's hand another squeeze. "How did they get away?" Obviously her father had been terribly wounded, but the clan—the clan should have been there. Except she'd seen no bodies, smelled no mass of human blood.

"I don't know," her mother said with a renewed sob. "I wasn't honestly paying that much attention after your father threw him out of the house." She pulled Regis closer, resting her forehead against his.

Aniya had to look away. Her heart hurt far too much, seeing her parents like this. Knowing her father's wound was too serious to heal in time. Knowing there was nothing she could do other than be there with them.

"A-Aniya," her father said with a cough, giving her hand a weak squeeze.

She lifted her gaze obligingly, both glad and pained to see him finally looking at her.

"The clan," he said, "needs ... a leader ... now."

No. "No, Dad," Aniya said, shaking her head, more tears escaping. "I can't—they wouldn't listen to me even if I tried." This couldn't really be what he wanted to say to her now, could it? "Dad, please," she said, hoping to change the subject. Or put his mind at ease. "I'll ask the twins to come home. I'll figure something out. Just ... just don't worry." But what could she say? What could possibly put the mind of a dying Alpha at ease?

"They have their own clans, honey," Florence said, her voice strained. "Your father hasn't wanted to say anything, but, he's been worried. He was hoping—*we* were hoping—you'd find a mate, and produce an Alpha for us."

But it's too late.

Aniya heard the words hanging between them like a gong in her ears.

For the life of her, the moment her mother said *mate*, an image of Maddox came to her in her mind and Aniya knew. She knew she'd never take a traditional mate. Which meant she'd never have cubs—or at least, not purebred cubs. Alphas were always purebred. But she couldn't say any of that to her parents now—or ever.

"F-find—" Regis cut himself off with a rasping cough. "Find ... a way," he said finally. When he met her eyes again, she saw tears looking back at her. "They're our responsibility…"

"R-Regis?" Florence whispered, desperation in her draining voice.

Aniya's eyes widened as her father's chest fell on an exhale and his hand went slack in hers.

****

Maddox stopped when he realized he'd crossed a fresher path of the poachers' scent than the one he was already following. He'd begun to pick up lingering, sporadic scents of cougar in the area, meaning they sometimes used this part of the forest as a hunting ground. A sign he severely disliked. But the new trail veered away from the one leading him toward the felines, for which he was grateful. Even if he used the largely legitimate excuse of tracking poachers, he'd have a hard time explaining incidentally ending up at the cougars' border.

So he altered course and renewed his chase. He'd closed a lot of distance. He would intercept them soon.

Several minutes later, the wind shifted direction and brought their scents more directly Maddox's way. On the breeze, he caught the smell of something that sent ice through his veins.

Cougar blood. Mixed with silver.

The blood wasn't Aniya's, he knew that instantly. It was no longer fresh, either, though not by much. All the same, they had wielded a silver weapon against one of Aniya's people. That *had* to be why she'd been summoned home. She could easily have run across these monsters in her flight, and what then? The pocketknife the first one had pulled on her before most definitely wasn't silver. She wouldn't have been expecting it.

Maddox's blood began to boil and he pressed forward, close enough now he could almost hear their voices. He needed to catch them. Needed to rip them apart. For reasons that extended beyond his responsibilities as Alpha—though those responsibilities were coming in to play the deeper the poachers walked as well. While at first, their direction could easily have been a random choice, it was beginning to seem like these poachers were headed toward his pack. As if he didn't already want to kill them badly enough.

Only it didn't make sense. How would they know where to find even *one* shifter den? Let alone *both* of the dens in the area? On some level, this hunt had to be purposeful. He'd never known humans to make a habit of hunting with silver weapons. It simply wasn't practical from an uneducated man's perspective.

Regardless, the poachers were nearly past the neutral hunting grounds the shifter species shared. Maddox could no longer afford to merely follow and see where they led him.

Lifting his nose to the wind in order to scent the area ahead, he took solace in noting none of his pack were nearby. At least not yet. It was also midday, which meant that could change anytime. Holding firm to his concern for his pack, driven by the scent of the drying cougar blood, Maddox broke into a run once more.

He burst past the final bit of shrubbery hiding him from his targets, who had stopped for some reason beneath a large tree, and let his angry growl slip free as he tackled the familiar one head-on. It was that man, the poacher he'd encountered in the city the previous day, who smelled of cougar blood.

The other poacher cried out in shock, leaping backward and out of the way.

Maddox and the first one crashed to the ground, but Maddox maintained control of his own descent and easily leaped over the man's flailing arm. He landed on his feet in front of the bastard's face, teeth bared, making damn sure the man knew what was coming.

"Phil!" the other poacher called as he scuffled around. He wasn't fleeing, but that didn't surprise

Maddox.

"Fuck! Get this fucking thing away from me!" the one named Phil exclaimed, trying awkwardly to shove himself backward.

Phil's hand landed in the dirt as he braced himself and Maddox dove for his arm. It was the same arm that had struck Aniya. The arm he should've just ripped off right there in the street. Phil jerked back, but Maddox still managed to sink his teeth into the man's flesh. Just not exactly where he'd wanted. Phil cursed vehemently and brought his other fist down on Maddox's head. It wasn't the most comfortable of hits, but Maddox held on, jerking and growling for good measure.

The bastard was going to pay for whatever hurt he'd put Aniya's people through.

For whatever blood he'd planned to shed in Maddox's pack.

He and his friend would pay with their lives.

Maddox was so intent on ripping pieces off Phil he nearly missed the single warning sound he wasn't meant to hear. He cocked his ears as he caught the telltale whiff of gunpowder in the air. With a sharp jerk of his head, he released Phil's arm, earning another pained outcry from him, and spun to dodge even as the forest echoed with the explosion of a gunshot.

Chapter Eight

No one had agreed with Aniya's decision to pursue the poachers, but in the aftermath of her parents' deaths, she'd learned she had no choice.

Unable to stay in the house another moment, Aniya had run outside, her vision blurred with fresh tears and scarred by the sight of father's and mother's lifeless bodies. She'd never thought her father would be murdered. She'd never expected to watch her mother die, as mates do, just moments later. It was too much.

In need of some kind of distraction, and recognizing her grief didn't override the looming danger of the poachers, Aniya had asked around until she found a clan member who'd seen them. He was wounded too, she realized. But his wound wasn't fatal. A fact that had brought her some relief until she'd learned how he'd gotten away—how he'd gotten *them* away.

Her own clan member had sold out the wolves.

He said he'd lied and told the poachers the wolves were weak. *"I told them if they took the wolf leader out too, and didn't come back here, we'd let it go. We wouldn't come for them."*

Even now, shifted back into feline form and running through the forest, Aniya felt the sting on her flesh from how hard she'd slapped him. She wanted to exile him for what he'd done. On principle, as a shifter, and also as a woman who wanted nothing more at that moment than to burrow into Maddox's arms and cry for days. But she had no authority to exile anyone—she wasn't an Alpha. And not only was Maddox not immediately available, but thanks to one of her own, he might be in imminent danger.

So she ran.

Her heart thrummed in her ears with each smack of her paws in the dirt. She ran as fast as she could, as hard as she dared.

She was still running, following the trail of the poachers as it led ever closer to the wolf den when a gunshot shattered the natural tranquility of the forest.

Aniya's heart nearly stopped. A vision of Maddox, bleeding and naked, on the forest floor, blinded her line of sight. *No!*

Not him. She couldn't lose him too.

****

Maddox cursed himself, his uncontrollable yelp of pain still hanging in the air, as he regrouped from the bullet that had nearly embedded itself in his hind end. If he'd been a few seconds slower, he'd be crippled. Instead, it hurt like hell, but the bullet had only sliced over the top of him. It would heal, but he'd need to shift to accelerate the process, and since the damned thing had been silver, even that would hurt like a mother.

"You fucking missed, Larry!" Phil snapped, having found his feet and now holding a dirty cloth to his bleeding arm.

"Give me a break! I was trying to avoid *you!*" The second poacher, Larry, lifted his gun again and Maddox charged. As he'd hoped, Larry panicked and shot wide.

"Jesus!" Phil exclaimed, throwing himself out of the way as Maddox aimed for Larry next. "He's a fucking beast!"

Maddox got his jaw on Larry's dominant hand, simultaneously knocking the gun askew, and tossed his head until he heard the cracking of fragile bones. Larry shouted, writhing, and rolled in toward his newly-injured hand as soon as Maddox moved away.

"Pull yourself together, goddammit!" Phil cried. When Maddox returned his attention to the larger poacher, he found Phil had managed to tie the cloth around his arm, for what little good it was doing. Phil extracted his knife—the very same knife, Maddox saw, that he'd used on the cougar he'd stabbed. It still had flakes of blood on its silver blade. "Fucking monster," he said. "I'll gut you. Just like I did that old cat."

Old? Had he gone for the Alpha? Maddox had never met the cougar Alpha, but he knew the cat was supposed to be a little older than his own father would have been. And this poacher had attacked him? He took *pride* in that?

Maddox growled again with renewed anger. Maybe he'd gotten the drop on an elderly Alpha, but he was about to learn what an Alpha in his prime could do.

"Phil, man, I think you just pissed him off," Larry said, his voice still burdened with pain.

"Good." Phil tightened his hold on the knife and lunged forward, swiping, forcing Maddox to rear back or lose an eye. "That's right, beast! *I'm* the big guy on cam—"

Without warning, Ty burst from the bushes in Maddox's peripheral vision, snarling viciously, and tackled Phil to the ground. The silver blade went flying and more blood splattered into the air. Phil had managed to block with his injured arm, but Ty got a good bite in all the same.

"*Fuck!*" Larry cried, jumping aside and scrambling for his gun. "Another one!" He pointed his gun at Ty and Maddox snapped sharply, quickly earning his attention even as Maddox moved forward again. Larry pulled the trigger, but his aim with his opposite hand was poor and Maddox easily evaded the shot.

Ty slammed sideways into Larry, having been

kicked off by Phil, and another gunshot rang out.

"Ty!"

Ty yelped, scrambled off the fumbling poacher, and moved quickly to Maddox's side. He didn't appear to be injured. *"My ears! Alpha, I may never be able to hear again!"*

Well, if he could still make jokes, he was all right.

"For the love of fucking God, Larry," Phil cursed, "shoot the fuckers! I need a hospital!"

"You take Larry," Maddox told Ty. *"Don't get shot."*

Together, they bared their teeth as Larry attempted to square his shot. His heartbeat was far too erratic, his arm was shaking, and his angle was lousy. Maddox was confident they could rip the bastards apart without further injury to themselves.

He wasn't counting on the ominous cry of an angry cougar as she pounced from the tree overhead.

Neither was anyone else.

She landed on Larry, her momentum knocking them both into Phil, and all three of them tumbled to the ground. The men fell in a tangle of limbs, curses, cries of pain, and fresh blood. Aniya dragged her claws down Larry's shoulder, narrowly missing when she went to sink her teeth into his bicep. Her jaw clamped on empty air, just centimeters away from Phil's face.

"Is ... is she...?" The confusion in Ty's voice was blatant.

Maddox ignored it. *"Now!"* He charged forward before either poacher could get their feet beneath them. His hip still hurt from the clip he'd taken minutes ago. He wasn't going to let them do worse to Aniya.

The difference in their species prevented him from communicating with her in his animal form, but she seemed to read his intent perfectly. Using Larry as a springboard, she arched into the air and around until she landed on her paws, facing Phil and growling. Maddox was honestly surprised by the intensity of her growl. But he didn't have time to be as he caught Larry by the sleeve—and a bit of his upper arm—and yanked him away, in the opposite direction of Aniya.

Larry went stumbling and rolling unceremoniously as Ty quickly moved to put himself beside Maddox, but eyeing the scene with Aniya and Phil.

Maddox wanted to tell Ty to trust her. More specifically, not to attack her, but there wasn't time. For the moment, he was going to have to place his own trust in his Beta and hope the other wolf would understand that, at least in this, the cougars were their allies. Maddox returned his focus to Larry, who was coughing up dirt, but then Phil spoke again and his words caught Maddox completely off guard.

"N-No," Phil stuttered. "You—or that other one—said if we got them, you'd leave us alone!"

"What?" Ty's stunned question echoed Maddox's sentiment perfectly.

Maddox looked back in time to see Aniya's fur ripple as she shifted. He wanted to shout for her to stay in her feline form, where her strength and agility were strongest, but to do that he would have had to shift as well and then the point would be moot.

Phil took half a step back when Aniya straightened, fully naked, and leveled an expression full of hatred and heartbreak directly at him. The pain in her eyes gutted Maddox.

"He doesn't speak for me," she said with a growl. Her hands curled into fists and she took a step forward. "My *father* spoke for me. Before you murdered him." A tear stole down her cheek.

"Ty. Take this one." He didn't mean to make it an order. The pain on her face, the pain in her expression, the pain in her scent, it was too much. Maddox couldn't focus on Larry and save her at the same time.

Then Phil lifted the knife he'd managed to retrieve at some point and, with a derogatory curse, swung out to slice her open.

Maddox moved on instinct. He shifted mid-lunge, caught hold of Phil's swinging shoulder, hauled him back into a chokehold, and snapped his neck. Phil's corpse hit the dirt with a dull thud.

"Ph-Phil!" Larry screamed. He moved to scurry forward, but Ty, additionally compelled by Maddox's inadvertent order, cut him off. In two quick movements, Ty managed to rip the other poacher's throat out, ending the fight. And the threat.

Maddox returned his attention to Aniya and scowled at the sight of several more tears running down her cheeks. He gave no thought to stepping up to her and wiping them away with his thumbs. "Aniya," he said gently. When she lifted her gaze to his, he forced the next question past his lips, even though he was fairly sure he'd pieced the answer together already. "What happened?"

Chapter Nine

"No," one of the patrol guards hissed for the hundredth time.

Aniya defiantly crossed her arms over her chest. She hadn't expected any of the clan to like this idea. Hell, when Maddox had made the offer—and after the shock had worn off—*she'd* rejected it. Initially. Until he'd wrapped his arms around her and explained all the reasons why it made the most sense for their situation. Both personally and as a clan—a pack. *Okay, the terminology will still be tricky.*

"Aniya," a female, the mate of the patrol guard who'd been wounded on the night of the poacher attack, spoke up. "Think about what you're saying. That's … that's asking a lot."

"I know," Aniya said. "I know it is. That's why I've taken the time to talk to everyone about this individually over the past week." She drew a breath and looked around. What was left of her father's clan had gathered, at her request, in the open backyard of the now-empty house. After the attack that had killed her parents, and the fight with the poachers, she'd returned and exiled the cat who'd sold out the wolves. Surprisingly, when she'd explained her reasoning, none of the others hesitated to support her.

This, however, was entirely different.

What she and Maddox were proposing was an unheard of change in lifestyle. *Nothing* would be the same. And he'd admitted he expected pushback on his end too. That, at least, made her feel better. Because at the end of the day, her father had asked her to look after their people. She didn't know a better way to do it than this, as ridiculous as it was. By the very nature of being born female, she could never be Alpha, and without a leader, even if they tried to stay together, they were vulnerable. If they scattered, in search of clans that might take new faces in, they risked unknown dangers.

She desperately hoped she could convince them to recognize that too.

"This forest is our home," Aniya said, projecting her voice. She'd told them all this already, but they needed to hear it again. "I'm not asking anyone to move. But we all know it's only a matter of time before something happens if we ignore the problem we face without an Alpha." Her throat threatened to choke on the word, so she took a breath. "We *need* an Alpha. You know it. I know it. My father knew it."

Another guard interrupted her. "Your father would throw you out if he heard this!"

Aniya cut a glare at him even as a couple of others gave him their own looks of displeasure. "My father asked me to take care of you," she said. "This is the best way for me to honor that wish."

"The *wolves*?" another voice exclaimed.

Looking around again, Aniya repeated, "I trust Maddox. He's more than willing to take us all in."

"Of course," the guard from earlier said bitingly. "More territory for them."

Aniya opened her mouth, but another cat beat her to it. "If they're as bad as you think, won't they just take our land by force, then? So wouldn't this be smarter?"

Aniya wanted to say Maddox wouldn't do such a thing, but she recognized the woman's point. So she kept silent. Letting someone else offer even a spark of favor in her direction couldn't hurt.

"*Smarter*? They're *dogs*!"

"Please don't tell me that's what this is," Aniya

interrupted. She couldn't stop herself. "Who cares about that? We're not incompatible. We've been neighbors for centuries. This feud has been in our *heads* for as long as any of us can remember, but have any of us seen any bloodshed?"

No one had an answer to that.

Their eldest member finally spoke up from the back of the small crowd. "Why?" she asked. "Why do you trust this wolf so much? Why should *we*?"

Silence reigned as the group waited for Aniya's answer.

She swallowed her nerves and dared to bare her secret. "Because I love him. Because he's asked me to be his mate, but neither of us feels it's right to take that step until our people are unified."

Aniya swore the shocked gasp that carried over the gathered group was louder than a group their size should have been able to produce. It took all her courage to keep from looking away, but she needed them to see that she wasn't ashamed. She'd never once been ashamed of her heart. If her heart told her Maddox was the answer, then Maddox was the answer. Sure, it was crazy for a werecougar to be in love with a werewolf. But she'd crossed that line two years earlier, when she'd first laid eyes on that flawless male body and known she couldn't leave the clearing until she'd wrung it dry.

Now, finally, for the first time, her wild ways just might be coming in handy.

****

"Here?" Aniya asked, surprise in her voice, when Maddox pulled her to him after they stepped into a familiar clearing.

"Here," he murmured, his lips brushing the skin beneath her ear. "It's appropriate."

She shivered in his arms and tilted her head,

granting him access. "It is. I think you might have claimed me that day, actually, and I just didn't know it."

Maddox vibrated with a silent laugh. Sometimes he felt the same way. But they were both going to know it after tonight. Here, in this clearing where they'd first met, he was finally going to claim his chosen mate. This beautiful, vivacious werecougar who always kept him on his toes.

It had been nearly two months now since the night the poachers attacked their forest. Since her father, her Alpha, had been murdered. It hadn't taken Maddox long to have the groundbreaking—and controversial—idea of merging their groups into one tribe. "Tribe" being the term they'd decided to use since neither could agree on abandoning or adopting the other's. Implementing that idea, however, had taken some work. *Lots* of work. He suspected it would be years still before everyone was really settled, but for now, they'd made good headway.

The cougars and the wolves were no longer at war. They were two species, united under one Alpha, living side-by-side in one shared territory. Learning to get along as allies, where he hoped in time they would be friends. But this was a good start.

Second, however, to the start of the life he would be leading from this night forward with Aniya. He'd never imagined he would love a woman as much as he loved her. From the crown of her head to the soles of her feet, and every delectable inch in between. Which he intended to spend his time indulging in tonight, he decided as he rolled her beneath him on the grass and pumped his aching, starving cock into her tight, hot center.

Aniya moaned and wrapped herself around him, ankles locked behind his ass, nails digging into his back. He growled and wedged an arm behind her back to hold her tighter as he drove himself deeper.

"*Yes!*" Aniya cried with a gasp, jerking her hips up to meet his thrusts. She was close. That was good.

Maddox kicked up the pace, not afraid to be a little rough since he knew she liked it, and was rewarded with another, louder outcry of pleasure. He felt his own body tense, the release building, and buried his face in the crook of her throat. Her body pulsed around his dick as he pounded into her, his rhythm slipping in favor of satisfaction, and as she grabbed a fistful of his hair, her walls clamping tight, Maddox sank his teeth into her neck.

His release tore through him with a force he'd never known, causing his entire body to surge against her, and Aniya muffled her outcry by leaning up and sinking her own teeth into his neck in return. Another wave of ecstasy ripped over his body, and hers, and they held each other tight, their hips blindly grinding and rolling on a seemingly endless orgasm.

Only when it finally subsided, the tension in their bodies finally fading, did Maddox and Aniya retract their fangs from each other's throats. Maddox ran his tongue over the wound that was already bruising on her skin, knowing it would scar, and he nearly shuddered when she did the same.

Fuck... He'd never felt anything so deliriously fantastic in his life. He'd never dreamed the mating process was actually that powerful, even though he'd heard rumors it was unlike anything else.

"*It really was ... amazing.*"

He lifted his head, removing his arm from her back in order to balance himself above her, and grinned. "Amazing, huh?"

Her eyes widened. "I-how—" She frowned. "I *thought* that. And yes. But still. How did you—?"

The breath rushed from his lungs as he realized what she'd said. Moreover, as he realized her point. Was that possible? In human form? And across species lines? Making sure to hold her gaze, Maddox kept his lips locked as he said, *"Baby, we're making history."*

Her lips twitched before the realization dawned in her eyes. "Oh, my God," she mumbled. "I heard that…" Then she smiled. *"We made history in this clearing two years ago, wolf. Catch up."*

He laughed, rolled off her, and tugged her onto his chest. "I fucking love you, Aniya," he rumbled before capturing her lips in another wet, lingering kiss.

She moaned and melted against him, her hands splayed over his shoulders. *"Never let me go, Maddox."*

Maddox wrapped his arms around her as he deepened the kiss, a wordless promise to do exactly as she asked. Because she was his, finally and forever.

The End

GUARDING WHAT'S HERS

Kait Gamble

Chapter One

Merlin's Cave, Tintagel, England

Saengdao 'Cammi' Willows picked a path along the wall of the cavern, listening to the echoing voices being carried along with the gentle gusts of wind. The scent of the sea air should have been invigorating.

Instead, all that rushed through her veins was burning annoyance.

Impatience had her drumming her fingers along the stone.

Bloody tourists.

Trembling with anticipation, she circled the little space again, trying to look natural. Like just another random visitor to the mythical location.

The place where Merlin legendarily brought Arthur up as a child. While others might have been entranced by the beauty of the landscape or the ruined remains of the castle, Cammi was focused on the cave.

The past decade of her life had led to this.

It had taken countless hours of plotting and literal blood, sweat, tears, getting around mind-boggling traps and deciphering incomprehensible clues and decayed maps. All to bring her here.

Now.

Surrounded by people soaking up the hype, pretending to feel the history there when they had no idea just how close they were to real magic.

How crazy would they go if they ever found out that everything so many of them dreamed of and feared lived among them all this time?

The thrum of magic through her veins always got worse around areas of power and at the moment, it didn't help the excitement and anxiety already pinging around her system. And she was only half-human. Cammi couldn't imagine what she'd be like if she'd been a full-blooded fae.

The magic here was so thick she could taste it.

This had to be it. The end of the long winding trail she'd followed that had been rife with dead ends, traps, and near-death experiences.

This had to be the place.

Cammi scratched the skin being rubbed by the coarse rope circling her neck. As if her Seeker nature wasn't bad enough, she had this damned thing to deal with.

Just had to get involved with a sorceress.

Not that she'd had much choice. Lavinia had shown up one day and before Cammi knew it, gold had crossed palms, an actual noose was around her neck, and she was stuck. The witch hadn't believed that her impulse to seek and find would be enough to make her follow through with the quest and thought a proper motivator would help.

With the way it had been tightening lately, Cammi knew the spell caster's patience was growing thin.

Because it was just that easy to go about searching out a dragon's hoard and then breaking into it.

It wasn't that she never had before. Three times before, four if one counted the instance she'd been lucky enough to practically fall into one. Based on her reputation as a relentless treasure hunter, Lavinia had darkened Cammi's door.

She walked the same circle around the cave. What she had to do next had been planned to the minutest detail and she itched to just get it over with. Who would have thought there would still be so many people milling around late in the day?

Needing to break up the monotony and trying to keep her gaze from locking on the points she'd have to concentrate on as soon as it could be afforded, she took a deep breath and shuffled along behind an elderly couple.

Cammi nearly tripped on a rock when a deep, melodious voice echoed around her. The chamber nearly pulsated with the low tones. Softly at first. The notes were comforting, almost cajoling. The tune carried on in words she didn't understand but wanted to hear more of.

Who was singing?

She knew humans liked to sing and play instruments within the stone walls as an experiment, perhaps? It seemed odd to her but there were some among them that were sensitive to magic and this place would certainly draw them in. Tease them with a taste. Inspire them to reach out. Taunt them to try to find it.

But this, this was different.

The voice wasn't mortal. It couldn't be.

Cammi, and everyone else, stopped in place to

simply listen. Or was it more than that?

Looking at the humans, she saw they seemed to be frozen. Mid-smile, part way through a comment, breath stilled in their lungs, it was as if time had simply stopped. At least, for them. Mimicking their inertness, she searched for the source and found it to be coming from the other entrance to the cave.

With the blinding sun behind him, she couldn't see much more than a misshapen silhouette. But she could discern enough to know he was tall and broad besides having the most incredible voice she'd ever heard.

Curious that another non-human should be there…

Unless they knew this was the only time the hoard could be opened. Without the right tools, however, they would never be able to get in. But if word had gotten out that she was prepared, they could hope to usurp her prize. An irritating possibility that had happened to her before.

Even without the sorceress's noose around her neck, she couldn't allow it. Couldn't afford to. Her integrity as a Seeker demanded successful retrieval. As did her sanity.

But did any of that really matter with her life on the line?

Cammi slowed her breathing and kept her eyes focused on the silhouette while doing her utmost to seem petrified like the rest. Thank goodness for the charms she carried around with her. In her line of work, it never hurt to have a little extra protection.

Especially when dealing with the tasks and beings she encountered daily.

Rings bearing stones etched with warding runes, bracelets of unicorn hair, even tattoos of dragon blood.

Cammi possessed them all, making her a walking good luck charm if there ever was one.

But why was she thinking about them now?

Her gaze darted to a slight figure on the other side of the cave. Training her eyes on the 'tourist,' she watched. Her vigil didn't take long to warrant success. Even if he hadn't fidgeted, who carried a Discman in this day and age? It did make her laugh when they tried so hard to figure out the culture of the human world and just got it so very wrong. It was what made half-bloods like her invaluable for moving between worlds.

And this one wanted to know what she had.

She narrowed her eyes at him. *"Stay out of my head."*

His eyes widened before lifting his eyebrow just enough for her to notice. *"Try and stop me."*

Moron.

Cammi wasn't going to play games with him. Not when a dragon's hoard was waiting for her.

She could deal with him when she had to. At the moment, she had other things to focus on.

Like whoever was singing everyone into a trance. Or Lavinia and the stranglehold she had on her. Or getting past the wards that were sure to be up to keep everyone and everything away from the treasure.

Thank goodness dragons were extinct or that would be another colossal hurdle to leap.

Sweat trickled down her forehead, inching ever closer to her eyes. Cammi willed it to stop before it started to inhibit her vision.

Chances were if these two were here, there were more. And since she couldn't detect them immediately, they were likely to be more dangerous than the joker with the Discman.

It was the upcoming Cull. It was driving everyone

crazy looking for any advantage to escape obliteration.

The cycle of destruction and rebirth was elegant, in its way. Eons could pass without a Cull. There would be tension between the different races and clans, but for the most part, there would be peace. But then, when populations grew large and power built too high, a sensation would start to niggle at the gut. Instinct would whisper at the back of the mind to look for ways of surviving, be it by collecting artifacts and therefore power or by making alliances. The urge grew daily until either oblivion or the impulse faded. With the power held by their kind and long lives, it was the only way to keep the balance.

For beings like her, slipping through the cracks came quite easy. Like gravitated toward like. Witches and warlocks built covens of mind-boggling might. Vampires, werewolves, and others like them banded together before hurling themselves into war in the hopes of a few surviving.

It didn't always work. The extinction of the most powerful—dragons—had proven that.

But for halflings, who belonged on neither side of the veil, things were less defined. For her part, Cammi stayed out of politics and alliances and just did what she could to survive.

Which meant doing the odd job for unsavory types to bring in the gold just to eke out a living.

And, unsurprisingly, a Seeker wasn't exactly in demand unless it was for something like this.

It was an all-or-nothing kind of life.

And these … frauds … thought they would just jump in at the last second of a decade-long search and steal the prize?

Not while she still breathed.

The singer had walked inside the cave and

Cammi had to force herself not to flinch when he stepped in front of her.

He still sang his entrancing tune as he studied her. The words caressed her skin and whispered to her mind as he tried to figure her out.

Cammi knew what he saw. A lowly half-elf. Her mother was an Asian human and had named her Saengdao, starlight in her language. Probably because of her pale-silver hair and eyes. She more than likely had no idea that names meant something to the fae. They defined who they were. And not just metaphorically. The name had cursed her to seek best by the light of the stars.

Tall and lithely graceful, the singer was clearly elven and very beautiful. Overwhelmingly so. His mouth especially. Full-lipped and with a sensuous curve that almost made it seem like only he was in on a secret joke. He didn't even try to blend in, though she doubted he could if he tried. His skin was pale on fine bones and his mop of hair the purple-red of wine.

Smiling at her, he winked.

The tune changed now. Became commanding. The humans all started to file from the cave. The Discman hesitated but fell into line, almost robotically obeying the song. Had the singer added more power to it?

She wiggled her finger to check she was still okay.

His hand gripped her arm before she could feign being one of the herd. "You can stop pretending. I know you're unaffected."

His voice was as seductive as his song.

Caught, Cammi met his gaze. "Who are you?"

"No one to be trifled with." He watched the last of the stragglers disappear before dropping his dark gaze to meet hers. "We're going to help each other tonight."

"Are we?" She glared up at him. "I doubt very much that I'll need your help."

Cammi's palms started to sweat as the demand to complete her task began to take over. She needed him gone. Now.

"I've followed you, little dove. I know you've got everything you think you require to break into the dragon's vault. But you're missing something. Something I have."

She turned to face him. Her research had been nothing short of methodical. There was nothing she needed that she didn't already possess.

"Nice try."

"Maybe this will convince you that I want to help." He held up an ornate silver blade etched with an intricate design.

Cammi shied away from it but he held her tight.

He murmured something before flicking the blade at her neck.

The noose dropped away.

Eyes wide, she ran her hand over skin that hadn't been free from the irritation in far too long. "My ... benefactor will not be pleased you've done that."

He sneered. "Does it look like I care? Now I've helped you out. You can do the same for me."

"And what's that?" She didn't have long before Lavinia would realize she was free.

"Promise me fifty percent of what we find and I'll tell you what order to put the stones in."

"I already know what order to do it in." Cammi clenched her hands as she tried to stay calm. The hoard was inches away and it could all be hers now that Lavinia couldn't exert her control. The things she could do with what she found in there... There might even be something to give her an advantage in the Cull. But first she needed to rid herself of this male. Could she incapacitate him? It was possible, but it was also apparent he had formidable powers of his own to be able to negate Lavinia's just like that.

"Time's ticking, dove. By my count, we only have a few seconds in the window left."

"Your name, first."

He sighed and said, "Salix," then held out his hand. "Do we have a deal?"

Cammi stifled a laugh. As bad as her name was, at least she wasn't named after a tree. She went to grasp his hand but stopped just a hair's breath away. "If you tell me something I already know or try to cheat or mislead me in any way, I'll leave you to the traps inside."

"Very well."

They pressed their palms together and a flash of light and heat sealed the deal.

"Now tell me the order." Cammi practically vibrated with excitement as he pointed to the far wall.

"Lyngurium."

She waited.

Salix sighed again. He pointed to the walls as he told her which stones needed to be placed in it. "Batrachite. Dragonite. Mermaid's tears."

It was in the reverse order of what she'd learned. Could she be wrong? What would he have to gain from lying? Unless he was trying to keep her away from the treasure?

Dark energy began to crackle around them.

"Lavinia is going to have a few words for you when she gets here. I suggest we get in there and get our prize before she arrives."

He had a point. She just had to wait for the sun to lower to the precise point and make her decision…

Cammi drew the first stone out of the air the same

instant the sun hit the gem she'd placed at the entrance. The refracted light pinpointed the exact locations for the keystones' placement.

When she placed the yellow stone in the wall and went the other way from what Salix had told her, she could feel his alarm even before he started yelling.

Cammi darted around the space, slipping the deep-blue chip of mermaid's tear that had nearly cost her an arm to retrieve into the slot and waited.

Nothing happened.

Livid, Salix's face had darkened, revealing bloody veins just under the surface and the rest of his monstrous true form. "You fool! I told you what order they were to go in!"

She knew better. Didn't she? After a decade of obsession, Cammi had to believe she did.

A crack of power rocked her back on her heels just as a rush of wind swept through the cave. It wrapped itself around her, whipping Salix back against the stone. A blaze of deep red appeared at the entrance but was quickly extinguished by the maelstrom that had formed around her.

Lavinia hurled something that looked like a thunderbolt at her, but when it should have lanced through Cammi, the wind repelled it, sending it back toward the sorceress.

As the air was sucked from her lungs and her skin was shredded by the whirling sand and rock, Cammi couldn't help but think Salix had been smart to keep his distance. That maybe he had been right all along...

She was aware of screaming. Was that her voice pleading for it to stop? To make it go away?

With a crack of thunder and a flash of lightning, everything then went mercifully black.

Chapter Two

Aldric hated this day. Every year non-human idiots would arrive at the cave to join the human ones only with the idea that they could get into the dragon's vault.

And every year they failed.

Except this one.

The clever little halfling managed it.

He watched her now in the mirror he held in his palm.

Secure in a bedroom, she slept. And had been that way for almost twelve hours. He might have gone a little overboard with the storm in the cave but he'd been caught by surprise.

Aldric put the scrying mirror back in his pocket and stretched. Watching her was both boring and fascinating. A strange mix. One that was quickly losing its novelty.

With morning about to dawn, he was done waiting for her to finally wake.

He strode through his apartment, taking a moment to look out at London spread like a canvas outside the floor-to-ceiling windows. Procuring a penthouse apartment in the Shard hadn't been easy but, as he'd learned over the years, the right amount of money thrown at anything had a way of opening doors. He continued to the second level and the only other bedroom other than his own, waved his hand to dispel the locking ward, and then entered.

She was tiny and curled up near the edge of the bed as if she'd never had anything bigger than a sliver to sleep on.

That thought didn't settle well with him as he studied her face. Even in sleep she looked serious. He found himself wondering vaguely if that scowl was ever-present. Even still, she was delicately beautiful. Pale as moonlight and fine-boned, there were old scars on the skin that was left exposed by the sheet. They decorated her flesh as did the many protective tattoos. Had she lived such a hard life?

Aldric bit back the anger that came with the thought someone might have inflicted the wounds that had left their marks on her willingly.

He'd find out soon enough.

He leaned in to let loose a quick bolt of energy a breath away from her cheek.

She lurched back, immediately on the alert. As he suspected, her silvery eyes were just as captivating as the rest of her.

The eyes of a thief, he reminded himself.

"Who are you? Where am I?" She looked down at herself and clutched desperately at the low draping sheet but not soon enough to hide her pert breasts from his gaze. Color blazed her cheeks and lent their fire to her eyes. "Where are my clothes?"

"I'll be asking the questions, if you don't mind."

There was a quick flare of feminine interest when they returned to him, but it was quickly, and expertly, extinguished. "I do mind!" She gripped the fabric keeping her body from his view tightly to her as she darted from the bed to the wall of windows on the far side of the room. She focused on the scene outside, pointing, keeping the attention off herself. "I'm in London? How did I get here? You had no right to kidnap me—"

Aldric pinched the bridge of his nose. Females. Hysterical, the whole lot of them. "Can we just stop with the theatrics? I know where you were and what you were trying to do."

Her silvery gaze narrowed with suspicion. "And you took the treasure when I opened the vault and kept me too? As what? A prize, I suppose. Or did you think I would open up another for you?"

"I don't need you to open *my* vault, you pompous little halfling. And a prize?" He raked his gaze up and down her small form, making sure it was nothing but scathing. "You have got to be kidding me."

She stilled. With her back ramrod-straight and her face frozen as she stared at him. After a second, the shock turned to wide-eyed awe. "You're a treasure dragon?"

That angered him even more. "No. Sorry to disappoint."

Indignant, she stomped toward him. "But you said the vault was yours."

"It *is* mine. The gold dragon it once belonged to gave it to me in favor of more high-tech options. Maximus thought it was outdated a millennia ago."

"But..." The little halfling looked confused. Lost, almost.

"But what? Sad that the fortune you thought awaited you wasn't there and hadn't been since before you were born?" He loomed over her, enjoying the way she stumbled back before she dug her heels in once more.

"I wasn't breaking in for me."

Aldric arched an eyebrow as he studied her every facial movement. "Weren't you?"

Emboldened, she straightened her shoulders. "I was being forced to."

He kept his expression neutral. "Really."

"I was! Lavinia, a sorceress of the East Isles, forced me to do it."

"Are you sure you're not lying to save your own skin?"

She nodded, more than likely aware the lies she'd already spoken could be used against her and didn't want to add more to her crime.

"That's interesting because I saw your friend remove the noose." Or had he been her lover? Aldric found he didn't like the idea.

"He wasn't a friend."

"Looked quite friendly to me. He was helping you, wasn't he? Why would a non-friend give aid?"

His captive glared at him, murder burning clear in her eyes.

Aldric continued, the air in the room crackling with electricity. "Then the sorceress arrived looking rather annoyed just before I rescued you from their combined ire."

Sullenly, she continued to glare at him without comment.

"Am I wrong in assuming you betrayed them both?"

"It's hardly betrayal when you fight back against the ones who coerced you," she fired back.

Aldric was impressed. At least a little. She had a spine. It was a little malleable, sure, but it was there. "As I see it, you tried to break into my vault and it was only through my great magnanimity that you are here alive and able to lie to me about your reasons for doing so."

"She forced me to do it, he was trying to make a deal to get half of whatever is in there, and I thought all dragons were gone—"

"So, there would be no harm in a little larceny?"

"It would have been a victimless crime! Who would it hurt if I got a little something for myself for once? All my life I've been nothing but a retriever." She snorted. "I would have been lucky to be treated as well as a dog!"

She glared at him. "Just once I wanted something for myself. Perhaps an advantage in the Cull. I saw the chance, and I would have been an idiot not to take it."

"You are aware that dragon's hoards are notoriously dangerous to break into."

Her chin tipped up. "I had that in hand."

"Did you?" He let his gaze flick around the room pointedly.

She jabbed her finger in his chest but quickly retracted her hand at the zap of sensation that jolted through them both. Clearing her throat, she glared at him. "I got in, didn't I?"

"You got through my first ward." Aldric let amusement curl his lips upward. This verbal sparring was almost … fun?

"I got in," she reiterated. "Which means the prize is mine."

"Sorry to disappoint, but there's nothing in there worth taking, and certainly nothing that will assist you in a Cull, unless you want trinkets I'd collected over the years. My good armor, perhaps, worn during the Battle of Agincourt … good times…"

She gaped at him. "There's nothing in there?"

"Not nothing. I just said. My armor and other antiquities that would no doubt interest a museum or perhaps a private collector. But not gold and gems as I assume you'd imagined."

"You're telling me I just spent a chunk of my life, been threatened on pain of death to get into a vault, and there was nothing in it?" Laughter bubbled out of her. "Nothing…" She dissolved into a fit of giggles that weakened her to the point of nearly toppling into him.

"Attempted robbery is no laughing matter,

halfling."

Wiping away her tears, she sniffled. "Don't call me that. My name is Cammi."

Warrior. A suitable name for the fiery slip of a woman. He carefully stepped back, putting space between them but not before his gaze was drawn to the gooseflesh on her arms and the beaded tips of her breasts. Unfortunately, the delicate scent of her lingered, tantalizing his sense of smell. "I don't care what your name is."

She shrugged. "I got nothing, so no harm, no foul. Now, if you'll give me back my things, I'll be on my way."

The thought of her leaving and him returning to his dull routine didn't appeal. "You owe me a debt."

"I owe you nothing. You took me from the cave without my permission or knowledge. I asked you for nothing."

He stepped closer. "Didn't you?"

Cammi pulled herself up to her full height and managed a look of haughty indignation even undressed as she was. "I did not."

"You don't recall pleading? Begging anyone, anything, to make it stop?"

Her expressive eyes widened. "You heard that?"

"Of course, I did."

Fierce color brightened her cheeks. "But it was your trap! It's like if Dr. Strange created a giant vortex that was going to swallow the earth but then turned around and said, 'Don't worry, I'll save you!' and then turned it off and expected everyone to call him a hero."

"You can tell this Dr. Strange that it's been tried and has never worked." Perplexed, he shook his head. "And it's hardly the same thing. I'm not asking you to call me a hero. I'm calling you what you are. A thief.

You tried to break into my vault, and despite my good judgment, I rescued you from not only my traps but the people you betrayed. You. Owe. Me. If not for one, then for the other."

Her jaw dropped before she snapped it shut and she glared at him. "What are you?"

"What does it matter?" Clearly, if he wasn't a treasure-hoarding dragon he wasn't anything.

"Because it does."

"What I am is irrelevant. It doesn't change anything you've done." Aldric swung around and strode back out, slamming the door behind him.

****

Cammi stared at the door, her lungs fighting for breath as if she'd been trapped under the surface of the ocean and had finally broken through.

What the hell just happened? One second, she'd been breaking into a vault filled with untold riches that would change her life forever without having to give any of it up to Lavinia or that other elf, then the next, she was in an opulent apartment overlooking London arguing with the most infuriating male she'd ever encountered.

Not to mention one of the most attractive.

Big, broad, darkly handsome, well-dressed, obviously intelligent. He looked like he could have just come home from a board meeting and had discarded his jacket and tie, unbuttoned the top couple buttons at his neck and rolled up his sleeves. The sight of his sculpted forearms and tanned skin at his throat made the blood throb in her veins. Even the scar on his cheek held an enigmatic appeal. And his eyes. Startlingly blue, it was as though they held the electric charge of what she felt whenever he looked at or touched her.

She snapped herself out of it. Not that it mattered. What was she thinking? He was still holding her captive and that was unacceptable.

What was he? A warlock? A demon? His finicky demeanor and uppity attitude would fit either. He could easily be a goblin with his covetous nature, but he was as far away as you could get from being short, green, and big-eared.

But just as much of an ass.

Cammi bit her lip, trying to get herself to concentrate. It didn't matter what he looked like, she needed to know what he was if she was to get away from him.

A slow turn around the room told her nothing. It was clearly a guestroom, if only a step above a prison cell. It was luxurious, to say the least, but stark-white linens and plain concrete walls didn't exactly make the ambiance welcoming.

She took a moment to look at the window. It made up one entire wall and let her see London from a point of view she'd never seen before.

What must it be like to be, quite literally, above everything?

Closing her eyes, she sighed. Not that she'd ever know. She had to get away and back to her life.

As mundane as it was, Cammi lived life the way she wanted and nothing, besides a blood clause in a contract, something that would never happen again, would change that.

The whole mess with Lavinia had just reminded her that as careful as she thought she was, it was never enough.

And her captor seemed like the type who would keep her on her toes. He'd been around a while, as his comment about Agincourt would have her believe, so he would be worldly and had probably dealt with his fair share of shifty characters. Which would make him formidable. If not in body but in mind as well.

Again, specifics about him would be wonderful.

But was she was going to get any? Probably not.

She lightly touched her hand to the door and was immediately rewarded with a zap of energy.

Booby-trapped. As expected.

Cammi shook her numbed hand as she weighed her other options.

The window would be as well, though escape that way was out of her skill set. What she wouldn't give for some Sky cakes right now from her favorite bakery. A few seconds of flight would definitely ease the fall, even from this height.

She didn't need to look down at herself to be reminded that she had nothing but her skin on under the sheet. What did surprise her, however, was there were no new cuts or bruises anywhere on her body. After the storm in the cave, she'd been sure her flesh had been flayed from her bones.

And yet, her skin was relatively smooth. Cammi had been breaking in and out of places most of her life and her body bore the scars of mistakes and mishaps that had come with the jobs.

Guess she wouldn't have any reminders of this one.

Not that she needed one. The biggest feat she'd ever managed and it had amounted to nothing.

Except incarceration. By some hot, exasperating male.

All that was enough to burn itself in her memory.

Cammi's attention drifted toward the windows again. Perhaps jumping to her death would be preferable to being kept there? He'd obviously wanted her naked otherwise wouldn't he have provided her with clothing? And there was only one reason for wanting her naked.

She'd sworn by every goddess old and new in both worlds she'd inhabited that she would never succumb to a male. She'd seen what loving her father had done to her mother. The nights she'd listened to her mother crying, pining for her lover who had abandoned her and their child, had ingrained a deep aversion to the opposite sex.

Of course, she probably had a mate she was fated to but she'd made sure to stay away from any entanglements. Even went as far as to avoid them. If there was any hint of a spark, she would head in the opposite direction.

And her captor? He made her skin prickle and her body throb with unwanted compulsions.

She looked out the window again, unsettled by what she felt just thinking about him.

Cammi touched the glass and was rewarded with a stronger shock than the door had given her. Snorting, she took a step back. It was just a zap. If she breached the barrier and got through it fast enough, then that would be it.

She gazed at the world below.

London would have its fill of creatures from the other side of the veil. She could find someone who was willing to help her, at least to find some clothes and a way back, surely.

There was only one way to find out.

"This would be so much easier with my charms," she muttered. Cammi backed up against the far wall. She quickly dropped the sheet and kicked it aside.

This would only hurt for a brief moment. The glass might have been thick and reinforced against a human, but she should get through it just fine. When she hit the ground, however, it would hurt for a bit longer. But a healer would be able to patch her right back up again. It would be a while before she'd able to work, but she'd be free.

Freedom was all that mattered.

Taking a few deep breaths, Cammi pushed off the wall and ran as fast as she could at the window. Using her elbow as a point, she rammed it into the glass.

As she suspected, the pain was immense—almost immobilizing—but then it stopped.

And the fall began.

The air immediately thickened and electricity wrapped around her.

Daylight eclipsed and an ear-shattering roar came from above just an instant before clawed feet gripped her within them. Then a sickening jerk as her momentum changed and she started to travel upward.

Since twisting around in the rough, tight scaly cage without tearing her skin off was an impossibility, Cammi turned her head as far as she could. Only to be forced to duck from the fierce gusts of wind that sucked the breath from her lungs. It didn't take long to work out the rhythm of the gusts and she managed a peek at huge leathery wings and a long neck and tail. Huge plates of scale such a dark blue they appeared black.

It couldn't be.

Too stunned to struggle, she clung limply as the dragon that held her craned his head to glare at her with angry, electric-blue eyes.

Their piercing gaze was the last thing that passed through her mind before a surge of power rocketed through her and knocked her unconscious.

Chapter Three

Aldric stared down at the halfling.

Had she gone out of her mind? What was she thinking jumping through the window like that?

She was tougher and much crazier than he could have ever believed.

What if he hadn't noticed or hadn't been able to transform? What if he'd been a wood elf or a selkie and therefore completely useless in the air? What then?

Fool of a female.

He had sensed her testing his wards, but he hadn't been expecting her to try anything as insane as jumping through them and the glass. Not when they were so high up. He'd obviously underestimated her desperation to get away from him. What did that mean? Had she done something that warranted such fear?

Or was it him she wanted to get away from?

Was he so repulsive?

He wasn't keen on either idea.

The thought of keeping her unconscious until he figured out what he was going to do with her popped into his head and put a wry smile on his face.

Another notion wiped it off just as quickly.

Why had he saved her?

Again?

Aldric studied her face as he pondered. She had to be the most maddening and irritating creature he'd encountered in all his very long life. And utterly fascinating. A distraction from his staid and predictable life.

That had to be it.

She was a spark that had caught his attention.

Nothing more. Soon it would fade and he'd move on to the next diversion.

In the meantime, he'd enjoy the interlude.

Even if it did mean protecting her from herself.

How could someone so self-destructive have survived the things she had?

He'd been intrigued enough by her to look into her life and had been going through the information he'd managed to dig up about her before her swan dive out the window. Cammi had led quite the life. An impressive one for a halfling. If given enough time, Aldric believed she could steal every treasure in the world.

And yet she held no wealth.

How odd.

From what she'd said earlier about wanting something for herself just this once, he'd gathered that her acquisitions had been on the behest of someone else. Someone who gained all and left her with nothing.

The injustice of it all irritated him. He was a fair man. More than. There was nothing he liked more than for people to get what they deserved.

It was what kept the universe in balance.

It was why he'd captured Cammi in the first place. She'd tried to break into his vault and therefore deserved to be punished.

The more he learned about her, however, the less inclined he was to keep her.

For that reason, at least.

She intrigued him.

"I'm getting sick of waking up with you staring at me."

Even if she was exasperating. Her voice put a wry smile on his face yet again. "If you stopped doing things that required you to be incapacitated, you wouldn't have this problem."

"You could have just let me go."

"Or you could say thank you, this time."

"For what? Locking me up again?"

"For saving your life. *Again.*"

She sat up, once again indignant. "I was going to be fine."

"You don't know that. Not only did you get a good zap from the wards, but we're sixty floors up. You'd have made one hell of a mess on the pavement."

The look she gave him was completely unimpressed. "I've been through worse and come out the other side just fine."

After weeks of intensive magic and rehabilitation. Did the woman have no sense? "There are some things no magic in the world can bring you back from, little one." He should know. The weight of those he'd lost over the years was an ever-growing burden on his shoulders.

The look in her eyes softened but her words didn't. "Why do you care?"

"I am only going to say this once, so listen well. There is precious little in this world that I care enough to save. And you, I believe, are worth the effort. With a Cull coming, I'd rather the good stay and the wicked go."

She blinked up at him. "But you … I'm a thief. You obviously think I'm trash."

"I never said that."

****

Cammi stared up at him. He hadn't. Not explicitly, but he looked down on her. It was clear in his every word and glance.

And he had no right considering he was a liar.

"You lied to me."

He raised his eyebrows. "I did not."

"You said you weren't a dragon."

The corners of his sensuous mouth curved slightly upward. "I said I wasn't a treasure dragon."

"But you *are* a dragon." Getting slightly breathless, Cammi sat up straighter. "You're supposed to be extinct."

He crossed his arms. "Sorry to disappoint you."

"Not disappointed…" Not in the least. Now his haughty attitude made sense. And all the electricity everywhere. And the weird tornado in the cave. Her jaw dropped again. "You're a storm dragon."

His smile was wry. "Finally figured that out, have you?"

She didn't care that he was being an ass. She was looking at a real live dragon. "But how? Everyone knows that dragons had all been destroyed, what, two Culls ago?" For over a thousand years, they were thought to be gone from the world.

He shrugged. "Not all of us."

"So, there are more?"

He peered into her eyes and did a great job of making her feel even more naked. "Does it matter? Or are you interested because you want to hitch yourself to one?"

"What's your problem? I'm just curious. No one has seen or heard from a dragon in millennia and now I find out there are still some out there."

He stood tall over her. "The reason there are any of us alive at all is because no one knows about us. Understand?"

"I'm insulted." How could he think that she would endanger an entire race? What did he think she was? An idiot?

"I just want to make sure we're on the same wavelength."

Now that he wasn't insinuating she was a moron,

his gaze swept lower over her body. For someone who didn't think she was a prize, he sure liked to look at her. What annoyed her even more was that her body responded to his attention as if he'd actually touched her.

She crossed her arms over her chest, hoping to hide the way her nipples had tightened. What was wrong with her?

So, Cammi went on the offensive. "If you want to keep your existence a secret, why are you keeping me here? And why tell me anything at all? It seems to me if you're so desperate to stay hidden from the world you should have just left me to your trap."

"Maybe I should have." His expression stayed bored but his eyes threatened to burn a hole through her head.

"So why did you?" Did he see something in her worth saving?

He actually looked as perplexed as she felt. "I don't know? Reflex?"

So much for that thought. Cammi sat, staring up at him in equal parts awe and vexation. "Will you let me go if I promise not to tell anyone your little secret?"

"*Little*?" The diminution of what he'd told her didn't amuse him as much as it did her. "No. Not until I know I can trust you."

"And keeping me here is going to endear me to you, how?"

The galling male shrugged.

They stared at one another for a few long seconds before he broke the silence. "Are you hungry?"

She nodded. "And cold."

"I've got clothes coming for you."

"Oh."

He stared at her, his eyes blazing. "You thought I was a pervert who wanted a stranger lounging around his home naked?"

She couldn't stop the color from flooding her cheeks.

"I see."

"I don't know anything about you. For all I know, you could have been a lust demon, you have the looks … and the … the…" Cammi's voice withered and died in her throat. What had possessed her to say that?

"The what?" he prompted, appearing interested in what she had to say for the first time during their short acquaintance.

"I … I…" Clamping her mouth shut before she said something even more stupid, Cammi wrapped the sheet tightly around herself. "You seem like the type of man who is all about the propriety, and yet here I am practically nude, about to have a meal with you and I still don't know your name."

As far as topic changes went, it wasn't the smoothest, but it seemed that he was going to let it slide. At least for now.

"Aldric."

The name certainly fit him. Stately. Old. Fusty.

"You have something to say about my name?"

She shook her head. "A pleasure to meet you."

Aldric said nothing but nodded in acknowledgment. "Would you like to come out now or would you rather wait until after your clothing arrives?"

"What's wrong with the clothes I had?"

"They were destroyed, but for a few scraps." He motioned to the door. "I have them still, if you'd like to see."

"I believe you." Hiding in the room was ridiculous after he'd seen her naked at least twice now. If he was going to do anything, wouldn't he have done so by now? Chewing her bottom lip, Cammi sighed. "Turn around."

Looking a bit puzzled, he did as she asked. Cammi quickly folded the sheet then wrapped it around herself sarong-style, tucking the end securely between her breasts. "Okay."

Aldric peeked over his shoulder before turning fully. "You know, you could have borrowed my robe or something."

Cammi shrugged and picked up the hem of her makeshift outfit clear of her feet as if it was a fancy gown. "This will do for now. You said something about food?"

She caught the slight shake of his head as Aldric took the lead through the apartment. Walking closely behind him was a mistake. The scent of him. Was it some sort of expensive cologne? Pheromones? Something concocted by some alchemist on the other side?

Whatever it was, Cammi's entire body reacted to the scent of him to the point she had to grit her teeth and hold her breath before she grabbed him and pressed her nose, and everything else, against him.

It wasn't natural. It couldn't be. He was messing with her mind.

Fighting her every instinct, she followed him down the stairs and to the first floor and nearly sagged with relief when they finally had space between them.

She wandered a little ways both to get some air and to get a better look at the apartment. Calling his home an apartment was a huge understatement, however. Cammi was right when she thought the place was luxurious. But the predominantly bare room she'd been in previously only hinted at the luxury that Aldric lived in.

Paintings and sculptures she recognized from artists on both sides of the veil decorated the huge space.

But what eclipsed even those were the massive windows that formed the outside walls. One room flowed into the next around the core of the building, giving the place an airy feel. The abundance of natural light and the view enforced the feeling that she was on top of the world.

"Your home is fantastic."

"Thank you."

Cammi couldn't help the little giggle that bubbled from her lips.

"What?" Aldric narrowed his gaze at her.

She let out a breathy laugh. "It's just that you so obviously like to look down on everyone. Not just me."

Aldric smirked. "I'm a dragon. We like to be up high." He motioned for her to follow. "What would you like to eat?"

She expected him to go to the kitchen but instead he pulled out his phone. When she gave him a questioning glance, he shrugged. "There's an excellent restaurant in the building and I don't keep much in the kitchen."

The problems of the wealthy…

"I'm fine with whatever you want to get." She cleared her throat. "Thank you. For this and for everything."

"That sounded rusty."

Couldn't he just let things slide just once? Fighting the urge to stick her tongue out at him, she walked over to the windows. "I do appreciate it. It's just been a long time since anyone has looked out for me."

He nodded as he dialed and made a quick order.

Guess she wasn't going to get anything fancy. But what did she expect? She wasn't his date. She was his captive.

Still, he was treating her with care and consideration she didn't exactly deserve. If the shoe were on the other foot, she'd probably be a raging bitch. She'd worked hard for what little she had. If someone tried to take any of it, she would do whatever it took to protect it.

Guilt wasn't a feeling she liked to experience. And it was definitely not a good thing for a thief to succumb to. But it was what was pooling like acid in her gut right at that moment.

He was only doing what he deemed was necessary to defend his home and she had no right to complain.

Not that she really had anything to whine about so far. He'd been a good host, considering. She sure as hell wouldn't be feeding or clothing someone who'd broken into her stuff and invaded her home.

And she knew what it was like to keep a secret. Big ones. Living among beings with whom she didn't belong wasn't easy. Cammi never fit in anywhere and had ended up giving up even trying. Anyone she did have to associate with usually had no idea who or what she was. And she worked to keep it that way.

Only Aldric had known she was a halfling probably from the moment he'd laid eyes on her. Was that an Ancient thing? Perhaps he'd been around for so long that he just knew everything.

The thought brought another smirk to her lips. Why wouldn't he have an inflated ego if that was the case?

His character started to fit together in her mind.

When Cammi dared another glance at his reflection in the window, she found him already studying her with the same intense regard as before.

She turned to face him, but before she could say anything, a quick buzz rang through the room.

"The food is on its way up." Aldric's scrutiny roamed over her again, this time in a more lingering way.

Again, her body throbbed as if she could feel the heat of his hand against her skin.

"Cammi?"

She snapped her attention to his face.

"The table is that way." He pointed with an elegant finger to the opposite side of the apartment.

It probably wasn't the best idea to let anyone see her dressed as she was. She could imagine Aldric having an apoplectic fit at any rumors even hinting at impropriety being whispered about him.

Giggling over that, she turned the corner.

****

Aldric couldn't help but watch the hypnotic sway of her hips as she walked away and only snapped out of it when she turned the corner.

She was doing her utmost to tempt him, that much was clear. Every look, every gesture. Even her laugh. Tinkling and enchanting even when she was the most irritating female. What angle could she be working? Did she think he had more valuables hidden away? Was she one of those females who just wanted to bed a dragon?

His body throbbed at the thought of having her under him, skin flushed and crying out his name.

No.

Whatever her motive, he couldn't trust her.

Even if his teeth ached from grinding them together, trying to keep his libido in check.

He sniffed the air and found her scent still lingering. Growling, Aldric shook his head and stalked toward the elevators. He had to get a grip. She would be out of his life soon enough. Then things could get back to normal.

Why had he revealed himself to her? It was stupid. There was a reason why he'd led a reclusive life up in the tower. Having others lie to keep his secret was an ugly necessity that he didn't like to force on anyone. It was just easier to stay away.

Perhaps he should call one of his alchemist friends and have them create a draught or charm or something that would wipe her memory of him? Then they could both get on with their lives. It seemed the most expedient solution.

Aldric was curious about her, however. Not just because he wanted to see more of her beautiful body. He'd been distracted enough by her that he nearly flew into the side of the Shard while trying to get a better look at her legs. But her life interested him as well. What he'd learned of it so far was fascinating.

He found himself wanting to hear stories about her adventures. Even if it was just to hear her talk. Hell, he'd listen to her recite the alphabet if it meant hearing more of that soft, husky voice of hers.

Aldric punched the wall next to the elevators and let the throbbing pain wash over him. What was wrong with him? He glared at the fissure in the stone his fist had created.

Women were a passing fancy. Perhaps they would get naked or maybe they wouldn't, but he wasn't going to let himself get crazy over it.

Over her.

There was no point.

He had a mate out there. Somewhere. Or perhaps he didn't. Maybe she'd been a victim of the Cull. Long gone. Either way, it didn't matter if he wanted Cammi or not. It wouldn't last.

The doors to the elevator pinged. He stepped back to wait for them to open. Aldric cocked his head as they parted.

Something was wrong.

He sidestepped and gripped the clawed hand that shot through an instant before it tore into his throat. Aldric dragged the beast toward him and broke its neck before it had the chance to do anything more than growl.

Bloody werewolves.

That begged the question, why? Why show up now? Why attack now?

Aldric immediately locked down the elevators and doubled up the wards around the apartment just as he felt attacks coming from almost every side.

Cammi!

He dashed through the apartment. Did this have something to do with her? Were they after her or was this an orchestrated attack against him?

The tower was veiled against notice from humans but an Other would have seen her insane attempt at flight earlier. A sorceress definitely would have been able to or could have just as easily been notified of such an event. If he had been her, his sights would have been set on finding the one who had betrayed him as well.

Positive this was retribution against Cammi's duplicity, fear gripped his heart. He might not have known her long, but he didn't want her hurt. Not while he was there to protect her. Not to mention, an attack on his home was nothing if not personal.

Did they even realize the fury they courted?

If they'd witnessed him saving her, they had to know.

What kind of idiot attacked a dragon in his own home?

Rage erupted up from somewhere deep and dark inside. His instinct to protect what was his roared through him. His beast howled to be let loose. To destroy the intruders. To protect what was his.

Aldric refused to relinquish control. He needed to

think while his beast was all instinct.

Cammi stood at the window, glaring at what looked like a small army of harpies, giving them a very uncomplimentary gesture.

Sighing, he dashed in front of her and pushed the harpies back with an electrified blast before turning to glower at her. "What do you think you're doing?"

"Telling them to go away. Why? Did it look like something else? Because I can be a lot more articulate with both hands."

"Antagonizing them isn't going to help things. We're in this mess because of your stunt with the window. Until you came along, no one even knew I was here."

She scowled at him. "If you hadn't brought me here in the first place, I wouldn't have had to try to break out."

"And if you hadn't been trying to break into my vault, I wouldn't have had to."

"I told you that it wasn't my decision."

"It was to keep going after you got free of the witch. Now come on."

The instant he closed his hand around her bare arm, however, his world tilted and shook on its foundations, nearly knocking him down to his knees. His dragon roared with approval and clamored. To break free. To take control.

To claim his mate.

Cammi's wide eyes clashed with his own. How could this be? This *thief* was his mate?

Chapter Four

This had to be a mistake. Did destiny make mistakes? Because this was a big one.

How could she be fated to him?

Him.

He was irritating and overbearing. Stuffy and boring.

When she'd been younger and entertained the idea of having a mate, it was through rose-colored glasses and with the hope he would come and rescue her. To take her away from the horrible life she'd been forced to live. To be the one constant in her life that she'd longed for, who was handsome and loving and utterly perfect.

That guy never showed up.

She'd suffered and scraped and survived. All on her own. She didn't need him. Or anyone else.

But when Aldric touched her … it was as though the planets aligned. Everything felt right. And she knew he would do anything to keep her safe just as she would do whatever it took to do the same for him.

She continued to stare at him. Her mate. And she'd tried to rob him. Of all the ways to meet the one she'd been fated to be with.

Cammi cringed. The entire course of her life had been nothing short of disastrous. An explosion of fire against the warded glass jerked her back to reality. They could discuss the future and possible relationship afterward. There wouldn't be a future if their attackers had any choice in the matter.

Aldric was right. It was all her fault that they were under siege.

It had to be Lavinia. Who else would be so angry? Unless it was someone Aldric had wronged and had finally been able to track him down. Could they be why he was so secretive about himself?

At any rate, her first instinct was to do whatever would enable her and her mate to survive. She turned to Aldric. "I don't suppose you have any of my charms?"

His eyes had darkened as he watched the harpies swooping against the glass. They practically glowed when he returned his gaze to hers. "A few."

"Can we get them?" Cammi didn't like the vulnerability she felt not having them. And in this fishbowl of an apartment, any advantage was better than none.

He led her back up the stairs to the room opposite to the one she'd been in.

Aldric's bedroom. The dragon's lair.

It was bigger than the one she'd been in. Definitely more sumptuous. He was a man who liked his creature comforts, apparently. The room was decorated in deep ruby-reds and warm, inviting wood. So completely different from the rest of the ultra-minimalist home. It had been so unexpected, Cammi simply stood and stared for a long moment.

The room was incredibly sensuous for a man she thought so cold. Perhaps there was some fire under that icy façade after all.

"What?" Aldric had crossed the room to open a door that had been disguised as a giant mirror and had turned to find her staring.

"Nothing." She strode to where he was and peered past him. The new room was bigger than she imagined. And was filled with weapons and charms the likes she'd only ever imagined. "You're okay showing me all this?"

Aldric held her gaze and she couldn't help but acknowledge the link she felt. "You are my mate. If there's anyone I can trust, it's you."

Hearing him say the words made her heart swell even as she fought against it. She wasn't supposed to fall into the clutches of a male. She couldn't allow it. Cammi had never planned to meet her mate, let alone fall for him. It went against everything she had trained herself to believe.

So then, why did it feel so right?

What if she couldn't hold up her end of the bargain? Aldric was ready to trust her at the drop of a hat, but could she really be entrusted with anything? Cammi knew she *wanted* to do everything she could for him. It was instinct. But would she be able to follow through? She spent most of her life just muddling through, wreaking more destruction than anything.

If there had ever been a time to sort herself out, this had to be it.

Biting her bottom lip, she desperately turned her gaze away to scan the room and the treasures within. She pointed at the preternaturally gleaming sword nearest to her. "Is that what I think it is?"

The moment gone, Aldric's face went blank. He picked it up and swung it with surprising skill. "Yes, it is." Clearly deciding it wasn't something he'd need, Aldric placed it back in its sheath before picking up several other items. He pointed to a glass case. "Your charms and any others you wish to use can be found in there. Are you handy with a blade?"

If it would keep them alive, she would certainly learn to be. "I think I can figure it out."

Aldric didn't look so sure.

She straightened her spine. Now wasn't the time to hide behind bravado. "I'm more of the stealth type.

My size and being half-human doesn't exactly make me a challenge face-to-face."

He leaned down and looked her directly in the eyes. "You are a formidable opponent, Cammi. I've seen what you can do."

Pride surged. "You think so?"

His smile grew slowly. "I think the idiots who've come here tonight are in for a world of pain. Between the two of us, they will never know what hit them."

His confidence was contagious and she couldn't help but smile back as the tower shook around them.

Of course, they had this. She wasn't without skill and she had a dragon on her side.

****

His mate.

It all made sense. The impulse to save her. The unquenchable desire to touch and smell her... Aldric fought the urge to touch her again even if it was to reassure her. He needed to keep his head on straight if they were going to get through this and he wasn't sure if he could keep control of his dragon. The urge to claim her was nearly as strong as the one to protect her and to obliterate whatever and whoever it was that came between them and that goal.

Now was hardly the time to be entertaining thoughts of her naked under him. Over him. Enveloped tightly around him...

The growl he let out made Cammi jump. She still seemed as dazed as he was that they were fated. There would be time to figure that out later. Hopefully in a way that would appease the dragon raging and clawing to get out.

Gritting his teeth, he handed her a few more weapons. Mostly things she could use from a distance. "These are grenades. Press this"—he showed her the little indentation on the golden orb—"and you'll have three seconds before it explodes. This one will release a blast of fire, good for werewolves, goblins, and just about everything else pervious to flame." Aldric stuffed it into a pack with several others. "The silver ones will freeze everything within a five-foot radius. Be sure to get clear of them because it will freeze *everything*. The bronze ones will bond things within the blast radius together."

Cammi nodded. "Got it."

He critically eyed her clothes. It didn't look like she was going to get the new ones in time. "Not very practical in a fight."

She tugged the sheet tighter around herself, doing her best to secure it. "I doubt you have anything that would fit any better."

Aldric mentally filtered the list of items he had that might even come close to fitting her and would work in this occasion. "I might have something."

He motioned her to follow him to the four armor-laden mannequins he had on the other side of the room.

Methodically, he peeled off the layers, tossing the unwanted bits to the floor. When he had his prize, he found her staring at him with undisguised surprise. "What?"

"This stuff is obviously worth a fortune and precious to you, and you're throwing it around like it's nothing."

"Your life is more important to me than things or money, Cammi."

While she stared at him agape, he tugged the long tunic over her head and helped her get her arms through the sleeves while doing his damnedest to ignore the silk of her skin. Breathing slowly and shallowly so he didn't get distracted by her tantalizing scent, he forced himself to concentrate. The relatively short sleeves almost reached her wrists and the hem hung below her knees, making it look like an ill-fitting dress. Aldric then found a belt with a scabbard and the accessorizing dagger and fastened it around her waist. When it was all secure, he tugged the long sheet away to give her legs the freedom to move.

His mouth went dry when he noticed he could see clear through the fine chainmail and couldn't help but stare at her hard nipples poking against the metal.

Tearing his attention away was one of the hardest things he had to do, especially with his dragon roaring in his mind to touch. To taste.

Aldric cleared his throat. "The metal is charmed and is virtually impenetrable."

"Except maybe by eyes." She looked down at herself but shook her head when the tower quaked again, this time accompanied by the shattering of glass. "Doesn't matter. I've taken on worse in much less."

Did he want to know? A barrage of mental images of her battling stark naked wasn't something he needed at that moment.

"Stay close to me." He would do everything he could to keep her safe.

She met his gaze. "I will." It was a promise.

Aldric held her gaze for a moment. His mate. All these years and she fell into his lap. Just like that. And nothing was going to take her away. Not now. Not ever.

"Ready?"

She nodded but stopped him as he started back through the door. "But what about you? You're not going to wear armor?"

Cammi's soft voice dragged him back to reality. Was that concern?

He smiled, touched by her unease. "I won't need

it."

Aldric led the way out. He was pleased when she followed his example and took quick, quiet steps behind him. When he motioned for her to stop, she did so immediately. Her big eyes asked him why, but he shook his head. He just needed to see what was going on.

He could hear activity below and knew at least a few creatures had managed to get inside.

There was an agonized scream that died as abruptly as it had torn through the air. His traps were working well. Cammi had a look of barely disguised glee when there was another.

His mate was quite the enigma. One he was going to enjoy puzzling out.

Aldric pressed his palm to the wall to close any gaps in the protective barriers and therefore blocking any more from entering. At least for the moment. He motioned Cammi to follow. They needed to get rid of the ones already inside.

There was a calm rage that overcame him when he saw a werewolf reach up and tear his claws through a painting he'd cherished for centuries. Idiot mongrel. Meanwhile, a delicate-looking female dashed through the room, picking up items here and there and sticking them in her pockets and bags.

As far as attacks went, this wasn't the most terrorizing.

If this was the worst he had to contend with, Aldric would do so with ease. He motioned Cammi to stay where she was. She gripped his arm as he turned around, stopping him. Cammi nodded to the kitchen and the man sauntering from that direction.

From the glowing red eyes, it was safe to assume he was a vampire.

Why the hell would they be working together?

Unless they thought they could get something for themselves out of this.

But what? Surely, they had to realize that even entering a dragon's home without invitation was a very bad idea. Stealing things or harming those within was absolutely beyond the pale and subject to the harshest of consequences.

A hard, feminine voice broke the stillness. "I know you're here somewhere Cammi. I don't know how you did it. We all thought you were a destitute little Seeker. This is truly a surprise."

Cammi mouthed, "It's Lavinia," to Aldric. Not surprising.

The sorceress continued, her voice coming from just below them. "I'm disappointed you didn't share your obvious success with me. I wouldn't have felt the need to put the collar on you if I knew you were this successful. And this powerful."

She thought Cammi was capable of his traps and wards? Aldric arched a brow at Cammi and she pressed her hands to her mouth to stifle her laughter. The witch was in for one hell of a surprise.

"How did you manage that dragon illusion? I'm assuming you betrayed that elf who helped you, true to form, who then came after you and threw you from the building. But how you managed to save yourself and create that dragon baffles me. I'm not too proud to say I'm jealous." Her voice started to fade as she turned a corner. "Not too jealous, mind. I would have made a more impressive dragon. One that was a bit more … awe-inspiring."

Aldric bristled. He'd give her *awe-inspiring*.

Cammi shook her head. He knew the witch was trying to goad her into action but she wouldn't expect a real-life dragon to appear, would she? His dragon agreed.

Aldric turned to Cammi to let her know what he was thinking.

His heart stopped and his dragon threatened to tear him apart from the inside when he found the space next to him empty.

Chapter Five

Cammi didn't need a bond with him to know what Aldric was thinking at that moment. Not that she could blame him for wanting to tear Lavinia and her little minions to pieces. But his ego was getting in the way.

He might be a high and mighty dragon, but he'd been living in his ivory tower for so long he probably had no idea what the witch was capable of.

She'd handle this. Her way.

While Aldric was listening to the ranting, she started rigging the area with the grenades he'd given her. It was better than sitting around listening to the crap Lavinia was spouting.

It pissed her off hearing what the witch thought of her. How beneath her Cammi was. As if she didn't know that already. A halfling Seeker with no true power of her own? How could she not be at the bottom of the food chain?

She wrapped the last little orb with a golden thread she'd found in Aldric's hidden room. It probably belonged to Queen Titania's sister's butler's friend and was worth more than her life, but Cammi had seen a need for it.

Wadding a little in the button, she carefully looped the thread around the ball before securing it to a door handle. Aldric's home didn't give her that many options. She never thought she'd complain about clean, simple design.

Several metal banister posts got the same treatment, leaving her with a handful in her bag. That set, she let the ball of thread unravel as she crept down the rest of the stairs.

The situation wasn't helped by the guilt nibbling away at her gut either. She'd brought this down on Aldric. Until she came along, his existence was quiet. Probably peaceful.

Then in came Cammi.

Like a wrecking ball.

If she could fix this, their relationship could start off on a more even keel because, at the moment, Aldric held all the cards. Not something that made her comfortable. If they were going to be bonded, she wanted to be an equal partner.

Cammi stopped moving.

What the hell was she thinking? She didn't want a mate. She didn't need one. Her life had been long, hard, and meager, but she'd done it on her own. So what if she'd slowly go mad because she wouldn't bond with him? It would take a long, long time before that happened.

As if she needed the added complication of an overbearing mate tossed into the mix.

This would be a show of strength. She didn't need him to protect her. If anything, *he* needed *her*. With his old-world mannerisms, he probably wouldn't strike Lavinia if it came down to it because she was a female. And she would take full advantage of that.

Shaking her head, Cammi cleared the bottom steps and made it around a corner without being spotted. Wishing she had her shadows charm, she painstakingly inched her way around the room. What she wouldn't give for a more traditional design at that moment. Having wide open spaces was great … until you got attacked and needed to find cover.

Using furniture and statues as cover, Cammi got behind the werewolf. Comparatively, he'd be the easiest to take down. Especially when he was currently swilling what was sure to be insanely expensive alcohol like he needed it to live.

Aldric would thank her for this.

Cammi lay down almost flat, balancing herself on her hands and toes as she moved closer. Unfortunately, the too-large tunic scraped along the marble floor.

She froze. In the vulnerable position that she was, chances were stacked against her getting away. Holding her breath, she waited. Cammi could reach her dagger in time—possibly—if he attacked. It wouldn't be pretty, or easy, but she could handle herself.

He paused, tipping the bottle upright as he listened.

Cammi forced her quickly fatiguing muscles to keep still.

When he sniffed deep, she almost rolled onto her back to grab the dagger. He stuck his nose in the neck of the bottle and inhaled again. Savoring the aroma. Relief caused her to sag a little but she held her ground.

When he tipped the bottle back again, Cammi took the opportunity and leaped to her feet. Using the chair, she jumped up onto his neck and wrapped her legs around it. She slammed her fist against the bottom of the bottle and pushed it farther into his mouth, using the liquid and her legs to gag him.

He ripped and tore at her. Thankfully the tunic held against the razor sharpness of his claws though she was positive she'd have some ugly bruises the next day.

She threw her weight to the side, twisting his neck. When she felt the pop, Cammi knew it was over and toppled him silently onto the sofa.

It was a quick matter of taking the bottle out of his mouth, to avoid a further mess, covering him with a throw and some cushions, and moving on.

She looked up to where she'd left Aldric and

caught sight of his furious face an instant before he disappeared in a blur of movement.

What? She'd saved what was left of his brandy and took out one of the intruders. That was two-to-zero in her book. He'd better hurry if he wanted to catch up.

As she took cover, she caught sight of him on the other side where the vampire was looking through his collection of books. From the look that crossed Aldric's face when the vampire touched them, he wasn't too happy.

Aldric grabbed him and she spotted how the would-be thief's body shuddered and spasmed. He'd been electrocuted and was likely dead before he hit the ground. Aldric stood over the smoldering body as he glowered at her.

Was that a challenge?

So what if he had powers? She had brains. And, thanks to him, a few new toys.

He motioned for her to come back to him. Why? Things were working out quite nicely as they were.

Lavinia was still ranting about … something. Not that it mattered. All she spouted were things that would distract her. Cammi needed to focus. That left her and the other witch. As long as nothing else got in.

Shaking her head, Cammi signaled he should go around to get the witch while she went after Lavinia. Aldric shook his head and pointed at her then at the ground at his side again.

Was he crazy? He wanted her to risk going over there just so he could play the big hero?

Aldric pointed again but when she glared back at him, he dashed across the space in the blink of an eye. What Cammi hadn't expected was the serpent he stomped on just inches away from biting her.

"What the hell do you think you're playing at?"

he growled in her ear.

A tremor skittered through her. He'd been trying to protect her, not boss her around. "I thought…"

"I know what you thought," he bit out. "This isn't a game, Cammi."

She pulled herself to her full height. "I know it's not. But how can I trust you when I know nothing about you?"

Aldric gripped her shoulders. "Know that I am your mate and nothing short of death will stop me from protecting you."

"And I'm trying to protect you. You don't know anything about her or what she's capable of. I do. That, and with your lord of the manor act, how can I know you'll be able to take her down?"

He looked utterly baffled. "What?"

"What if you have to hit her?" It sounded ridiculous to her own ears now, but Cammi kept going. "Could you?"

He looked at her as if she was crazy and in that moment Cammi wasn't sure that she was completely sane either.

But his face softened inexplicably. "It's a big change, I know," he murmured. "If only we'd had a chance to bond before this happened."

That would have made thing easier? Sure, they'd be better attuned to one another. Cammi had heard stories of mates who could read each other's minds and trace the other over vast distances. Would they be like them?

Or would the extreme need to protect the other be a hindrance? It was bad enough now that she worried about his safety as well as her own. If they were bonded, wouldn't the urge be much worse?

But at least she would get where he was coming

from and that would be a huge advantage.

Too late now.

"Who's this?" Lavinia had rounded the corner and spied them with curiosity clear on her angular features.

Tall and willowy, the sorceress appeared fragile enough that a stiff wind would break her. Experience told Cammi that was the furthest thing from the truth.

The obvious attraction in Lavinia's gaze as she studied Aldric ignited the impulse to grab her by her auburn hair and throw her out the nearest window.

Aldric closed his hand over her shoulder as if he could read what she was thinking.

The witch's eyes caught the move. "I never knew you had a lover. You seem so stressed and … unlikable, I assumed that was due, in part, to sexual frustration. You *are* full of surprises today, aren't you?"

Cammi shrugged Aldric off. "I don't know what you think you're getting by coming here, but I suggest you leave."

Lavinia's face turned hard. "Look who's tough now that she's got backup."

Aldric stiffened behind her but thankfully said nothing.

Stepping in front of Aldric, Cammi squared off with the witch. "I'm not the one who had to show up with a team to help her take on one little halfling."

Laughing, Lavinia tore her gaze from Cammi to look at the man behind her once again. "I get it now. This is his place. Does he even know what you are? What you do? What you dragged him into?"

Aldric chuckled.

"What's so funny, handsome?"

"You." Aldric's voice rumbled into Cammi's back. "You think you can break into my home and threaten what's mine and get away with it?"

"I think I might," came her haughty reply.

A low growl came from the man behind her. One that belonged to a creature much, much bigger. "Wrong."

Chapter Six

Cammi couldn't say that she didn't enjoy the look of terror that came over the witch's face when Aldric transformed. *She* was still in awe from what she remembered, and the sheer size of him alone was awe-inspiring.

But as much as she wanted to stop and gawk, there were two spell-casters that needed to be disposed of.

Darkness descended upon them when Aldric spread his wings and destroyed the lights. Suited her just fine. And definitely gave them the advantage over the witches.

Movement caught the corner of her eye and Cammi spotted the other witch. She'd dropped everything she had pillaged and stood wide-eyed and jaw loose at the dragon that filled the space, and she was scrabbling in the darkness to get away.

Taking advantage of the opening, Cammi hit the easy target with an ice orb an instant before Aldric released a blast of electricity-laced blue fire at her, vaporizing her in an instant.

Darkness, it seemed, didn't hinder him in the slightest either.

Aldric wheeled around, looking for Lavinia, smashing out the windows with his tail to give himself more space to maneuver.

For a moment, Cammi stared at the space left open where the glass used to be. But the creatures on the other side, the ones that hadn't been stupid enough to get cooked by the barrier, still couldn't pass Aldric's wards.

She counted a couple of harpies and a vampire

left outside. Seeing Aldric in all his glory, they'd have to be fools to try to take him on.

That left the sorceress.

Lavinia had broken through the shock though the terror she experienced at facing down Aldric was clear in her pallor and glassy eyes.

"I—I didn't know…"

Of course, she hadn't. If she'd had any inkling of what she would face, Lavinia would never have shown up. A charge filled the air, but it wasn't from Aldric.

Cammi screamed for him to take cover as a blast of green blazed from the witch, aimed directly at his head. He countered with a blast of his own. The resulting heat seared and blistered Cammi's skin until she had to take cover.

It gave her an opportunity, however.

Using the crashing as more glass and stone was obliterated with Aldric's next move as camouflage, Cammi ducked around. Aldric seemed aware of where she was and kept relatively still as she darted around his legs and past his tail to get to the other side of him.

Lavinia's focus was on the dragon bearing down on her. No matter what she hurled at him, Aldric was able to counter it. Easily.

How could Cammi tell him that Lavinia was more than likely trying to lull him into a false sense of security? Did she need to? Surely, Aldric knew what she was up to.

In case he didn't, she'd make sure she had his back.

While he kept Lavinia's focus, Cammi edged closer toward her. There were a couple of grenades left in her bag, a fire and a bonding orb, her dagger, and her tunic. She'd make do with them.

Cammi hadn't been kidding when she'd told

Aldric that she'd made far less work in her favor. Now wasn't the time for reminiscing, however. She edged behind an armed statue to try to figure out a strategy. One idea would be to lob everything she had at Lavinia and hope one of them would incapacitate her. And that was including the spear and shield the statue held.

But a look over her shoulder told Cammi that it wasn't likely. It was possible one of the creatures outside could tell Lavinia where she was. Did Aldric have a ward for something like that? She got the feeling they were being watched with great interest. How were they going to stop them from telling the world dragons still roamed among them?

Cammi couldn't let that kind of information get out. It was bad enough the damage they were doing to the tower. How was that *not* going to be on the news that night?

Giving the sorceress a quick glance and seeing she was still establishing Aldric's power, Cammi headed to the blown-out windows. She tested the wards with her hand and felt the familiar charge of energy. Aldric was in for a world of questions if they got out of this in one piece.

But like the last time, she was able to get through it. It was painful, but that would give her an advantage.

It occurred to her that it might have been because he was her mate that she was able to get through his barrier with minimal damage. Then an idea hit her, putting a smile on her face.

Cammi carefully slid the spear out of the statue's grip, careful not to make a noise. Not that it mattered with the literal firefight and enormous dragon wreaking havoc. It was a simple matter to tie the golden thread around the spearhead then loop the end around a pillar. With it secure, she cut her thumb on the tip, smearing her blood on the head and the shaft. That done, Cammi then mockingly motioned to the vampire and the harpies.

"Can't get me, can you? I bet that just pisses you right off, doesn't it?" She recognized one of the harpies as one she'd run into before. The hag had stolen a relic that Cammi had spent ages working out the traps for.

This was going to be good.

She danced just out of reach, swinging her butt at them, enraging them all the more. Cammi used her movements to disguise her pulling the bronze orb from the bag and holding her thumb down on the trigger.

Predictably incensed, the harpy started attacking the ward and encouraged the others to do the same.

Exactly what Cammi hoped for.

The moment they did so in unison, Cammi acted. Throwing the bronze ball toward them, she quickly followed the same path with the spear. The orb did its job and exploded with a flash of orange, binding them together with the spear, which thanks to her blood had pierced the ward. She grinned in triumph at the gelatinous glob dangling from the golden thread like fish on a hook, keeping the world below from knowing what was going on far above.

With them out of the way, Cammi was free to focus her attention on Lavinia.

Aldric had circled the core of the building, destroying everything in his wake. Cammi mourned his collection, much of which was little more than shards and splinters now.

And all because she had brought this chaos into his life.

Putting that thought aside for later, Cammi reached into the bag and closed her hand around the last orb. She needed to lure Lavinia upstairs so she could use the ones she had planted along the way.

Aldric let loose a world-trembling roar that shook the remaining glass from their panes, sending them shattering to the floor.

Or she could let Aldric deal with her.

Rebuking herself for such an uncharitable thought against her mate, Cammi picked up a chunk of cement and hurled it at the sorceress. If she could just get her attention, she just might be able to give Aldric an opening and they could end this.

Luckily, he was keeping her busy enough that all she was capable of was launching quick blasts of energy and not something more devastating. Neither of them looked as if they were tiring. She had no desire to see who would first.

She hurled another chunk only to have it bounce off whatever shield Lavinia had put up around herself. Cammi searched for something, a thought, an item, anything that could be used to distract her focus on Aldric.

Mind working overtime, Cammi's gaze shot to the stairs as an idea hit her.

She needed an ice orb.

Confident she could get around without being noticed, Cammi gave up trying to keep cover and ran for the stairs. After seeing how the other ones had worked, she hoped her hunch would be a good one.

Carefully undoing her knots, Cammi grabbed the closest one and ran back to where the two ancients were doing battle. That Lavinia had the ability to keep Aldric at bay was frightening, to say the least. The realization she was toying with him chilled her as if she'd used the orb on herself.

She couldn't be more powerful than Aldric. Wouldn't logic dictate he was toying with her as well?

It didn't matter. There were two of them against

her.

Cammi watched for a moment, tried to gauge movement on both their parts to figure out the best angle of attack. It took a fraction of a second for her to act.

Thanking the gods for wet English weather, she activated and threw both the fire and ice orbs simultaneously. The water in the air froze just as quickly as the fire melted it, providing a wet path from Lavinia to the electric wards guarding them from the outside world.

The charge blasted along the newfound path, through the witch, knocking her off her feet and throwing her backward into the puddle. The current continued to use her as a conduit but didn't prove powerful enough to keep her incapacitated for long.

She fought the electricity charging through her and was strong enough to push herself up a short way and aimed what was sure to be a ruinous assault at Aldric.

Cammi dove on top of her, shoving her into the water and holding her there even though the current tore through her as well.

She fought to get a scream past her locked jaw. "Aldric! Blast us!"

Aldric had spun to rivet her with his electric gaze. But Cammi could barely see him as the pain of the charge lanced through her, seizing all her muscles. Luckily, her added weight was enough to keep Lavinia from moving.

But not from hitting Cammi with a debilitating spell. Combined with the pain from the voltage from the water, Cammi's vision started to narrow. But she was still aware enough to note that the witch's power began to swell. Whatever attack she planned was going to be a powerful one

"Do it!" she screamed through her gritted teeth.

Whatever happened, she would have protected him.

Her dragon did as he was bid.

His eyes locked to hers, he unleashed his electrified fire at them.

The world exploded into a sea of agonizing blue-white before collapsing and enveloping Cammi in blissful darkness.

Chapter Seven

Cammi could see the blinding white before she even opened her eyes. It didn't matter. What she couldn't help but focus on was how there wasn't a single ache in her body. Not a niggle at her neck. Not a crick in her back. No pain. Anywhere. She'd never felt this good before. Surely this was the afterlife. There was no way she could feel healthy and whole after what she'd been through.

Unless it was all a dream?

That had to be it. The only place she could feel this good and have found her mate was in a dream.

But since when was the ramshackle cot she called her bed so comfortable?

Almost afraid of what she would find, Cammi cracked open one eye.

The room was pristine white and blinding in its brilliance. She lay on cloudlike pillows and the biggest bed she'd ever seen.

Definitely unlike any hospital she'd ever encountered.

So, where was she?

Cammi stretched cautiously, even eventually wiggling her toes, and found everything in working order. Not only that, but she felt as if she'd slept a week and could now conquer the world.

"It's about time you woke up."

The familiar voice put a smile on her face as she turned toward it.

Aldric sat on a chair next to the bed. He looked as calm and cool as ever, though more serious than she'd thought possible. How could he get *more* serious?

"How long have I been out?"

He muttered something that sounded like *too long* but he gave her a shake of his head. "Why did you do that?" he growled.

He was angry at her? "Do what?"

"In effect, you sacrificed yourself for me. You had no idea what my dragon fire could do to you and yet you all but begged me to flame you both."

"We had to get rid of her somehow." It had worked, hadn't it? "She's gone, right?"

"Yes." His voice was still tight.

"Then it was all worth it."

"You could have died with her, Cammi." His voice was tortured.

"But I didn't."

"You're just so damned smug, aren't you?" Aldric unfurled his long, lean body from the chair and started pacing. "You have no plan, no idea, you just jump in half-cocked and hope for the best."

Pointing out that she'd made it through just fine didn't seem like a great idea at the moment. Cammi flipped her hair over her shoulder. "I figured since we're mates your fire wouldn't hurt me too much. Like your ward didn't."

"So careful thought, testing, and consideration went into your hypothesis, did it?"

The scorn in his voice wasn't lost on her. "You know as well as I do that there wasn't time."

"No, there wasn't."

"So I was right in what I did."

"No."

The triumph that swelled her pride withered just as quickly as it had appeared. "We made it out just fine. In my book that's a win."

He whirled around to stand before her, using his

imposing size to intimidate. "You don't get it, do you?"

"What's there to get?"

Aldric exploded. "That I could have lost you! For all you knew, you could have ended up a smoldering pile of ash like Lavinia is now. *She* could have killed you even if I didn't!" He scrubbed his hand over his face. "I have spent millennia looking for my mate and this is what fate has given me."

Cammi shot to her feet, standing on the bed to take away his height advantage, wholly unconcerned she was once again stark naked. "And what's that?" she asked, knowing he could probably list her imperfections. A ridiculously long litany, without a doubt.

He moved closer, his gaze wandering over her nude form before meeting her eyes. "A tiny, maddening thief who cares nothing of her own safety."

She stepped forward, jabbing him in the chest with her finger, ignoring the heat coming off his body and the pleasurable zaps she received with the fleeting contact. "And I got a starchy, stuffed shirt who cares more about his things than anything else."

"Wrong!" he roared. Aldric gripped her head. "All I care about is you!"

Tangling his hands in her hair to hold her tight, Aldric tilted his head and devoured her mouth with shattering sensuality. Cammi immediately pressed herself against him as if her body couldn't stand being apart from his any longer. She gleefully threw herself headfirst into the pleasure his kiss gave her.

What was she doing?

She shoved at his shoulders, forcing him to break the kiss. Breathless, she stated, "But you hate me."

Aldric was just as starved for air but managed to breathe the words, "I never hated you."

"I tried to steal from you."

"A mistake. Besides, you never got a thing."

"I would have."

He brushed his lips against hers. "You wouldn't."

"I'm a halfling."

"So?"

"But…"

He leveled his gaze at her. "Cammi, I have no doubts, I want this. You. But I need to know that you are willing. That your reservations can be silenced."

Could they? She'd been against this all her life, but now that she'd found her mate, found him to be intriguing, and formidable, and gorgeous, and infinitely desirable, she began to doubt the wisdom of her old oath. He'd fought to protect her. Even after what she had tried to do.

With Aldric, she felt whole. Like puzzle pieces. He was her serious, solid, other half. That part of her that would keep her grounded.

Did he feel the same about her?

Was she his other half? The part of him that had been missing?

That he was giving her the choice made her heart swell. Deprived of their mates, Others would slowly wither away crazed, as surely doomed as if they faced a Cull while in a trance.

"If it's time you need…" Aldric forced himself to give her space. The trembling in his body told her just how hard it had been for him to do so. "I will endeavor to give it to you. Whatever you need…"

She tugged him close again, enjoying the heat radiating from him. "I'm not the one I'm worried about needing time. Are you sure you want to hitch yourself to this?" Cammi motioned at herself.

He laughed roughly. "I've thought of nothing but *hitching* myself to this"—he ran his hands up and down her sides—"since I first saw you."

Shocked at his innuendo, Cammi burst out laughing. "So, you do have an improper side after all."

****

Cammi's tinkling laughter was an incredible sound. Especially after watching her nearly roasted alive by his own fire. It was a nightmare that flashed through his mind in a constant loop. Watching the sorceress burn away until there was nothing left but ash had been satisfying, but witnessing Cammi's skin incinerate had been just short of demolishing his sanity.

It had taken over a week of single-minded dedication from some of the finest healers he could find to patch her up. Had she even noticed her pristine new skin? He hated that he could see her tattoos being burned away with her flesh when he closed his eyes.

He opened them again.

For a tiny halfling, Cammi was resilient. Strong. And probably right about being somewhat immune to his abilities because they were fated to be together. If they had been bonded, would she have been hurt at all?

Aldric would never forgive himself for not searching harder for her in the first place and perhaps forgoing this whole ugly scene altogether. If he had, Cammi might have been spared the life she'd obviously endured all this time.

But she was alive and well and in his arms.

His mate.

Finally.

Cammi could be exasperating, sure, but she was strong, smart and so very sexy. And so naked.

Having her so close was ravaging his self-control, but he refused to give in to the dragon clamoring inside him just yet. Aldric needed to know Cammi was willing—not just willing—but as eager as he was to be claimed. That she wanted him and wasn't just giving in to fate. Not that he believed she would *just* give into anything.

"Cammi…"

"Yes?" She blinked her big, silvery eyes at him innocently. If he'd only just met her he wouldn't think butter would melt in her mouth.

But he knew otherwise, didn't he?

His dragon tore at him from the inside as Aldric fought him back. "Cammi," he rasped. "I need to know this is what you want."

"It is." She peered into his eyes and he saw something glowing there that warmed his heart. "I never thought I'd find my mate. And when it took so long to find you, I convinced myself that I didn't need you."

"And now?"

"There is a very specific need I feel right now."

He would wager it was the exact same thing he was feeling too. "Tell me it's not just because we're fated to be together."

She seemed to think about it but shook her head. "It might be part of what I'm feeling, but I think we both know that nothing could compel either of us into doing anything that we didn't want. Otherwise, wouldn't we have sought each other out ages ago?"

"Don't remind me," he muttered. "Because of my stubbornness, you were stuck thieving to survive."

Cammi pressed her lips against his, effectively silencing him. The sensation of her tracing her tongue along the seam of his lips chased all thoughts from his mind.

When she pulled back, her eyes were heavy-lidded and smoky. "Let's forget about all that." Cammi brushed her lips against his. "Do you want me? Because I want you." Another gentle kiss. "Just you."

Her soft declaration snapped the last remaining thread of his control. Aldric tipped her head back so he could plunder her mouth to his satisfaction. Hunger he'd never known raged through him. Everything he was made of was on edge with need for her.

Cammi wrapped one leg around him, then the other until she had wound herself around him with the same apparent need as she kissed him back. The blast of desire that hurtled through him was nothing short of cataclysmic. That this tiny female had the power to bring him to his knees was both awe-inspiring and terrifying. For a dragon who'd been alone for so long, it was humbling. Exhilarating.

Aldric trembled as he lowered her to the bed. Nothing had ever felt this important.

For the first time in his long and illustrious life, there was a twinge of performance anxiety. What if it didn't work? Even worse, what if she didn't like … it? Him?

Cammi didn't allow him to dwell. Lying back on the bed, she smiled up at him. "It's not fair that I'm completely naked and you're not."

Aldric didn't need asking twice. The appreciation and unabashed lust in her eyes as he peeled away his clothing spurred him on. By the time he stood before her just as naked, he was more than confident she enjoyed what she saw.

Her gaze raked over him from head to toe and back up again, her expression rapt as her eyes dropped back down to his groin.

She sighed with what sounded like appreciation. "Every inch of you is beautiful."

"No more than you."

Cammi blushed but held out her hand to beckon him closer.

Aldric took it and let her tug him over her. Let her set the pace. Her earlier admission that she'd had no interest in men before him both pleased and alarmed him. He needed to be gentle not only because she was so much smaller than him, but because he figured it was more than likely her first time being intimate with a male.

An honor she bestowed upon him that he wouldn't take lightly.

She arched up against him as he dragged one hand over her skin, mentally cataloging every inch of her flesh. Every scar, every bit of her that made her giggle or sigh. Aldric wanted to know all of it.

The taste of her, the scent of her, what made her scream in pleasure.

And he would.

Lowering his head, he took the peak of her breast into his mouth.

****

Cammi breathed his name as the pleasure threatened to swamp her. She'd read books, seen movies, and heard tales whispered about how magical just a touch or a kiss from the opposite sex could be. Not to mention the pinnacles of ecstasy that could be attained by the act of sex itself.

She thought it all swagger and hyperbole.

Until now.

Being close to Aldric alone was a heady experience.

His touch sparked all sorts of wondrous sensations that crashed through her. But the flick of his tongue over her hardened nipple sent a streak of purest pleasure pin balling through her.

Cammi's head swam and her senses clamored as she experienced so many new and incredible sensations all at once. Then he let loose a spark of electricity that zapped into her breast and darted through her to explode low in her belly. Dazed, she lifted her head to look down and found him watching her reaction carefully.

"Do that again," she moaned.

Aldric grinned and lowered his head once again, to do as she bid.

He randomly alternated between infinitesimal shocks and breaths of hot and cold air as he sucked and licked, keeping her in a constant state of awareness and winding her body tight with pleasure.

Until Cammi couldn't stand it any longer. She couldn't stop the cries of delight as her body detonated in orgasm.

It was a long while before she could focus her eyes again. Cammi was aware of him at her side, watching her, gently pinching her nipples and sending tiny jolts of electricity into her breasts each time he asserted pressure.

The way the electricity raced through her body, ricocheted, and collided with one another before slowly dissipating was incredibly erotic.

She wanted more.

Wishing she could reciprocate with something as amazing, she dragged him closer. "I want more Aldric. I want everything."

His eyes darkened. "I'm trying to be gentle. I'm not wrong in thinking this is your first sexual encounter, am I?"

"You're not wrong." She kissed him, hoping it would tell him what she wanted. What she couldn't articulate. Cammi drew back to gaze at him. "But I want my mate to enjoy himself too."

He chuckled as she writhed against him. "Believe me, I am."

That put a smile on her face. "I think I've proved I'm tougher than I look." She insinuated herself under him, loving the deliciousness of his weight on her. "I don't need gentle. Make me yours, dragon."

The low growl that came from him rumbled through her. Now they were getting somewhere.

His hands grew rougher, more demanding as he slid them down her body. The currents flowing from him streamed through her in electrified waves of sensation until every cell in her body felt energized. When he parted her thighs and delved between them with his fingers, she thought he would hit her with another bolt. Aldric grinned at her wickedly.

Cammi barely had a chance to register it let alone try to figure out what it meant before she felt the power drawing out of her. It coursed ever faster toward his fingers, leaving tingling trails in its wake. To pool buzzing in her clit.

Then it burst.

The shock of sensation had her screaming into his chest as another orgasm ripped through her. But Aldric was on the move. He licked a path of fire down from the valley between her breasts, over her stomach, stopping briefly to dip his tongue into the little hollow there before sliding lower.

Cammi's breath caught when he flicked the tip of his tongue over her folds. She arched against him when he sucked the sensitive little bundle of nerves between his lips. But when he zapped her clit with a tiny bolt of electricity, she screamed her delight and surprise at the sensation. The charge rippled through her body and down her limbs.

She lay dazed under him for a long while, marveling at the sensations and the connection she already felt with Aldric. When he slid back to her side,

Cammi couldn't help staring into his face in wonder. It was so easy to see how anyone could get addicted to the feeling. Especially when she had a wicked storm dragon toying with her.

Aldric's smile was wolfish. "Think you can take more?"

"Think you can give me more?" Cammi raked her nails down the hard muscles of his chest. Then his abs...

Biting his lip, Aldric hissed when she ran the tip of her finger along the length of his cock. "Most definitely."

She did it again just to watch the tremors ripple through him. The sense of power it gave her was heady. That she could make a dragon tremble at her fingertips was incredible.

Cammi met his gaze, then lowered it just as quickly, suddenly shy despite what they'd already done.

"What is it?" He tipped her chin up so she met his gaze.

"I want to ... I don't know how..." Cammi cleared her throat. "I want to please you."

Aldric gave her a gentle kiss. "You *are* pleasing me."

Feeling ridiculous, and knowing heat burned her cheeks, Cammi forced herself to continue. "I want to make you feel the same way you make me feel. But I don't have any powers ... or anything."

"You have plenty of magic, my little thief." He curled her hand around his erection and couldn't help the groan that escaped him. "This is the power you have over me."

His cock, so hot and hard in her hand, fascinated her. He was thick. Her fingers couldn't meet with him gripped in her hand. Steely and silky, Cammi found she liked the texture of him. Another deep groan came from deep inside Aldric when she tentatively caressed him, and it was the sexiest thing she'd ever heard.

She did it again to see if she would get the same response. This time she got a growl as tension tightened his body.

Cammi continued her to pump him in her hand as she explored the length of him. She marveled at the beauty of his body. How amazing he felt. How he responded to every little movement and squeeze.

That was, until he pulled her hand away.

His chest was heaving and his eyes were tightly shut. She ran her hand over his chest and found his heart pounding against his ribs. "Did I do something wrong?"

Aldric opened his eyes to level his burning blue gaze at her. "Absolutely not. But if you don't want things to end too soon, you have to stop."

That put a smile on her face.

He rolled her under him. When she parted her thighs to cradle him between them, he nuzzled her neck with a chuckle.

The feel of Aldric so big and solid against her was amazing. The differences between them in size and strength was sure to be a continual font of delight for Cammi. Aldric seemed to enjoy having her against him as well. His clever hands found every spot on her body that made her tremble with pleasure or ache with desire.

His kisses caused her head to spin and only added to the maelstrom of sensation that threatened to devour her. The sensation of his cock, hard and grinding against her, made her crave in a way she'd never imagined. And the fact that touching him was like being in contact with a live wire gripped her senses like a drug. When she was sure she was going to go mad, Cammi forced her eyes open to look at him.

Aldric.

Her mate.

There was no doubt in her mind that she'd found him and that this was what she wanted. He was whom she wanted.

Aldric was the part of her that had been missing.

Dragging him down for another soul-searing kiss, she hoped he understood what she felt. What she was trying to convey with the kiss.

He drew back a little to look into her eyes. She could see in the startlingly blue depths he felt it too and this moment was just as profound for him.

In the end, no words were needed.

Aldric dropped his head to crash his mouth into hers once more. Cammi arched up under him, needing to feel him against every inch of her. His hair-roughened skin abraded hers in a way that set off sparks of fire everywhere it touched. Writhing against him wasn't getting her enough sensation.

Cammi needed more.

Sensing her desire, or perhaps no longer able to leash his dragon, Aldric raised himself just enough to get his hand between them and notched the broad head of his cock between her wet folds.

His eyes searched hers when she went still. This was it. The last chance to back out.

Cammi clawed his shoulders as she pushed her hips upward, slowly impaling herself on his thick erection. She felt the tremor that rocked him as surely as if it had been her own body. Then again, perhaps it had been a combination of them being ravaged by sensation.

Aldric gripped her hips and slowly pushed the length of him inside her. What little resistance he met disappeared with a pinch of pain.

Then he was deep inside her.

She stared up at him in wonder. Feeling so full of

him. Of emotion. It was incredible.

His eyes were dark as he watched her. Even now, he was concerned for her well-being. She'd never felt better but had the gut feeling he could improve on that exponentially.

Biting her lip, she shifted her hips and was rewarded with a shock of sensation and a groan from him. Cammi rocked against him again, and this time Aldric helped her untutored movements until they established a relentlessly deep, grinding rhythm.

Cammi dropped her head back, closed her eyes, and she savored everything he did to her. Every sensation. Stretched around his cock, she met his thrusts, loving the groans rising from his throat and that buzz of pleasure that grew with every plunge he made inside her.

He seemed aware of the building tension in her and his thrusts became more determined. "Come with me, Cammi…"

Tingling had already started in her fingers and toes, rolling up her limbs. All the energy seemed to converge behind her belly button and, for an age, it pooled there.

And then exploded.

Screaming, she clung to him as he slammed into her. He held himself deep. The pulsing heat inside her as he came was accompanied by a burst of electricity from him that shot through her.

The bursts of pleasure eventually faded, leaving Cammi dazed and the most relaxed she'd ever been. At the same time, she felt him. Not just inside and against her, but in the back of her mind.

He lifted his weary gaze to meet her stunned one. "I feel it too."

"I guess it worked. We're bonded." She said it with a sense of wonder.

Aldric gently grazed her skin with his hands. "If you wanted further proof."

Cammi followed his gaze and found her arms lined with the most delicate pattern. Silvery blue, it looked as if her arms had been painted with light. She knew it was the path his power had taken and had marked her as his. Her chest was the same, and she was willing to wager her back and legs were decorated as well. The marking looked to have originated from a bright point over her heart and flowed from there.

"My tattoos…" The loss of them was in no way comparable to the delicate markings now on her skin. "It's beautiful."

"Only made more beautiful by the woman it is on." Aldric kissed her shoulder. "How do you feel?"

"Wonderful." It was as if his power now flowed through her veins as well. Cammi smiled at him but gasped when she met his eyes.

"What's wrong?"

She gripped his face so she could get a closer look. "One of your eyes has turned silver."

Aldric smiled as if the news pleased him supremely.

"Why do you look so smug?"

"It's proof I belong to you." He kissed away the moue of confusion from her lips. "You've marked me as I've marked you." Aldric's fingers traced the pattern along her collarbone. "Didn't you know?"

She stared into his eyes for a while longer. "I did … sort of. I wasn't sure if I'd mark you. I thought you had to have some sort of power to do that."

Aldric tipped them to their sides, keeping them locked together. "Didn't I tell you you had power?"

Smiling, she pressed her face against his chest. "I guess I do."

"Never doubt me."

Cammi couldn't help but laugh at the return of his haughty attitude. "Never?"

He shook his head. "Just as you should never doubt I will do everything I can to give you whatever you want. Your old life is over."

Not having thought that far, Cammi's eyes widened. No more scraping by or risking her life? The first part sounded wonderful ... the second...

"No more thieving." His voice was implacable.

"But—"

"Cammi. I don't want you risking your life foolishly. What could you possibly need that I can't provide?"

He was right about that, except there was one thing she wanted to do. Needed to do.

"But I owe you a debt." She gave Aldric a wicked smile as she wriggled against him. "I have to rebuild your collection..."

Aldric's laughter turned into a groan but didn't argue when Cammi dragged him in for a kiss.

"Perhaps I can be persuaded," he muttered against her lips as her hands started to roam.

Cammi proceeded to persuade him very well.

The End

THE LIBRARIAN AND HER DRAGON

Doris O'Connor

Chapter One

Annie

The peace of the library was shattered by the roar of motorbikes. Their vibrations rattled my cup of peppermint tea on its dainty saucer, and I frowned at the disturbance. As if it wasn't bad enough this particular motorcycle club had decided to pay our sleepy village a visit, they had to come and disturb my peace at my place of work too.

Not a day went by that someone didn't come in with a story to tell about the leather-clad hunks who rode through the streets as though they owned the town. Not that they'd done any actual damage, but their reputation preceded them. As a relative newbie—I'd only been in residence for a few years—I'd never witnessed the destruction they apparently left in their wake before I'd arrived, but this was getting old, fast.

The doors flung open and the whole lot sauntered in. The leader lifted his helmet off his head as he approached, and I swallowed hard.

Talk about a slab of prime male meat. He had to be well over six and a half feet of tightly-packed muscle and I couldn't tear my gaze away from the way his biceps bulged as he put his helmet down and straightened back up again slowly. A well-trimmed beard covered a strong jaw, which led to a corded neck and broad shoulders that strained the leather encasing them. Slim hips, powerful thighs, and an impressive bulge completed the look. Definitely easy on the eyes, if you went for that sort of brute strength. I preferred the intelligent, geeky type myself. Still, in the interests of honesty, I had to confess a woman could drown in the warmth of his brown eyes. They drew together in a frown as he noticed me. I briefly wondered what he saw as he devoured me with his gaze. I sure didn't warrant that much male attention, usually. Not that I thought I was hideous. I scrubbed up pretty well when I wanted to, and I was comfortable in all my wobbly bits, but I was at work and the way this guy was checking me out just wasn't on.

"Can I help you?" I adopted my most professional voice and fixed a polite smile on my face as he came closer. Jeez, he really was tall. I craned my neck to stare up at him. He didn't answer me, like any normal person would have done. Oh no, the mountain of a man loomed over my desk and sniffed the air. *Sniffed*. How dare he? It was hot in here with the ancient air conditioning on the blink, for sure, but I didn't smell.

A rumble rose from his massive chest, and when his dark gaze finally reached my eyes, I could have sworn flames danced in their depths.

Maybe the heatwave we were experiencing had fried my brain or something.

"You're new." His deep voice washed over me, made my hackles rise, because he was still undressing me with his eyes.

"You're rude!"

A muscle twitched in his neck, and the whole library went quiet. You could have heard the proverbial pin drop, and my overdramatic co-worker's loud gasp rang in my ears. Barbara rolled her chair closer to whisper in my ear. Not sure why she bothered. Her whispers were akin to other folks' normal tone of voice.

"You can't speak to him like that. Goodness only knows what his gang will do now."

I barely resisted the urge to roll my eyes. Really, it was pathetic the way everyone feared these *Dragoons*. What sort of name was that, anyway?

Too late I realized I said the thought out loud, and I squirmed under the stranger's heated gaze. *Jesus*—intense much? And there went his eyes again, definite flames, and it might be my imagination, but the heat just went up several degrees.

If I was given to flights of fancy and I was one of the heroines I liked to read about in my stash of paranormal erotic romances on my Kindle, I'd have said he was a shifter who'd found his mate. His nostrils flared, and he leaned right into my personal space.

Now, I was sure I was supposed to swoon here and go all mellow and spout nonsense like, "Take me, I'm yours," but this was real life, not fantasy.

My knickers might be soaked through, because, let's face it, the guy was hot, but that sure didn't mean I was going to make it easy for him.

No, siree, not this librarian.

"Have I got something on my face that needs closer inspection, or have you simply forgotten your glasses at home, Mr...?" I raised my voice, waiting for him to reply, but he continued to stare at me as though I was some sort of fascinating microbe under a microscope. Barbara made a strange noise as though she couldn't get enough air into her lungs, and I picked up a sheet of paper and fanned the woman, lest she pass out on me.

Our local paramedics were overworked as it was in the middle of tourist season, and they did not need to attend to a call out because she succumbed to hysterics again.

What would I say in the report, anyway? Woman passed out due to hot, brooding guy at desk? When he still didn't say anything, I did roll my eyes, which earned me a raised eyebrow. Oh, he was one of *those.*

"And for your information, I've been holding this position for the last three years, so I'm hardly new. Now, unless you have a book to return or wish to borrow one, please move aside so that I can deal with an actual customer. You're holding up the line."

Not that there was one. The members of the women's reading club who had been holding their weekly meeting here were all squashed in the opposite corner, clutching their books to their bosoms like the proverbial pearls.

Maybe we would need that ambulance after all. Mrs. Peacock looked almost as scandalized as when the stalwarts of our community had found out that I was stocking *that* book.

Mr. Grey might do nothing for me, but who was I to stop women from wanting to read him? I had far hotter and more accurate stuff on my Kindle, for sure.

I jumped when the brooding hulk dropped a

leather-bound copy of Tolstoy's *War and Peace* on the desk in front of me.

"I came to return this."

A cloud of dust rose off the desk, and I swallowed the resulting cough tickling the back of my throat. Once I could see again, my mouth fell open because this book looked ancient. I'd have known if we had something this old in our collection. My heart started to beat faster. How I wish we *did* have this in our tiny library.

"Oh, I say."

I ignored Barbara's stage whisper and traced my fingers over the leather-bound exterior. Every fiber in my being urged me to open up this treasure and to immerse myself in what had to be first edition. How on earth had a leather-clad biker got hold of this?

"There has to be some mistake, Mr…?" I raised my eyes and promptly wished I hadn't, because the far too alluring stranger was still too close. So close that the heat emanating from his big body scorched my skin and I took an involuntarily inhale. I couldn't help it. He smelled just *so* damn good.

Smoky, like a good, old-fashioned bonfire—not the vile, cigarette kind of smell—mixed in with a hint of sweat and a dark musky scent, which wasn't any cologne I recognized. One that got me all hot and bothered though, and that made me angry.

At myself and this hunk, who still hadn't told me his name and dared to waltz in here, tempting me with books and … *damn it.*

"Gideon." His voice dropped lower, taking my stomach with it, and I struggled to get my brain to work as lust short-circuited my synapses. Sweet Jesus, I wanted to climb this man hunk like a tree and never let go.

What the ever-loving high kinks is happening here?

"What?" I grimaced at the most unlike-me squeak I managed to produce and cleared my throat to try again. Before I could, however, the brooding hulk smiled. I was struck by how white and even his teeth were before I lost myself in that sinful curve of his lips, and the surprising dimple which showed in one cheek.

"You asked me for my name, Annie."

I jerked in surprise that he knew mine. Before I could make a complete fool out of myself and ask him how he knew, I remembered my ID badge dangling on its lanyard over the girls, which once again seemed to snare his attention.

So flipping typical.

"My name is Gideon. Gideon Jackson the Third, to be precise, but who's counting?" He winked at me and then spoiled it all by continuing. "Annie Taylor. Suits you. Tell me, is that Annie short for anything or...?" He reached out to touch said ID and I slapped his hand away.

"Private property, mate. Don't touch what you can't afford. And it's *just* Annie, thank you very much."

Another rumble came from his big chest, the likes of which I'd never heard before. It was akin to the deep, throaty roar of a motorbike. Clearly, I had bikes on the brain, but that sound shouldn't come out of a human's chest. No animal's chest either; none that I'd ever met, anyway, not even in the zoo.

"I wasn't aware you were for sale, *just* Annie."

He did *not* just say that. My fingers itched to plant my fist on that annoyingly perfect and straight nose of his, and to wipe that knowing smirk of the guy's face. I refrained—barely—the good old ladies would have hysterics, and I was too aware of this guy's minions lurking behind him, huge grins on their faces, as though this was the most amusing interchange they'd ever witnessed. Damn the lot of them.

"I'm not. How dare you insinuate—"

"I'm only drawing the natural conclusion from your comment of not touching what I can't afford, and…" He stepped back and made a big show of studying me. "I could most definitely afford you."

That did it. I saw red. In the absence of a weapon, I picked up the tome and lobbed it at his head.

A collective gasp went into the air from the ladies in the library, his cohorts hooted in laughter, and the annoying man hunk simply ducked, which meant the heavy book sailed over his head and *kadunk*ed on the floor with a loud thunk.

The librarian in me winced. Lord only knew what damage that had done to the book's spine, and I shot out of my chair, rounded the desk, and gingerly picked up the book again.

The wolf whistles that erupted as the action made my pencil skirt rise up my legs rung in my ears, and too late I realized we were now surrounded by the entire group of bikers. I glared at them all in turn and then took a step back when this Gideon advanced on me.

"A man could get jealous over the way you're clutching that book."

He smiled at me, and I shoved the offending piece of literature at his impossibly broad chest.

"Here, have the damn thing. It's not one of ours anyway. I…" Our fingers brushed as he grasped the heavy object, and whatever I was going to say fled my brain. The spark of electricity zinged up my digits and woke up every erogenous zone in my body, and a few I didn't know I had.

What the hell?

I bit my lips to stop myself from uttering those words out loud. Especially as he looked at me as though I was dinner. That was really the only way to explain the intense hunger in his eyes, as he pinned me in place with his sheer will. I didn't think I could have moved if my life had depended on it. A ridiculously fanciful notion, I know—*oh, believe me, I know*—I wasn't the sort of woman to drop her knickers for any man, but...

Yeah, said items of underwear were in serious danger of self-combusting. Maybe I was more like those heroines in my book after all. Heaven forbid!

At least I wasn't the only one affected. A quick glance at his groin showed that bulge had rather grown in dimension, a bit like the man himself, who appeared to have gained a few inches. He seemed taller, wider, altogether more menacing somehow, yet I wasn't afraid of him.

"Gid, remember where we are."

The growled words from one of the men circling us sent shivers down my spine, because that voice didn't sound human. Not that I could tear my gaze away from the man hunk in front of me to check who had said that, because his eyes bled back to a warm amber, and after a deep inhale, he shook his head and appeared back to his normal self. Or rather just a devastatingly handsome, if incredibly cocky specimen of a man, who I absolutely under no circumstances wanted to climb.

If I said that to myself often enough, I might even believe it.

"You haven't checked inside, so how can you be so sure it isn't?"

My mind dragged itself out of the gutter with some difficulty as his words registered.

"I don't have to check. I know the books we have in our library, and—"

"Annie, actually…" Barbara hopped up and down behind the man hunk like a rabbit on speed. If I hadn't seen it with my own eyes, I wouldn't have believed it.

"What?" My reply might have been a tad too curt, but really. What the hell *was* her problem?

Gideon raised one eyebrow in that devilishly effective way men had, not that I'd ever noticed anyone doing that before, and it did not have any effect on me. Well, not the one he was no doubt hoping for. Made me want to lob the tome again and make sure I didn't miss this time, and I didn't even believe in violence.

"Well, that looks like an original copy. A bunch of them went missing a good thirty years ago. Look in the inside cover for a stamp, my dear."

She was still bouncing, and it was starting to make me feel queasy, or maybe that was just the effect being this close to man hunk—*I really must stop calling him that in my head*—was having on me. We were practically breathing each other's air, and what was it with the urge to lean in to all of his muscles and drink in his masculine scent? Was this what heat stroke felt like? The air conditioning must have given up its ghost completely because perspiration collected under my over-generous boobs and ran down my spine. I could only hope I wasn't leaving sweat stains on my blouse. That would be so unattractive, not to mention unprofessional.

That thought pulled me up faster than anything else could have done. I was here to do a job, and like it or not, that meant dealing with this Gideon person. Reluctantly, I forced my attention back to the book in my hands and sure enough, there on the inside cover was a faded stamp. I squinted at it and could just about make out the words.

Property of Rabbenstall Library 1873

My mouth fell open. Good Lord, that couldn't be right. That was the year the library opened.

"*How* did you get this?"

Chapter Two

Gideon

The little human did have the most expressive face. While she didn't say it out loud, her mistrust was written all over her features. It made me want to turn her over my knee and spank that luscious butt of hers for making assumptions about me and the rest of the *Dragoons* for that matter. The days of causing havoc on the sleepy streets of Cumbria had long passed, yet folks had long memories and mud stuck, as they say. My dragon roared, all ready to spit fire, and I had the devil of a job containing the beast. I couldn't believe I'd almost lost it earlier when her soft skin touched mine.

Of all the places I had to find the one woman I was destined to be with—the universe was having a great big fucking laugh at my expense giving me a human mate—it had to be here in the library, my one safe haven. I loved books, always had, and my father used to despair at the amount of time I'd spent in the library as a child.

Being a dragon had its advantages when it came to sneaking in and out of places unnoticed, that was for sure. Magick was a wonderful thing once you learned how to use it. Only reserved for the elders of the clan now, but I'd come into my powers early and had used it shamelessly for my own needs.

Not that I would be able to do that anymore. Not as the Alpha and certainly not here. Not with my *mate* working here. Fuck me sideways, I had to get out of here, or my dragon would want to claim her, consequences be damned.

Leonard, my second in command of the clan, cleared his throat and shook his head at me. The most infinitesimal of moves, that none of the human occupants would notice, but I got his warning loud and clear. Since my father chose to abdicate his responsibilities, I'd relied on Leonard to show me the ropes. I never wanted to be the next Alpha, thought I had years yet, but then Mum had been run off the road by a drunk driver. Caught in her human body and with no access to her own kind to help her shift, her injuries had proved catastrophic.

By the time the rest of the clan had managed to get to her, it'd been too late. She'd died peacefully in my father's arms, and the best parts of him died with her.

We all knew he hadn't just retired from his responsibilities. He'd flown off into the distance to die, to join the one woman he couldn't live without, and we would never see him again.

Emotion clogged my throat, made my dragon roar inside, and my reply came out much more forcefully than I'd meant it to.

"If you were mine, I'd put you over my knee for the assumptions you're concocting in that pretty head of yours."

That brought her head and ire up so fast it was a wonder she didn't give herself whiplash. Had she been a she-dragon, I'd be doused in a stream of fire already, and my dragon curled itself into a satisfied ball and grinned. I failed to see what was so damn amusing about all of this. Even Leonard's stern features cracked into a grin, and I heard Annie's co-worker's whispered exclamation loud and clear.

"Oh, I say."

My mate, of course, had no such compunctions to keep her voice down.

"How dare you." She looked all set to throw the book at me again but then seemed to think better of it and hugged the damn thing to her chest. The action pushed her impressive rack up and my already hard cock ached seeing the way her breasts strained across the fabric of her sensible blouse. No doubt in reverence to the heatwave we were experiencing, she'd left the first two buttons of her blouse undone and the shadow of her cleavage brought my primitive caveman side to the forefront, kicking and snarling. My dragon was all too on board with the erotic thoughts bombarding my brain. All that passionate fury she unleashed on me would make for one hell of an explosive ride in the sack.

I did like my women snarky and intelligent, and little Annie Taylor was just the kind I went for. I supposed there were small mercies in that. Gaia might have set me up with someone I wasn't at all compatible with. The goddess was known for her mean streak, especially with those she considered shirking their duty, and I was all too aware that my refusal to join the clan and procreate hadn't gone down well with anyone.

Dragon numbers were dwindling fast and we were desperately in need of fresh blood, but a human?

Damn it all to hell and back.

"You try and lay one finger on me, and I'll have you arrested faster than you can say 'misogynistic asshole.'"

My dragon's amusement fled, and I took a step toward her before common sense won out. I was too volatile to have this out with her right now. This was a discussion to have in private, and we would have it, but not yet.

"Little Annie, I'm many things." Try as I might, I couldn't keep my dragon's growl out of my voice, and no doubt she saw the beast in my eyes. Her eyes widened, for sure, her breathing sped up, and fuck me, if she didn't grow wetter. Her sweet feminine musk hit my nostrils, damn well near drove me insane with the need to sink my cock into her and claim her in the most primitive way.

Jeez, meeting my mate clearly had turned me from a reasonable, intelligent, modern man to, well, not what she was accusing me of, but... Somehow, I managed to engage my brain cells and ground the next words out through gritted teeth. "I have never, nor will I ever force myself on a woman, or belittle her opinion, as misguided as it might be."

She spluttered for air and looked all ready to interrupt me, so I didn't give her a chance.

"I found that book and many more in my father's collection when I was going through his things, and I felt it only right to return this to the library. I'll pay any outstanding fines, of course, so kindly work out how much they are and send me an invoice. You'll find me on the computer. I have a membership here."

I forced myself to step past her and the boys fell in line behind me without a word. I sensed their amusement and their silent excitement at the fact that their Alpha had found his mate, and I told them all to *"Shut the fuck up."*

Their joined laughter echoed in my head, and I revved the engine of my trusty Harley hard to drown out their thoughts.

"You did well keeping it together in there, son." Leonard's thought came through loud and clear and I nodded at the approval in his voice.

"Why the fuck do I have a human mate? What the hell do I do with that?" I sent that thought to Leonard only, or so I'd intended, until everyone laughed inside my head.

Scratch my earlier thought. This damn Magick was a pain in the ass.

"Ride it with it, son, nothing else you can do. Dragons mate for life. All you have to do is to convince

that little spitfire that you're the one for her."

I glared at Leonard before I pulled my visor down and took off while telling the rest of them to go take a hike. What I needed to do was to get away, to shift, to let my dragon soar and fly and work out some of this pent-up frustration while I came up with a plan to convince an unsuspecting and fragile human that she was indeed a dragon's mate.

****

Two weeks later, I was no closer to figuring that one out. Somehow, I doubted my turning into her stalker would help my quest, yet my dragon wouldn't and couldn't stay away from his mate for any length of time. The beast was getting more and more volatile, and when I barely stopped myself from creating a freaking forest fire, I knew something had to give. My sanity, more likely as I soared high in the air above the forests surrounding Rabbenstall and released a stream of water I'd sucked up from the nearby lakes. It took several fly-overs to bring the fire under control and I winced at the firefighters who shook their heads at the sky.

Gaia only knew what it must look like to have water descend from a cloudless sky. Little Annie was watching too. My damn scales itched as her gaze followed me around the sky. It was almost as though she could see me such was the accuracy of her gaze, but that was impossible. Cloaked as I was, I didn't even leave a shadow when I flew across the sun, yet still, her expressive brown eyes seemed glued to my flight path.

She was also in a great deal of pain. The closer I flew to her, the more intense I felt it. Toothache was a bitch at the best of times, but this was more than that. Even without my dragon senses and being so utterly tuned into my mate, I'd have known something was wrong. She was running a fever, and her muscles tensed as she rode out the waves of pain. She would *so* pay for not looking after herself better, once she was mine.

Her co-worker—*what was her name again?*— Barbara handed her some painkillers and a glass of water and my gut twisted at seeing the desperate way she swallowed them down.

Why the hell hadn't she been to see a dentist? I knew my card was on the noticeboard in the library because I'd placed it there myself in an effort to drum up some business when I first set up my practice. It was still there and even if it wasn't, my practice had been thriving, and I had a waiting list a mile long. Then again, the only other dentist in the area was a human so ancient and set in his ways, he gave dentists a bad rap all around.

I clung to the side of the clock tower and cursed a blue streak in my head as my claws dislodged the old rubble.

"Oh goodness, me, the mayor really needs to do something about that." Barbara shaded her eyes to look up the clock face, and Annie grimaced.

"Well, it's old and the council doesn't have the necessary funds. Let's hope the summer fete we have planned will bring in some much-needed cash. What we need is a local celebrity that will bring in more of the tourists or you know … ow." She held the side of her mouth and my dragon growled his annoyance. Her head flew up and her gaze zeroed in on my location with unerring and unsettling precision. Maybe there was some dragon blood in her ancestry somewhere because she sure as hell shouldn't be that attuned to me without the mating bite. I'd pored over the ancient volumes of dragon mating rituals involving humans in my father's library for hours in a vain attempt to find some answers to my dilemma, to no avail.

Waste of time it had been, and I was beginning to

wonder whether my time wouldn't have been better served looking into Annie Taylor's history in greater detail.

All I had been able to ascertain, with the help of Leonardo, who was the computer whiz kid of my clan, was that Annie had been left on the steps of an orphanage when she'd been a day old. They'd never found her mother or father, but, at least she'd been adopted by a human family. An only child, she'd been doted on by her adoptive parents until their early demise in a freak train accident when Annie had been away at University. She'd never finished her studies and had chosen to settle here in our sleepy little town in the heart of Cumbria, securing the position of librarian.

It was a wonder I hadn't run into her before now. Then again, clan business as well as my dentistry had kept me busy. One way to avoid wondering about whether my father was still alive out there.

Seemed both of our lives had been touched by tragedy, so we had that in common.

"Did you hear that?" Annie asked while continuing to stare at me.

"What, my dear?"

"That deep rumble coming from the clock tower?"

Barbara looked at her as though Annie was losing the plot.

"No, but I do hope we get some rain soon. That should dispel this suppressing heat. What we need is a good thunderstorm, or the next time a wildfire breaks out, we might not be so lucky. Lord only knows where that freaky rain came from, but thank goodness it did. That fire could have been nasty."

Guilt sat in the bottom of my stomach. I was supposed to protect my clan and the humans we lived amongst, not endanger them with my dragon's instability.

"Yes, well, it could have been thunder, I suppose." Annie winced anew, and Barbara clucked her tongue.

"You really ought to go and see a dentist. I've heard good things about the one in the village over. Daring Smiles, it's called. You should go and visit them, dear."

Annie recoiled in seeming horror. "I hate dentists, I told you that. This will pass. It always does. I just need stronger meds, that's all."

I could've no more stopped my dragon's snarl at that stupid comment than I could have stopped breathing. My mate had a rip-roaring infection setting in and would lose that damn tooth if she kept this up.

"Oh, I say." Barbara, too, looked up. "I do believe that was thunder. I heard it too this time. What odd weather we're having. Anyway, think on it. As for the summer fete, there are the *Dragoons,* I suppose."

Annie's scowl grew deeper and she shook her head.

"A bunch of leather-clad Neanderthal bikers is not our local attraction, dammit. Even if they do seem loaded."

I swallowed another growl at her assessment of my clan. While it was true that the Alpha before my father had been into all sorts of nefarious dealings which had earned the *Dragoons* their reputation as troublemakers, that'd been eons ago. When that fucker had been successfully outed, after my father challenged him to a duel in the skies over Cumbria—a battle that had gone down in human history as an epic thunderstorm—the *Dragoons* had stopped their criminal ways.

There was little left of the feared MC of old. We mainly got together to ride for pleasure and our charity work in Carlisle had taken off big time. Not that the news appeared to have traveled down to sleepy Rabbenstall. One of the worst hit during the *Dragoon*-inflicted terrors, and the locals were slow to forget the history.

I was keen to change that, and this fete would prove just the right venture for that. Something to discuss at our next meeting, if I ever managed to get my head out of my pants.

"Well, think on it, dear. Their leader did cough up for that rather large invoice you sent him."

Another bone of contention I would have to take up with my stubborn mate once she was mine, and mine she would be, come what may. She just didn't know it yet.

Chapter Three

Annie

Strange weather indeed. That rumble I kept hearing was no thunder. It was an animalistic sound that made my heart skip a beat. Not in fear but excitement, which made no sense at all. Then again neither did that feeling of being watched. I shaded my eyes from the sun and looked up the tower again, certain that something or someone had to be there, yet all I saw were bricks and mortar.

I was losing the plot because I swear I could smell him. That unique combination of smoke and virility that was Gideon, the proverbial pain in my butt. Ever since he'd shown up in my library, he'd robbed me of my much-earned peace, my sanity, and my sleep. No wonder this toothache was getting to me. Everything seemed worse when you didn't get enough sleep, and mine was disrupted night after night by erotic fantasies of the leader of these damn *Dragoons* taking me any which way you could think of and plenty that should be and probably were illegal. I'd worn out my favorite dildo, for pity's sake, and still was as horny as a cat in heat.

Why now and why him was utterly beyond me, and the man wasn't playing fair. I had deliberately set the fine at the rather ridiculous amount of three hundred quid, expecting him to show up and dispute it. That would have given me the chance to tell him what for, but instead, the infuriating man had paid it by bank transfer almost the minute I'd emailed him the information.

Barbara had been as gobsmacked as me, and I did have to listen to a lecture of how unethical my behavior had been. Charges were usually capped at a maximum of seven pounds, which was what we kept in the end. The rest we donated to the Rabbenstall Restoration fund. I had stated as much in my follow up e-mail to which I had yet to receive a reply. He was rude as well as infuriating, and far too damn handsome than any man had a right to be. It didn't help, either, that he was indeed a library member and his record showed the variety of books he'd borrowed over the years. The man's reading tastes were eclectic and varied, and he and I had several favorite authors in common.

I was beginning to realize I may well have misjudged him, and that grated. Still, if the man didn't show up, I could hardly apologize, could I?

A shooting pain from my tooth took my breath away, and I tried and failed to hide my wince.

"Really, now, my dear, enough is enough." Barbara grabbed me by the elbow and steered me back inside the library. Before I knew what she was doing, she'd ripped a card off the noticeboard and shoved it at me.

"Here, these are the details for that dental practice. I suggest you get in your car now and drive over there. They're open until six tonight and if you hurry, you'll just catch them. I don't want to see you back here until you've got that tooth seen to, and before you say you can't turn up without an appointment, think again. You're an emergency, so just park yourself on their doorstep. From what I've heard, he always takes on emergencies. Now, shoo, be off with you. Don't make me pull my trump card and remind you that I'm your superior here."

Barbara put her hands on her hips and glared at me. I had to give it to her. As silly and annoying as she could be, she was technically my supervisor, and I didn't want to get into trouble and lose my job.

"Okay, okay, I'm going. No need to be so damn bossy, but if I die of a heart attack in that dentist chair, it will be all your fault."

"Oh, balderdash. Scoot." She gave me a shove back out of the revolving door for good measure and the full heat of the relentless sun hit me in the face when I looked up the tower. Strange, I didn't sense anything there now. I was going loopy, that was what.

In truth, I knew deep down Barbara was right. I didn't feel at all well, pretty certain I ran a fever rather than simply being hot due to the heatwave, and that couldn't be good. It took me several attempts to start my car, and by the time I finally pulled out, I was sure I was melting. I briefly considered stopping at home to change into shorts and a strappy top to attempt to cool down, but if I did that, I knew full well that I would pop some more painkillers and avoid going to the dentist.

So, I set off for the neighboring village and with every twist in the road, my stomach churned until I thought I was going to throw up. I didn't, though Lord only knew how not, and managed to pull into the last available parking space outside Daring Smiles. The place was tiny, if welcoming, and I forced a smile on my face for the young woman who came out with her daughter in tow. The little girl held a big lollypop and was wearing a sticker pronouncing how brave she had been.

Well, well, well, a dentist who still gave out lollypops to kids. Hardly encouraging good dental hygiene. What the hell was I letting myself in for?

Taking a deep breath in, I pushed open the door and came face to face, or rather face to chest, as I'd swapped my high heels for my comfortable flats for the drive, with the nemesis of my dreams. None other than Gideon Jackson the third. What an utterly absurd name that was. The third what? Robber of women's sleep?

Dentists? Hang on… What?

"You're the dentist?" I croaked my question even as the white coat and name tag confirmed who he was as clearly as the certificates on the wall.

"Madam, we're about to close, and you haven't got an appointment, so…" A pert blonde appeared from behind his massive shoulders like a jack in the box and gestured for me to leave. Something I gladly would have done could I have got my feet to follow the commands of my brain. They didn't seem to want to catch on, however. Rather, the room spun and I was dimly aware of the blonde's gasp, before Gideon, the freaking dentist, scooped me up against his chest as though I was a child. How strong was this guy? I was no lightweight, let me tell you that, yet he didn't seem to strain at all as he carried me off to goodness only knew where.

"She does. Sorry, Glenda, I forgot to tell you. I took the call earlier."

I opened my mouth to protest but one look at his forbidding expression and the fire swirling in his amazing eyes stopped my protests. His gaze softened when I sagged against him, and the strangest feeling of rightness settled over me.

I didn't catch the details of what he and this Glenda woman discussed next, and I may have well have zoned out there for a bit. I really did feel like shit and it felt so damn good to be taken care of. I'd find my feminist side again when I was feeling better. Leaning my sore cheek into the heat which poured out of Gideon's skin—the man was a walking furnace—soothed the intense waves of pain somewhat. Anything to make it stop, really. A door opened and shut, and then we were on our own. I barely had time to register that he lowered me into a dentist chair before his face filled my vision.

"Right, that's Glenda gone, so let's have a look at what you've done to yourself, little goose."

Goose? Oh no, he did not just say that. I opened my mouth to give him what for and promptly screamed in pain as he touched my inflamed tooth with whatever he had in his hand.

"Easy there, I've got you. Oh, fuck it."

My eyes widened at the growled exclamation uttered in that deep, gravelly voice and then heat engulfed my face, the likes of which I'd never experienced before. Pain followed, so intense and all-consuming that I couldn't even scream, or perhaps I was, in my head anyway. Whatever was happening to me wasn't normal, that was for sure, because Gideon's gaze drew me into the swirling fire he created between us. He murmured words in an ancient-sounding language I didn't understand and then it was over.

I shook my head to clear it and glared at the man who was still towering over me.

"What in the hell did you just do to me?"

He at least had the good grace to look uncomfortable at my question and when I pushed myself up, he moved out of my way.

"Get away from me, you, you…"

"How's the tooth, Annie?"

That question threw me off balance completely. How was my tooth?

****

Gideon

She really did have the most expressive face and I suppressed a smirk, which no doubt would earn me a slap to the face if she saw it. My dragon had no such compunctions. He was positively strutting under my skin, eager to come out and show himself completely to our mate but I feared that would send sweet little Annie screaming from the room. Not exactly good for business if that happened. I was painfully aware I'd broken more rules than I cared to remember, both human and dragon, but I couldn't leave my mate in pain like that if I had the power to heal her. If I needed any more proof that this little human spitfire was my mate, I had it right here. It shouldn't have been possible for me to heal her completely otherwise, not with the deep infection that had set in. Had I used traditional methods, she would've had to have taken ten days of strong antibiotics, for sure, and might still have lost the tooth. At the very least, it would have meant root canal treatment and a crown, and as my little goose was clearly terrified of dentists, she'd never have agreed to that.

Annie poked her tongue at her teeth, judging by the cute little bulge she was creating in her cheek, and I hid my smile at the astonishment on her face.

"It doesn't hurt anymore? How is that?" Astonishment turned to suspicion. Her eyes narrowed and I was utterly fascinated by the frown line which appeared between her eyes. Man, I had it bad. Then again for a shifter, it was easy. When we found our mates, we were biologically programmed to fall head over heels in love. And it was love I felt, mixed in with a healthy dose of lust, of course, but the foremost emotion tightening my chest with longing was the need to protect this woman. I would literally kill for her if I had to, die even, and I finally understood why my father had retired from his duties after my mother's death. As infuriating as Annie Taylor was, the world seemed brighter with her in it and my life would never be dull. Regardless of what she felt or didn't feel for me, she was the only woman for me until the day I died. And as dragon, lifespans lasted centuries. Yeah, that was one hell of a long time. How to explain all that to a human.

"Stop staring at me as though I'm dessert and answer the question, you, you, impossible man. What did you do to me?" She touched her cheek and then studied her hand. "There was fire and shit."

The speed which with she jumped off the chair would have done any shifter proud. She studied herself in the mirror on the wall, waves of anxiety pouring off her as she checked herself over.

"How is that even possible? I'm not burned, but there was fire." Her gaze connected with mine in the mirror and her confusion hit me in the gut with the full force of a speed train. "Dammit, talk to me. Tell me I'm not going mad, please."

"You're not going mad."

Annie spun around, hands on hips, and glared at me. I swallowed hard and fisted my hands by my sides to hide my emerging claws. Her fury batted against my dragon's fire, and I could barely hold him back. I knew she stared into his flames reflected in my eyes, felt myself grow an inch, especially as it wasn't fear I sensed from her. Astonishment, curiosity, and above all annoyance, as confirmed by the way she stepped right into my personal space. So close that her breasts brushed my chest. She groaned, my dragon growled, and I shoved my hands into the back pockets of my jeans. Anything to stop myself from touching her, because if I did, there was no way I could stop the shift, and that wouldn't end well. My dragon stood at well over twelve feet and with his wings fully extended you could easily triple the width. My practice would be torn to shreds.

Mercifully, she seemed as affected as I was by our close proximity, as she scowled, stepped back, and wrapped her arms around herself, as though she too had trouble keeping her hands off of me.

If only.

"That's all you've got by way of an explanation, Mr. *'You're not going mad'?*" She mimed quotation marks around that sentence and the sarcastic spin to her voice only served to make me harder. I so needed to shift, or fuck, and neither seemed on my cards in the near future, dammit.

She looked me up and down slowly, and heat rose in her cheeks when her gaze lingered on my groin. The short white coat I wore at work did nothing to hide my boner and the way she bit her lip…

"Jesus, woman, don't do that. Makes me want to kiss you and as I value my gonads, I don't think any such move on my part would end well for either of us." Try as I might, I couldn't keep my dragon's growl out of my voice. Annie blanched and tore her gaze away from my dick.

"Damn right, big boy. I don't know what the fuck is happening here, and that"—she gestured to my groin and made a sound somewhere between a moan and grunt—"is not coming anywhere near me." She shook her head. "I won't sleep with you, so you can just stop all this mumbo jumbo and take those contacts out. It's pathetic. Are you a dentist or some form of wannabe magician? I should report you for—"

"For what?" My furious snarl interrupted her as I took a step toward her and she stepped back. I took another step and so on, a game we continued until her back hit the mirror and she was forced to crane her neck to look up at me. While I was careful not to touch her, this close to her, her scent wrapped itself around me, soothed the savage needs of my dragon, and he became a little easier to manage. The same couldn't be said for my unruly cock. I'd have zipper marks along its length at this rate, especially as she grew wet for me. She might fight her attraction to me, but she wanted me. *Thank you, Gaia.*

I forced my mind off imagining how sweet she would taste or the sounds she'd make as she came under my tongue and got back on subject.

"Tell me, little goose, what would you report me for? The fact that I saved your tooth, and you're now healed? Yes, saved." I dropped my voice on that last word because she looked all set to argue with me some more. "You left it so late to seek treatment you'd have needed a shitload of antibiotics and might still have lost that tooth. At the very least, painful and invasive procedures to fix it." Tears shimmered in her eyes, as it no doubt dawned on her that I was right, and dammit, my anger fled seeing those. I gentled my voice and stepped back to give her room. "I get the whole being afraid of the dentist thing, but, *Jesus*, woman, don't jeopardize your health like that. You have no idea how ill you were or could have become. You need to take care better of yourself or so help me, I'll tan that backside of yours until you listen to me."

That earned me a shove to the chest like I'd hoped it would. Not that she achieved to move me at all, but my little speech had worked. The gut-wrenching tears were replaced by fury as she glared up at me.

"You lay one finger on me without my consent and I'll have you arrested for assault."

I couldn't help my smirk at the slight distinction she made without seeming to have realized it.

"Who says I wouldn't have your consent, little goose?"

That shut her up momentarily. Seeing her speechless gave me a secret thrill and I knew I was grinning like a loon when she finally found her voice.

"You're so full of yourself, aren't you? If you

think for one minute that I'll submit to any man, let alone *you,* then you're even more deluded than your stupid stunts."

"You just haven't met the right man to submit to yet, my sweet goose." I stepped back further and sure enough, she erupted.

Arms flailing in her agitation, she stamped her foot and growled. The cutest, most ineffective little growl, but nonetheless it made my dragon insanely happy to hear it. Our children would sound like that. The thought of her round and heavy with my child made my grin deepen. We seemed light years away from that, but a man can dream.

"How fucking dare you, and stop grinning at me." She poked her index finger into my chest repeatedly as she spoke. "And do *not* call me a goose."

"Why not?" I asked. "You remind me of one, after all."

For the second time today, she appeared lost for words.

"That's... You're so rude. I know I'm not some stick-thin model type, but I'm not round and I neither waddle nor quack or whatever the hell geese do, so how dare you."

I crossed my arms over my chest and cocked an eyebrow at her which only seemed to infuriate her further.

"Wrong again, little goose. I call you that because geese are fierce little warriors when the need arises. Romans used them as guards after all, and your spirit sure matches that. As for your curves..." I paused and deliberately let my gaze wander over her figure. "I love your body, and I can't wait to mark it when you finally stop fighting us. I want to suck on those tits and bury my cock between them. Can't wait to see them bounce while

I fuck you so hard I'll ruin you for any other man. I love flesh to hold on to while I torture my woman with pleasure, and make no mistake about it, Annie Taylor, you are mine. Every delectable, wobbly inch of you is mine."

Her mouth worked silently, and her breathing sped up, her heartrate a rapid beat at the base of her throat. When she finally looked up at me, her dilated pupils told their own story, so I pushed on. Might as well get this out in the open.

"I know you feel this too. This connection between us, and I also know you don't understand it, won't believe a word of what I'm about to say next, but you, Annie Taylor, are mine. Whether you want me or not, I'm not going away and I'm going to spend the rest of my life making you see that, if you just let me in. I know I sound like some caveman asshole, but I'm really not, and there's a good explanation for all of this."

Annie snorted and shook her head. "You're full of shit, that's what you are, and I'm leaving. If you can't give me a reasonable explanation, then."

I stepped in front of her, barring her exit, and placed my hands on her shoulders. I felt her gasp all the way down to my toes as the connection between us arced in almost palpable bursts of electricity.

"I'm not full of shit, Annie. What I am is a dragon shifter and you're my mate."

Chapter Four

Annie

Of all the things he could have said, that had to be… No, he was messing with me, wasn't he? Yet, as I stared up at him utterly speechless for the third time in quick succession—*believe me, that doesn't happen often*—I couldn't deny the sincerity that poured off of him. He wasn't lying. He truly believed every word he'd just said, words that my befuddled, lust-short-circuited brain was still trying to assimilate. The heat emanating from him alone made me feel faint, fragile, and feminine all rolled into one. His hands touched my shoulders only lightly, and yet I felt their heated mark like a brand, and then there were his eyes. If they were contacts like I'd first assumed, they had to be super sophisticated ones, the likes of which didn't exist. As I stared up at him, his eyes bled from brown to swirling embers of fire to lizard-like slits and then back to normal in front of me.

"You … that's not possible." From somewhere I found my voice, a breathy, thready, and high-pitched version of my voice, but hey, I managed to form words and I was damn proud of that.

"Breathe, Annie, slowly, you're hyperventilating." The deep gravelly tone cut through my confusion. That sure explained my lightheadedness, and I didn't resist when he steered me back to the chair and his hand between my shoulder blades pushed my head between my legs.

"Slowly, sweetheart, in and out with me. That's my brave little goose."

I should be outraged at his continued calling me that, but the way he said that, all soft and tender, as though I was precious to him, yeah … maybe it wasn't that bad being called a goose. I rather liked that he saw me as a warrior and as for the rest… I was glad my hair was hiding my complexion because my face had to be resembling a beetroot. Why was his dirty talk such a turn-on? On any other man, I'd have kicked him in the balls, but when he said it … damn, every wicked fantasy I ever had come to life. My pussy sure liked the idea. If I got any wetter I would leave a stain on my skirt, and as for my knickers … yeah, might as well not be wearing any. It was damn infuriating the way that man effortlessly tapped into my needs and desires, as though he was in my head. Which he couldn't possibly be, but then what did I know? He was a dragon shifter, he said, and did I really entertain the notion that he was, that shifters existed and I was his *mate?*

That thought got me even more hot and bothered, because if that was the case, then heaven help me. If it worked the same as it did in the paranormal novels I loved to read, then he literally wouldn't leave me alone. And why the hell did that not bother me more? I was a modern, independent woman who didn't need or want a man, let alone a mate, wasn't I? It also meant I just couldn't give in and let him scratch that itch which had been building ever since I first clapped eyes on the man hunk, 'cause that would give him entirely the wrong idea and I wasn't that woman. Never had been a prick tease.

"There you go, up you come, baby."

A gentle hand cupped my chin and helped me to sit up, and time stood still as he studied me, breathed with me, and slowly my mind cleared.

"Back with me, I see, just Annie."

The reference to our first meeting made my lips twitch in amusement and his answering smile lit up his harsh features. A woman could literally drown in that smile and I had to get away from him.

"I never went anywhere, and I'm still not sure I believe you. If you're really a dragon, then show me. Go on, I dare you."

A burst of heat emanated from him, hit me square in the face, and I held my breath as his dragon showed in his eyes. There was no doubt in my mind that was what I saw, but still. I needed to see him in his other form for no other reason than that I needed to reassure myself I wasn't having some form of fever-induced hallucination. I pinched myself to be sure, and Gideon swore and rubbed the patch of abused skin on my arm. Heated tingles traveled up from that innocent enough contact and I squirmed on my seat as they settled in my clit. I swore that bundle of nerves swelled, ached to be touched, and my internal walls clenched on thin air, desperate to be filled.

"Don't do that. You're not dreaming. You're really here and yes, I used my Magick to heal you. I shouldn't have, broke countless rules, but I couldn't see you suffer like that. Not when I had the means to put an end to it."

"There are rules?" I sounded like a parrot, but he didn't seem to mind as he smiled down at me and then traced his thumb over my lips. I gasped at the contact of that roughened pad against my lips, and his dragon roared. The most amazing, deep-throated rumble came straight from his chest and made every feminine cell in my body sigh.

Dammit, that was so sexy.

Without meaning to, I leaned in closer, and it was Gideon who pulled away, even though every fiber of his being appeared to scream his reluctance.

"Yes, of course there are rules. For me, more so than any ordinary shifter. I'm the Alpha of my clan. I'm supposed to be leading by example. I—"

"Clan, Alpha? You mean the *Dragoons* are…?"

He scrubbed a hand over his face at my interruption, but he didn't seem annoyed, more resigned and for some inexplicable reason, that made me want to apologize. "Sorry, I didn't mean to, that is, hell, I'll just shut up now."

Gideon laughed and shook his head at me. "Woman, I find it hard to believe you ever truly shut up."

I harrumphed at that and he sobered.

"And that's okay, I've no desire to change who you are."

"You have no idea who I am," I countered, and he sighed.

"True, so perhaps we should start to get to know each other a little better, say over dinner at my house? Healing you took a lot of my energy, so I need to eat, and preferably shift, but I can't do that here."

My mind was still stuck on the shifting part. Holy shit, I so wanted to witness that. Regardless of what may or may not happen between us, I'd have to be a fool to turn down a chance to see that.

"Why can't you?" I asked.

"My dragon is way too big to do this safely here. I'd destroy my surgery and scare countless humans silly and that's not what I want to do."

A thought occurred to me and I shot to my feet in triumph.

"I knew it. It was you, wasn't it?" When he didn't reply and just patiently waited for me to clarify, I rushed on. "The clock tower. I thought someone, or something was there, and I heard your dragon and … hell no, did you cause the forest fire?"

Gideon looked most uncomfortable and eventually nodded.

"Not one of my prouder moments. I'm new to this, controlling my dragon when all he wants to do is claim his mate." He ran his hand up and down my arm as though he needed to touch me, and in truth I craved that contact too. It helped ground me in the reality of the situation. Not every day a girl found out that the hot bod man hunk she'd been lusting after was a dragon shifter. If I repeated that to myself often enough it might eventually sink in, right?

"What do you mean, new, and how could you?"

Gideon shrugged and pulled away. Dammit, if I didn't miss his touch on me. What the hell was that about? I should be running away from here, not asking him questions and getting to know the man.

"I also put it out again."

"The rainfall out of a blue sky, that was you?" It wasn't so much a question but a statement, because it had to have been him. Something else dawned on me too. "So, you can what, cloak yourself or something?"

In answer, Gideon raised his arm and I whistled through my teeth as the tanned, corded limb disappeared in front of my eyes.

"Wow." I breathed that one word and his dragon grumbled anew. It sounded like a most satisfied and pleased-with-himself growl that made me grin.

"Yes, he likes to impress you."

"Your dragon is a smart ass."

Another more menacing-sounding rumble came from the big chest in front of me and I rolled my eyes.

"Are you sure I'm not dreaming all this?" I asked, and Gideon laughed and held his hand out.

"Positive, but come with me and I'll show you." When I hesitated to do so, he disarmed me completely by adding, "Please? I really need to shift."

In truth, he didn't look too great right now and

my heart gave a funny little lurch in my chest.

"Okay, but I'm driving so that I can get away from you if I need to."

Gideon murmured something I didn't quite catch, but he straightened and nodded. He really was tall when he did that and some more of my objections melted away.

"Of course, I didn't expect anything else. Just follow my bike."

My heart sped up a little more at that thought. Did that mean I could have caught a ride on the back of his Harley had I not insisted on driving? Not that I was dressed for tearing around the countryside on the back of a bike.

"Ready?" he asked.

I wasn't at all sure I would ever be ready, but I nodded anyway and followed him out of the building. There was something surreal about watching him do the mundane shutdown things like switch off his computer, set the voicemail, close the blinds, and finally set the alarm, before he kick-started his bike and put his helmet on.

Something else occurred to me and I blurted that question out.

"How old are you?"

He half turned to me and I could see the amusement in his eyes.

"Thirty-four, a mere babe in dragon lifespan terms." He sobered and the sadness which appeared in his eyes took another chink out of my armor. "I shouldn't have been the Alpha for a good long while yet, but shit happens, right?" He revved the engine, effectively cutting off my next question, and I got the hint loud and clear. Not something he was either ready or willing to discuss now, and, of course, that only served to make me more curious.

I got behind the wheel of my car instead and drank in the sight that was Gideon's fine ass as he expertly took the tight corners of the Cumbrian countryside. I was pretty sure he was holding back too, in deference to my clapped-out car. I had no idea where we were going, as we went off the main road and deeper into the forest than I'd ever ventured before. Mainly because this was private land and I whistled through my teeth as it dawned on me who that land must belong to. Eventually, we pulled up into a clearing next to a lake. With the mountains on one side and surrounded by forests, it was the idyllic location and also utterly deserted.

A sliver of fear slid down my spine as I climbed out of my car, and I shook it off almost immediately. The man was a dragon, for pity's sake. If he wanted to hurt me he could have done so ten times over and there wasn't a thing I could have done about it.

He climbed off his bike somewhat stiffly and his earlier words came back to me. He needed to shift and Lordy, I hadn't even thanked him for healing my tooth. I could have kissed the man just for taking my pain away, never mind anything else.

Before I could think too much on it, I blurted out what was on my mind.

"I'm sorry."

He looked puzzled, as well he might, and worry clouded over his eyes. No doubt he was thinking I'd changed my mind or something, or was about to throw a hissy fit. I'd had a far few after all.

"I mean, I never thanked you for healing me." Heat blossomed in my cheeks when he didn't say anything, just cocked his head to one side and studied me. I wondered what he saw, what made me so damn special in his eyes, and then he smiled and my heart missed a few beats.

"My pleasure, little goose." He gestured toward the house. "Go on in, the door is open and it's much cooler in there." I belatedly took in the imposing stone building. It looked huge and above all ancient with little turrets, like a mini-castle. The sun reflected off the multitude of mullioned windows, and I took in a sharp breath at the sheer beauty of the place. Tourists would flock here if they knew it existed, which of course they didn't, for very good reasons, as it turned out. His earlier comment of being a mere babe in dragon terms came back to me.

"When you said how old you were, how long exactly do dragons live?" I asked.

There it was again, that shadow of sadness which crossed his features, made him tense as though this was a hard subject for him to talk about. The urge to cross the distance between us, to offer comfort in any way, drove me hard, so I folded my arms under my boobs instead. I barely knew him, so I shouldn't be this affected by his emotions, but there it was. No doubt another side effect of supposedly being his mate.

Gideon cleared his throat and the hoarseness of his voice as he answered made my stomach drop.

"We can live for centuries. The oldest dragon in our clan was five hundred years old before she passed on." He smiled grimly at my gasp of shock. "Alijah was very much the exception. She was a grand old lady and a true leader. All went to pot when her son took over."

He grimaced and rotated his shoulders. It was obvious he needed to shift, but I needed answers right now.

"What do you mean it went to pot?"

Gideon huffed out a laugh. "You've heard the

stories of how the *Dragoons* were." He waited for my confirmation and I nodded.

"Yes, when you first reappeared here all the locals were living in fear, and I ... well I might have jumped to conclusions about the whole lot of you when I first met you." I scuffed my toes in the gravel we were standing on, suddenly all too aware of how prickly I'd been.

"It's okay, Annie, I get it. My father got it too. That's why he challenged that so-called leader, whose name has been erased from our history due to his conduct, to a duel. That was the epic thunderstorm of all storms the locals still talk about too."

My eyes widened at what I was hearing. I'd heard the stories of the storm that lasted days. There was even a historian's account in the library.

Gideon smiled again, but it didn't reach his eyes.

"My father won and the *Dragoons* as it were disappeared. He felt it best if the MC relocated, so the clubhouse is now in Carlisle, and we've worked hard to turn it all round. Look up the Bikers against Bullying campaign and you'll find us there. Well, any kind of charity work, really. The *Dragoons* are also not just dragons, if you're wondering. The core, the ones you saw me ride with here, are. They're part of my clan, but the actual MC is run by a human. He knows our history, of course, but most of the brothers in Carlisle are humans with one thing in common. A love of bikes and a desire to do good. I help out when I can, but I've always preferred books over people and my passion was dentistry. Hence, I chose that profession and I should have had years of not worrying over all the clan stuff, but that's a story for another day. I really need to shift, so..."

Before I could say anything to that astonishing account, his clothes melted off him in an instant. My tongue quite literally got stuck to the roof of my mouth because a stark-naked Gideon... Lord have mercy on a girl. There wasn't an ounce of fat on his body. He was all sleek muscles, sinews, and smooth skin, apart from the smattering of hair on his chest which narrowed into the most enticing happy trail leading down to his cock.

Now, let's be honest here, that part of a man's anatomy can never be called pretty, but Gideon in his fully aroused state... Where was the cold shower when you need it? He was big, but not huge as I'd half expected, and was relieved to note. His male musk hit my nostrils and damn it all to hell and back if I didn't want to sink to my knees in front of him and lick that drop of pre-cum from his swollen head. Mercifully, before I could act on that impulse, the air around Gideon distorted and in a flash of blue fire, he changed. Had I blinked, I would have missed it. As it was, all I could do was stare in awe as the most magnificent dragon I'd ever seen—*yeah, okay, I have nothing to compare him to, but cut me a break here*—shook his massive wings and took off into the air with a grace I wouldn't have expected from a creature that big. He flew across the sun and his scales shimmered and sparkled before he dove into the lake and disappeared from view. Seconds later, he re-emerged, blowing a stream of fire out of his nostrils. He did a few more laps across the lake and soared as high up as the mountain at some point, when I lost him from view. Presumably, he cloaked himself to be safe, because he would be visible to all that high, and then he sat down in front of me. The ground shook with his landing, the vibrations of which traveled up through the soles of my feet.

"Wow."

Dragon Gideon flashed his razor-sharp teeth at me in what I assumed was his version of a smile in this form and then bent his long neck until his horned head was right in front of mine. His forked tongue tasted the air and a whoosh of his scent hit me. Just like the man, the dragon smelled of earth and fire, sunshine and wind, and all things free, and I took a deep breath to savor his scent. He just smelled so damn good. If he could bottle that and sell it as aftershave, women the world over would swoon.

Okay, maybe not all women. We all had different tastes, for sure, but I certainly felt like swooning. And I'd never swooned in my life.

He inched closer until there were mere millimeters between my nose and his snout, and I lost myself in the expression in his eyes. I saw Gideon in the dragon, much like I'd seen the dragon in the man earlier and the sheer wonder I was witnessing hit me anew.

"Can I touch you?" I whispered that question and Gideon's tongue flicked out and licked that spot under my ear that made me go to mush every time. It tickled and aroused in equal measures, and I tentatively lifted my hands and placed them either side of his huge head. Much to my surprise, his scales felt soft and warm, much like a snake's would. I'd held one once when the local primary school had taken over the library in an effort to make it more appealing to the youngsters. Storytime had involved a man with real-life snakes and lizards and had been a huge success. I really must arrange another session soon, if the budget allowed for it.

A deep-throated rumble rose from my very own dragon's chest, and emboldened by his reaction, I let my hands wander. Over the ridges on the back of his head down along his long neck to his shoulders, where more wicked-looking spikes set between his wings. The perfect handholds were I to climb on his back. Now, where had that thought come from? And even if he'd let me, I was hardly dressed for the occasion. Why hadn't I stopped at home and changed into shorts again? Oh, yeah, my tooth. That ache seemed to have been light-years ago, and I closed my eyes and rested my cheek against Gideon's side. Reassuring warmth enveloped me as he brought his wings up and folded them around me. He curled his tail too, keeping me in a dragon embrace I never wanted to end. When I eventually opened my eyes, I looked straight into his, as he'd swung his head around too and nudged me closer to his back. It was almost as though he wanted me to climb on his back.

"I'd love to, but I can't. Not in this outfit."

Dragon Gideon grinned and before I knew what was happening, my skirt and blouse disappeared and I was in one of my itty bitty, strappy summer dresses that I only wore around the house. He'd also Magicked away my bra and, holy moly, *my knickers*?

I thumped his side, rather ineffectually, it had to be said, 'cause feeling the breeze go up my naked legs to my bare pussy was rather a nice feeling. Still, there was no way I was climbing on his back sans knickers.

"Gideon Jackson the third, you give me back my underwear right now."

A stream of hot air puffed across my face as dragon Gideon huffed, but sure enough, I felt something covering my essentials. Not the comfortable pair I'd put on that morning, though, but one of my secret stash of Victoria's Secret lace which I'd indulged in, just in case I ever found a man in Rabbenstall I wanted to do the horizontal shimmy with.

I narrowed my eyes at Gideon and shook my head. "Not what I meant, and how do you do that anyway?"

He shook his massive shoulders and gave me his best dragon grin again. Damn the man. We would have to have a serious discussion about what was and wasn't acceptable when using his powers around me. For now, the temptation to climb on his back and ride him was too great to resist. No sooner had I managed to clamber up and grasped hold of the spikes he took off. I screeched not in fear, but utter exhilaration as the air whooshed past me. He stayed low at first, as though he was worried about my reaction.

Sure enough, he glanced back at me and when I couldn't help but grin at him, he really let loose. As he soared higher and higher, the small, still sane part of my brain did wonder why I wasn't afraid. It was a long way down, after all, but it never once occurred to me that I could fall, or he'd drop me. Where that innate certainty came from, I couldn't have told you. This just felt right and it was the most exhilarating thrill ride I'd ever been on, and trust me, I'd tried them all. I'd always loved the adrenaline rush that came with conquering the scariest ride a theme park had to offer. None of them compared to this though. The feel of a warm body between my legs, Gideon's powerful muscles as they clenched, and released, the sound of his wings flapping, the fresh air in my face which whipped my hair around my head… Words couldn't describe this feeling, and for as long as I lived I would never forget this magical half hour or so, as we climbed and fell as close as two beings could be without actual intercourse. That thought got me all hot and bothered again, and by the time we finally set back down, my mind was most definitely firmly in the gutter. Catching another glimpse of Gideon's naked self so didn't help, neither did the heated intensity in which he studied me when he turned around. Dressed in faded jeans and a white t-shirt, which barely stretched over his muscular, tanned biceps, and with his feet bare, he looked good enough to eat. I was all too aware I must have looked like the proverbial scarecrow and I tried in vain to tame my hair.

"Here, let me." Gideon stepped closer and my eyes widened when I saw what he was now holding in his hand.

"Is that my hairbrush?"

Gideon smirked and stepped behind me.

"Dragons have Magick. It comes in handy for small things like this. I couldn't transport something big, but clothing and knickknacks I can move. Now hold still, little goose, and let me do this for you."

"There is no need to—"

"Hush, woman, this is clearly bothering you, and it'll take me mere moments. I'm told I'm quite good at brushing hair."

Somehow that comment irked me, and my reply came out far snarkier than I'd intended it to. "Had plenty of practice with your floozies, had you?"

The soothing brush strokes stopped, and I felt his sigh all the way down to my toes.

"Believe it or not, I haven't been with a woman for a very long time indeed."

"Hah, as if. *Ow*."

The swat to my ass really stung, and outraged, I spun around to give him what for but the expression on his face stopped me. He looked so sad all of a sudden. So, I settled for glaring up at him and rubbing the burning spot on my left ass cheek with my hand.

"You do that again, and you'll be singing soprano, mister."

A wry grin kicked up a corner of his sensual mouth before he twirled his finger in an unspoken request for me to turn around again. I did so reluctantly, and only because my hair still needed sorting.

"I mean it, Gideon," I said.

This time he laughed and resumed brushing my hair with firm, soothing strokes, which really shouldn't turn me on more, but he'd stepped closer to me, so his delicious scent surrounded me.

"Duly noted, little goose. However"—he lifted my hair off my shoulder and leaned in to whisper the next words into my ear—"we both know that there will be a next time, because you, woman, are too bratty for your own good. What's more..." He pulled back and tugged my head back by my hair so I had no choice but to follow or risk losing a clump of it. "You like it, or you'd have already tried to kick me in the balls."

I opened my mouth to refute that ridiculous notion, but the knowing glint in his eyes and the way his nostrils flared stopped me. No doubt he could smell my arousal, which should have been mortifying, but right now simply served to make me hotter. Before I could make a complete fool of myself, my stomach rumbled loudly and broke the sexual tension between us.

Gideon laughed and stepped away from me. "There, that'll do. We best get you inside and feed you."

With that, he walked off, leaving me to stare after him. My choice was clear. Accept what he offered or get back into my car and leave.

Chapter Five

Gideon

My dragon snarled under my skin, furious at my walking away from our mate, but I was firmly in charge of my beast after my shift. Regardless of what my animal half thought, this had to be her choice, made when she was not under the influence of the shitload of pheromones my dragon threw her way every opportunity he got.

It had never set well with me, this ability to attract human women whenever I chose to. Not since my teenage years, anyway. I was no saint, and as a horny-as-fuck teen, I'd made plenty of use of it, but I'd like to think I'd grown up a bit since then. Fucking for the sake of it was all well and good, but it left you empty inside after a while, and having grown up with the example of my mother and father devoted to each other... Yeah, that was what I wanted and never thought I'd find.

I hadn't even realized how much I wanted that until little Annie Taylor appeared in my life. I banged the front door shut behind me and forced myself to carry on walking to the kitchen. Cooking was one of the things I'd always enjoyed and as I perused the contents of my fridge, my chest tightened when I heard that door open and shut again. Flames licked around my hand curled around the fridge door, as my dragon, too, breathed a sigh of relief. Annie's sweet scent announced her arrival in this part of the house as clearly as her loud gasp.

"Jesus, are you trying to burn the place down?"

I pulled her scent deep into my lungs to satisfy my dragon and the blue flames receded. Having picked up the stuff I needed for my go-to quick meal of

Spaghetti Bolognese, I turned to face her with a grin.

"I'd only do that if the flames were red or orange. Blue doesn't scorch a fly."

She bit her lip and regarded me warily, so I stepped closer to further illustrate my point. Annie's eyes grew round when I held out my hand and let the blue flames dance between my fingertips.

"Touch it and see for yourself," I said.

I was half expecting her to come out with a snarky reply, but she surprised me by reaching out and lifting her index finger and then tentatively raised it to mine. My dragon grumbled his approval and I closed my eyes as my dick jerked painfully against its denim prison. It was sweet fucking torture indeed, to have her touch me in any capacity, let alone to mingle with my dragon's fiery core.

"Wow, that's... Wow." She interlaced her fingers with mine and when I opened my eyes, it was to see her staring down at our digits in utter awe. The flames danced between us, traveled halfway up her arm and mine, and the sweet musk of aroused woman hit me in the gut with the full force of a sledgehammer. I had to clear my throat to get my voice box to work, and when I did, I knew I didn't sound entirely human.

"Yeah, one word for it."

I had to pull away lest I pounce on her and take her right here in my kitchen. It would be a matter of moments to flip up the tiny skirt of her dress, push the scrap of lace out of my way, and bury my aching cock deep inside her ripe little pussy. She wouldn't resist me, but I wanted more than a quick fuck, dammit. I wanted it all. Her submission freely given because she chose to be with me, not because my damn dragon made her horny.

Annie's breathing grew labored, her heart beat a drum inside her chest as she seemed to wait for me to pounce, and when I didn't, she frowned and pulled a shuddery breath into her lungs.

"So, you said something about feeding me?"

I nodded and gestured toward the vegetables and mince that I'd pulled out of my fridge. "Yeah, spag bol okay with you?" I asked.

"One of my favorites." I heard the smile in her voice and sure enough, when I looked over, she was regarding me almost whimsically, head cocked to one side.

"What?"

"Nothing, it's just when you said you were going to feed me I was expecting frozen pizza or something, not you cooking from scratch."

I raised an eyebrow and set to chopping the onion in front of me. "I happen to like cooking, sue me."

A lighthearted laugh was my answer this time and I swallowed a groan when she stepped up next to me and playfully bumped her hip into mine.

"Let me help, and I would sue you, that is. Not sure what you're worth though. I mean you live in this grand old place and all, but that doesn't mean anything. I should know. Rabbenstall is full of history, which is crumbling around our ears because we can't afford the upkeep."

I passed her the mushrooms to cut and threw the onions into a pan to brown.

"True enough, and you know, Barbara was right. You need something to pull in the crowds. The *Dragoons* could put up a bit of a show if you like. We do so regularly in Carlisle."

The nimble fingers slicing the mushrooms stopped and I felt her surprise.

"You would do that? I mean after everything I said and…"

I put my hand over hers and needing to get my point across, pulled her in closer.

"In a heartbeat, Annie. All you have to do is ask me."

I threw the mushrooms into the pan and finished slicing the rest of the veggies before I tossed it all together with the mince and put the pasta in the boiling water.

I was all too aware of her watching me the entire time, her brows drawn together in a frown.

"It can't be that easy?"

I turned the heat down and faced her with a grin. "Why not?"

"Because, well, this just doesn't happen, okay?"

"What doesn't?" I countered. When she didn't reply, I turned the heat down more and tugged her along with me.

"Come on, let me show you something, little goose."

She dragged her heels a bit, but she did follow me into the living room and the huge fireplace which held the memories of my childhood. I picked up my favorite picture of my parents and held it up for her to see.

"My parents were fated mates and they were together for seventy-five blissful years before..." I cleared my throat, emotion clogging it anew, and *my* mate put her slender hands over mine.

"What happened? I mean, something did, right, something awful? You don't have to tell me, it's just..." She stopped talking and traced my parents' faces with her index finger. "They look so young and happy here."

I forced out a short laugh. "They were. That was taken on their thirty-fifth wedding anniversary."

Annie's eyes widened, and she shook her head. "No way, they don't look older than early thirties, at the most. You're pulling my leg."

"Plenty of things I'd like to do to your leg, little goose, but pulling is not one of them." I couldn't help it. My voice dropped an octave, imagining those luscious thighs of hers wrapped around my head as I ate her out. As though she followed my train of thought, her breathing sped up. The most delightful blush appeared on her cheeks and she squirmed on the spot.

"You can't talk to me like that." That breathy response only served to make me harder, and I tugged the photo out of her hands.

"I can talk to you any way I want. You're mine, sweet little Annie, but I'm really fed up of talking right now. Let me show you how good we can be instead."

I dropped to my knees and nuzzled into her soft belly, earning myself a groan of need from the woman in front of me.

"What are you, I mean … the food."

I huffed a laugh and flicked my hand to turn off the stove. "Can wait, I'd much rather eat *you* right now."

I sensed her acceptance seconds before I heard her breathy whisper. "God, yes, please."

My dragon roared his approval and I moved us onto the comfortable couch in front of the fireplace before she'd even stopped giving me her consent. A mere thought removed her lacy panties, and I blew a stream of blue flames across the quivering, pink flesh in front of me. Hearing her moan in response and seeing the way her pussy clenched and released more of her sweet musk meant any restraint I might have been capable of flew out of the proverbial window. My claws ran out and dug into the soft flesh of her hips as I held her still and tasted her. Her essence exploded on my taste buds, made me hungry for more, and allowing my tongue to fork, I set to work. I swirled it around her clit, coaxing that little nub out of its hiding place while lapping up her arousal and probing her inner walls at the same time. Annie clamped down on me, and her fingers pulled at my hair as she ground her cunt against my face. The sounds she made as she climbed those rungs of arousal were such a fucking turn-on it was a minor miracle I didn't come in my pants there and then. This wasn't about my release, however, but hers. When I pulled away slightly and released more of my fire, she screamed and flew headlong into an orgasm which was a delight to witness.

My sweet little human mate gave it her all, writhing under my tongue when I lapped at her gushing pussy and pushed her into multiple releases with my fingers and tongue.

"Oh, God, oh, God, I can't … no more… Yes, yes, *yes*."

Her screams of pleasure echoed around the building, and my dragon drank his fill, imprinting himself on her body, her very soul, as I drank every last drop of her cream while growling my approval into the quivering pink flesh. Only when her hands fell away and she lay there shuddering in aftershocks did I let up, but not before I'd speared my tongue into the little hole I needed to claim to make our mating complete. That tight ring of muscle clenched around me, while I pushed two fingers into her pussy, found her sweet spot, and wrung one last climax from my girl. She clamped her thighs around my head and screamed as she flew again.

****

Annie

Oh, my God, oh, my God, oh, my God. Those three words bounced around in my lust-hazed brain on repeat as I struggled to draw breath into my restricted lungs. Pleasure consumed me, intense, overpowering flames of ecstasy the likes of which I'd never experienced before. What Gideon could do with his tongue ... and as for his fire. My pussy clenched anew as something cool touched it, and over the roaring in my ears as I slowly floated back down to earth, I heard the deep rumble of my dragon's voice.

"There, all cleaned up now. I've got you, little goose. Just rest for a while. There's plenty more to come."

Somehow, I managed to laugh. A somewhat hysterical bark of a laugh for sure, but if he thought I could do that again, he had another think coming. Everything felt tender down there, oversensitive, and the rush of cool air against my heated pussy lips as he flipped the skirt of my dress back down made me groan.

I cracked an eye open and swallowed another moan because that action meant I got a full and close-up view of his groin as he straightened up.

"I... That doesn't look comfortable."

Gideon laughed, and I forced my gaze up from the long, hard imprint of his cock testing the strength of his denims, over the washboard abs clearly delineated under his tight t-shirt, up to the strong Adam's apple which movements utterly fascinated me, until I reached those sinful lips which had given me such pleasure moments before.

"You know it's rude to do that to a girl before you've even kissed her."

One of his eyebrows shot up in that devilish way he had and those lips of his curled in a wicked grin while his amber eyes crinkled up the corners in amusement.

"Didn't hear you complaining a minute ago, girl, but by all means, let's rectify that."

Before I could process those words, he'd pulled me to standing and that sinful mouth descended on mine, stole my breath, my last bit of resistance as he grasped my ass cheeks to hoist me higher up his body while he licked across the seam of my lips.

I opened up to him without any conscious effort on my part, and it was the most natural thing in the world to lock my hands behind his neck and to wrap my thighs around his hips. We both groaned into the kiss because that move settled my bare pussy right across his cock. Need flared to life between my thighs with a speed that left me lightheaded. It shouldn't be possible for me to be this ready to come again, not after the myriad of releases that very tongue now exploring every crevice of my mouth had given me.

When I kissed him back, his dragon's roar of satisfaction rumbled through me, settled in my clit, and then I stopped thinking altogether as instinct took over. I clenched my thighs around him and shamelessly rubbed myself over his hard erection, soliciting another one of those clit-clenching growls from my dragon. Blue flames engulfed us, testament to how on edge Gideon was. His claws ran out, pierced my skin, and that sweet sting of pain sent my hips into a frenzy as I chased another orgasm building inside me.

Gideon tore his mouth of my lips, his breath as labored as mine was, and I stared into the eyes of his dragon. More flames engulfed us, which should have terrified me, but it just seemed right somehow, as we stared at each other.

"Jesus, woman, I need to stop, before I can't." He attempted to set me down, but with a strength I didn't even know I had, I held on.

"No." My eyes widened at the sound of my voice. Hoarse and guttural, it didn't sound like me at all, yet I'd never felt surer that this was me. Heat rose deep within my belly in swirls of purple until flames licked from my skin onto his.

"Fuck, I knew it."

I dimly wondered what the hell he thought he knew before flames engulfed me. Pain sliced through every part of my body and then I was free. Air rushed past me, and when I opened my eyes, it was to see my reflection soaring above the lake.

Only it wasn't me who stared up at me but a purple/blue/green dragon. I attempted to shriek, but a stream of orange fire erupted from my mouth instead. I lost control and would have gone face diving into the lake had much larger claws not grabbed me and pulled me to safety.

Gideon, it had to be, thank God. That was my last thought before everything, mercifully went black.

I came to in a darkened room and sat up with a start only to be pulled back into a warm, and thankfully human body.

"Easy there, little goose, I've got you. Here, drink something."

A side light came on and Gideon's worried face appeared in my vision. He held a glass of water to my parched lips and I eagerly drank.

"Slow sips, baby. Don't want you being sick, now do we? That's it. That's my beautiful little dragon mate."

I attempted to slow down my sips, but it was hard to do. Why was I so thirsty, and hang on, what had me called me?

My heartrate kicked up and I pushed against his broad chest to sit up. That meant the sheet covering us both fell, and I pulled in a sharp breath as my nipples pebbled in the cool air of the room. At least they were nipples not scales and… "Oh my God."

As relieved as I was to hear my voice was back to its normal cadence and I wasn't breathing fire, I still had a hard time processing any of this.

"What in the hell did you do me?" I sought refuge in anger, for surely this had to be all his fault.

Gideon frowned and rolled out of the bed. My traitorous nether regions clenched in need as I saw his tight buttocks before he pulled on a pair of joggers and covered that perfection, dammit.

"I might have known you'd blame this one on me, woman." A hint of his dragon showed in his voice and my other half stirred and spit. A plume of smoke left my mouth and I clamped my hand over my mouth in horror.

Gideon crossed his arms over his massive chest and smirked.

"And there she is. I didn't do this, little goose. That was all her doing."

"Hers?" I mumbled that reply between my fingers, not at all sure I ought to be taking my hand off of my mouth.

Gideon sat back down on the bed and did it for me. With his gentle and extremely reassuring strength, he pried my fingers off my lips and then leaned in for a kiss. A mere brush of his soft, firm mouth over mine, yet it grounded me in the here and now and the restless thing inside of me retreated.

"Yes, hers. Your dragon's beautiful, and dare I say it seems even more volatile than you."

"My dragon?" I couldn't seem to stop parroting everything, but really, that was just impossible.

Gideon smiled and skimmed his knuckles along my jaw, over my collarbone and lower. When he reached my nipples, I hissed in pleasure, and his dragon growled. An answering rumble came from my chest, and I stared down at myself in abject wonder.

"I didn't do that."

Gideon cupped my chin to make me look at him and the tenderness I saw in his gaze took my breath away.

"I know, sweetheart, that was her." He dropped a kiss on my nose. "Breathe, baby, it's okay."

I took a much-needed breath at that gentle reminder and the tightness in my chest eased. "How, I mean, I would have known?"

Gideon sobered and regarded me thoughtfully. "Not necessarily. You were adopted, right?"

I glared at him but nodded. "Yes, but how in the hell do you know that? Oh, let me guess, your *Magick*."

Gideon shook his head and scrubbed a hand over his face. "Not this time, no. Just a case of one of the *Dragoons*, who happens to be good at hacking into computer files."

"You checked me out?" I winced at the screech I managed to produce. Nails on chalkboard sprang to mind. Add to that my hearing, which was definitely sharper than it used to be, and yes... Not the most comfortable combo.

Gideon grimaced and tapped his ear. "Thanks for that. That cleared out the wax for sure. Have mercy, woman."

"Sorry, but, *really*?"

I attempted to glare at him, to feel the rightful anger I should be feeling, but try as I might, I couldn't. Seemed all I wanted to do was lean in to Gideon's strength and finish what we started earlier. My pussy tingled, my breasts ached, and Gideon's nostrils flared as I grew wet for him.

"I had my suspicions, so yes, I looked into your background. Don't tell me you didn't at least Google me?" he asked. Heat rose in my cheeks and he laughed. "Thought so. Bet it pissed you off to no end when you didn't find anything, right?"

This time, I did glare at him. "Yes, and why the hell didn't I?"

Gideon shrugged.

"I value my privacy for obvious reasons. I practice under Gideon Daring. Had you Googled him, you'd have found me. Well, the me I'm prepared for the public to see. The real me is buried in the dragon archives here in my father's library. I dare say the truth about your parentage is to be found somewhere in there too. That's if your father reported it. I assume your dragon comes from your father."

"Why automatically assume that? That's so typically chauvinistic. Why couldn't my mother have been a ... mmph."

His kiss shut me up very effectively, and by the time he finally let me come up for air, I had a hard time remembering why I'd been all annoyed.

That wasn't the only thing hard. His erection prodded my leg, and he hissed between his teeth when I stroked the heavy length through his joggers.

"I said that because no she-dragon would ever abandon her young like your mother did you. They are fiercely protective of their young." That stopped my exploration of his cock, and I frowned, all too aware that I'd jumped to all the wrong conclusions—again.

"And male dragons aren't? Is that what you're saying? They what, get humans pregnant and just abandon them?"

Gideon's dragon roared his annoyance and I resumed stroking the shaft pulsing under my fingertips. He was so big and hard, my pussy clenched in need, and I couldn't stop touching him. It was utterly insane, this need which was driving me, yet it felt so right.

"That's not what I'm saying, woman. Stop

twisting my words. Assholes are everywhere, that's all I'm saying, and, yes, some dragon shifters won't think about any possible consequences when they use humans for sex, but it's not the norm. Certainly not in my clan. Our young are too precious to not cherish them and their mothers, human or otherwise." He paused, and that flash of sadness crossed his features again.

I reached out to touch his face and a shudder went through his whole body.

"You're thinking of your mother, aren't you?" How I knew that, I had no idea, but Gideon blinked and sighed.

"Yes." He scrubbed a hand over his face and I held my breath at what he was going to say. "You asked me earlier what happened."

He stared into space and his erection lessened under my hand, testament to how deeply this still affected him.

"She was killed, wasn't she?" I asked even though I knew the answer deep in my bones.

"Yes, she was run off the road in her human form."

I gasped, and he smiled grimly at my response.

"Drunk lorry driver took her out. Her injuries were so severe that even our combined clan Magick couldn't save her. My father might as well have died with her that day. The light went out of his eyes and he retired from his duties as Alpha soon after." Gideon shook his head and his gaze cleared and focused on me.

"That's when I had to step in. I should have had years yet of just being a dentist and not having to deal with being the Alpha, but I didn't hesitate to step into the role, even though Daddy's boots are mighty hard to fill."

My heart turned over in my chest at the way he said *Daddy*.

"Where is your father now?" I asked.

"I don't know, little goose. He took himself off. Dragons mate for life and without my mother, he didn't want to live anymore. I've no idea whether he's still alive, but I hope if he is he's managed to find some solace and if he isn't then he's with Mum, and they're happy again."

I blinked away tears at the heartfelt emotion that came through with his words.

"I miss them, you know."

I nodded, and he smiled and kissed my nose. "And I hope this answers your earlier question."

"What question?" I was somewhat distracted by the way his cock was once again hardening under my hand.

"When you, once again, I hasten to add, made assumptions about me and referred to my floozies." Heat rose in my cheeks as I recalled that conversation and I sought refuge in snark.

"Well, what was I to think when you're so good at sorting out women's hair?"

Gideon laughed and shook his head at me, and I was rather relieved to see that cloud of sadness lift off his shoulders.

"I've had no time for women, floozies, or otherwise, and if you must know, I used to brush my mother's hair for her whenever my father wasn't around to do it for her. It was too long for her to manage on her own."

"Oh, right."

"Something I'll gladly do for my own mate, if she'll let me."

His cock jerked as he said that, and I bit back a moan as the implications set in. He meant me, little Annie Taylor, and I wasn't at all sure what to make of that, so I simply grabbed him harder, hoping to distract him from this serious conversation. Gideon grumbled. "Stop doing that, or we'll never get to eat, and I'm hungry now. All this emotional unburden will do that to a man." He winked at me as he said that.

It was on the tip of my tongue to say, "Forget about the food," when my stomach and my dragon grumbled in unison. It was the oddest sensation. Gideon laughed, straightened, and held out his hand.

The minute I took it, peace settled over me, and what was more, I was clothed. Another summer dress sans underwear, of course. I rolled my eyes at him but didn't object. My nether regions were too sensitive to cover them, and besides, he'd seen it all already.

Heat rose in my cheeks at that thought and my belly gave a little flip all of its own when I looked up and saw Gideon's expression.

The tenderness in his eyes, as though I was the most precious thing he'd ever seen … good grief almighty, that did things to me. I was angry with him, wasn't I? Yet I found myself grinning up at him like a loon.

"What is your obsession with keeping me out of underwear, Gideon Jackson?" I tried for a reproachful tone but failed miserably because that came out all breathy, and sure enough, he winked at me, leaned down, and stole a quick kiss.

"Like I said, sue me, woman. Now, let's eat."

Chapter Six

Gideon

Watching my mate eat was an exercise in torture. Not only did she thoroughly enjoy her food, the noises she made as she sucked the spaghetti into her mouth... I couldn't get the image of those full lips wrapped around my throbbing dick out of my head. What was more, I knew full well it was her newly released dragon playing games with mine. I could see the shades of purple in her eyes, the challenge they held, and my dragon roared his approval.

It was with a certain amount of relief I saw her push her empty plate away and rub her belly.

"That was so good—what?"

A blush crept across her cheeks as her dragon self receded and her human side took over, and I reached across the table to link our fingers together.

Annie bit back a moan and her musk increased, calling my dragon to finish what we'd started, but we still had things to discuss and I was all too aware that my little goose's mind had been blown enough for one night.

"I was just thinking that I should escort you home. It's getting late." Darkness had fallen in earnest while we'd been eating, and the dining room was cast in long shadows only interspersed by the soft candles I'd lit on the table.

"You want me to leave?" She tried to pull her hand away, but I wouldn't let her.

"No, that's the last thing I want, but I thought it might be what you need."

A flash of purple heat hit me in the face as she erupted, and I grinned. It was so damn good to see her embracing her fiery half rather than be afraid of it, though I'd have to teach her to control it better. Folks on the whole weren't ready to know that dragon shifters existed.

"You don't get to tell me what I need, Gideon, not after… Dammit, stop."

She glared into thin air as though she was having an internal debate with her dragon half and I swallowed a laugh. The carafe of water on the table promptly upended over my head, dousing me in ice-cold water.

"What the fuck, woman?'

I shook my head to clear it of the water, but I wasn't really annoyed, more damn proud of the quickness with which my mate was coming to master her abilities.

Plus, her face was a picture of shocked awe.

"Did I do that?"

"You know damn well you did," I said. "I should put you over my knee and, oh, no, you don't." I countered her move to tip the wine bottle over my head with one of my own and she shrieked when her glass of water landed squarely in her chest. Not the wisest of moves for my sanity, as the wetness rendered the fabric of her dress transparent and I got a clear and enticing view of her full breasts. They shook in her outrage, or so I thought, until her laughter registered.

"What's so damn funny?" I asked, but my lips twitched too. Seeing her this happy and carefree; hell, yeah it was worth enduring that ice-cold dousing for.

"You, you're all wet and oh, so menacing, like a wet puppy or something."

"A puppy?" My dragon roared his fury at that comparison, and sure enough, the little minx's she-dragon appeared briefly in her eyes.

"Yes, where is your big, scary dragon now, you

… argh."

I yanked her off her chair and over my lap before she'd even stopped talking, and rained a few hard swats on her still-covered behind. She screeched and squirmed, but I trapped her legs between mine and one hand behind her shoulder blades held her down while I lifted her dress and exposed her delectable ass cheeks. The possessive animal in me growled seeing my handprints already imprinted on her pale skin.

"Let me go, you. Dammit, I'm not a child."

I laughed and continued to swat her ass, accentuating each swat with my words.

"I'm … well … aware … you're … not … a … child…" I paused briefly to pull the exhilarating musk of aroused woman into my lungs, satisfied to note that she'd stopped fighting me and had gone limp over my lap. My cock jerked against her soft belly and she gasped. I brought my hand lower to cup her soaked pussy and she panted her need.

"So fucking wet for me already. I love how responsive you are to me." I paused and swatted her ass again, much harder than before. The way she rose into each loud spank as though eager for my touch made me blurt the next words out. "I love you, Annie Taylor."

I rubbed the heated flesh in front of me, and my little dragon moaned and lifted her head up to look at me. The longing in her eyes made my chest tighten in emotion and my dragon retreat into the farthest corner. He didn't do the mushy stuff, and I smiled at his grumbling in my head. There was no sign of Annie's dragon half either, just a woman looking at a man, and our connection arched between us.

"You're only saying that to get into my knickers." Her breathy reply made me smile and I shook my head. I cupped her wet pussy and she squirmed and clamped her thighs around my hand.

"At the risk of pointing out the obvious, you're not wearing any knickers, sweetheart."

Annie attempted to glare at me but gave up when I slid one finger into her tight sheath.

"You're not playing fair." Her internal walls clamped around that digit and she groaned. "Besides, you're only saying that because of some weird mating dragon mumbo jumbo and I want more than that. I ... oh, don't stop please."

I'd slipped another finger into her channel and thrust them in and out, mimicking what I wanted, needed to do with my cock, and she went a little cross-eyed. I took her right up the edge and then stopped, eliciting another deep-throated moan from her.

"Dammit."

Withdrawing my fingers completely, I swatted her ass and then helped her to stand up. Seeing her all flushed and needy had to be the best sight yet. I patted my lap in an unspoken invitation for her to sit down, but I might have known she'd take that one step further. The little minx straddled me, so that the wet heat of her pussy settled right above my hard cock and we both groaned.

She started to rub herself against me, and I fisted my hand in her hair and dug my free hand into her hips to hold her still.

"Enough, woman, or so help me I'll claim you right here and now and show you what it means to be my mate."

She pursed her lips at me and grinned. "Yeah, so you keep saying, yet you still haven't done that. Me thinks you're all talk and no action you, big, bad dragon, you."

My dragon did roar at that, and my fearless mate matched him with a super cute growl of her own. Annie smiled at me and ran her hands over my face.

"Please, I wish you would … show me, that is."

I held my breath at what I saw in her eyes. Acceptance, longing, and dare I say it, love? Instead of answering her, I put all of my pent-up emotions into the kiss I gave her. Annie didn't disappoint in her reaction. She kissed me back and passion exploded between us. How long we kissed, I couldn't tell you, but eventually she broke away, and tears shimmered in her eyes.

"I don't understand any of this and it shouldn't be possible, but I think I love you too. Please tell me this is real?"

I cupped her face with one hand and rested my forehead on hers while I removed my joggers with a thought. Annie gasped but lifted up, and my cock sprang to life between us. Poised at her entrance, her heat called me, but I held her still and stared into her eyes.

"Believe me, this is real, my love." A tear rolled down her face and I kissed it away while slowly lowering her onto my shaft. The feel of her hot, tight cunt sliding down my dick tested my resolve to do this slow, to give her room to adjust, but I needn't have worried. This woman was made just for me and the sounds she made as she impaled herself all the way, gushed for me to aid the slide of my dick into her depths, told me she was so on board with this. We both stilled when I bottomed out inside of her, and when our gazes locked, we simply stared at each other.

"I promise I'll spend the rest of my life showing you how real this is. I love you, Annie."

I flexed my hips and Annie gasped and tightened around me.

"You better, and I love you too." She smirked and rose up, making us both groan in pleasure as she dragged her internal walls along my shaft. I let her set the pace for a while as she chased a release which almost sent me over the edge too, but I needed to finish inside her ass to complete our mating, so I counted backward in my head as she shuddered around me and bit my neck. My dragon roared his approval and my incisors lengthened, ready to mark this woman as mine forever. I stood up with her in my arms, and swiping the contents of the table onto the floor with one hand, I laid her back on the polished wood.

She arched her back and grinned as I magicked the dress off her until she was exposed in all of her naked glory. Her nipples called to me, hard little beacons of want, and I bent my head to give each rosy tip the attention they deserved. Annie locked her legs behind my butt in a vain effort to imprison me, but I was in charge now, so I pulled out of her and pushed her legs up and out to give me a full view of her quivering cunt.

After taking her hands, I wrapped them around her ankles and growled my instructions. "Keep them there, or I'll tie you up."

A shocked-sounding moan came from my girl, but she complied, wide-eyed, and I kissed her soft belly. I continued my path downward until I reached her wet pussy lips.

"Hmm, so wet and delicious and all mine, aren't you?" I looked up from my bounty to see her watching me.

"Yes, I'm all yours. Please, whatever it is you have to do, please just do it."

My dick jerked, my dragon growled, and she gushed more of her juices for me. They trickled down from her pussy toward that tight ring of muscle I needed to breach to complete our bonding. Using my fingers, I used her natural lubrication to wet that hole. She moaned when I pushed my slickened thumb through that ring, and her eyes clouded over in need. Purple flames danced in their depths as her dragon took over and I knew mine would reflect my dragon's flames as the two halves got ready to join.

"I need to claim this hole too, my love."

Her dragon answered me loud and clear, and Annie nodded. It was all the confirmation I needed, and I let my dragon soar. My claws ran out, as I thrust into her tight pussy, coating my dick in her juices before I ran it down to her anus and pushed in. Annie gasped and lost her hold on her ankles, not that it mattered, not when I slowly and surely claimed her body and soul. Our dragons roared, our fires mixed, and instinct took over for both us. As I pulled all the way out and then slammed back in again, Annie's nails scored my back, her incisors lengthened, and she met me thrust for thrust as our joined climax built, hotter and faster than anything I'd ever experienced. I hollered my release when it came and spurted my seed deep inside her ass as I sank my teeth into her shoulder, dimly aware of Annie following suit. Every inhale of her scent, the taste of her blood, the feel of her sucking mine cemented the age-old bond between us. When we both finally came down from the high, our dragons retreated, and we smiled at each other.

"You're mine now, my sweet little goose."

Annie's eyes widened in shock and I heard her response in my head loud and clear.

"Oh, my God, you're in my head. How is that possible?"

We both thought it together.

"Magick."

Epilogue
Annie

Three Years Later

The annual summer fete was in full swing and all around us the villagers of Rabbenstall mingled with the influx of tourists this event inevitably brought to our little village. Ever since the *Dragoons* had put on a motorbike cross rally for the first fete after my mating with Gideon, this had become an event the tourists flocked to. That first fete had generated so much income, helped along by my mate's clan's monetary contribution, of course, that Rabbenstall's old buildings had been restored to their former glory. It was a work in progress, of course. We fixed one thing and something else went kaput, but such was the nature of restoration.

It hadn't been the only work in progress, by any means. I rubbed our latest one still hiding in my barely visible bump and hugged our surprise to me like the precious gift it was.

"Have I told you lately how beautiful you are, mate?"

Gideon's deep voice in my head made me grin, and shielding my eyes against the sun, I looked up into the cloudless sky to see him soar high above us as he kept an eye on the masses of humanity spilling along our streets. He wasn't the only one up there by any means. The *Dragoons* took the safety of these events very seriously, and while their human MC brothers performed tricks on the ground, the dragon ones kept watch. Not that I had eyes for any of the other magnificent dragons circling overhead. No, besotted little me only had eyes and ears for Gideon, whether he was in his human or dragon form.

"You don't look too bad up there yourself, husband." I sent that thought to him and grinned as the sun glinted off my wedding band. While our mating bond was stronger than any human cultural tradition would ever be, I was still damn proud to call myself Mrs. Gideon Jackson, or rather Mrs. Gideon Daring, as our wedding certificate stated.

So much for my feminist views. Gideon, God bless him, had assumed that I would want to keep my own name, but as I had pointed out to him, what would be the point in getting married if I did that?

Gideon had spun me around and that sex had been one of our most inventive yet. Oh, yeah, let me tell you being a dragon makes for an interesting sex life. We never did find out who my real parents were, but it didn't really matter. As Gideon's mate, I'd found a whole new family and the way the clan had welcomed me with open arms had been delightful.

Humans could learn a lot from dragons, if you ask me.

"How is my son?"

"Your daughter is just fine, thank you." I stuck my tongue out at my impossible mate and earned myself a strange look from Barbara, who stood next to me at the library stall.

"Gah, a bug flew into my mouth. Don't you hate it when that happens?" I asked.

Gideon's laughter in my head joined Leonard's. Gideon's Beta crossed his arms over his big chest and grinned, his eyes on a flustered-looking Barbara. Heat stained her cheeks and I pulled in a sharp breath.

Leonard and Barbara? Surely not. The ancient dragon shifter hadn't mated, this was true, but Babs?

Leonard's dragon growled at me, Barbara

dropped the iced tea she'd been holding, and Gideon simply laughed in my head.

"Stanger things have happened, little goose."

Well, that was certainly true. One thing you could say about living in Rabbenstall. Life was never dull.

The End

EAGLE'S SEDUCTION

Elyzabeth M. VaLey

Chapter One

Kit revved up the bike's engine. Adrenaline pumped through him, traveling from the tips of his toes to the top of his head. He licked his lips, tasting the wind. Dipping to the right, he nearly grazed the asphalt. Had it been any other time of day, he would have heard a few cries of distress, perhaps even a few insults from other drivers at his manic maneuvers. Currently, however, there was not a soul in sight. Even the sun kept its distance, still a mere orange glow peeking through the dirty buildings, too shy to show its face.

He sped up. Feeling the powerful engine reverberating beneath him was almost as good as flying, but driving through a city as if there were no rules was an aphrodisiac. It was him against the concrete jungle. Ahead, a traffic light blinked amber. Kit grinned and bent, tucking in his elbows at the side. Every inch of him tingled with anticipation. Could he make it before the light changed?

She came out of nowhere.

He gripped the brake but there wasn't enough time. His world slowed and narrowed, everything but her fading as the inevitable collision crawled forward. Time ceased to exist. He took her in. Faded jeans, matching black tank top. She faced him, her pixie cut bobbing around her face and framing luminous blue eyes that screamed at him to halt.

His fingers dug into the handlebars, but the machine didn't respond, moving too fast to change course. Her backpack plummeted to the ground, landing with a solemn thud. Their gazes locked. Kit took in a shuddering breath, bracing himself for the impact. It never happened. Her clothing crumpled onto the pavement as an owl soared into the sky. Its cry of distress echoed in his ears and his eyes teared up, a mixture of relief and awe running through him.

His bike came to a sudden standstill, sending him flying over it and onto the road. He rolled for a few feet, friction burning his arms, torso, and legs. Finally, everything ceased. He lay on the ground, staring at the changing sky.

An owl.

Grateful couldn't even describe how he felt. Had it been any other shifter or a human, he would have killed them, but that little bird just flew. He twisted his head to look at her belongings. She probably wouldn't return for them, or at least, not until she redressed. He'd take them with him and give them to her, apologize, and offer some kind of compensation. It was the least he could do.

Slowly, he sat up. His body ached unpleasantly, but nothing seemed to be broken. Time to get moving before people started showing up and asking questions. Going to his bike, he checked it for any major damage. One of the mirrors had shattered when it had toppled over, but other than that, the machine seemed intact.

Satisfied he could ride again, Kit collected the shifter's bag and clothes. His fingers tightened around them. A shirt, no bra, pants, and a black thong. Her essence wafted up his nose, hypnotic, mesmerizing, calling to him to get closer and making his dick twitch. He groaned and stuffed everything into his motorcycle's saddlebags. It hadn't been long since he'd gotten laid, so this must be the way his mind chose to celebrate being alive. He could work with that.

Kit paused. There was something else caught under his wheel. He reached for it, curious. His eyes widened and his eagle slammed against his chest, reminding him of its presence.

"It's just a feather," he mumbled.

He ran his thumb across the soft, brown surface. Goosebumps sprouted across his arms and his bird cried out a song he'd never heard but recognized.

The mating call.

"Don't be ridiculous. It's just a feather."

The response was another hard jolt that traveled down his spine and through his limbs, bringing on the familiar ache he experienced before shifting.

"Not here," Kit growled.

His bird complained loudly, his cries of distress bouncing off Kit's skull.

Mine. Mine. Mine.

"We don't know her."

Sticking the feather into his pocket, Kit mounted the leather seat.

"But we'll find out."

Chapter Two

Kara collapsed onto her bed. She shook from head to toe, every inch of her aching with the speed of her shift and the circumstances. She shut her eyes, hoping the tears leaking from the corners would go away.

The accident replayed in her mind. She'd heard the roar of the bike, but it had been miles away. Or so she thought. Suddenly, he was upon her. The message in his gaze was distinct: *I'm sorry but I can't stop this.*

Her options were equally clear: die or fly.

Her body changed at a rate she'd never known was even possible. Bones bent, joints realigned, and feathers sprouted. She was up and gone in seconds.

Curling into a ball, Kara took in measured breaths. The move had been reckless, but the alternative was becoming road kill. She preferred to live.

****

She woke up with a jerk.

"Shit."

She sat up in bed. How long had she been out of it? She reached for her phone to check the time and grasped nothing. Realization sunk in. She'd lost everything. Her backpack, which she'd been forced to leave in the middle of the road, had all her valuables. Heat flushed through her body and anger pumped into her veins. Her phone, her books, even her clothes. All of it gone.

Heartbeat pounding, she made her way to the kitchen where the numbers on her microwave blinked green.

"Almost eleven o'clock already?"

Running her fingers through her hair, she sighed

heavily.

"Thinking on an empty stomach is impossible," she murmured, recalling her mother's old saying. "During a crisis, eat first, think later."

Kara snatched an apple from the fridge and sat down at the breakfast bar. It was all she'd be able to stomach. Grasping the notebook and pen she kept next to the telephone, she opened the pad to a new page.

Cell Phone

Wallet with two credit cards, driver's license, and fifty dollars.

Small makeup bag with skull print on it.

Sunglasses.

A book on astrophysics and a notebook.

She tapped her lip.

"What else, Kara?"

Taking a bite out of the apple, she stared at the page, nervously bouncing her knee.

"Now what?"

Considering the neighborhood she lived in, someone had probably taken her backpack. Of course, the money was probably gone, but maybe she could get her phone, textbook, and class notes. Heck, she'd be happy if she only got the books back. She had less than a week to study for her last three exams before graduation, which meant she wouldn't have enough time to rewrite notes and she knew her friend's weren't as good. Furthermore, if she didn't graduate, she might not be able to do her internship. Her stomach cramped painfully.

No. She was too close to her goal to let anything stop her. She would call the police and report the accident. Maybe they would find a witness who would know what had happened to her belongings.

Kara covered her face with her hands. Who was she kidding? If she went to the police, they'd ask her why she'd left the scene of the accident.

You see, officer, I shifted and had to leave all my stuff behind. I really had no other option.

They wouldn't believe her.

"Fuck," she swore.

She wracked her brain for solutions.

Go to the road where it'd all happened?

Cold sweat slithered down her back.

Too soon.

Call a friend? No point in doing that.

She bit her lip. What if she called her own cell phone? Would the thief pick it up? Drawing the landline toward her, she dialed her number.

Ring. Ring.

"Hello?"

Her stomach flip-flopped at the sound of the sexy, masculine voice. The animal within her stirred, making her nerve endings tingle.

"Hello?" Kara said.

"Hi. Who is this? Are you the phone owner?" the voice on the other side asked.

"Yes," she replied. "I suppose you have my phone or you wouldn't be answering."

He chuckled. The rich sound made her heart pick up its tempo and her owl preen, sending tiny darts of arousal to her pussy.

"Can you describe your belongings to me, or can I ask you a few questions?" he asked.

She frowned. "What are you? The police? If I'm calling this number it's because I'm obviously the owner."

He laughed openly and a giddiness she'd only experienced in her teenage years slammed into her. Her pussy throbbed and she glanced down at her lap. Why hadn't she bothered to get dressed?

"Just humor me. It won't hurt and that way we can both be sure I have your stuff."

"Fine." She rolled her eyes. She supposed he made some kind of sense. "Shoot."

"What kind of phone do you have and what's your background image?"

"I have a cranky old iPhone5 with a red cover and a shitty battery which doesn't last more than two hours. The picture is of a gray owl with big yellow eyes."

My niece after her first shifting. Kara smiled, recalling the shock in the young girl's eyes.

"Great. And your backpack?"

"Black, a little worn at the edges. Inside I have my wallet with my driver's ID, a makeup case with skulls printed on it, red-framed sunglasses, a book on business administration and a notebook." She paused. "Oh and a set of keys."

"What does the keychain look like?"

She took in a deep breath. Her owl fluttered wildly at her chest, making her dizzy. What the hell was wrong with the creature?

"Is this really necessary? I just told you everything else that was in my bag."

"Just trying to make sure. I wouldn't want to give someone's house keys to a stranger or a crazy boyfriend."

"First, I don't have a boyfriend. Second, it's a little Lego RD2 *Star Wars* key ring."

"So, you like *Star Wars*, huh?"

"What?"

"Never mind. It sounds like I have your stuff, little owl. Including your clothes."

She almost dropped the phone. "Excuse me?" Had he just called her *little owl*?

"You don't need to sound so pissed."

"Pissed?" she echoed.

The knot of anger in her stomach, which she'd forgotten about at the sound of his voice, returned tenfold.

"What do you mean I don't need to sound pissed? You interrogate me, mock my film choices, and call me pet names. How do you even know I'm an owl? Are you the asshole who almost ran me over this morning? Because if you are—"

"I'm at *Coffee First,* Kara. Do you know where it is?"

"Yes, I know where it is. How the fuck do you know my name?"

"Whoa, calm down," he said.

"What?" She jumped up, her chair toppling over. "Are you giving me orders?"

"No. Are you okay? I just heard something fall."

"I'm perfectly fine, except I have some arrogant asshole hijacking my stuff and insulting me over the phone."

He laughed again, the sound full of warmth. Kara curled her hands into fists.

"How dare you?" she said.

"Listen, I'm sorry. I didn't mean to be a jerk. I was just teasing. How long will it take you to get here? I have an appointment at noon."

She let out a long breath. *Think rationally.* Kara glanced at the rest of her school material piled on her coffee table.

He had her possessions and she needed them.

"I'll be there in fifteen," she said.

"Great. See you in a few."

"Wait, what's your name?"

"Name's Kit."

"Kit? What kind of name is that?" she blurted

out.

"The same kind as Kara."

Kara dug her fingertips onto the counter, focusing on the bite of the granite and pushing her sarcastic retort aside.

"And how am I supposed to recognize you?" she asked.

"Don't worry, little owl. You will."

The line went dead.

Chapter Three

Kit smiled at the hovering waitress. This was the third time she'd come by to ask if he needed anything. Considering the size of *Coffee First,* it was comical. The coffee shop had a grand total of eight tables, two big easy chairs, and a breakfast bar. Her interest in him was obvious and normally he'd have cashed in on the moment, but not today. His thoughts revolved around only one woman: Kara. His mate. He still couldn't believe he'd been so lucky. Never, in his wildest dreams, did he imagine he'd find her. Those kinds of things always happened to others, like his brother or his friends, not him.

Yet, here he was, waiting for her to walk through the door.

Fifteen minutes hadn't elapsed yet but every time the bell at the front chimed, he looked up. Unfortunately, the damn place was buzzing as customers dropped by to pick up orders or enjoy a quick bite to eat before heading to work. Morning had finally caught up with the city and people ran to and fro, rejoining the frantic rhythm of the gray world around them. Kit glanced at his watch.

Seventeen minutes.

She was late. Had he made her so angry she'd decided not to show? He ran his fingers through his hair, combing it back. He didn't know what had possessed him, but he'd been unable to stop the ribbing. And the *little owl* pet name? He'd put his foot in his mouth on that one, but it'd slipped naturally.

The door opened and a young woman dressed in a pin-striped suit walked in. She had the right height and build as well as the same pixie cut as his mate, but one look at her face, and he knew it wasn't his Kara. Kit glanced away.

How much longer was she going to take? He finished his coffee and frowned. He should have probably chosen something else. Tension and caffeine didn't mix and he was getting jittery.

"Keep it together, man," he whispered under his breath.

He toyed with the strap of Kara's backpack, which rested at his side as a quiet testimony of reality. Kara wasn't a dream.

He wasn't ashamed to admit he'd gone through her stuff before receiving her call. His reasons were both selfish and gallant. On the one hand, he wanted to find a way to return her things. On the other, he yearned to learn more about his mate.

"Good morning."

That voice. Kit's head snapped up. There she was. His heart cartwheeled and his eagle cried out in victory. She stood at the bar, her back to him, appraising the cakes on offer.

His woman was petite, with a cute bubble butt, but a waist so tiny he feared crushing her if he squeezed too hard. She wore her hair short with streaks of red, and she dressed informally, in jeans and a flowing shirt.

Kara spun around.

Her beauty stole his breath but her eyes were something from another world. Big and bright, they seemed to peer into his soul. His pulse quickened and his eagle sprinted through his system, the need to shift and claim his mate becoming almost unbearable. Was she feeling it? Was her little owl fighting to come out and claim him?

Kit closed his fist, his talons digging into his palm.

Wait.

He took in a deep breath. Sweat slithered down his spine. Control. He had to maintain the reins on the animal.

As much as his eagle had made up its mind, he needed Kara's consent and she appeared to be anything but happy as she marched in his direction. Tension rolled off her in waves.

"Kit, I suppose." She tilted her chin defiantly, daring him to disagree with her.

"Yes. A pleasure to meet you, Kara." He extended his hand, thankfully normal again, but she didn't take it.

"I never imagined the guy who almost ran me over would also be the one to collect my stuff."

Kit lowered his arm, motioning for her to take a seat. She ignored him.

"I apologize for this morning. I was driving recklessly."

"No shit, Sherlock."

Kit stifled his laughter. "You've got quite the temper, don't you?" he said.

"I'm sure you'd be pretty pissed if you were in my position."

"I'd apologize, but in reality, I'm glad I almost killed you."

Her eyebrows almost touched her hairline. She threw her hands up in the air.

"Just as I suspected. You're insane." She pointed to her backpack. "Mind handing it over? I have things to do that don't include chatting with a madman."

Kit patted the dark bag. "Actually, I thought we could talk for a bit, and get to know each other better."

Kara's nostrils flared and she crossed her arms across her chest, clearly unaware of how the gesture

271

made her breasts stand out. They were small, but perky. His cock stiffened. He could hardly wait to get her in private. Kit's eagle whistled impatiently.

Soon.

"Why would I do that?" she asked. "You almost killed me and now you won't give me my stuff. The last thing I want to do is sit here and speak to you."

Kit frowned. A little resistance and bantering were fun when it came to women, but this open hostility bordered on ridiculous.

"Come on, you're going to deny the connection between us?"

Fire blazed in her eyes. "Connection? I don't know what you're talking about."

Chapter Four

Kara dug her fingertips onto her ribs. She needed to stay grounded. Her stupid owl was acting all kinds of crazy, and the itch to shift or throw herself into this man's lap was becoming almost painful.

Connection?

What she felt went beyond that. It was an edgy tremor that traveled from the nape of her neck to her stomach and took residence there like bubbling lava.

It'd started the moment she'd walked into *Coffee First* and had spotted him sitting next to the window. She'd stalled at the bar, pretending to look for a pastry, buying time so she could get rid of the sudden rush of maddening lust racing across her veins.

He stood out like a sore thumb. Kit was a giant of a man, too big for such a small, cozy place in which hanging light bulbs, plants, and pastel signs were the norm.

Too badass.

Biker boots, black jeans, and a t-shirt which stretched across his pecs and made her want to tear it off him and expose him to her gaze to see what else he hid beneath, because surely, he didn't only have tattoos on his arms. Then there was the long, blond Mohawk and thick beard, which made her hands tingle with the need to touch.

However, his eyes were what undid and fixed her resolve at the same time. They were a light brown, almost amber in color, and the way they looked at her sent the churning fire in her stomach rolling and spreading across every inch of her skin. Her owl squeaked in delight, pecking at her heart to let go and shift.

No.

Kit spelled trouble with a capital T and right now, she was trying to stay away from anything remotely similar. She had dreams and aspirations and a man wasn't in the picture.

"Connection or the primal urge to mate. Call it what you will, little owl," Kit said, flashing her a set of pearly whites which stood out against his tanned skin.

Of course, the man couldn't be missing a tooth or two so I'd find him repulsive.

She took a deep breath. She'd endured this nonsense for far too long. Time to make things clear.

"I have no desire to mate with you. Now, give me my stuff before I call the police."

His grin widened, and spreading his arms across the back of the seat, he lifted her backpack and dangled it on two fingers.

"You want it? Have a seat and chat with me. That's all I'm asking, unless you prefer we leave and cut to the chase."

Her owl twittered in approval at his suggestion. Kara swallowed a groan. Treacherous beast.

"Give me my stuff now. There's no connection and no mating happening here. If you think I'd ever go into bed with a guy like you, then you need therapy."

He didn't retract. To her dismay, he moved so close she could see the specks of gold in his eyes and smell the coffee on his breath.

"Why are you fighting it? Haven't you dreamed of this moment?"

"What do you think I am? A damsel in distress?"

She didn't give him time to respond and, leaning over the table, she lunged for her stuff. A large hand squeezed her ass. Gasping loudly, she scurried upright.

"What do you think you're doing?" she demanded.

"Just giving you a helping hand," he replied. "You're short. I thought I'd give you a boost."

"This is harassment."

Kit laughed. "It would be if it weren't because I'm attuned to your arousal, little owl. Lust is pumping through our blood hard and fast, our birds begging to fly together and perform the mating ritual. You want me as badly as I want you."

She shook her head but her damn bird was screeching for release and her libidinous body ached with a throbbing rhythm that demanded to be satisfied.

"Give me my belongings."

"Your wish is my command, little one." He handed her the black school bag. "Unfortunately, I have to go, but this isn't the end of our conversation," Kit stated.

"If that's what you want to believe, suit yourself," she said, shouldering her backpack. Kara turned to leave.

"Don't forget your clothes," he said.

She spun around. Kit held out the jeans and shirt she'd been wearing earlier in the day. Scowling, she took them from him.

"And my underwear?"

"Oops." His eyes held a playful glint. "I must have forgotten it at my hotel room, but you could accompany me and we can go get it. Although the idea of knowing you might not be wearing any panties makes me drool."

"You're disgusting," she said, even though liquid pooled between her thighs.

"And yet I'm your mate. Isn't life full of hard … things?"

His gaze dipped and she mistakenly followed it.

Her eyes widened at the impressive bulge in his jeans. Heat crept up her neck.

"G-goodbye."

Devilish man chortled. "See you soon, little owl."

Not if she had any say, he wouldn't.

Chapter Five

Kara punched the cushion. She'd sat on the couch to get some studying done before lunch but she couldn't focus. Her body was on overdrive, her thoughts relentlessly returning to Kit.

Mates.

Ha! That was probably what he told all the girls to get them in the sack. Then once the deal was done, it'd be a quick apology and farewell. Not that it mattered. She had no interest in him. Kara shut her book with a snap.

Fine, she was attracted to him, but she didn't have time for a quick roll in the hay with some jerk. She had to be studying for exams. Her degree was her long-term plan, not romance. Unlike most shifters she knew who secretly or not-so-secretly craved a mate, she'd never cared.

If she'd learned one thing from her parents, it was that hard work paid off. She'd been working her ass off to be able to graduate with top grades and she was almost at the end of the race.

She looked at the family picture hanging on her wall. She loved them, but unfortunately, they didn't understand her. They expected her to stay home and work in the family business forever. Her dreams involved making airplanes and living abroad.

Sighing, Kara glanced at her watch.

Currently, however, she had to deal with the cards she'd been dealt. No one in her family knew what she was studying or her future plans. Her mother's tantrum when Kara mentioned studying engineering was still fresh in her mind, so she never mentioned it again.

Instead, and to appease her parents, Kara pretended to sign up for Business Administration at the nearby community college, but the reality was that she drove two hours each way to be able to study Aeronautical Engineering. For them, she had an easy life. She went to classes in the morning, studied for a bit, lent a hand in her parent's business for two hours, and went home.

Kara rubbed her eyes.

Her timetable was much more complicated. She'd managed to schedule most of her classes in the morning, so she was usually done by two o'clock. After, she'd eat something quick and return to help out in the shop for a few hours. Next, she'd head home, do some homework, take a nap and then she'd go to her second job, waitress at Moon Point, the infamous shifter bar. Once she got home from work, she'd study for another few hours before crashing in bed and getting up at five again to repeat the whole process.

Most of the time she was exhausted, but luckily, when it was exam period classes were canceled, so she could focus entirely on studying and didn't have to worry about commuting, but still, she was sick of lying and making up excuses. Finishing her degree was her number one priority in life. Period.

Kara checked the time again.

"Let's go."

Grabbing her backpack and keys, she left her apartment and called the elevator. The only good thing about going to work today would be that the bustle of the shop would keep her thoughts from straying to Kit. Her stomach fluttered and her owl hooted dejectedly.

"He's just some guy," she murmured. "Stop acting all irrational."

The elevator pinged and the doors slid open.

Kara shuffled back a step and did a double-take.

Her animal rattled noisily against her chest in ecstatic joy.

"Kara?"

His gaze swam over her face as if he couldn't quite believe she was standing there. Her owl rammed against her flesh and a wave of dizziness hit her.

Mate.

Kara clenched her teeth. Her scalp itched, the first forewarning sign of a shift.

No.

"What are you doing here, Kit?" she asked. Her voice came out low, and sensual. She scowled.

Kit's eyes lit up.

"Well, I'm a contractor and I had come to see an apartment they're selling on the seventh floor and which a friend had told me about."

"Oh."

So it was a coincidence. Kara swallowed. The doors to the elevator began to close, but Kit placed his booted foot between them, halting their progress.

"Weren't you going down?" he asked.

"Not with you, I'm not," she replied. *Not when my owl has some kind of crush on you.*

He chuckled. "Scared of riding with me?"

"No, but you're so big I don't want to be squashed."

Placing her hands on her hips, she glared up at him, pretending to be angry when really she felt ashamed. Could her insult be any lamer? And damn it all, she liked big and tall and muscular, and Kit had it all. Unlike her ex, the eagle shifter probably wouldn't have a hard time fucking her standing up, back to the wall and arms pinned above her head. Her breath shortened and her cheeks burned.

Kara, keep your thoughts together.

Kit laughed. "So you're definitely scared."

"Move over," she snarled, squeezing into the small space. "I don't fear anything. I was simply being polite and thought you'd prefer to have more room," she lied.

Kara wasn't frightened of him, what she feared was her reaction to him.

"A fearless woman. My favorite kind," Kit said.

Their arms brushed together and electricity raced across her every pore, hardening her nipples and making her vagina swell.

"Also, an aroused woman."

Her head snapped up and she looked at him. "No—"

"I can smell you," Kit growled. "You can deny your feelings, little owl, but your body is telling another story."

"Leave me alone."

He moved fast, positioning himself so she suddenly found herself caged between his arms, aware not only of his size but also his scent. She inhaled sharply. Images of freshwater lakes and pine trees conjured in her mind. Her owl thrashed within her, desperate to fly loose.

"Tell me why you are fighting against something so natural, Kara?"

Kara gazed into his eyes. The whites disappeared, becoming a dark golden hue and the pupils had dilated and darkened. Within, she saw the animal. Proud and bold, the eagle beckoned her to respond. Kara's breath hitched and her head spun.

"I—"

His lips descended on hers. Hot and hard, they showed no mercy. She didn't need coaxing. Kara opened up to him like a flower eager for sunshine. Their tongues tangled together, licking, sucking, moving with an ease she'd never experienced on a first kiss. Grabbing her by the waist, he dragged her closer. His erection bumped into her and an involuntary moan escaped her. He slipped a hand beneath her ass, and she fisted his shirt. She held onto him, her reluctance forgotten and replaced by the need to delve deeper into him.

The elevator jerked to a stop, breaking them apart.

"Kara."

He cupped her cheek, gazing down at her with adoration and undisguised lust. Stunned, she stared at him.

Mate. Mate. Mate.

Her owl fluttered giddily. The tattoo of her frenzied heart echoed in her ears.

No way. This isn't part of the plan. Can't be.

"If you touch me without my permission again, I will call the police."

Without waiting for his response, she ran out of the elevator and onto the street.

Chapter Six

Kit walked into the shifter bar, Moon Point. It was as rowdy as he remembered and made him feel immediately at ease. A group of men shouted at the game playing on the screen, while others dealt cards around a plate of nachos with cheese and beers. Two couples, in what appeared to be a double date, toasted loudly and embraced. The place smelled like oil, alcohol, and animals. Not exactly a five-star joint, but just what he needed to get Kara off his mind for a bit.

Or at least, to try to relax and figure out a way to win Kara over. He wanted more. However, she seemed to want nothing to do with him.

Granted, they'd just met, but they were mates. Things should be simple: sex, mating dance, and live happily ever after.

All right, perhaps he was oversimplifying things, but still this whole I-don't-want-you-but-my-pussy-is-drenched was ludicrous. Why fight something that came so naturally?

He took a stool and waved at the bartender, a lanky man with a braided beard and a goatee. Kit rubbed his temple. He'd figure things out. Normal women couldn't resist him and his mate wasn't going to be an exception.

"Hey, what can I get you?" the barman asked.

"Hi. Do you have any Guinness? And is Lee around? He told me he usually arrives around this time."

"The manager?"

"Yeah."

"He hasn't come in yet, but he should be here soon." The guy smiled and filled his glass, and presented it to him.

"Things have changed around here if Lee is late for work," Kit said.

The bartender laughed.

"I think his husband keeps him busy," he said, taking his beer again, which had now taken on a ruby-red color, and topping it off.

Kit chuckled. Unfortunately, he hadn't met the famous lion shifter, Alkaline. He'd had a deadline to meet last year and he'd missed the couple's wedding.

He placed the drink in front of Kit. "That'll be eight dollars."

Kit paid and thanked the server. He took a sip and shut his eyes in appreciation. Maybe, once Kara accepted their inevitable mating, they could organize a dinner date with Lee and his husband. Kit sighed. Not thinking of Kara was clearly impossible.

"Well, well, well, what's a little bird doing at a shifter bar?"

Kit spun around at the sound of the familiar voice.

"Lee."

Standing, he pulled in the puma shifter for a hug. He took in his friend. His blonde hair was slightly longer, and he'd gained a bit of weight, but he looked good, more relaxed. Besides, there was a sparkle to his gaze he'd never seen.

"You're looking good, my friend," Kit said.

"That's because you haven't seen me in, what, three years?"

"It hasn't been that long. I saw you at Sisu's wedding."

"Yeah, that was two years ago."

Kit winced.

"Really? Damn, time does fly. I'm sorry, man."

Lee clapped him on the back and sat next to him.

"No worries. At least, we've kept in touch. It's not like you dropped out of the radar or anything." He shrugged. "Life gets busy. It happens to all of us."

"Yeah. And then some of us go, get married, stop being workaholics, and arrive late to work." Kit waggled his eyebrows.

Lee grinned. "You'll have to meet him, Kit. He's—" Lee sighed. "I can't even." He lowered his gaze self-consciously.

"Man, you're drooling."

"Ha-ha. You will too when you meet your soulmate."

Kit swallowed. Should he say anything? He took a sip of his beer. Surely, Lee would have some advice for him, wouldn't he?

"Well, as a matter of a fact," Kit began.

Lee's eyes widened. "So that's why you look like something the cat just dragged in." He snickered. "No pun intended."

"Yeah, I think I've found her, but she doesn't want me," Kit spat out. He scrubbed a hand over his face, the day's tension finally catching up to him and creating a hollow ache in his chest. His mate didn't want him. His throat closed up and his head started to pound. What was he going to do?

Lee whistled low. "That story sounds way too familiar. You wouldn't believe the fight Alkaline put me through. Is she human? Shifter?"

"Shifter. Owl," Kit said. He raised his hands in defeat. "I just don't get it, Lee. We're soulmates. This is the kind of thing every shifter spends their life searching for, especially women. I mean, it should be easy. She shouldn't be fighting me every step of the way."

Lee wrinkled his brow. "Are you listening to

yourself, Kit? This is the twenty-first century. Women have goals and aspirations other than finding a mate and bearing children. I know your upbringing was unusual, with your parents and all—"

"Don't." Kit stopped him, palm raised. He didn't need to be reminded of his family history. He knew it all too well. He wasn't the child of a mating and his mom didn't want him. He hadn't found out who his dad was until he was almost in his twenties.

"In any case, my point is, mating is more than primal attraction. We are not animals. We're people. There are complicated emotions behind all of us. Maybe she wants you, but she's afraid."

"I get it, but what do I do?"

"Speak to her. Take her out on a date. Court her."

Kit stared at him. "Do you even know what you're asking from me?"

Lee snorted, his eyes shining with mirth. "Come on, man. You're telling me you're not able to keep it in your pants?"

"Not where she's involved." Kit shook his head and took a long swig from his beer. "There's also a problem," he admitted. "I don't have her number."

"You don't?"

He shook his head.

"Ran into her twice today, but didn't ask for it." Quickly, Kit explained how he'd met Kara and when he'd run into her at the elevator.

"Wow. So you almost ran this girl over, tried to seduce her like a caveman, and finally, managed to kiss her. I'm surprised she didn't slap you or kick your balls."

Kit nodded. "Me too. Except, she's so tiny, Lee. She's like a fragile porcelain doll. Except, she's not fragile. You know what I mean?"

"Not at all." Lee's eyes filled with glee and Kit

glowered at him. "But tell me more," he rushed to add.

"She's petite. Short, tiny waist, small tits, but a nice little bubble butt. Don't even know how we're going to, um, you know."

"Too much information, man."

Kit rolled his eyes.

"In any case, if she weighed 200 pounds, I'd still be all over her. It's her face that has me mesmerized. She's got these great eyes, Lee. I've never seen anything like them. They're a luminous blue, almost as if she were peeking right into your soul and bringing out the best in you. And she's smart, man, she's studying —"

"Wait, does she have short, black hair? Like up to her chin?"

"Yes."

"Fuck me. What's her name, Kit?"

"I haven't told you? Kara. Why?"

Lee burst out laughing.

"What's so funny? Do you know her?" Kit stood up.

"Your mating is definitely in the stars, man." Lee wiped an invisible tear from the corner of his right eye. "Know her? Kara works for me. She's the head waitress here at Moon Point. And you've been so intent on your misery, you haven't noticed she's out there, working."

Lee spun in his chair and waved his arm, encompassing the bar with the gesture. Kit's jaw dropped. Kara stood at the back of the room, taking a table's order. His eagle soared within him, making the room spin.

Mate.

He took a step in her direction. This was fate. Lee grabbed his arm.

"Don't. She's already turned you down several times. Do you really wanna cause a scene here? Let me offer you an alternative plan."

Kit's eyes narrowed. His instinct told him to go over there, throw Kara over his shoulder, and get out of there whether she wanted to or not. But Lee was right. They weren't animals. He needed a strategy. He looked at Lee.

"All right. I'm all ears."

Chapter Seven

Kit waited for Lee. He leaned against the brick wall, absently watching a rat dig into the large garbage containers. Sweat rolled down his back, the unforgiving summer unwilling to offer a slight breeze even at this hour. The yellow light above the rear exit of Moon Point quivered, the bulb probably close to dying. A metal door creaked in the silence and Lee emerged from within.

"All right. Everyone has gone home for the night except her. She's in my office, studying. You're going to enter through the kitchen, then cross the main area and to the right of the bar. You'll see the door toward the changing room and office."

"Great. Thanks, Lee."

"No worries. I'm sure had you been here, you'd have helped me with my mate." Lee handed him a set of keys. "Lock the door once you're inside. You know this isn't the best neighborhood."

"I'm aware," Kit said. "And to think she spends her night studying here."

"She says she can focus better. At home, she only falls asleep, or so she's told me." He shrugged. "Good luck, Kit. Though really, all you need is patience." Lee squeezed his shoulder.

"Thanks."

Quietly, Kit opened the door and went inside. After locking up, he padded through the quiet bar. The air reeked of cleaning products, but another, much more agreeable scent stuck out. Kara's. His sense of smell wasn't as good as a wolf's but he could still pick her out in a crowd if he needed to. His eagle shrieked erratically. He wanted her as badly as he did. His heartbeat raced, rushing in his ears. He could see light coming from under a door. The office. His hands became clammy and he stopped to take in a deep breath.

Slow and easy. Patiently. Give her time.

Kit opened the door.

"So this is where you hide at night."

Kara shrieked and jumped to her feet. Her pen clattered to the floor.

"How did you get in here?"

"Lee let me in."

"Lee?" she echoed, disbelief painted in her features.

"Yes, we're old friends and when I told him about you, he did me a favor."

Her nose scrunched up and her lips became a thin line of anger.

"I'll have a word with Lee tomorrow, but as for you. Please, leave me alone. How can I make your thick, ginormous skull understand that I want nothing to do with you?"

"My brain gets it, my heart and my eagle don't."

"Well, send them the memo." She glanced down at her books. "I have a lot to study and you already ruined my morning. Leave me alone." She bent down to retrieve her pen and returned to her text.

Kit shut the door behind him. The room, which wasn't too large to begin with, became smaller, more intimate. It was just him and his mate. His vision shifted, becoming sharper, as if he were on a hunt and had to locate his prey. This time, there was only one thing he wanted to devour: Kara.

His mate appeared to read but her eyes didn't move and the vein on her neck throbbed erratically while her chest rose and fell quickly. She could pretend all she wanted, but she wasn't immune to him. He took a step in her direction when Lee's words returned to haunt him.

Show her you care. Demonstrate you're interested in more than just fucking her. She's like a frightened animal, Kit. You can't pounce on her. You must give her time to adapt.

"So, what are you studying?" Kit asked.

"Business admin. Why are you still here?"

"Business?" Kit approached her slowly. "You know, this morning, when I was looking at your stuff, I went through the book you had in your bag. I think it was the same one you're reading now. It's interesting because the cover does say *Principles of Modern Business Administration*, but I could have sworn the content had something to do with physics."

"You went through my stuff?"

"I was trying to find a way to get in touch with you before you called."

"Of course." She rolled her eyes and returned to her studying, chewing on the end of her pen.

"So, what are you really studying?"

"Business."

"Really?"

"Leave me alone," she snapped.

"Why are you hiding what you're doing?" he retorted.

"I'm not hiding anything and it's none of your business."

"It is my business. We're mates and I'm trying to get to know you, Kara. Come on, let's make an effort."

"I'm not mating with you, Kit. And I am making an effort in trying to get you to leave." She pointed at the door.

Kit ignored her. He eased into a chair and picked up a book titled, *Exploring Management*. He flipped through the pages.

"Cepheid variables swell and contract, using—"

"Give me that."

She lunged at him, snapping the book from his hand, which fell on the desktop with a clatter.

"What is wrong with you?" she growled. "I told you to leave it."

"Why the mystery? You should be proud about studying something so complicated."

Her nostrils flared and she pursed her lips as if holding in a scream. "It's none of your business," she said.

Kit set his jaw. Something funny was going on. When he'd originally seen the book in Kara's bag, he hadn't thought much of it, but now, it seemed his mate was adamant on keeping her textbooks a secret.

"Who doesn't let you study this?"

"What?"

"You evidently enjoy it, because this is not the kind of thing you study for pleasure. So, allow me to rephrase my question. Who are you hiding it from? Who doesn't let you be you?"

Her eyes widened and her cheeks reddened.

"You wanted to have sex, didn't you? This whole mating thing is nothing more than primal sexual attraction, so let's do it."

Chapter Eight

"Excuse me?" Kit leaned forward in his seat. Had he heard her correctly?

"You call it mating. We both know it's sex. You're hot and I'm hot. So let's do it. Get it over with and then you can leave."

She peeled off her shirt, standing in front of him in a silky red bra. His cock jerked alive, blood rushing to fill it. He shook his head.

Keep it together.

His little owl was trying to distract him from asking more questions she didn't want to answer. They needed to take this one step at a time.

Her bra landed on his lap and he looked up. Her breasts were a handful, with long, pink nipples that begged for his mouth. Kit swallowed. It would not be easy.

"What are you waiting for?" Kara asked. "Are you going to fuck me fully clothed?"

"I don't like to be rushed," he said.

Kit rose. He would play her game, if only until he was able to recollect his thoughts. He took off his shirt and folded it. Ideas rifled through his brain. He needed to regain control and he had to do it quickly.

Kara wanted to have sex and distract him from knowing more about her. Lee was right. He would have to arm himself with patience, but it was clear it'd be the only way to get his mate to open up to him. Otherwise, theirs would be a relationship based solely on the physical and he wanted more. It'd be what he'd always dreamed about: a mate who understood him, who was on the same wavelength as him. He knew the possibility stood in front of him and he wouldn't let it go. A plan formed in his mind.

Finally, he slipped off his jeans. His cock jumped out, thick and already leaking pre-cum. His eagle screeched in anticipation of what was to come.

Not yet, my friend.

He went around the desk. Kara glanced up at him. Her lips parted in expectation. Kit ignored her and sat down on the leather office chair. Kara's brow lifted.

"So you expect me to do all the grunt work?" She placed her hands on her hips. They were slim, just like the rest of her. Kit dipped his gaze to her pussy. She was aroused, the evidence glistening under the light like raindrops on grass. He couldn't wait to be inside her. He palmed his cock, spreading his juice.

He clenched his teeth. *Be strong.*

"No, babe, you're going to suck me first."

"What?" She scowled, but she was unable to stop the tip of her tongue from traveling over her lips. Greedy little owl. Kit grinned.

"If my cock is gonna fit in your cunt, it has to be dripping and the best lubrication I have around here is your mouth."

"I'm pretty wet already," she admitted, wringing her hands.

"Let me check."

"No," she cried.

Kit guffawed. "I'm gonna be shoving my mouth and my cock up your pussy but you don't want me to see how wet you are?"

She gave him a death stare. "Fine. I suppose you're right."

"I love hearing you say that. Stand here." He pointed to the space between his legs. Shyly, she went to him. Kit ran his fingertips down her spine. She arched her back.

"Spread 'em," he told her, placing his hand between her thighs.

She did as he asked and he cupped her pussy. He whistled appreciatively.

"Fuck, you are soaked." Kit sniggered. "And you didn't want me or anything to do with me, right?" he asked, sliding his fingers across her nether lips.

"Nothing," she replied.

He circled her hole, gently pushing the tip of his finger inside. A low whimper escaped her.

"Absolutely nothing," he agreed. He entered her fully and she moaned, thrusting her hips at the same time. God, she was tight. "You're dripping, but I need you to be gushing."

"Keep doing what you're doing and I'll get there," she replied, rolling her hips.

He flicked her clit. She gasped.

"Little owl is close, isn't she?"

She nodded.

"You've been horny all day, haven't you, Kara? Thinking about my cock inside you."

He introduced another finger.

"Yes," she gasped.

"Two fingers and you're already putty in my hands? I don't know how you're going to manage with my dick."

He stood up, pressing his front to her back, his cock nudging her from behind.

"Kit," she murmured.

"Yeah, babe?"

"Fuck me."

"Soon."

Kissing her neck, he enjoyed the shiver that racked through her. His mate. Bending his head, he inhaled her fragrance. She smelled sweet, like a coniferous forest after a spring shower. A surge of affection mingled with possessiveness. He'd win her over.

He pressed a third finger into her, curling them over her G-Spot. Kara whimpered and rolled her hips, rubbing her ass against his cock. Kit drew in a shaky breath. If she kept that up, he'd lose control, and he couldn't. Not yet. "Don't do that," he warned her.

"Why?"

Pulling out, he spun her to face him and sat her atop the wooden desk. Kara's lips curved into a sensual smile.

"Do me."

Kit sucked in his cheeks. Was he dreaming? Did this woman truly belong with him?

"You're gorgeous," he said, his voice coming out in a hoarse whisper.

"Quit the sentimentality and fuck me."

He swallowed drily. No, she wasn't his yet. Soon.

Grabbing his cock, he slid the thick head across her slit, relishing the way it parted her lips. Kara threw her head back and spread her legs further. He repeated the movement, moving his length up and down her slick folds.

"Kit, stop teasing."

Tension crept up his neck. Dear God, he hoped his plan didn't bomb. He took a step away from her.

"Kit?"

"You know, little owl, since you won't tell me what you're hiding, I've decided I don't want to have sex with you right now."

Chapter Nine

Kit breathed slowly through his nose. This was probably the hardest thing he'd done in his life. His chest throbbed with a keening ache, and a sorrowful cry filled his ears. His eagle was not happy.

Kara sat up, an incredulous look on her face. "You don't mean that. Your dick looks like it's going to burst."

It probably would the moment he got out of here.

"I meant every word. I'm gonna leave you like this. Hot and bothered and thinking about my cock and how much you want it." Unable to resist, he tabbed the mushroom head against her clit and watched, fascinated as a dribble of liquid slid from between her slit and onto the dip of her ass. "You're going to masturbate, Kara, and you're going to fantasize about me, but it won't be enough, little owl." He grazed her clit with his thumb, making her jump. "You'll imagine me stretching you, filling you completely, ramming into you until you can hardly breathe."

She grabbed his arm. "You can't do this. I have three exams coming up. I need to study and if we don't have sex I won't be able to focus."

"For a business exam, right?"

"No, I mean, yes."

Kit chuckled. She couldn't even lie properly.

"When you're ready to explain more, call me, little owl. Meanwhile, you're going to have to deal with the arousal."

"This is ridiculous," she stated, crossing her arms.

Kit laughed. It sure was, but he wasn't about to tell her that.

"You know what is ridiculous?" he said, instead. "You thinking we could have a wham-bam, thank you ma'am. I can see your owl reflected in your eyes. Your feathers are coming out," he said, gently caressing the nape of her neck where indeed a tiny fluff of a feather had sprouted. "We're mates, whether you like it or not. We both have a lot to learn, and this is just the first lesson, Kara."

Leaning over her, he kissed her cheek and grabbed his neatly folded clothing.

"Here is my number," he said, taking a pen and scribbling it on the corner of her notebook. "When you decide to speak, give me a call. I'll be waiting."

Quickly, Kit redressed. He didn't look at Kara, but he could sense her gaze on him, angry and frustrated. She had no idea how badly he wanted her, but he wanted a mate, not just a quick fuck.

"So you really are leaving," she said when he was at the door.

"I'm a man of my word, little owl."

"Good riddance," she said.

He chuckled.

"Talk to you soon, babe."

Without another word, Kit walked out. Stifling heat punched him in the face, mingling with the reality of his situation. Kit forcefully rubbed his knuckles against his head.

"Shit," he growled.

Kara's pussy scent wafted to his nose. His cock jumped, confined as it was against his jeans. He didn't even know how he'd managed to stuff it back into his pants. Force of will, he supposed.

If his little owl wanted to play games, so be it. He hated the idea with a passion, but if she wanted him to be the big, bad predator, then he'd comply. When he caught her, though, he was never letting go.

Chapter Ten

Kara didn't move for at least five minutes. She dug her nails onto the cheap wood, leaving half-moon marks.

How dare he just get up and leave her like this? She looked down at herself. The image of his cock grazing her pussy jumped to the front of her mind. Her owl beat its wings against her chest, sending it into palpitations.

Mate.

No.

Asshole. Yes.

Kara jumped down and redressed. She wiped down the table and reorganized her books. None of it mattered. She had three more exams coming up. The last round before graduation and her internship in France, away from her family and Kit. A ball of lead landed hard in her stomach and she shivered, a sudden cold feeling taking possession of her body.

No, this wasn't about Kit. She was upset about leaving behind her family. She rubbed the heel of her palm against her chest. She'd cried when she'd made the decision to move abroad. Reality was catching up with her.

Kara opened one of her books and started to read. Her vision blurred, her thoughts straying back to her encounter with Kit. She covered her face with her hands. His face popped behind her lids. Glittering eyes and a smile so bright, she craved to see it every day. But she'd never see it again. Sudden, overwhelming sadness overtook her and her eyes filled with tears.

"No," she cried.

He was a stranger. A man she'd just met. No one important.

"Study, Kara. This is what you've always wanted."

But the smell of sex permeated the air and his image changed to what she'd seen a few minutes ago. Chiseled abs, colorful tattoos covering thick arms and pecs, a tapered waist and a dick so big she feared it wouldn't fit. Her clit twitched.

"What the heck is wrong with you?" she yelled.

You'll imagine my cock stretching you, filling you.

Closing her eyes, Kara stroked her pussy. She whimpered.

Shit. Shit. Shit. She was doomed.

****

Kara glanced at her clock. Six AM. He'd been galvanizing on his bike at that time yesterday so he was probably awake and if he wasn't, well, too bad. She couldn't take it anymore. Unable to focus on her material, she'd gone home. She'd taken a shower, hoping to relax and catch some sleep, but instead, she'd masturbated. Her libido didn't decrease. She'd fallen into bed and done it again, replaying every single one of Kit's words. She'd fallen asleep for maybe a half an hour before she'd woken up again. She'd taken a cold shower to no avail. Had a cup of tea, watched some TV, and attempted to study again. Nothing. She couldn't rid herself of the cavorting desire to be with him.

Picking up the notebook where he'd scribbled his number, she dialed. It'd just be sex. A quick hanky-panky and she'd be on her way.

"Hello?"

"Kit."

"Hey, little owl."

"You were right," she blurted out. "I'm studying something my parents don't approve of, engineering, and that's why I'm hiding it."

"Your parents don't approve of you studying for an engineering degree?" he echoed.

"No. They want me to work in the family business."

Kit swore. "What is wrong with them? Don't they realize how brilliant you are? And the possibilities you could have in life away from this gritty neighborhood?"

The corner of Kara's lips lifted and warmth spread across her limbs. It was nice to have someone on her side unconditionally.

'Thanks," she said. "No, they don't get it. I think they worry about me leaving. I want to work for Airbus and—" She clamped her mouth shut. *Too much information.*

"And?"

"Nothing. Let's meet up and fuck." She swallowed. "I'm desperate. I have three exams coming up, Kit. I need to be able to study. Please, help me."

She sounded frantic, but she didn't care. She couldn't afford to lose any more hours. She had to get rid of this maddening arousal.

There was silence on the other end of the line. She could almost hear the wheels of Kit's mind turning. She'd said too much and now he was wondering how he could use it to his advantage.

"I've masturbated twice and I can't stop thinking about you," she said, hoping to distract him.

"I know, babe. I haven't been able to get rid of my erection." He sighed. "I'll be there in thirty minutes. I know the building, but what's the number?"

She gave him the details and hung up. She looked around her. Thirty minutes? What was she supposed to do in that time?

Kara was fluffing up the bedroom pillows when the doorbell rang. Taking a deep breath, she headed for the entrance. Sex. This was all about the primal urge to fuck. Nothing else. She threw the door open. Emotions clashed within her like waves against the shore. Her owl fluttered its wings, battling to jump out and perform the mating dance. Goosebumps sprouted on her flesh and liquid rushed to her core at the same time. Her knees wobbled.

"Hey," Kit said.

"Hi."

He smiled and it was almost as if everything around her ceased to exist.

"Can I come in?"

"Sure. Sorry."

Kara moved out of the way and allowed him inside. She observed him. Somehow, even though her apartment was tiny and Kit was large, he moved around as if he'd visited her hundreds of times, as if he belonged. The thought scared her.

"Can I get you anything to drink?"

"A glass of water would be great. Is this your family?" he asked, looking at one of the pictures on the wall.

"Yes, Mom and Dad and my older brother."

"They look, um, traditional."

"They are," she agreed. "Ice?"

"Please," he replied.

She dug out a few cubes from the fridge, taking the opportunity to collect her thoughts. As soon as he'd drunk the water, she'd jump him. All these questions unnerved her, not to mention, she was wasting time.

She emerged from the kitchen and found him settled onto her couch, browsing through one of her books.

"So what kind of engineering is it that you're studying? Thanks," he said, taking the glass from her.

"Aeronautical," she replied.

His eyes rounded.

"Wow, babe. And your parents aren't proud?"

She pressed her lips, allowing the familiar surge of anger to pass. Too many personal questions for someone who wasn't going to be part of her life.

"Can we talk about something else? Or just have sex?"

Kit took a long gulp of his drink. "So you want to get down to business?"

"Yes."

His gaze traveled up and down her body, snaring on her breasts, before dipping lower. Her pussy pulsed in response.

"Tell me what you've been fantasizing about," Kit said.

"What?"

"You said you've masturbated twice. I want to know what you were thinking about."

"Why?"

He smiled broadly and offered his hand. She hesitated. Sex, she reminded herself. They were only talking and having sex. She slid her palm into his and he tugged her onto his lap. Gently, he grasped her chin and tilted her head so they made eye contact.

"Because, little owl, if I can, I'm going to make them come true."

A delicious shiver raced across her spine. Kit leaned in and kissed her, softly. She dragged her fingers into his hair, drawing him closer, but he didn't respond the way she wanted him to. He took his time to trace the contours of her lips, before finally sliding his tongue against hers and initiating an erotic danced which fired every cell in her body. Moaning, Kara pressed closer. She rocked her hips against his erection, wishing to devour him and taste every inch of him until they fused into one being. Her pulse beat erratically, her flesh sizzling with uncontrolled erotic energy.

Kit pulled back. "Tell me," he demanded hoarsely.

Kara pressed her cheek to his, her mouth almost at his ear. "You fucked me against the wall."

"Very doable," he said, sliding his hands beneath her robe and cupping her ass. He pinched her bottom. Kara yelped.

"What else?"

"And over Lee's desk. Hard. Fast. Stretching me like you promised you would."

Kit groaned and opened her garment, exposing his breasts to his gaze.

"Can be managed," he said.

"And you?"

He blinked, apparently taken aback.

"I imagined all of it and more, little owl." He pinched her nipple and she gasped.

"Fuck me," she pleaded.

"Soon."

Her nipple disappeared into his mouth. Kara bucked her hips.

"Harder," she encouraged him.

He swirled his tongue around the nub, then sucked deeply.

"Yes," Kara cried out, rocking against him. "Fuck me, Kit."

He switched breasts and reached between her legs, sliding his index and middle finger across her labia, parting it.

"I don't think you're wet enough," he said.

She gaped at him. "Come on. I know you're well-endowed, but do you really think it won't fit?" She chuckled incredulously.

Kit picked her up and placed her on his feet. "Look at your size and now look at mine."

He unzipped his jeans and his cock sprung out. Kara swallowed. His erection was impressive, proudly standing out in a nest of neatly trimmed golden hairs. The veins on the shaft stood out and the swollen head leaked pre-cum. Her mouth watered.

"I don't even think it'll fit your mouth," Kit said, rubbing his thumb across her bottom lip.

"Is that a challenge?"

She glanced up at him. His eyes mocked her.

"Take it as you will, little owl."

"Let's make a bet," she offered.

"I'm all ears."

"If it fits in my mouth, you fuck me."

"And if it doesn't?" Kit asked.

Smiling, Kara kneeled in front of him. "That won't happen."

"Wait." Kit sat down and offered her a cushion. "You might be down there a while."

"Arrogant bastard," she muttered, but she took the pillow anyway.

Kit spread his legs. Kara worried her bottom lip. His cock was huge. She wanted to drive him wild and to the brink of exasperation to show him how she'd been feeling, but she had to take things slow or otherwise, he'd win. Wrapping her fist around the shaft, she found she could barely encircle it.

"I told you," he said.

"I haven't put it in my mouth yet," she replied.

"You can hardly fist it."

"You want me to give you a blowjob or not?" she asked.

"I'm sorry. Please proceed."

Holding his dick, she traced the thick vein from base to top and teased the slit, relishing the taste of his pre-cum. Rolling her tongue across the smooth edges of the crown, she tried to wrap her mouth around it. Too soon.

She kissed the head again, sensually resting her lips over it and sucking in lightly. She heard Kit's sharp intake of breath. He liked it. Knowing he was enjoying the experience made her wet and she repeated the action. Kiss by playful kiss, she slid down the side of his shaft. When she reached the bottom, she swirled her tongue across his balls.

Kit gasped and she moaned in response. Kara repeated the process until his dick glistened with her saliva. Finally, she took the meaty flesh into her mouth, slowly working her way down.

"That's good, baby," he whispered.

Her pussy tightened at the praise and she inched more of him in, carefully breathing through her nose to avoid gagging.

"Yes," Kit groaned.

His hands hovered over her head, but he didn't take control and she appreciated it. His hips seesawed back and forth.

"You have to stop, Kara."

She ignored him. He was close, his dick throbbing against her tongue.

"Kara."

The warning in his voice was unmistakable. Reaching for his hard sacs, she squeezed them and slipped her pinkie into the crack of his ass.

Kit growled. Long strings of cum spurted into her

mouth, and she eagerly swallowed as much as possible, loving the taste of his essence. Finally, she released him. Leaning against the coffee table, she took a moment to regain her breath.

"How am I supposed to fuck you, now?" he asked, keeping his eyes closed.

Kara laughed. "I'm sure I can find you something else to do in the meanwhile."

He glanced down at her. "Don't worry, I have my own ideas. You've got a little something there."

Kit pointed to her chin. Keeping her gaze on him, Kara swept the remnants of his seed with her index finger and sensually licked it clean. His nostrils flared.

"My turn."

Faster than she'd imagined for a man who'd just orgasmed, he picked her up. She shrieked and involuntarily kicked her books and the glass of water, sending them flying in all directions.

"My books," she cried out.

Kit placed her on her feet and she ran to the kitchen to grab some paper towels.

Chapter Eleven

While Kara went to the kitchen, Kit hurried to collect her scattered books. Fortunately, water had spared all of her books, except one. He picked it up. A few drops had blurred the ink of what appeared to be an agenda but the words still stood out to mock him. He clenched his jaw.

September 15th. Flight to Paris. 12 AM.

If he hadn't already orgasmed, he was sure his dick would have shriveled. For a moment, he thought it was merely a holiday but the words *hello new life* occupied most of the page and even through the wetness, were still legible.

Kara was leaving. Starting a new life in Europe. Kit shut the book with a snap. She was still keeping information from him.

"Are they wet? Please tell me they're okay." She returned, waving paper towels. Kit handed her the agenda.

"This one got a little water on it, but the rest are fine," he said. "Here."

Taking some towels from her, he dried the hardwood floor and took the chance to cool down. She wasn't his yet. This encounter was merely to get off and for her to be able to study. He knew her exams were important but so was their relationship. He clenched his teeth. No wonder she didn't want to have anything to do with him. She was leaving. Kit breathed heavily through his nose. *Patience. You're jumping to conclusions.* Maybe she had a perfectly good explanation, or perhaps it was a holiday. *Hello new life.* Bullshit. Taking in a deep breath, he made up his mind. He'd give her one last chance to explain.

Getting to his feet, he noticed she hadn't moved and was staring down at her open agenda.

"Is it ruined?"

Kara jumped and looked at him. A panicked gaze crossed her eyes. "Yes. It's fine. Here, give me that."

She snatched the used papers from his hands and headed to the kitchen. Kit narrowed his eyes. She knew what he'd seen. Would she speak about it? He watched her in the kitchen, nervously rummaging through the cabinets.

"Would you like some more water?" she called.

"No. I want you to come here so I can lick your cunt."

She froze and turned to face him, eyes wide.

"Are you frightened?"

He watched her chest rise as she took a deep breath.

"No."

She returned to the living room, head high and shoulders squared, daring him to bring up what he'd seen. Kit wrapped his hands around her waist and drew her in for a kiss. He wasn't gentle, pouring all his frustrations into the moment.

You're mine, little owl. Mine.

She melted against him, her arms locking around his neck and her body searching for his heat. Kit reached between them, cupping her pussy. He groaned.

"You're so damn hot. How fast do you think I can make you come?"

"In less than a minute," she declared, rubbing against him like a cat in heat. His cock twitched, already returning to life.

"I say thirty seconds flat."

"Another bet?" A smile played on her kiss-stung

lips and her lust-filled gaze dipped.

"No, just some fun." Gently coaxing her onto the couch, he spread her legs, exposing her to his gaze. His eagle soared hard and fast against him and he grunted. All in due time.

"I want you to count," he told her.

"What?"

He slid his index finger over her slit and she moaned.

"Count, little owl. One Mississippi, two Mississippi."

"Kit, this is—"

"You want to come, don't you?"

He teased her opening with the tip of his thumb.

"One Mississippi," she said.

"Good girl."

He pushed his index finger inside her, rotating it and then pulling out.

"More."

"Count."

"Three Mississippi."

Kit entered her again. He fingered her slowly, enjoying the view of her body splayed out for him and the way her juices dripped down the crack of her ass. Maneuvering them around, he placed her legs on his shoulders and pressed his face to her pussy. Kara gasped loudly.

"Five Mississippi."

He licked her from top to bottom, groaning at the tangy taste. His cock lengthened.

"Don't stop counting."

"Si-six. Kit, please."

He flicked her clit with the tip of his tongue and circled it slowly.

"Oh God."

"Seven," he spoke against her folds.

"Eight," she murmured, rocking her hips.

Kit chuckled. He traced her lips, teased her hole, and returned to toy with her clit. Kara bucked. Pressing two fingers into her, he began to fuck her.

"Number, Kara."

"Twelve."

Suddenly, he withdrew his fingers and replaced them with his mouth. He lapped at her juices and fucked her with his tongue. Kara's moans turned louder and urgent.

"Don't stop," he growled, swatting her ass.

She squealed.

"Fifteen."

"Sixteen," he corrected.

"Please, Kit. I need to come."

"I love hearing you beg, little owl, but I suppose you deserve your orgasm."

He easily slid three fingers into her, groaning at the pressure of her walls against them. His cock throbbed in anticipation. Kit pumped slowly into her, steadily gaining speed until her legs were shaking and a sheen of sweat glistened on her flesh.

"Thirty," he murmured.

Pressing the flat of his tongue against her clit, he grazed it with his teeth. Kara screamed and her pussy walls contracted, her orgasm rushing through her and flushing her flesh. Feathers sprouted at the base of her hairline, grazing her collarbone, her owl clearly wishing to be released. His throat clogged with emotion. How dare she still doubt their mating? Kit took a step back and stroked his cock. He was hard again, ready to fuck her and claim her, but he had to hold it. She had to tell him about Paris so they could build a future together.

"Fuck me, Kit," she said, huskily. "I want to feel

your cock inside me."

"I could. You're wet and open. I'd fit perfectly."

She sat up, brow furrowed. "So why don't you?"

"What's in France?"

"You read my agenda."

"It fell open on that page. Kara, just tell me about it. I'm your mate."

She scowled. "No. It's none of your business."

"Then I'm leaving."

He shrugged and swallowed his sigh of frustration. Why did she have to be so difficult?

"You know? You're all, tell me this, tell me the other, but you won't give me any information about yourself."

He stopped picking up his clothes and looked at her. "All you need to do is ask, babe."

For a moment, she appeared shocked. She quickly recovered, replacing her features with a mask of indifference.

"I don't because I don't care, just as you shouldn't care about me. You don't know me. You only want to fuck me."

Kit laughed. "I believe you were the one who called me."

"It's the stupid mating, which is nothing more than an urge to have sex. My owl likes you and that's it."

"Of course." He quickly redressed.

"But I've had my orgasm, so you know what? You can walk out and never come back."

He watched her shrug on her robe and wrap it tightly around herself as if it were some kind of protective shield. Stomping to the door, she threw it open.

"Get out."

Kit stopped at the threshold. She turned her cheek

away. He chuckled.

"Do you really think it works like that, little owl? That I'll walk out and you'll never see me again? Granted, I don't know much about mating, but I know one thing, Kara. This isn't just some random hookup. There's no other woman for me and there never will be. If you'd open up to me, you'd see how good we can be together."

She finally faced him. "Leave."

He shook his head. "As you wish. You have my number."

Chapter Twelve

Kara weaved around the tables, scanning to see if she could take anything to the kitchen. So far, she'd managed not to drop anything at work, but honestly, it was just a matter of time. She was jumpy and tired.

After Kit left, she'd slept a bit, but woken soon after with a pit in her stomach and a deep-seated ache in her chest. She'd interpreted it as hunger and cooked something, which had ended at the bottom of the trash can.

If she weren't careful, her thoughts would stray to him. She could still smell him, taste him, and envision him standing in front of her in all his naked glory. She yearned for his heat, pined for his presence. It unnerved her. She didn't need anyone. For goodness sake, she was moving to another country so she could fulfill her dreams. She wasn't going to stay behind for some random dude just because it brought tears to her eyes every time she thought about not seeing him again.

No.

She'd get over him, just like she'd gotten over her sadness at saying goodbye to her family.

The biggest problem she had right now was her relentless arousal. Two hours after her orgasm, her owl had started jittering and flooding her mind with images of them together.

Kara sighed.

If only he wouldn't make everything so difficult. Why couldn't he be like other guys? A quick fuck and they would be done. Uh-uh. Kit wanted to know her better so he invented stupid games in which she always lost. It was terribly unfair. Her only consolation was that he wasn't getting any sexual gratification out of it. Well, except for the blowjob she'd given him. Her mouth filled with the memory of his taste and she pressed her lips into a thin line. She'd enjoyed every minute of it.

"Hey, you okay?" Jay, the sous-chef, tapped her on the shoulder.

She smiled at the young man with green eyes and dirty-blond hair. Jay was friendly and easygoing, not high-strung and obsessive. Why couldn't Kit be more like the coyote shifter?

"Yeah, I'm fine. Just a bit tired. You know, exams and stuff."

"Ugh, that's something I don't miss. You were studying business, right?"

"Yes," she lied.

"Tough degree." He shook a whipped cream can and topped the chocolate ice cream. "Good luck."

"Thanks," she said. At this rate, she'd need it.

"Dessert table five," he called out.

"Mine."

Kara placed the items on her tray and returned to the main room. Her breath stuck in her lungs and for a moment, the room spun. He was here.

Her owl screeched in joy. Kara chewed on the inside of her cheek, battling with the turmoil of emotions assaulting her. The items on her tray teetered dangerously.

"Work first," she muttered.

She'd serve her dishes and afterward she'd figure out what to do next. She crossed the room, heat creeping up her body at every step. He was watching her.

The moment she fulfilled her order, she searched for him. He sat at the bar, unabashedly staring at her. He'd braided his Mohawk, which made his eyes stand out and gave him a perilous look. Hi colorful ink peeked brighter than ever from beneath the sleeves of a gray shirt she was confident was too small for him. Her breath quickened and her owl pecked at her heart, sending sharp pangs traveling across her torso.

"Stop it," she muttered.

The fact he was here wasn't romantic. It bordered on stalker behavior, especially when she'd told him repeatedly she wanted nothing to do with him. Curling her hands into fists, she stomped in his direction.

"What are you doing here?" she hissed, standing so close she didn't miss the spark in his eyes when they made contact with hers.

"Having a drink," he replied, lifting his glass.

"Couldn't you have it somewhere else?"

"I happen to like Moon Point. It's the best shifter joint in the area."

"It's also where I work."

Slowly, his lips curved into a mocking stance. "That's none of my business," he said.

Kara's jaw dropped. She fished her brains for some kind of retort, but her mind drew a blank. Her owl banged against her ribs, wings tickling her insides and claiming her attention.

Kiss him.

No.

Kiss him.

Her gaze dropped to his lips. Smooth, firm, with a slight indentation on the bottom bow, they were far from perfect. They tasted heavenly. Her nerve endings tingled. She swayed forward.

Kiss him.

His mouth parted.

"Asshole," she said instead.

His laughter resonated in her ears even as she swerved away from the kitchen and into the bathroom.

She went into a stall, locked the door, and sat on the toilet. Sticking her fist into her mouth, she stifled a scream. Between the animal within her and him, she was bound to go crazy.

She stared at the teeth marks on her hand. It would have been so easy to give in to him.

Mate.

Her owl reminded her.

A stranger who had come to rob her of her dreams. A threat.

You don't know that.

It was what Mom did with Dad. She wouldn't let the same thing happen to her. After standing up, she unlocked the door and washed her hands. She combed back her hair and stared at her reflection in the mirror.

"You've got this, Kara."

He was at the bar, so she wouldn't have to deal with him. She'd pretend he wasn't there. The corners of her mouth dropped. Why did she feel it'd be easier said than done?

Chapter Thirteen

Kara didn't even look toward the bar when she emerged from the bathroom. She didn't have to. Kit sat at the table previously occupied by the couple she had served dessert to.

"What did you do with the customers who were sitting here?"

"Absolutely nothing." Kit sipped at his drink. "Apparently, they had to leave. They mentioned something about a trip to Europe, but they wouldn't elaborate."

Kara glared at him.

"They paid their bill though, including a tip." He nodded toward the one hundred dollar bill sitting under one of the glasses.

"So extorting me is not enough, now you also bribe people."

"You're so dramatic," Kit said. "I merely wanted to eat something and enjoy another drink. Is that a crime?"

"It should be," she muttered.

Kit's eyebrows shot up. "Do you think this is any way to treat a customer?"

"I'm actually being nice," she replied.

He chuckled. "How do I get you to be *really* nice?"

"By leaving."

"Not happening. I actually wanted to order some food. When I can't fuck, I get peckish, don't you?"

"What do you want, Kit?" She clenched her jaw.

Kit grinned. "Have I touched a sore spot?"

Kara didn't reply.

"All right, I won't dig into it. Since owl is apparently not on the menu, I'll have some mac n' cheese."

She pursed her lips.

"And to drink?"

"Another beer will be great. Thank you, Kara."

Giving him a brief nod, she swept around and marched back to the kitchen. Frustration gnawed at her insides, mingling with unspent desire and her owl's restless mating call. How much longer could she take this? Kara hung her head. She needed a few hours to herself so she could think and reevaluate. She wouldn't give up France, but perhaps they could come up with an alternative. Anything to keep the intensity of her emotions at bay.

Somehow, she managed to serve Kit and continue about her work regardless of his scrutiny. Midnight was fast approaching when the heat of his gaze vanished. Unable to stop herself, she looked toward where he'd been sitting. His chair was empty. She grabbed her apron, wringing it in her hands to hide their sudden quaking.

"Hey, Gile, where'd the guy sitting at that table go?" she asked the bartender.

"The hottie with the Mohawk?"

Kara nodded.

"He headed to the back with Lee."

"Oh."

She let out a breath she hadn't been aware of holding. What was wrong with her? She wanted to stay away but as soon as he actually left, she panicked. Stupid owl. She chewed on the inside of her cheek. She had to put a stop to all this.

"Focus, Kara."

Forcing herself to move, she cleaned up his

dishes and continued her shift. She was in the kitchen when Lee walked in.

"Kara, are you staying tonight?" her boss asked her.

"Yes," she replied. Because home meant memories of their time together. Surreptitiously, she tried to look behind her boss.

"If you're looking for Kit, he's left," Lee said.

"No, I wasn't looking for him, just making sure all the tables are clean."

Lee smirked but didn't comment.

Kara sagged against the wall. Who was she fooling?

Chapter Fourteen

Turning off the light in the dining hall, Kara made her way to Lee's office. Light filtered through the crack in the doorway. Her owl swooped and her heart hammered fast. He was here. Slowly, she opened the door.

"Hi, little owl."

She dragged in a breath at the sight of Kit. He sat behind Lee's desk, bare feet propped up and biceps glistening beneath the white glow of the lamps. He placed his hands behind his head, throwing more muscles into display. Her pussy moistened. Would this ever stop?

"What are you doing here?" she whispered. "And why are you shirtless?"

"I was waiting for you and I went flying. I needed to think."

"About what?"

"Us," he said.

"Didn't I tell you I wanted nothing to do with you? To leave me alone."

"You did, but you're a poor liar and I'm stubborn. A lethal combination."

"I wasn't lying."

"Perhaps not at first, but you are now."

Kara swallowed. Was she that transparent?

Kit smiled smugly. "In any case, you said you needed to study and you couldn't think when you're horny, so I want to help you."

"How's that? By bringing me to the brink and leaving me strung?"

Kit smirked.

"No, not anymore, my little owl. I've realized

how important your studies are for you and I wouldn't be able to forgive myself if I stood in the way of your dreams."

She narrowed her eyes.

"What do you get out of this?"

"Your happiness."

"That's it?"

Kit chuckled. "I'm hoping you'll accept our mating by the time I'm done with you." He grinned confidently.

"And if I'm not?"

"Then I'll help you this week and leave."

"Help me this week?" she echoed.

"You really do think this will just go away after we have sex." He put his feet on the ground and leaned over the table, clapping his hands together. "This isn't transitory, Kara. You'll cool down after we fuck, but for a whole week? And without mating?" His lips quirked. "Our birds are desperate to be with each other. This is just to appease them, a placebo of sorts."

Kara swallowed. Under normal circumstances, she would have refused but she couldn't. She wanted Kit. Every inch of her body craved his touch until she couldn't think. Besides, he was giving her what she wanted. Sex and the possibility to move on after her exams. Slowly, she nodded.

"You've got a deal," she said.

Chapter Fifteen

Kit smiled. The tension in his body dissipated, replaced with a boundless desire. His mate had said yes. His eagle soared, ecstatic, and he felt the familiar tug before shifting.

Easy.

She'd said yes to sex and yes to keeping him close for a week, but she hadn't accepted their mating yet. He stood up and offered her his hand.

No matter. That would come soon enough.

She slid her hand into his bigger palm, and he tugged her into his arms, bending her backward so he could devour her mouth. She didn't resist, arching against him with a moan that had his already hard dick turning into stone.

"Next time, I'll take things more slowly," he murmured, nuzzling her ear while slipping his hands under her shirt and bra. "Now, I just want to be inside you."

"Yes."

Untangling herself from his arms, she made quick work of her clothes. Kit's breath caught.

"Let me see how wet you are," he said. Running his fingertips across her thigh, he coaxed her legs open and cupped her pussy. "You're already soaked."

"You've made sure to keep me hot and bothered all night," she said. "I could feel your gaze." She placed her palms on his chest, flexing her fingers across his pecs. Pleasure raced across him. His mate was touching him, caressing him intimately.

"I watched you and imagined this," he said. "Me, fucking you atop Lee's desk, just like you'd fantasized about." He picked her up and set her on the table.

Rotating two fingers inside her vagina, he spread them.

"I don't want foreplay, Kit. I want this." She tugged the hem of his jeans with one hand and grabbed his aching dick with the other. Kit groaned.

"And I'm going to give it to you, babe."

Quicker than he'd ever done so, he was rid of his jeans and kicked them aside. His cock curved upward, the mushroom head red and angry, desperate to be inside his woman. He grabbed the condom he'd prepared in case his mate accepted his terms.

"You were expecting me to say yes," Kara said.

"I wasn't sure, but it never hurts to be ready." He tore the package.

"Wait." Kara clutched his arm. "Are you clean?"

He nodded.

"Me too. And I'm on the pill." She ran her fingertips across his length, stroking it gently. "I want to feel you inside me, like you promised." She circled his waist with her legs, drawing him closer. "Stretching me, filling me."

Kit groaned.

"Are you sure?"

"Positive." She rubbed her folds against him, making his cock slick with her juices. Kit pulled her into a sitting position and kissed her hard. Placing the head of his cock at her entrance, he entered her, inch by glorious inch. His eyes almost rolled to the back of his head at the tight squeeze of her cunt. Her nails dug into his arms and he forced himself to stop.

"Am I hurting you? Am I going too fast, little owl?"

"No. Don't stop," she mewled, moving her hips. "It feels so good."

"Yes."

Firmly, he thrust the rest of his shaft into her.

Kara gasped, her body bowing upward. Kit savored the moment. He was fully seated inside his mate, her pussy tightly wrapped around him. Slowly, he drew back. Kara moaned.

"Fuck me hard, Kit."

Her lust-filled gaze beckoned him to do as she asked. He started to thrust into her, gradually picking up speed and watching in awe as feathers sprouted at the nape of Kara's neck.

"Admit it, little owl," he growled, digging his hands into her locks. He slowed his movements. His vision shifted and he knew his own animal was making its presence known. "We're mates."

Kara swallowed. Reaching up to him, she cupped his cheek.

"Yes," she gasped. "You're my mate."

At the confession, Kit erupted, ecstasy both emotional and physical crashing against him like a tidal wave. His mate.

****

Kara sat on his lap, her head resting on his shoulder, her breathing slow and steady, though the feathers on her neck hadn't disappeared. Kit brushed a kiss on her shoulder and she shivered. He nuzzled her neck, inhaling her fragrance and branding it into his heart. He wanted more, but as of that moment, he was content just to hold her close.

"Kit," she said at length. He cracked his eyes open. The urgency in her voice was unmistakable, though she didn't look at him.

"I'm going to Toulouse in France. I have an internship lined up. It's my dream."

"I understand."

"No, no, you don't. This, us, it can't happen."

"Why?"

"Because I'm moving abroad, far away from here."

"So? I'll move with you."

Kara pulled away from his embrace. Her large eyes searched his face. "You can't do that. You can't give up your family, friends, job, dreams, for a woman you've just met."

"Why not?"

"Because, well—" She chewed on her bottom lip. "It's what my dad did for my mom. He had aspirations and when they mated, it all went to hell." Kara shook her head. "It's wrong."

Kit cupped his mate's cheek.

"Kara, did you ever ask your dad if he was unhappy?"

"No, but—"

Kit raised an eyebrow.

"He wanted to be an astronomer and she wouldn't let him, just like the selfish bitch didn't want me to study engineering." Kara clapped her hand over her mouth. "I'm sorry."

"There's nothing to be sorry about." He ran his thumb across her lips. "I'm actually pretty thrilled that you're finally opening up to me. I probably should have fucked you sooner."

Kara narrowed her eyes and slapped his arm. "Yes, you should have, but I'm not opening up to you. I can't, Kit. We have to keep this thing superficial. Just sex. Strangers having sex."

Kit threw his arms up and groaned.

"You still don't get it, do you, little owl? You are not a stranger to me. Sure, I don't know what you have for breakfast or what your favorite book is, but I know what's in here." He pointed to her heart. "Mating is primal and urgent but it happens when two animals recognize a soulmate, a kindred spirit in another person. You are strong, independent, a fighter, a survivor, like me. You are full of hopes and ambitions for the future. You are what I have always dreamed of, little owl." Kit sighed. "You know, when we met, you asked me if I thought you were a damsel in distress and this might, er, emasculate me in your eyes, but the truth is, I'm the one who needed saving. I've been yearning for my soulmate ever since I discovered you could be out in the world somewhere. I had all but given up, living a frantic lifestyle in which I searched for ways to substitute the hole in my heart. I was missing you. I've felt more alive these two days than I have in years."

Kara's gaze softened. "Is that why you have nothing tattooed over your heart?"

Kit smiled. "You see? You know me even if you think you don't. Yes, I was waiting for the right design." He brushed his lips across hers. "It'll be an owl."

"But France, Kit. I'm not going to give it up."

"Have I asked you to?"

She stalled.

"No," she said softly.

"And I won't. I respect you, Kara. You had a dream long before I came along. It'd be pretty shitty of me to ask you to throw it out the window."

"My mom—"

"I'm not her, babe. Besides, I've always wanted to go to Europe."

"But what will you do?"

"Don't worry, little owl, I'm resourceful."

She opened her mouth, then shut it.

Kit laughed.

"Run out of excuses to push me away?"

"I guess so," she admitted.

Kit raised his arms in celebration. "About time,

because my next tactic was to fuck you silly until you begged me to go with you to France."

"I think you should try that anyway." Her eyes twinkled mischievously. Kit nuzzled her neck, relishing her intake of breath.

"You don't need to ask twice, my precious little owl."

Epilogue

The sun was barely awake, its rays little more than splashes of yellow and pink mingling with drifting blues. They walked in silence, hands firmly entwined. A crisp wind caressed Kit's scalp and he took in a deep breath, inhaling the blend of oak and pine, earth, and water. The sound of birds waking up from their slumber echoed alongside the murmur of a nearby river. Excitement coursed through him. This was it.

"Are you ready?" he asked.

"More than ever," Kara replied. She glanced at him. Her eyes were bright, her skin flushed. "I've been looking forward to this."

Kit wrapped his arm around her waist, bringing her closer. She leaned on him.

"I've been waiting for this moment since I met you," Kit said.

They continued to walk in silence, leaves crunching beneath their sneakers as they made their way deeper into the forest.

"Here," Kara declared, running toward a bubbling stream. She glanced upward. "Look at the sky. It's both night and day. You can see some stars but the sun is chasing them away."

Kit didn't follow her gaze. He kept his eyes on his mate. A radiant glow seemed to envelop her and already he could see feathers interspersed with her hair.

"My beautiful, little owl," he murmured, unable to keep his voice from cracking with emotion.

Kara smiled at him. Her eyes shimmered. He spread his arms and she stepped into his embrace. Placing her palms on his chest, she stood on her toes and kissed him lightly.

"I love you, Kit," she said.

His stomach fluttered and his pulse raced as it did every time she pronounced those three words.

"I love you too, Kara."

Beaming, no doubt radiating his own sense of peace and happiness, she slipped out of her coat, dress, and shoes.

"Catch me if you can," she said, winking.

Transfixed, he watched her shift. Her petite frame reducing itself into an even smaller size, her bones and muscles realigning, transforming into a cute, brown owl. It hooted at him and took to the skies.

"Run, little owl, because you know I'm going catch you and make you mine for good."

Quickly, Kit removed his clothes and shifted. He flew high, taking advantage of the clearing. Kara watched him from a branch, her large eyes taking in every one of his moves as he swooped and dove, courting her. Abruptly, she screeched and ascended. Kit streaked ahead and pitched. Turning her back to him, Kara presented her talons. He took them with his own, locking them. Together as one, they cartwheeled through the sky, plummeting to the ground at an alarming rate. However, just when they were about to crash, they broke apart.

Kit landed first. Shifting into his human form, he lay on the grass, grinning from ear to ear. Kara followed him, alighting on his belly. Hooting once more, the little owl shook and shifted.

Laughing, Kit tangled his fingers in her hair and brought her down for a kiss.

"You're mine, now," he whispered against her lips.

Kara tugged at his bottom lip. "Permanently," she agreed.

The End

MAKE HER PURR

Sam Crescent and Stacey Espino

Chapter One

It was too early for a fight.

Titus picked up his pace, running through the familiar, old-growth forest. His paws barely made a sound as he raced on all fours to the source of the commotion. The thoughts of his packmates clouded his head, one of the many annoyances of being Alpha.

"What's the problem?" he asked as he neared. Many of his wolves had made a ring around the threat. As Alpha, it was his call to finish the job.

He pushed his way through the others, emerging in the center of the ring.

A human?

She was half-naked, her long, pale hair tangled around her arms as she lay in the dirt.

"Is this your threat?" He scoffed, turning to his beta for clarification.

"She's on our territory. Every human's a threat," said Axel.

He growled his displeasure. Barely sunrise and he

had to deal with this shit? *"A human girl in the middle of nowhere? No visible weapons. She's not a damn threat."*

"So, you're telling me she hiked for hundreds of miles on her own. Without even a backpack?"

Titus turned back around to examine the girl again. A few weeks ago, they'd had to deal with an unruly group of drunken hunters. It hadn't ended well for those men. But it had been the first human sighting in years. Their territory was so far off the grid, amid dense rainforest and steep mountain ranges, that they rarely had to deal with trespassers. Their only concerns were rival packs and the occasional bear trying to throw its weight around.

The human peered up at him, her entire body trembling from fear or the cold, he wasn't certain. He breathed in her scent. Those big blue eyes did a number on him, ripping open his armor and leaving him vulnerable.

"Are you going to kill her or do you want me to do it?" asked Axel.

He left the ring, his heart racing, his wolf agitated yet never more focused. That scent. The human was his mate. Titus shifted into his skin, stretching out his muscles and running both hands through his unkempt hair. It had been months since he'd shifted.

A human? What the fuck did that mean? He was forty-three and had expected to find his fated mate over a decade ago, but tried not to focus on it as the years kept passing. The woman he imagined bonding with was a she-wolf, one worthy to take her place by his side in the pack.

He didn't know how to deal with this new revelation.

"Boss?" Axel had shifted into his skin, a look of concern on his face.

"What?"

"Want me to kill her?"

Despite his confusion, one thing had never been clearer. No one touched his mate.

"She's not to be harmed. Bring her back to the camp."

His beta threw his arms up. "Back to our camp? She's a worthless human. End this now."

"Since when do I take orders from you? If one hair on her head is out of place, you'll answer for it." Titus returned to the ring, his wolves baring their fangs at the girl ... his mate. He had to remember how to act as a human, how to converse and behave. Although he was a shifter, split between two worlds, he'd never embraced his human side as other shapeshifters had. The Black Rock Creek Pack had always inhabited the harshest expanse of wilderness, going back for generations. It was survival of the fittest, and he knew never to show weakness, not even within his own pack. The fact made him worry for his mate. The little human wouldn't be accepted. And it would be a full-time job keeping her safe from all the forest predators.

"What's your name?" he asked.

Her voice was barely a whisper, soft and feminine. "Lilly."

"I'm called Titus. Where did you come from?"

She shifted into a sitting position, the rags she wore barely covering her full tits. "I was traveling with a group but got separated weeks ago. I've been surviving on berries and roots." Lilly looked around at the wolves, her lower lip quivering. "Please don't let them hurt me."

He bent down and tilted her chin up. She was breathtaking, and all he could think about was fucking her. "You're safe with me. I'm taking you to my camp. We have more than enough food and supplies for you."

She touched his leg as he attempted to walk away. "I'm scared. Please don't go."

Titus planned to let his pack handle her so he could get his thoughts together. There was so much to think about, and his emotions were getting the better of him. After all these years, the gods had sent him a woman. He felt blessed and cursed all at once. She's wasn't a she-wolf, but he'd deal with it. His entire life was devoted to Lilly now.

****

Lilly wrapped herself around Titus's arm as they hiked through the forest. It was hard and thick with muscle. The wolves had scattered in different directions, but she knew they were close and watching.

"Are you hungry?" he asked.

She nodded.

"We have plenty of meat. You'll never be hungry again."

She expected to wake up from a dream. This was way too easy. Worst-case scenario, she expected the Alpha of the Black Rock Creek Pack to try to kill her, and at best, she hoped they'd lead her to their camp. But Titus had taken a liking to her, looking at her like a man possessed. She wondered if he was acting and leading her into a trap. Or had her flirtation actually paid off?

"I don't know what I would have done if you hadn't found me," she said, holding his arm a little tighter. Never mind tracking, she should get an Oscar for her performance.

He growled and the sound traveled all the way down to her clit. She wasn't supposed to have feelings for the enemy. But the enemy wasn't supposed to be ripped to fucking perfection with dark eyes that tore down all her barriers. The Hawthorn Clan had sent her to find their missing elder, and her plan to infiltrate Black

Rock Creek had gone better than planned.

She knew why they'd sent her. It wasn't just because she was one of the best trackers.

Lilly was disposable.

As one of the few unmated females in the pack, she was quickly ordered by her Alpha to find and retrieve their elder. He was a valuable asset, coveted by other shifters. Her Alpha believed he brought power to his pack, giving them strength and a leading edge. If a rival stole him away, they'd benefit from Oslow's power. She was ordered to get him back at any cost.

She remembered her Alpha's last words to her. "Bring Oslow back alive, or don't come home at all." Part of her wanted to tell him to fuck off. She could survive as an exile, and she had for most of her life. Even as a child the wolf pups wouldn't play with her. Adults barely tolerated her. Loneliness had always been her best friend. But she bit her tongue and followed orders, looking forward to the challenge and the chance to move up the ranks in the pack. She had something to prove, and the fact she was retrieving Oslow made it personal. He was the only wolf to treat her with kindness, standing up for her and teaching her hunting tactics when she was young. Now he was old and frail, and the only wolf in the pack who cared if she lived or died. She needed to find him and bring him home.

It was unpleasant traversing the forest with her delicate human feet. She craved to shift into her fur, not only for comfort, but to have her teeth and claws ready in case of trouble.

Her estimate wasn't too far off. They arrived at the camp less than an hour later.

"We live simply here, but you'll be cared for," said Titus. This pack really lived off the grid. There were no human structures, just a series of crude dens. They had a reputation for being cutthroat, one of the most lethal packs in the country. Other wolves rarely challenged them, and when they did, they never came out on top. She needed to find the elder and get out as soon as possible. It wouldn't take long for one of Titus's packmates to figure her out, no matter how good she was at playing human.

He motioned for her to enter a den, and she did as told, crawling in on her hands and knees. It smelled like him … the Alpha's den. Her body heated, her own traitorous desires distracting her from her mission.

"This is probably not what you're used to."

"It's nice," she said.

He sat next to her in the large den, the floor a thick bed of soft needles. "I'm not sure where to start," he said. "I never planned on any of this, but as soon as I scented you, I knew."

"Knew what?"

"That you're the only woman for me."

Holy shit. This couldn't be happening. The Alpha of the Black Rock Creek Pack was coming on to her. He probably wanted the novelty of fucking a human, but she still felt flattered by his attention. She needed to stay focused and carefully turn down his advances while trying to locate Oslow.

"You don't know me," she said.

"This isn't the city, Lilly. Things are different out here."

"What do you mean?"

"We don't date. We don't play games. Out here, we mate for life. There's only one female for us."

She giggled, trying to be cute. Alphas had an innate desire to protect and dominate, and she was going to use it to her advantage. "And you think I'm that mate?"

"I don't think, *I know*."

Lilly swallowed hard. He sounded sincere. Did her rival, the pack Alpha no less, actually think she was his fated mate? She wasn't falling for it. Her life had been a long series of disappointments. She'd learned one thing—she could only depend on herself, and she didn't need a man to feel complete. Being unmated at twenty-eight put her in an uncomfortable place in the pack. Other shifters treated her like she had an infectious disease, unable to understand why she lived alone on the outskirts of their camp. Getting too close to anyone only ended up badly, so she focused on becoming the best— hunting, tracking, and pack protection.

"What if I'm already married?"

He frowned. Titus took both her hands, examining her fingers. "No ring. Don't your males claim their women with rings?" His ignorance about humans was oddly endearing. Lilly had lived in both worlds and could blend as a woman or an animal.

"Sometimes."

His jaw twitched, and she wondered what he was thinking. "You were on my territory. I saved you from my wolves. I'm claiming you as mine."

Those words should be raising her hackles, instead her pussy pulsed and her heart pounded in her chest. Her inner beast wanted this, wanted him, but she knew better. She'd never be owned. Still, she played along for the sake of her mission.

"How can a human own wolves? Aren't they wild animals, impossible to tame?" As long as she was stalling, she'd have some fun with him.

"I guess I'm a good trainer."

"And you want me as a pet too?"

He took a deep breath, his large ribs expanding. Even though the den was a mix of shadows, his eyes were intense, staring at her with unblinking focus. "I want you for a lot of things, but not a pet. The gods sent you to me, I'm certain of it. That's why I found you in my woods. Do you feel anything for me, Lilly?"

She shrugged, tempted to play along, but knowing it would be her own undoing.

"I'll give you time. I'm a patient man."

Lilly pulled her hair over one shoulder, fiddling with the knots. She had to get alone so she could search for Oslow, but Titus wasn't budging.

He reached out and felt her hair. "Such a pretty yellow."

"It's called blonde," she said, unable to hide her smirk. She'd never met such feral shifters in her life.

"Is all the hair on your body the same?" He reached for the cotton shorts she was wearing, but she swatted his hand.

"You promised to be patient. That means no touching."

"But you're my mate." He leaned closer, his Alpha aura pulling her in. Was he going to kiss her? She was supposed to hate him and his entire pack. The Black Rock Creek Pack was the worst of the worst. They'd kidnapped their elder. But she'd be lying if she said she didn't crave to feel him pressed between her legs, his muscular body glistening in sweat as he fucked her like an animal.

"I need to get out of here." She bolted to her feet and rushed to the entrance of the den.

Chapter Two

Titus watched her leave his den purely to see her ass as she did. It was nice and plump and he couldn't wait to feel it nestled against him as he rode her pussy or after when she fell asleep in his arms. So many years of waiting, and he'd finally been blessed.

These feelings were shocking to him. He'd always dreamed of finding his mate. The scent he picked up around her was fucking incredible. Her human part, that was a little … tricky. He didn't want to hurt her and humans were so damn fragile.

His cock had never been this hard. The need to take her beneath him, spread her pretty thighs, and fill her tight cunt was so intense.

She's in danger.

He couldn't shake the feeling that she was scared, that she needed him.

Getting his head in the game, he climbed out of his den, which already had her scent lingering in, and came to a stop.

His pack had circled around her once again. *Fuckers.* Others stood by in their human forms. Lilly turned around, watching all of them. She looked petrified, but he also saw the determination in her gaze.

This woman.

This stranger.

She was a fighter.

A human surrounded by a pack of hungry wolves that wanted blood for her daring to come onto their land.

"Who are you?" Axel asked.

"I don't have to answer to you."

"You think you can come in here and just take our Alpha with your disgusting human pussy?" Danny, one of their strongest females, spat at her feet.

Lilly rolled her eyes and he didn't like how she seemed to be mocking them. She didn't understand that as a human there was no way for her to fight these people. They were all wolf shifters and she was a human who entered their pack.

"Enough!" He broke through the circle and crouched down with his back toward her. He kept his gaze on his pack.

"You're seriously going to allow this human access to our pack, to our way of life?" Axel asked. "If you're going to keep her alive, she should be in a cage."

Out of all of the men, Axel had always been closest to him. There had been a time he considered him a friend but just of late, Axel had proven his thirst for leading, for wanting to take over. To make this pack his own.

This pack was one of the most feared because Titus didn't have an agenda. He wasn't cruel to his people, nor did he go on the offensive. But he would protect his land and his pack with no mercy. Glancing toward Sean and Anna, a new couple in the pack, he noted they weren't hissing or glaring at his mate. They stood on the sidelines, looking, waiting.

Axel had a thing for Anna, but it hadn't been reciprocated, and because Titus approved of the relationship, Axel had been seriously pissed off. Every decision he made, Axel tried to overturn.

His friend and beta was starting to wear on his last nerve. The mating call was clear, and Titus knew that firsthand now. His beta was acting like a prepubescent pup.

In recent years, the power Axel had as beta had gone to his head. His friend needed to remember who was Alpha of their pack.

"She needs to be destroyed," one of the pack yelled.

"She could lure other humans here," another cried out. "They'll destroy us all."

He listened as they all started to yell at him.

They stank of fear.

The same fear that Axel had instilled in them. Without a strong, fearless leader, they had no hope.

"You will not kill her. Or harm her." He stood up tall, letting them all see his strength.

Killing Axel wouldn't be a hardship.

It would be so fucking easy, but he didn't want that.

He'd trained Axel, but the cocky bastard was power-hungry.

He wouldn't allow Axel to even think he could win. But he'd give him a chance to alter his ways. Hoped he'd have a change of heart.

"She's my mate," Titus said, letting his words sink in. The words seemed to echo through the forest canopy. Silence settled over the camp. It was unheard of—a wolf mating a human.

As a collective, they took a step back.

"If you hurt her, I'll consider that a personal threat, and you'll have to take me on. To fight against me. Are you willing to let that happen after all I've done for you?" He paused, letting them think about all the times he'd saved them. How he'd made their pack strong, fearless. They never had to worry about anyone or anything and that was because of him and his ancestors.

"No!" Axel's hand slashed through the air. He'd remained standing so close. Too close.

Titus made sure to stay between him and Lilly.

There was no way that Axel would take his woman or demand he cut her loose. Not after all the years he'd put off finding her for the sake of his pack.

They all knew he'd waited long and hard, forever putting the pack first.

"You choose a human over us?" Axel's voice rose so all could hear. "They are forever getting closer, determined to wipe us out with their technology. They'll kill us all given the chance, and you're going to take a human female as a mate?"

****

Okay, Lilly thought her pack was bad, but this was so much worse. The way the beta kept on back-talking and trying to instill fear from nothing was unreal. She watched him closely, seeing the insanity lurking behind his eyes, and her beast wasn't happy.

They all thought she was a human, which simply … irritated her now. Especially as she'd never been a human.

She was one hundred percent shifter, just not a wolf breed. They clearly all lived in the dark ages if they thought she wasn't a shifter.

There was no way she'd have survived this long and this deep in the fucking forest if she'd been a pathetic human. They had no idea what they were dealing with.

Humans were … animals.

She'd had a run in with them many years ago when she'd been a young shifter and loved exploring. Lilly had stumbled onto a human camp and they'd hunted her, shooting at her. It had been the scariest five hours of her life.

As an adult, she'd adapted and embraced her human side to benefit her pack. She could easily blend in to human society for supplies, information, and to understand their customs. If they stayed in the dark ages, only living feral, it would be to their downfall.

One thing she learned—she'd choose life as a shifter any day. There was no way she'd ever be cruel like humans were. She only wished her pack was more accepting of her, but she was a misfit, and that wasn't going to change.

She'd ventured far from everything she knew to find the elder her pack loved so much. He was special to her in so many ways. Studying Titus's pack, she saw they were all struggling with Axel's demands. This wasn't good.

She couldn't let them know what she was.

If they didn't have the elder, then she intended to leave. Glancing around at the group, she saw them all staring at her with fear and uncertainty.

The last thing she wanted to do was hurt them. They were just as innocent to human ways as their Alpha, and she didn't fault them for that. It was almost refreshing.

The beta was different. She sized him up. He was clearly strong, but she believed she could take him. Why was he so uptight?

Relax.

Show fear.

Be human.

Don't give them reason to think you're anything different.

She was good at trying to fit in. It was the story of her life. Being a wild cat in a pack of wolves was a special kind of hell. The Alpha female had pity on the abandoned cub, taking her in, and over the years she'd been … tolerated. She still felt alone every day of her life.

While she had no location on the elder, she'd have to blend in. To pretend to be human. What she did next went against everything inside her. She was a fighter. Growing up in a pack of wolves, she had to be. No one allowed for weakness and as she sank to her knees, placing her hands in the dirt, and forced tears to her eyes, she tried to remember this was for a good reason.

"Please don't kill me." She tried to appear submissive. Every single part of her wanted to kill this piece-of-shit beta. He didn't deserve to be by Titus's side. Her own thought surprised her. She came here already hating Titus, but he was already growing on her.

She scented the anger within Axel, the blind rage.

"I will do anything, but please don't kill me." She kept her forehead pressed to the earth, hoping that they would ignore her. That they'd pretend to never have seen her, but one glance at Axel, and something didn't sit right with her.

She'd stay with this pack for as long as it was necessary because she couldn't go home without Oslow.

Titus bent down next to her. He inhaled her scent.

"Get up, my queen." He gripped the back of her neck, not tightly, but tenderly. They stood, and he pulled her against his side. "If any of you think to take Lilly from me, then you're going to have to come through me. This is my choice, not yours. I will not have any harm come to her. Do you understand?"

They all nodded and even Axel took a step back.

She found that interesting.

Without another word, Titus turned and walked her away from the crowd.

"Is it safe?" she asked.

"Of course it's safe. You're with me. My pack won't give you any problems now."

"They're afraid of you?" She wanted to know more about this man who claimed to be her mate. Nothing could come of his claim. Her pack would never allow her to mate with a rival pack member.

And Titus didn't realize what she really was.

When he found out she wasn't human and not a she-wolf, he'd have a change of heart. Cats and wolves didn't mingle well. She knew that firsthand.

Even still, as he let her go, taking her hand, she couldn't help but admire his strength. He was gentle as he took hold of her. Part of her wanted to tell him he could be rough. She'd lived through a lot of broken bones in her life.

Pain was a friend to her. Something real.

They reached the edge of a low embankment and she released a gasp. There was a river just below, the water flowing with calm. It soothed her just watching it, and it sounded like the kind of lullaby she could fall asleep to at night.

"You've got a smell to you, mate." His cock was rock-hard but he didn't make a move to cover himself. "I won't bite, much. I promise." He winked at her.

Titus traversed down the river edge and walked into the water. The hard, defined muscles of his ass caught her attention.

Would it be so wrong of her to blend in?

To have a few days where she was simply this Alpha's mate? It was a fantasy, nothing more. It felt foreign to be wanted rather than living as the outcast. Why not indulge?

She'd never been a male's world before nor had anyone look at her with such hunger.

She loved his gaze on her. The way he seemed to caress her with his eyes. Whenever he looked at her, she knew without a doubt he wanted to do a whole list of dirty things, and what was more, she wanted it all.

The elder can wait.

We cannot.

Our people don't care about us.
It's why we're out here, unprotected.
They want us to fail.
They want to see us die.

Titus dipped beneath the water and seconds later broke the surface. He ran his fingers through his hair and smiled at her. Gods, he was stunning.

"Come on, baby. There're no sharks here."

She laughed and even as she was nervous revealing her body to him, she removed her clothes and padded toward the water. Stepping inside, she waited for Titus, who took her hand and pulled her in. This was like a dream.

Lilly wrapped her arms around his waist, staring into his eyes. His warm skin felt so good that she barely caught the purr before she emitted it. The last thing she wanted was for him to cast her out because of what she was.

She was being selfish right now, she knew that, but she didn't wish for this to stop.

After a lifetime of being looked at as a pariah, this was refreshing.

He held her close, his strong hands on her hips and waist. It soothed her to know that someone had her back.

"I've waited all my life for you, Lilly."

Her heart fluttered. "You have?" *Damn!* He was saying all the things she'd ever wanted to hear.

"So many nights I've laid awake, thinking about you, about finding you, claiming you, taking you as my own."

"And now?"

"I'm not ever going to let you go. I'll take care of you for the rest of our lives."

One of his hands sank into her hair, holding the

back of her head, but she didn't fight him as his lips touched hers. Instead, she closed her eyes, and for the first time in her life, she took the kiss that was so keenly offered.

Chapter Three

Titus had been driving himself crazy for the last few days. He had to tell his little human mate that he was a wolf. Would she be terrified? Want nothing to do with him? She was his ultimate weakness. But he'd be her strength, protect her from everything.

All he knew was that he'd never let her go. She'd have to learn to love him. The gods couldn't have gotten this wrong after so many years of waiting. A few times he'd build up the nerve to tell her, but she'd wander off again. She was a curious thing, forever exploring despite the dangers. Lilly said she needed time and space, so he didn't want to pressure her.

She hadn't questioned much, which was a relief for him. How would he explain why most of them didn't wear clothing or why they didn't live in human shelters? He wished he had paid more attention to human customs when he'd had the chance over the years.

At least Axel had kept his distance so far. In fact, Titus hadn't seen him since introducing Lilly to the pack. Hopefully he was thinking over his behavior and would come to his senses. Pack hierarchy had to be maintained at all costs. And Titus had no plans of stepping down from his position as Alpha.

Despite the unrest in his pack, he had to tell her the truth.

Today was the day.

They hadn't consummated their mating yet, and he didn't want the memory of that night tarnished with lies. He had to reveal his Alpha wolf to Lilly.

He followed her scent to the northern outskirts of their territory. Why had she come out this far on her own? There were too many threats in the forest for her to take off like this, so he needed to help her understand the danger when he found her. Humans may be on top in their cities, but they were at the bottom in the wilderness. He stopped when he couldn't find her, keeping still and listening to the sounds of the forest. She was near.

A dry leaf floated down from above. He looked up. Lilly was on a high branch looking at him, the wind picking up the tips of her long hair.

"How the hell did you get up there?"

She shrugged. "Just climbed."

"How?" The old-growth Douglas fir had no lower branches. It was impossible.

"I like to climb. Can you help me down?"

Wolves were not climbers, but he reached for her as she hung down from the branch and caught her as she fell. It felt amazing to have her back in his arms again.

He combed both his hands into her hair, holding her head steady. Titus stared into her blue eyes, mesmerized by his mate. All the she-wolves he'd known had dark hair and eyes. Lilly was unique. His treasure.

"Don't run off on your own. It's not safe."

"But I love the forest," she said.

"You're something else." He kissed her once on the lips. "Nothing like I expected."

She smiled. "And what did you expect?"

"Doesn't matter. You're more than I hoped for." This was it. He had to explain everything to her. "I'm not what you think I am," he said. "I'm different than you are. Haven't you noticed anything unusual about the way we live?"

"I guess."

He didn't let her go, terrified she'd bolt and want nothing to do with him. "First, I want you to know I'd never hurt you. Never."

"Okay."

He swallowed hard, then went for it. "I can change into a wolf. All of us can. We're a pack of shapeshifters."

She said nothing, only staring back into his eyes. He expected shock, fear ... something.

"Lilly?"

"Prove it," she said.

She continually amazed him. Titus backed up. "Remember, don't be afraid. My wolf loves you more than you can imagine." He commanded the shift to take over his body, his bones shifting, and fur replacing his human skin. Within seconds, he was a black Alpha wolf, the same one who'd first met her in the forest a few days earlier.

Titus walked around her, his wolf savoring its mate's scent. He licked her leg and she giggled instead of screaming. He took it as a good sign. When she ran her fingers into his fur, he growled low in his chest, his need to mate with her driving him crazy.

He shifted back into his skin where he had better control.

"That's it. That's my big secret, Lilly. There's nothing else."

"Well, I'd say that's a big one."

"Are you okay with it? You must have questions?" he asked, taking her hands in his. Titus couldn't read her. He was used to hearing everyone talking in his head as Alpha of his pack.

"How long have you known you're a wolf?"

"I was born this way, as was my father, my grandfather, and his father before him. Our pack goes back too many generations to count."

Sadness seemed to wash over her. "I have no family. No history. It's just me."

He traced her jaw with a finger. "You have me

now. Everything I am, everything I have is yours."

"I'm not a wolf. Why would you want a human mate?"

"I don't care what you are, Lilly. My wolf knew you were the one the second I scented you. The mating call can't be mistaken."

She pulled away from him. "You wouldn't say that if I wasn't a human. What if I was a bear or some animal other than a wolf? What if I was a cat?"

He tugged her shoulder, spinning her back around. "I wouldn't care. And you are human, so it doesn't matter. I'm completely devoted to you, Lilly. Unconditionally." Titus reached down and grabbed both her thighs, hoisting her against the tree. Standing between her legs, he nuzzled her neck. "If you'd allow me, I'd fuck you right here, mark you and make this official."

"No," she said. "Humans require a long courtship … weeks, months, or even years."

He scowled. How was he supposed to live side by side with his mate, the ultimate temptation, for years? "That's too long, Lilly."

She painted a line up his neck with the firm tip of her tongue, then shelled his ear. "I need more than a few days."

He closed his eyes and took a cleansing breath, trying to calm his beast. He'd never wanted anything more in his life. "How long, baby?"

"Soon. Just give me some space for a while. You've given me a lot to take in. I need to be alone, to think."

Titus set her down to her feet and nodded. "If that's what you need. Don't wander too far." He kissed her forehead once and then returned to the camp, leaving her alone. Hopefully she didn't decide mating with a wolf was a bad idea.

****

She'd been on the cusp of finding Oslow. And time was definitely running out. Titus wanted to make their mating official, but he had no clue she was a misfit wild cat from a rival pack. He thought he loved her unconditionally, but no such thing existed.

As soon as he was out of sight, she shifted back into her cat and continued her hunt. Oslow was so close she could taste it. She moved with stealth, so slow not even a leaf made a sound. Then she came upon it—a cave, an old bear den, and it was unguarded at the moment. The perfect opportunity for her to act. She rushed forward, her senses on high alert. Titus or his packmates could return at any time to check on their captive.

She shifted into her skin so she could talk to the old, gray wolf. Since she wasn't a she-wolf, she couldn't use telepathy like the others. "Oslow, it's me, Lilly." She fiddled with the latches on the iron cage he'd been held in. "You're going to head south, keep running, stay hidden. I won't be far behind. I'll find you and lead you back to the village." She released the final latch, and the gray wolf rushed out. "Quickly!" she called behind him.

Lilly leaned against the stony wall to calm her nerves. She'd done it. Oslow was free, but they weren't out of the woods yet. As soon as her enemies realized their prize was gone, they'd start the hunt. The Black Rock Creek Pack was faster and more experienced. They'd find Oslow within hours if she didn't lead him herself.

Once she returned to the village with Oslow, maybe her pack would finally show her some respect. Maybe she'd finally belong.

She walked out of the den and headed back to the

camp. She'd stall the pack and keep Titus entertained long enough for Oslow to get a good head start. He was elderly and his wolf wasn't up to the long, rugged journey. She had to think of strategies to get them home safely.

"And where are you going?" Danny, one of the dominant female wolves, blocked her path.

"Back to my *mate*. Can you move?"

"He mentioned you know the truth about us, but I don't see a marking on you. That means he's not your mate. Titus is just playing with his human toy. You'll soon use up your usefulness. Do you know who the rightful Alpha female is?"

"Move, bitch." Lilly wasn't in the mood for more bullshit. Certainly not some jealous she-wolf.

"Stupid, human. I could kill you right now. My wolf can cut you to shreds."

"I'd love to see you try."

Danny shoved her, probably expecting her to fall on her ass, but even in her human form Lilly was strong and well-trained. She jabbed Danny in the face with her right fist, making the she-wolf stumble. Then she slashed her across the cheek with her claws. Her cat began to overpower her thoughts, her feral nature emerging with her heightened adrenaline.

Danny held her cheek, the blood from her face marking her hand. Fear danced in her eyes. "What are you?"

Lilly looked down, her claws were still out, so she retracted them.

"A fucking cat?"

She smirked. The bitch was about to die, anyway. The Hawthorne Clan used her as a first line of defense along with some of the stronger males, knowing she never hesitated to kill. There was no way she would leave a witness, someone who could expose her. Besides, Lilly never liked the way she looked at Titus.

He's not yours to claim.

They charged each other, Lilly not holding back. She let out her aggression, punching, kicking, and clawing. Her fangs emerged and her pupils had shifted to slits, giving her better vision in the darkening forest.

"Lilly! Stop!"

She was straddling Danny, the she-wolf at her mercy. Lilly turned her head, her chest rising and falling rapidly. Titus stood nearby, waiting for her to comply. Only she wasn't his to command. Lilly turned and sank her fangs into Danny's neck, tugging until a morbid crack could be heard.

She looked at the Alpha again, blood dripping from her fangs. It was all in the open, and she goaded him, proud of her disobedience.

How do you love me now?

Lilly was done with this charade. These past few days had played on her emotions, making her dream up impossible fairy tales. This life wasn't for her. Titus loved a human, an act, something that didn't exist. She was a cat, a killer, a recluse. They could never be mated, and she could never give him heirs for his precious lineage since their animals were incompatible. Titus's love and acceptance was a tease, a fantasy that was never meant for her.

She got off the dead body and began to run in the opposite direction of Oslow, still determined to finish her mission and give him more time. It was all she had left. If she couldn't prove herself to her pack, what else did she have? With no birth family, no history, the Hawthorne Clan wolves were all she knew.

"Lilly!" He ran after her, but she knew she could outrun him. She'd always been fast. Tears blurred her vision, but she angrily wiped them away. She wasn't weak and she wasn't in love. There was no way she'd submit to the alpha wolf.

When he started to gain on her, she didn't see a problem with shifting at this point. He wouldn't be able to connect her to the Hawthorne Clan since she wasn't a wolf. They'd be safe from any retaliation. She leaped into her fur just before he caught up with her.

It felt like coming home, her soft paws hitting the forest floor, the sights and sounds becoming magnified. Lilly loved her cat, even if everyone else looked down on her. She didn't dare turn around to see the disappointment on the Alpha's face.

She dashed between the trees, in and out, and over roots and stumps. This part of the forest was unfamiliar to her, more north than she'd ever traveled. Within minutes, Titus was on her, his black wolf overpowering her. She struggled, biting and clawing at the wolf.

He'd kill her for taking Danny's life. And was probably disgusted that he'd considered mating with a cat. She had to fight for her life, something she'd been doing for a long time. And she was good at it, able to turn off pain and channel her energy.

But she'd underestimated the alpha wolf. It was huge and more powerful than anything she'd ever encountered, including all the males in her village. He had her at his mercy, and after weighing her options, she shifted into her delicate human skin. Better to die a woman. Less shame in being defeated.

The wolf followed suit and shifted into a man. Titus shackled her wrists at the sides of her head, and struggling was useless under his intense strength. "You're a shifter? A fucking wild cat? Why didn't you tell me?"

She scoffed. "Don't bullshit me, Titus. No wolf would be caught dead mating a cat."

"I don't understand. Why play human?"

Lilly needed to buy time for Oslow. Titus didn't realize she'd released his captive. He only thought his human mate had turned out to be a wildcat. And killed one of his pack.

It would be easy to flirt and lie her way out of trouble, but it wasn't so easy anymore.

Looking up into Titus's dark eyes, she realized this mission had gone terribly wrong.

She'd fallen in love.

Chapter Four

Titus had never been more afraid than seeing Danny fighting with his mate. What he didn't expect was to see Lilly's true colors. To many wolf shifters, cats were a pest, especially wildcats, only Lilly wasn't a pest.

She was real and beautiful, and the moment he looked at her, saw her true cat form, he'd become even more in love. It was like her cat called to his wolf and the ferocity with which she fought Danny had turned him on. He'd been worried for Danny, not his mate.

Yeah, he was a sick fuck, but he didn't care. All he knew was that he had to have Lilly, and soon. There was no way he could go another day without having her.

With Lilly trapped beneath him, her soft body struggling against his, he wanted her. To bite her, to claim her, to mate her.

"You're fucking perfect," he said.

The moment he spoke, she froze beneath him. "What?"

"You heard me. I'm not repulsed, if that's what you're thinking."

"I just killed one of your bitches."

"I don't care. Danny had it coming."

She frowned up at him. "You're not making any sense."

"Nothing in life makes sense." He released her hands and cupped her face. He ran his thumb across her lip but she attempted to bite him, which he found so incredibly cute. "You really are a wildcat."

"You've got to let me go."

"Why would I even dream about doing that? You're my mate and I've spent a long time trying to find you. I'm not letting you go that easily." There was no

357

way he'd be able to let her get far. The moment he saw her running, every instinct within him made him react. He had to follow her. He loved to chase and she was a sweet little prize.

"I've got to go. Please, Titus. You have to let me go."

He saw the tears in her eyes but he refused to budge. "I'm not falling for your crocodile tears anymore. You don't want to go."

"I've got to go."

"That's not the same thing," he said. "You don't want to go but you have to go. Why? You worried about what your pack will think?" He hoped she wasn't a spy for other wildcats trying to move in on his territory. "I need you to be serious with me right now, Lilly. It's the only way I can protect you."

"I don't need you to protect me." She tried to fight against him, but he was stronger, more powerful, and an Alpha.

He laughed. "Honey, you need me a lot more than you think right now. You've already killed one of my pack and the rest don't trust you. When they find out you're a cat, they're going to be begging for your head." He wouldn't let that happen.

To protect his mate, he'd slaughter anyone who tried to take her from him. Even if that meant taking on his own people.

"Then let me go."

"Can't do that."

She growled. "I'm a cat. This is never going to happen. We're incompatible. There's no such thing as mixed species mating or breeding. You know it. I know it. Stop fighting me on this." Lilly took a breath. "Okay, I get it, you want power. You're greedy for it. You're so fucking hungry you can't even see when someone is not of your species. Now let me go."

He frowned down at her. "I'm not hungry for power."

"Get the fuck off me!"

"No, you don't go throwing out accusations like that without telling me the truth. I'm not hungry for power, or for anything. I take care of my pack because that's what I'm supposed to do."

"You took him!" she blurted. Her voice echoed around the forest.

"I've not taken anyone. What are you talking about?"

"Don't lie to me, Titus. It's the reason I'm here. I'm the best damn tracker my family has. You have our elder and you can't have him. You want to suck him dry. To draw all the power to yourself to keep your pack strong. I don't want a weak man for an Alpha and you're weak."

He was a little taken aback by her accusations and he paused.

She kept on wriggling.

"An elder?"

"*Our* elder."

"I've not taken an elder."

"Liar!"

"Look at me, Lilly. We're destined to be mates. You should know if I'm lying or not."

"You couldn't tell that I was lying," she said, throwing that back at him.

He smirked. "Babe, you weren't lying to me. You simply didn't tell me the whole truth and you're a shifter so you're part human."

She kept trying to fight him, with no sign of wearing out. The feisty little thing would be amazing in bed.

"I don't have captives. I haven't trapped any elder. I don't need power given to me by anyone because I'm a fucking Alpha. I'm the one in control."

"He was locked up in a cage. I found him close to your camp. He was taken by one of your own," she said. "If you're such a great Alpha, you'd know about it."

None of this was making any sense to him. He was so confused.

Letting go of her hands, he held her face and kissed her lips. At first, she fought him, even trying to bite him. If they were true fated mates, then she'd relent. He knew she would.

Seconds passed.

Finally, the fight within her died. She stopped tugging on his hair, running her fingers through it instead, kissing him back. "Yes," she murmured. Her tongue trailed across his lips and he let out a moan, opening up to the kiss, meeting her halfway, tasting her.

She was everything he imagined she would be.

Fire and ice.

So perfect.

So hot.

So sexy.

She belonged to him.

Mate her right now.

Take her.

Fuck the fight right out of her.

She'll never want to leave.

He groaned.

Titus was so tempted to do what his wolf wanted but he couldn't. She believed he'd taken an elder but that wasn't the case. All these lies and misunderstandings needed to be cleared up first.

He'd heard of mystical elders, older beings with the power to pass on great wisdom and as such, great power as well. He'd truly believed it was just a rumor. Some fantasy story parents made up for their pups.

If this was true, someone within his pack had taken an elder and intended to use him against Titus.

Breaking from the kiss, he smiled down at her. "You can be angry at me all you want. You've got me now, Lilly. I can't turn back or turn away. You need to learn to trust me."

"And if I can't?"

"Then we're stuck, but I swear to you, I have never taken an elder."

She stared into his eyes. "If you didn't take him, who did?"

"Do you know where this elder is?"

She nodded.

"Please, trust me. I won't do anything to hurt him or you. Do you understand?"

"I ... I can't let anything happen to him. He's important to me. Oslow's a good wolf."

"I'll guard you and your elder with my life. I don't want to use him."

She nodded again. "Okay. I can track him. I tried to get him away."

"Then lead me to him. I need to know who took him."

"If you didn't take him, it means someone else did and they intend to take your pack," she said.

"That's the risk I'm not willing to take."

He lifted up off her and held his hand out for her to take. "Please, Lilly, trust in me. I want to do what is right for you. You're not alone."

She stared at his hand and he knew she struggled to accept his offer of help.

He waited though.

Being as patient as he possibly could, he left the

decision up to her.

Slowly, she reached out and he felt like he was on top of the fucking world when she took his hand. Lifting her to her feet, he wrapped an arm around her waist. "Thank you." He kissed her lips and released her. "Now, let's go find your elder."

She hesitated for a split second before turning her back on him and started into the woods. He kept his distance, making sure to give her the space she needed to track.

****

Lilly was exhausted. Fighting against an Alpha, trying to win, knowing she couldn't back down. Fear for Oslow's safety was what drove her. She had to get him away. When she found him in that cage, he looked weak. An elder needed to constantly be free to roam. To be one with all the elements so that he could remain strong. Without that connection, elders started to weaken.

Oslow was known for being one of the strongest elders and yet, he'd not had the energy to break out of the cage.

She had to believe Titus.

There was no choice left to her. Forever relying on herself was exhausting.

It had seemed strange at the time for him to even need Oslow. Trying to keep her cat hidden, she'd felt the power within him. Titus didn't need help from anyone, and the fact turned her on.

He was strong.

Powerful.

Fierce.

A true warrior, and one she was falling for fast.

Get your head in the game.

Not on him.

She had to focus.

Oslow was in danger and if Titus wasn't responsible, someone else was.

Please let it be the bitch I already killed.

Rushing forward, she smelled Oslow. He'd taken a seat and she smelled blood.

Not good.

Speeding up, she was aware of Titus staying close to her. Breaking through the tree line, she saw a narrow river, water rushing over rocks. The current flowed particularly fast but Oslow was at the edge on his stomach. He was covered in blood. Lilly dropped at his side, kneeling down in the dirt. His hand was in the water and he let out a groan.

"Oslow, sir, what is it? Please, let me help you."

"Honey, I need water," he said.

Cupping some water, she tried to present some to him, but he wouldn't take it.

"Here, let me," Titus said.

He easily lifted Oslow, resting the elder against his chest so that she could feed him water.

Oslow looked so pale and weak, it scared her.

"I should have known they'd send you," Oslow said. "They're so stupid not to see how strong you are." He let out a cough but she gave him more water, which he took.

"Please, don't say anything. Rest." Oslow had always been the nicest wolf she'd ever known. Even when everyone was spiteful to her, he always found a way of making her laugh. She adored him so much.

Oslow took more water and with each gulp, she saw the color returning to his cheeks.

She couldn't let him die.

"Who took you?" Titus asked.

Oslow chuckled. "You couldn't shake this one?"

"He wouldn't let me," she said.

"You know our pack won't let him near," Oslow said.

She bowed her head. They would scent Titus on her and the moment she delivered their elder, she'd be expelled, and she knew that. Still, Oslow's rightful place was with their kind, not being some slave for a bunch of wolves.

Oslow cupped her cheek. "You don't know why they hate you so much, do you?"

"They've never liked me. I get that. They think I'm the weaker species."

"No, sweet child. They always think wrong of the child. You're not weak. I am weak."

She frowned, looking at him.

"I was forbidden to tell you the truth. To keep my title and secure your position within the pack, I had to stay silent. You're my child, Lilly. You always have been. You're not a weak cat or a feeble one. You have great strength and wisdom and you're so much like your mother—in every way. She loved to travel. Wanderlust is what she called it. She was a shifter but she didn't have the desire to live in a pack. Cats generally keep to themselves. Once she gave birth to you, I never saw her again. Despite the secrets, you've always been my greatest treasure."

She froze, staring at Oslow. "You're my father?" It was outlawed for any of the elders to have a mate. Their sole purpose was to provide power to the pack that they were with. All of her life she'd been made to feel like an outcast. Like she'd been thrust upon the pack as some kind of disease.

Stepping away from Oslow, she stared at the water, somewhat shocked. She couldn't believe they would do this to her. Her entire life was a lie, and her thoughts were scattered.

"Lilly, I know this is a lot to take in," Oslow said.

"Is this why you were always nice to me? Because I'm your daughter?"

"I didn't want you to grow up without someone. Our world, it's cruel and harsh. I did what I did to protect you. If I didn't, they'd never allow a wild cat into the pack."

She felt tears fill her eyes and for the first time in her life, she actually felt weak, stupid. Shaking her head to clear all the thoughts going on inside, she stared at Titus. She had to focus on the task before her emotions destroyed her. "We need to know who would try to take over Titus's pack. Who had you?"

Titus let the elder go and he moved toward her. "Are you okay? You look shaken."

She stepped away from his concern.

Lilly was holding on by a thread. All this time, people knew and yet they treated her like shit. She had to deal with knowing when she returned her father, their elder, she'd never see him again.

It was all just a little too much and she had to focus.

"It was Axel," Oslow said. "That's what he called himself."

She saw the shock on Titus's face. Then his brow furrowed.

"No, it couldn't be him. He's my best friend," Titus said.

She heard the pain in his voice. The disbelief. She put a hand on his arm but he shook her touch away.

"Please, listen to him," she said.

Titus shook his head. "You've got it wrong. You have to be wrong."

"I know it's a lot to take in but Axel doesn't like the way you're doing things. He kept blathering on incoherently. He only sees his own agenda. He believes that he is far better than you. That he can do better by the pack. He wants the power to overthrow you, and when you're weak with your need to mate, he intends to strike."

She stared at Titus, knowing that she couldn't let anything happen to him. She wasn't ready to mate with him and because of that, he'd get weaker. She didn't have a choice. The thought of losing him made her feel sick to the core. She had to protect him.

Chapter Five

Titus always held on to the hope that Axel would come through, to prove himself a worthy beta. To find out he'd been planning a damn revolt behind his back was the ultimate betrayal. He paced back and forth, knowing he had to kill his friend, and was pissed off he was forced into this position.

What kind of male left an old man beaten and broken? It pissed Titus off to imagine his so-called best friend using his power against the weak.

Axel had kidnapped an elder, creating upheaval and enemies along the way. The bastard had planned every detail, even using Titus's obsession with Lilly to his advantage. He wasn't at his best, his wolf's need to mate with the wildcat off the fucking charts.

"Where would he go?" Titus was talking more to himself than anyone else, wondering what move he should make next. Axel had been MIA for days, so only the gods knew where he was.

"We can track him," said Lilly. "*I* can track him."

He turned to face her. "First, we'll get your father to safety."

She smiled, a barely there tilt of her lips. "That sounds nice," she whispered. "I've always thought I was an orphan."

"You're a woman now. Regardless of your past, all I care about now is you and me. The future." He ran his hand over her hair. Her happiness had a profound effect on him. Titus was completely in love with a woman he barely knew. A wildcat, no less. He couldn't wait to make their mating official.

"Axel wants to kill you."

"He can try."

She shook her head. "You heard his plan. He knows you're weak … because of me."

"I'm not worried, baby." He winked at her, not wanting her to worry or blame herself. "I have a place we can bring your father. Your village is too far. He'll be safe until after I deal with Axel."

They helped Oslow through the forest to a shelter he used on occasion when hunting. It was far enough from his camp that he wouldn't be sensed by the others.

"What is this place?"

"It's a relic from my grandfather's day. Hunters used to set up here until the wolves scared them off." He settled the old man on the twin bed, the springs protesting.

"He's still bleeding," she said.

Titus examined him. "Oslow, you need to shift. It won't be easy, but it's the only way your body will heal."

The elder nodded, then he closed his eyes, his entire body convulsing. It was painful to watch him shift. It didn't come easy, but after an excruciatingly long few minutes, he managed to change shapes.

Now he could heal.

Lilly knelt beside the bed, running her hands over the gray wolf's head. "We'll come back for you. Everything will be okay. I promise." Her eyes shimmered. Titus wanted nothing more than to be her hero, to fix all the bullshit going down. And he would.

"We have to go, Lily. He'll be safe until we come back."

She got to her feet, took his hand, and he closed the cabin door behind them. They rushed away from the shelter, not wanting to draw any attention to it. Miles later, they came to a stop. Lilly took a deep, cleansing breath, as if turning off her emotions and preparing for a fight. "Okay, let's do this. Let's find Axel."

"Why the rush?"

"What do you mean? You know what he's done."

"First things first." He ran the backs of his fingers down her arm. She froze. Realization settling in. Goosebumps spread across her skin and her cheeks flushed. The scent of her arousal perfumed the air, making his fangs prick his gums.

"You sure you want to fuck a wildcat?"

"You heard what your father said. We're more than compatible." Lilly was living proof that wolves and cats could procreate. He looked forward to having her pregnant and the mother of his children. And he didn't care what anyone thought of his choice.

"You're right. If we get this over with you'll be at your best. It's the only way to defeat Axel."

He licked his lips. "Lilly, I have no plans on getting this over with. I'll be taking my time."

She rested her palm on his chest, then raked her fingernails gently down to his stomach. Her touch made his cock even harder than it already was. "You're able to think about sex right now?"

"You have no idea the nasty shit I'm thinking of."

"Like what?"

He slid his hand along her curves, over her ass, and then around to cup her pussy. She moaned when he added pressure. "Such a hot little cunt." He slid his middle finger deep into her pussy, then added a second finger. She was already soaking wet. Titus grabbed her long, blonde hair with his free hand, tugging her head back sharply as he finger-fucked her. "You're not a human, Lilly. Do I have to be gentle with you?"

Her breathing was rapid and shallow, her eyes glazed over with lust. "I like it rough."

"Such a good kitten." He leaned down and suckled her tit. She dropped her weight onto his palm, wriggling for more of his fingers. He growled in his chest.

"Titus…"

"I've got you, baby. I'm going to make you forget everything."

He lowered her to the forest floor. Titus was thankful his mate was a shifter and not a delicate human. His wolf would be too difficult to tame. And he planned to enjoy Lilly.

Her hair spilled out, light against the dark leaves. Such beauty. He stared at his mate and all her luscious curves—those big tits and rounded hips. Titus knelt down and spread her thick thighs.

"You're my first," she said.

"I know." He couldn't smell another male claim on her. Titus would be the first and only male to enjoy her body. His territorial wolven instinct was deeply satisfied knowing she was untouched. Her pretty pink pussy glistened in the moonlight.

His mouth salivated, his cock leaking pre-cum. He got his face comfortable between her legs and lapped up her folds. She bucked and gasped, her arms reaching out to her sides. He continued to fuck her with his tongue, licking and sucking her sensitive little clit. She writhed beneath him, but he held her down, knowing it wouldn't take long for her to come.

He wanted to taste her, to hear her cry out in orgasm.

"You like that?" He looked up at her from between her legs. Her beautiful lips were parted, her breathing labored. "Tell me you want more. Tell me to eat your virgin pussy until you come all over my tongue."

"Oh, gods." She tossed her head back, her legs dropping open more. "Make me come, Titus."

****

The things he could do with his mouth were unreal. She'd never known pleasure like this. And she wanted more.

It felt dirty having a man, an Alpha, eating her pussy. The animalistic sounds he made proved he enjoyed every minute of it. Lilly had always been the one in control—strong, fearless, and ready to survive on her own at any given moment. She never expected a mate. But this wolf, this beast of a man made her feel safe and protected. Made her feel wanted. It was a high in itself to be able to let go and just savor the pleasure he willingly gave her.

"Claim me," she murmured. Lilly didn't trust her own voice. She was floating, the pre-orgasmic bliss taking her higher and higher.

"You know what you have to do," he said. Then he began to suck steadily on her clit, his arms stretched out along her sides. His rough stubble scraped her inner thighs. The pressure built, her womb coiling tighter and tighter.

He wanted her to come, and even if she tried, she wouldn't be able to hold off much longer. What she wanted was his cock, to feel him fucking her deep and hard. Claiming her. Lilly needed him to mark her, committing to her body and soul. Until their mating was official, it was still a fantasy. And she was still the little girl, the wildcat nobody wanted around.

Lilly pushed away her insecurities and let go, embracing the mounting pressure. Within seconds, she ignited, her body jolting as she arched off the ground. Wave after wave of heat and raw pleasure coursed through her veins, leaving her spineless. Only once she'd settled did Titus rise up to his hands and knees. His eyes looked feral, more animal than man, and it turned her on.

His shoulders were corded with muscle as he crawled higher up her body. He stopped to take her nipple in his mouth, then moved to her neck. He licked her pulse point, breathing her in.

"Are you sure it's the mating call?" she asked.

Another breath. "You smell like mine. Your blood is calling to me, calling to my wolf." He nuzzled her neck, licking, his fangs lightly nicking her skin.

"You can't own a wildcat." There was little conviction in her words at this point, but she feared being controlled.

"But I make you feel so good you'll never want to run off."

She fought the cloud of desire and pushed Titus off her. Lilly sprang to a crouch. "What's that supposed to mean?"

"You heard what your father said. Your mother was a cat. As soon as you were born, she was gone, regardless of the mating bond."

Lilly frowned, her hackles up. "I'm not my mother."

She knew it. He'd rather have a she-wolf. Titus thought badly of her race and she wouldn't be tolerated by a mate. She'd rather be alone forever.

"Relax, baby." He reached for her, and only then did she realize her fangs and claws were at the ready. She growled at him.

"I never should have killed Danny. She would have made the perfect mate for you." Lilly leaped forward, about to shift and get Oslow from the cottage. She'd bring him home and forget about Titus, his promises, and the way he set her body afire. She should have kept to the mission.

He caught her in mid-air. "*Ah ah ah.* You're not getting away from me so easily, little cat."

She struggled in his arms. "It'll never work, Titus! Admit it to yourself. One day you'll regret settling for a cat, I promise you that." Lilly punched him hard in the gut, and he groaned, his jaw clenching down hard.

"Enough." He shackled both her wrists, and she was helpless against the Alpha's power. "I'm not going to regret shit, and do you know why? You're my mate, Lilly. The only woman I'll ever want."

"I know what you think of cats. You compared me to my mother. She abandoned me!" Tears filled her eyes, and a pain she never realized she harbored was just under the surface. It spilled over, her body sagging against him.

Titus released her hands and pulled her close, his arms around her body. "It was her loss, Lilly." He stroked her hair, and she closed her eyes, savoring the simple kindness. "I don't hate your cat. I'm just scared. Scared to lose you, scared you'll regret accepting a wolf. I saw the pain in your father's eyes. I don't want that to be me." He kissed her forehead. "I love you. I want us to be together forever."

No words formed. The kaleidoscope of emotions had weakened her. In the past hour, too much had been thrust upon her. One thing she knew for certain—she was nothing like her mother. She craved a pack and wanted to belong more than anything. It was the reason she pushed herself, always convinced she had something to prove. The last thing she dreamed of was wandering the world alone forever.

Hearing *her* wolf talk about his own insecurities drew her closer to him. She was the Alpha's weakness. She'd never been anyone's anything. Lilly took a deep breath, reminding herself about the control she'd perfected over the years.

She dropped down to her knees in front of her

mate, taking his thick cock in her fist. Lilly looked up at him and licked her lips. He gave her pleasure, and she wanted to return the favor. To show him how much she appreciated his love.

Lilly wrapped her mouth around his girth and sucked until he groaned. Back and forth she fucked him with her mouth.

"You'll be the death of me," he said.

She felt a rush of power bringing the Alpha pleasure. He was at her mercy, trusting her as she'd trusted him. Her cat clawed to be released, her feral nature becoming stronger as her body heated with desire. She lapped up his length, loving his thick meat and musky taste.

"Whoa, baby. That's enough." He pulled her up to her feet.

She blinked away her cat pupils, refocusing on her breathing. "You didn't like it?"

He smirked. "Barbed tongue."

"Oh. Sorry."

They stared at each other. Not moving. Not speaking. Only their labored breathing among the night song of the forest. Desire snapped between them like a living force.

"I won't be gentle. Not now," he said.

"I'm a big girl. I can handle whatever you give me. Just make it soon."

He grabbed her by the base of the neck, pulling her in for a kiss. His lips were firm, his tongue probing. She opened for him, savoring the brutality and urgency of the kiss. This was exactly what she craved.

It was time to see just how compatible a wolf and cat could be.

Chapter Six

Titus had waited a long time for this moment. Forty-three years to be exact. He never, in all of his wildest dreams, thought his mate would be a cat. She was stunning. No doubt about it. Even with the threat of Axel hanging over them, he couldn't go another second without claiming her. It wasn't about being stronger. He wanted to bond with her. To have a partner in life.

He'd never let her get away or give her a chance to think that they weren't compatible. He knew they were destined for each other, deep down into the very essence of his being. Without her, he was nothing. The pack, they couldn't compare. His mate was his number one priority.

For many years he'd been warned that when it came to his mate, he'd risk everything to claim her, to be with her. He'd always thought it was lies, an overexaggeration of how important a mate was.

With Lilly, he felt it.

He was consumed by this desperate need to mate, to fuck, to claim. To have her submit to him. Breaking from the kiss, he trailed his lips down her body.

The scent of the earth and forest fueled him. He relished it along with the purrs she kept making.

The sounds she made went straight to his cock and he was hungry for more.

Sucking one of her nipples into his mouth, he bit down lightly onto the bud, hearing her cry out his name. He wanted to howl out in the night, but growled low in his chest, keeping focused. Sliding his fingers between her thighs, he found her wet heat and stroked, feeling her body quiver beneath his touch.

It was her first time but he was going to make sure she'd never forget it.

Changing to her other nipple, he teased her areola before taking that one between his teeth. She had full, heavy tits. He lapped at her skin, loving the taste of her.

All of his senses were on alert.

Mate her.

Take her.

Fuck her.

Claim her.

Now.

Do it now.

He needed this more than he needed anything else in the world.

Gliding down her body, he pressed a kiss to her sweet clit before sucking it into his mouth. He was tempted to rid her of that pesky virginity but he had to be patient.

When she was at the edge of bliss once again, he watched her body.

There were no more signs of her wanting to leave or having doubts. The flush on her cheeks, the rapid rise and fall of her chest—she was close. There was no way he'd ever allow his woman to question what she meant to him. He felt fucking consumed by Lilly.

She'd stumbled into his life and everything was going to change. No more loneliness, no more feeling deprived by the gods.

Lilly was the one with the real power here, not him.

He was at her mercy and he loved it.

My mate.

All mine.

No one else's.

He felt pride knowing this cat, this wild, beautiful woman, was all his. No one else would ever know how sweet she tasted or the sounds she made as she came.

Lowering her to her back, he spread her legs wide. Her pussy was pink and glistening, making his fangs prick his gums.

Grabbing his aching cock, copious amounts of pre-cum already leaking out of the tip, he settled between her legs. Sliding his cock along her slit, he got himself all nicely coated in her cream.

Wolves didn't need protection.

He didn't want to use a condom to dull the senses.

They were wild beings.

Lilly was his mate.

There was no way in hell that he'd ever be without her.

If their union ended with a little baby, damn, he'd feel so damn proud. Becoming a mate and a father all within a matter of days. This was his dream.

"Titus," she said. "Please."

He didn't give her a chance to change her mind. Putting the tip of his cock at her entrance, he stared into her eyes and slid to the hilt, tearing through her virginity, claiming her as his.

She cried out. The feminine sound hurt him deeply. He held himself still within her as her pain filled the air.

He wouldn't let her suffer.

Don't hurt her.

Wait.

"Oh, baby, I'm so sorry," he said. Cupping her cheek, he stared into her eyes, which had gone wide as he slid in deep. "I have to remember this is new for you."

"It's fine."

"It can't be fine if you're in pain. *Shit!*" He went to pull out of her but her nails sank into the flesh of his ass.

"I'm not made of glass. I'm not going to break. I don't want you to stop."

"I don't want to hurt you, baby. We can wait."

"The first time always hurts for a woman, Titus. Just give it a minute and it'll all be fine. I'm not the delicate human girl I claimed to be. Don't forget what I am."

He wanted to stop. To tell her *no*, but he didn't pull away. Lilly was right. Her shifter DNA wouldn't allow pain to linger. Her body would heal incredibly fast, even in human form.

She held him in a death grip.

Lilly's nails continued to sink into the flesh of his ass. They'd not broken the skin but if her body changed or at least her claws did, she'd cut him.

Taking possession of her lips, he nibbled at her mouth until she opened up. Plunging his tongue inside, they kissed harder, unable to get enough of each other. Their teeth clashed together, their passion scorching. Slowly, he felt her pussy start to grow even wetter, pulsing around him.

Lilly began to thrust her hips, riding his cock, wriggling for more.

It took every ounce of his control to not slam deep within her.

He wanted to fuck.

But he allowed her time to grow accustomed to his girth being inside her. Moaning against her mouth, he heard her growl. It sounded so strange coming from her lips. It wasn't a wolf growl but a feminine one.

"Please, Titus, I need you."

"You want me to fuck you now?"

"Yes, make me yours. Make me your mate."

The words were sweet music and as he pulled out of her only to slide back inside with force, he felt that linking. That bond of their bodies and the connection of their souls. Their inner animals came out to play as they mated together, doing what they should have been doing from that first day.

In his mind's eye, he saw her cat and it was beautiful. *Strong, confident, loyal.*

This was how they were destined to be together. They were as one.

The two of them from now until eternity.

She was his queen, his reason for existing. Her rightful place was by his side and he relished it.

"Yes, it feels so good." She writhed beneath him, anticipating each thrust of his hips.

Taking hold of her hands, he pinned them to the ground. Lilly wrapped her legs around his waist and he drove inside her.

She took everything he gave and moaned as she did. Her pussy spasmed around him with every thrust, taking them both closer to the edge.

He felt the first stirrings of his orgasm. The ache in his balls to fill her up. To make her take his cum so that they could have a baby.

His teeth grew long and as he sank his fangs into the flesh of her shoulder, he was rewarded by the spike of hers.

Mated.

Together.

Forever.

"I love you, Titus," Lilly said.

Now his world was complete.

****

Blood covered her thighs and mouth.

Lilly couldn't believe she was no longer a virgin but also that she was mated. She stood beside her mate.

She felt him. Inside her head. She'd never had a

connection with her pack, being a different species. Now she felted united, like she belonged.

It was strange how to describe him. His energy seemed to surround her with warmth and love. The initial penetration had taken her by surprise, but she was strong and wanted to see their mating through. It didn't take long for discomfort to morph into the most addictive pleasure she'd ever experienced. Having Titus inside her, bonding them, his thick cock driving home over and over was what she'd been craving for days.

Keeping hold of his hand, they entered the micro lake they'd found. They looked a sight after their mating and needed to wash up.

"I think it's only fair that I get to help you," he said.

He picked her up in his arms.

Rather than fight him, she wrapped her arms around his neck, staring into his eyes. This was the first time in her whole life that she'd ever allowed herself to trust anyone. No man had ever been allowed past her walls before.

"I'm scared," she said.

It hurt her to say those words. Tears filled her eyes.

For so long it had only been her. Her against the pack. Fighting for her life.

Titus paused. "Why are you scared?"

"I don't want to … fail you." Being vulnerable was not in her nature. This mating had opened up that path that gave her the courage to believe she could with him. Nibbling her lip, she couldn't look away.

He smiled. "You won't."

"I'm a cat."

"You're mine. Whenever someone tells you differently, you tell them that you belong to Titus.

You're his mate and I will tell them all that I belong to you. You own my heart, Lilly. Cat or not, I'll never let you go. You will never fail me."

He lowered them down into the water. It was cold and fresh, making her nipples pebble.

The sex had been so crazy. A whirlwind. The feel of him pumping inside her, stroking her with his cock. She wanted to do it again. And again.

Axel.

She couldn't enjoy the pleasure of his cock again until she found this traitor. How dare he think he could take Titus's place? Her mate's pack belonged to him and she'd never allow anyone to take that from him.

"I want to fuck you again," she said. "After we deal with Axel."

He chuckled. "Baby, once we deal with all the pack stuff, you're not going to have much choice. I'm going to fuck you every single chance I get." He ran his hand down her body, teasing between her thighs. She jolted.

She knew he was cleaning her the best way he could, but she was still hypersensitive.

Once he was done, his hand came to rest on her stomach.

"How would you feel about us having a baby?"

She laughed. "A little too soon, don't you think?"

"No. I've waited a lifetime for you."

Whenever he talked like that, she felt this fluttering within her heart.

She closed her eyes and allowed herself to relax, resting her head against his chest. This was what love felt like. She didn't want to ever lose this feeling.

Running her hands down his back, she gripped his buttocks, feeling his cock tighten against her stomach.

"Woman, we don't have time for more of that yet."

She giggled. "Would you deny me?"

"You know I can't." He held her even tighter, making her pulse with need. Her tits felt so heavy and her mind clouded with the thought of him taking her once again. Thanks to her shifter blood, she'd already healed. Her cat felt feral with need.

She leaned up about to kiss his lips, but froze.

"What is it?" he asked.

With a frown, she sniffed the air.

The scent was faint but there. Her tracking skills were second to none.

"I don't have bad breath, do I?" he asked, with a hint of a smile to his lips.

"Axel."

Titus tensed up.

"You can scent him?"

"I think so. I remember that scent. There's something else though."

"What do you mean?"

"Axel isn't alone."

She didn't like the twisted feeling in her gut.

Shaking her head, she made to pull away.

"Where are they?" Titus asked, holding her still.

"We must go and find them."

"Do you recognize the second scent?"

"It's familiar but I don't know why. I can't place it. Come on, Titus, or we're going to lose them." She looked at Titus and saw the apprehension in his gaze. "What is it?"

"I trained Axel," said Titus.

"So?"

"He's … he's been like a brother to me, Lilly."

"You're not going to be able to kill him, are

you?"

"I don't know. Does that make me weak?" he asked.

She placed a hand to his cheek. "Don't think. You're an Alpha, Titus. You'll know what to do. I'm your mate. If you can't handle it, I'll end him for you."

They were losing time. Axel's scent was getting weaker. She didn't know who the other scent belonged to. A hostage? There was blood. He could have a civilian from the pack or even a human. Seeing Titus confused, she couldn't move on.

Her cat paced in her mind, wanting out.

She craved to go on the hunt for the man who thought he could take the pack from her. Only mated a matter of minutes and already it was *her* pack*, her* people.

"I love you, Lilly," he said.

This made her smile. After they mated and she told him how she felt, he stayed silent. It had hurt but she knew he felt the same way. How could he not? They were together. They belonged to each other.

She tasted his lips and his hands moved to her ass.

Wasting precious time here.
Come on. We have someone to hunt and to kill.

She moaned and pulled away from the pleasure of his lips.

"We've got to go," she reminded. The honeymoon would have to wait.

"Shit, yes."

He was stalling and she hated knowing how hard this would be for him. It made her hate Axel even more for betraying a caring Alpha.

"A good Alpha questions everything," she said. "He takes his time. You're here for your pack. They matter the most. They can't do without you."

He nodded. "We need to turn. We'll be faster."

Titus kept hold of her hand, leading her out of the water. Even as they faced each other, their bodies splitting, she kept on staring into his eyes. Trying to offer him her strength. Whatever they were about to do, he needed her and she'd be with him, every single step of the way.

"Hello, sexy," Titus said.

His wolf rubbed against her side.

Her cat purred.

"Come on, let's go and deal with this. I'm ready."

Her cat moved him out of her way. *"Remember, I'm still your queen."*

She took the lead, following Axel's scent.

Chapter Seven

They slowed down when they neared their targets. Titus wasn't ready for this, but he had to be. He'd avoided dealing with his beta, hoping he'd been wrong about Axel. Where had he gone wrong?

How many times had they saved each other's asses? Before Lilly came along, he was the only other person Titus trusted completely. Now he didn't know what to think.

"Blood. Do you scent it?" she asked.

Now that they were close, all his senses were magnified. He even knew who the other person was. It was Sean, Anna's boyfriend. Axel had gone berserk, claiming Anna was his mate when Sean had already claimed her. His beta was probably going to kill him in revenge.

This wasn't good at all.

It was time to end this, to handle his responsibilities as Alpha, to eliminate the traitor.

"I'm going to shift," he said. *"Stay in your fur in case things go bad. You'll be able to get away quickly."*

"You don't know me very well, do you? I'd never run away and leave you behind."

His wildcat would be the death of him.

He shifted into his human skin and emerged from the underbrush. "Axel!"

His beta turned around and fell to his knees. He was wounded, his body covered in blood. "I'm sorry," Axel said.

"What have you done, Axel? You kidnapped and nearly killed an elder, and now Sean? Do you crave power that much? Did you never see me as a friend?"

Axel shook his head before falling forward onto the ground.

Titus whirled around when a commotion broke out behind him. Lilly's wild cat had its teeth around Sean's leg, and he cried out in pain, dropping the knife he held.

"Call off your bitch!" Sean shouted.

Titus looked to Axel, then Sean, the true story slowly taking shape. "That's my mate. And she wouldn't have attacked unless she felt I was in danger."

He stepped closer, kicking the knife away. "What are you doing out here, Sean?"

"It's not what you think."

"Oh? What am I thinking?"

"It was Axel. He's gone nuts. It was a jealous rage. I was only saving myself."

Titus tilted his head to the side, searching the man's eyes and only finding deception. He paced back and forth while the man whimpered, but he refused to ask Lilly to back off. She was in her fur, so her senses would be much more in tune right now than his.

"I assumed my beta was trying to overthrow my position. I shouldn't have been so narrow-sighted. All I want to know is why?"

"I'm telling you, Titus. It was all Axel. Ask the old man."

"What old man?" asked Titus. "If you're talking about the elder you shouldn't even know about, he only went on what you said. He doesn't know what Axel looks like."

"He tried to steal my mate!"

Titus shook his head. "I was a fool not to listen to Axel. Should I get the elder here to point out his true kidnapper? He is alive and well, after all."

Sean kept quiet, but Titus didn't need to hear any more. He approached Axel, rolling him to his back. His eyes fluttered open.

"You need to shift and heal."

Axel grimaced when he tried to move. "He set me up. When he tried to claim Anna, it drove me crazy. No one understood, except Sean. He wanted you to think I was the problem so he could take over the pack."

"Shift," Titus repeated. "We'll talk later. Everything will be set straight."

He watched as Axel struggled to change into his wolf, but he managed.

There was no way he could allow a traitor in his pack. Sean had gone just under the radar, secretly creating a wave of unrest.

"Let him go, Lilly."

She growled but complied. Sean immediately shifted and rushed off into the forest. Titus smirked at his wildcat. "I'll let you handle this one, my little huntress."

Lilly flashed her fangs, then darted into the forest after the wolf. He knew she could handle herself and wanted to show her that he trusted her as his packmate and queen. He'd also be right behind them in case there was more trouble than she could handle.

When he caught up with them, it was already over. Blood dripped from her mouth as she stood over the wolf carcass. She was perfect—beauty and power. The perfect mate to stand by his side as they led their pack. Together.

"I never should have doubted you. You're a huntress through and through."

"Like I said, I'm not delicate. I know how to handle myself," she said.

She approached him, the muscles of her cat strong and defined. Lilly licked his snout.

"Now what?" he asked.

"We begin. Everything starts now."

Lilly dashed away, and he followed. She stopped

in a quiet area of the forest and shifted into her skin. Her body was beautiful, all strong, soft curves. He paced around her, scenting her ripeness. She ran her hands through his fur, no fear, only anticipation snapping between them. He shifted to join his mate.

"What are we doing here, baby?"

"My father and Axel need time to recover. And we have unfinished business," she said.

"Such as?"

She smiled, turned, and walked away. Lilly peered back over her shoulder, teasing, knowing how much he wanted a piece of her ass. He growled, watching her every move. His cock reacted, despite everything they'd been through.

"Lilly, behave yourself. You shouldn't tease."

"I don't plan on refusing my big, bad wolf. Unless you'd rather wait for another day."

He still remembered her beautiful wild cat and the way she'd handled herself. She was vicious and capable, no less than any she-wolf.

"I thought you might be tired."

She shook her head. "I feel energized. Complete." Lilly circled him, running her hand over his back and ass. "I belong. I even have answers to where I came from. I couldn't ask for more."

"That's right. Your father mated with a wildcat, so we're not the first. We'll be able to have children."

"There's a difference," she said.

"Oh?"

"I never plan on abandoning you or our pack."

He tugged her against his body and kissed her hard on the mouth, completely in love with his woman. She was right. Today was the first day of forever. The unrest in his pack would finally be dealt with, and Axel could claim Anna as the gods intended.

"I want to fill you with my cum. Cover you in my scent." He ran his tongue along the rim of her ear until she purred.

"What are you waiting for, wolf?"

****

Lilly had spent twenty-eight years as a pariah. Even in her adopted pack, she was always cast aside, only of use when the others needed something from her. It was the reason she'd been determined to be the best at everything. Anything to become accepted. Loved.

It hadn't worked until she found Titus.

The Hawthorne Clan had done her an injustice, keeping her true identity a secret. She could have had a relationship with her father, but so many years had passed. At least now she knew her roots and could slowly build a friendship with the elder who'd always been kind to her. Now she knew why he was different from the rest.

Titus spun her around, his arms snaking around to cup her tits. Her nipples were sensitive and his hands were rough. He made her feel beautiful when she was certain he'd be disgusted by her wildcat.

"Doggy style?" he whispered in her ear.

"Obviously."

He pressed her back down and she got to her hands and knees, waiting for him to mount her. Her alpha. Her beast. Her mate.

He lapped up her folds, taking her by surprise. "Titus!"

"Let me enjoy myself." His tongue teased her pussy and clit, then circled her asshole, making her see stars. "Such a good kitty."

She clawed the earth as he toyed with her, nearly bringing her to orgasm. Then it was over, his strong hands gripping her hips as he positioned himself behind her. She felt the hard length press against her before he grabbed it and searched for her entrance.

As soon as he impaled her, she cried out, knowing they were so deep in the forest nobody would hear. She let loose, savoring the feel of his big dick pumping in and out of her pussy. She was hot and slick, savoring the fullness and bonding.

He pulled her long hair from behind and she growled in appreciation. Lilly wasn't a delicate-skinned human girl, she was all woman, all wildcat, and his roughness turned her on.

Titus fucked her hard and fast, never slowing. The man was a machine, all strength and muscle. She began to pant, knowing she'd come any minute. Each time he filled her, he pounded against her clit, making her gasp.

He reached around and teased her clit as he worked her, bringing her to another level of ecstasy. She'd never get enough of her wolf.

"Come for me, Lilly. I want to feel you milk my cock." He began to take her at a fevered pace, and she couldn't hold back another second. Her orgasm raced through her, detonating with enough power and heat to make her scream Titus's name over and over. "Take it all, baby." She could feel his cum filling her and, for the first time, she really began to envision life as a family.

They collapsed together on the leaves, their bodies spent. The forest was a thing of beauty, the trees rustling in the breeze, and the moonlight filtering over them like a fine lace. She always preferred nature over her ventures into human towns and cities. Titus's pack was the most feral she'd ever encountered, and she looked forward to learning their ways.

She tucked herself against his side, watching his chest rise and fall, feeling safe and grounded. Lilly was proud to be a strong female and huntress, and now she'd be leading a pack with her mate. It had never been fun being alone, and sometimes she just craved to be loved and cared for. Her mate filled that void. She knew that Titus would be able to handle himself in the face of danger. He'd die for her, and she'd do the same for him. They were a team.

"When will you tell the pack?" she asked.

"As soon as we get everything sorted with your father and Axel, I'll make the official announcement. I'm sure they'll be able to scent my claim on you before that though."

"And they'll be okay with it?"

"I know they'll love you. You have a good heart, and you'll be an honorable leader," he said.

"Just like you." She kissed his cheek, snuggling close, and she couldn't help but purr.

CLAIMING THE COYOTE

Roberta Winchester

◆

Chapter One

Channing

An explosion inside my skull. It's all I can remember.

What the fuck?

I can't see. My eyes are open, but nothing's there.

Nothing but darkness. And pain. A blade of agony slices through my head and face.

Where *am* I?

Twelve Hours Ago

"My tie is choking me," I gasp, yanking at the stupid knot wedged up into my Adam's apple.

"Stop *messing* with it, dude. And stand still. Music's about to start."

Rafe Ulric. Least sympathetic big brother in the

world. His soon-to-be new wife is perfect for him. "Your woman tried to strangle me with this thing, I'm telling you."

Rafe glares at me, his eyes flashing a warning. "She was trying to help you out, man. If you weren't such a barbarian, you'd know how to tie your own damn tie."

I'm not a barbarian. I'm a shifter, and a damn good one too. In my coyote skin, I can outrace, outpace, and outhunt Rafe any day of the week. He knows it too. But since our dad retired and made Rafe the Alpha, my big bro has been kind of a dick. He's my boss too, since he's Alpha and we own the family business together with our youngest brother Weylin—who, I'm happy to see, is standing next to me, shifting restlessly, looking almost as miserable as me.

The thing is, it's not just the tie that's bothering me. Or Rafe. Not really. And I actually like his bride, Corina, a lot. She's good for him, and vice versa.

No. What's bugging me is this damn *wedding.* Flowers. Cake. Music. Rings. Speeches. Vows.

Love.

Everything I'll never have.

Because the only woman I ever wanted didn't want me back.

"Hey, man, you okay?"

I blink, startled. Weylin is staring at me.

"Yeah," I lie. "It's this damn heat, choking me. Who the hell has an outdoor wedding in the middle of July?"

"*Shut. Up.*" Rafe growls under his breath, loud enough I'm pretty sure the closest row of people seated in front of us hears him. Our mom glances up and gives Rafe such a hostile look of warning his face flushes fire-engine red.

The music starts, a cheerful, classical piano score that sets my teeth on edge.

It's going to be a long, long night.

I straighten and force myself to smile. I mean, I'm happy for my brother and Corina. I really am. They've been through more than any other couple I know.

There's a murmur of rustling as all the wedding guests stand. The music gets louder and that's when Corina enters. She's even more beautiful than usual. I try not to imagine a different woman walking down that aisle, toward *me*—a woman with long, lush hair the color of coffee and almond eyes so deep and inviting you forget your own name when you stare into them.

The ceremony starts. Rings are exchanged. I try to pay attention, but I keep catching myself mindlessly staring off at nothing, pretending I'm watching.

Memories keep intruding. *Her eyes. Night after night, nothing but her and me on my bed. My name on her lips, crying out...*

She was mine for almost three years. Three. Years. I thought it was enough. I thought she was ready. I was dead wrong.

"And now, I introduce Mr. and Mrs. Ulric!" the officiant announces, hands spread wide over Rafe and Corina.

Everybody stands, clapping and whooping.

The happy bride and groom disappear into a throng of well-wishers. Bride and Groom. Wife and Husband.

A tide of envy rises over me. I'm going to drown in it.

"Come on, man. It's our turn." Weylin puts an arm around my shoulder and drags me with him into the throng of people. "We've gotta do our groomsmen duties. Photos, speeches, all that stuff."

Weylin and me, we're pretty tight. He's the only one who knows what I'm dealing with today. It's not like I enjoy talking to people about ... about *her*.

The Only One.

God, I can't even say her name.

"Come on," he says, clapping me on the back. "It's an open bar."

Weylin's crooked smile is contagious and makes me feel a little better. I can do this, I decide. I'm strong enough to get over Her.

We get through all the meet-and-greets, the photos, the speeches, the cake-cutting.

And then it happens.

I'm on my way into the reception tent. The canopy is lit with amber-colored lights, fending off the dimness that comes with early dusk. I'm heading to the bar, thinking about how I'm going to die a miserable death if I don't get a drink in my hand right now.

It's the voice that freezes me in my tracks. From somewhere behind me, I hear it.

"Hey, Channing."

I stop, close my eyes, reeling from the shock of it, allowing that smooth, smoky silk of her voice to soak into my skin and imprint into my memory. I must be hallucinating. Obsession is a terrible, unhealthy thing.

But then I hear the shuffle of steps through the grass and I feel the presence of someone standing in front of me. Goddamn it. It can't be...

I open my eyes. My heart stops. My breath stills.

The Only Woman.

Tala.

Chapter Two

Tala

It's the look in his eyes that's to blame. He didn't see me and he wouldn't have if I'd kept my mouth shut. But when I saw his face—those unearthly green eyes of his brimming with so much unchecked pain—I couldn't help it.

It's all your fault, Tala. My guilt over breaking it off with Channing has mutated into a monstrous thing. I can't even shift into my coyote form without thinking of him, though it's been more than a year since we've even had a conversation.

"Hey," he returns my greeting, his voice devoid of emotion—a dramatic contrast from the ravaged expression on his face.

"I'm sure you didn't expect to see me here," I say, trying to fake a nonchalance I don't feel.

"Well … yeah," he says, his gaze raking across my body. I know he's studying my uniform, wondering what the hell the local chief of police is doing at his brother's wedding.

"I'm here to keep an eye on things, is all. Relax," I tell him, before he can ask. It's not a lie, but it's not the entire truth.

His eyes narrow, his brow furrowing—I know that look. He's not going to leave it alone.

"Keep an eye on things? What the hell's that supposed to mean?"

I shrug. I don't want him to know, at least not yet. If I tell him the truth—that notorious murderer and shifter-hunter Bryce Holter has escaped from prison, Channing will get involved and he'll get hurt.

And that is exactly why I broke up with him—because I knew, with my job and his overprotectiveness, eventually he'd get himself killed.

When I tried to explain this to him, well … it went over like a lead balloon.

"Your brother sent me a wedding invite, anyway," I say, trying to veer the conversation into safer territory. When Rafe's new human wife Corina accidentally shot him last summer, mistaking him for a feral coyote, I was the one who tidied everything up with the authorities and made sure no one stumbled onto Rafe's secret. Besides, his secret belongs to all of us—Channing, Weylin, their parents, a few others in the community. Me, of course. I'm glad my parents are still living out west, where I grew up, so there'll be two fewer shifters to worry about now with Bryce Holter running around out here somewhere.

"Wait. Rafe invited you?" Channing spits the words out.

I pause for a second, reminding myself to act casual. "Well, yeah," I say. "I figured it couldn't hurt to drop by for a minute, right?"

Channing flinches, his thick eyelashes sweeping down as he shifts his attention to the ground between us. My breath hitches and catches in my throat. I've hurt him too much by showing up here. I should've thought of that but—shit. I've been too busy chasing down Bryce Holter to think of much of anything else—including how Channing would feel about seeing me at a wedding.

"I'm so sorry, Channing, I didn't mean anything by it. I'm sorry—"

"*Don't.*" He snaps his gaze up again, piercing me with those pain-ravaged eyes. "Don't waste your empty words on me, Tala. If you're so sorry, why didn't you say yes to me when I asked you to marry me?"

And there it is. He'll never forgive me for turning him down.

"I *told* you, Channing. My job is dangerous. I've pissed off too many psychos. Marrying me would be dangerous for you."

He blinks at me, looking stunned. "Tala. Look at me. Do you honestly think I can't take care of myself? I can take care of *both* of us."

He outstretches his arms as if he needs to show me how well-muscled he is. Even through the layers of his suit, his biceps are visible and defined. "No one is going to touch you, not with me around."

"Your strength won't protect you from a bullet, Channing. You know better than that."

"I'm not my brother. *You're* not going to shoot me, are you?" His tone is slightly teasing, but there's a rawness to it, a delicate balance between trust and mistrust. I get it, but he doesn't seem to understand my logic. Or maybe he just doesn't want to.

"If you're so worried about the dangers of your job, you should quit. I can take care of us, Tala."

"I can't settle down and play house, Channing, and you know it. I love my work."

"More than you love—*loved* me."

I'm not going to play into this. It's not like that and he knows it. I love my job, I love helping people. And I loved—*love* him, and that love is the reason I want to protect him by keeping him away from me.

"We were great together, Tala."

"I know."

"We could be again."

He hasn't moved on, not at all. I hadn't heard otherwise from anyone, but being here, in front of him, hearing him say these things—there's a whisper of doubt, of regret murmuring in my conscience.

"No, Channing. I—"

There's a crackle in the radio clipped to my duty belt. I hurriedly push the button before he can hear anything. The media will know about Bryce Holter by now, but as long as Channing is at this wedding and doesn't do any browsing on his phone, he'll have no idea until he gets home and turns on the news.

I glance back up at Channing and try not to look him in the eye. He's already suspicious, I can tell. "I have to go now, I'm sorry."

"Yeah, I get it." There's a simmering anger in his voice, and I know it's not my needing to leave that's pissed him off.

"Bye, Channing."

I don't know what else to say. I turn to go and suddenly his arms are around me, my face pressed into the rough stubble of his cheek, his strong hands firm against my back, holding me tight against him. He smells of cedar and sandalwood. The familiarity of it, saturated in memory, takes my breath away. I don't even try to pull away.

And then his lips are on mine, a warm, gentle, tentative kiss.

"I miss you, Tala." His voice is a harsh whisper.

There's a lump in my throat, choking me. Responding to him is impossible.

My police radio crackles again. "I need to go," I manage to say, pushing away from his embrace. "I'm so sorry."

He releases me and I go, walking as fast as I can without running toward my police cruiser.

"Tala," he calls out to me, but I don't turn back. I can't.

Chapter Three

Channing

There is no way in hell the woman has me fooled. Something is wrong. Big time. You'd think she'd be a better liar, watching criminals lie all the time. She's a fine cop, but damn.

Maybe it's just that no one knows her like I do. She's mine. She always will be, no matter what she does with her life. And there is no way she's staying home alone tonight, not with whatever's going on out there, making her lie badly to me.

I glance at my watch. It's ten PM. Late enough to duck out of this wedding.

I head out to my truck parked in the lot beyond the tent. The reception music—some godawful pop song someone must've requested—follows me as I make my escape into the darkness. I think I'm free and clear when I catch movement coming from under Rafe's truck, which is parked next to mine.

I freeze, suddenly remembering Tala's police radio trying to tell her something she didn't want me to hear. My instincts click into overdrive, the coyote under my skin champing at the bit, demanding release. I shut out the music, focusing on the scents and sounds around me.

And then the shadow under the truck emerges. I lower myself to the ground, preparing to shift and fight if I have to.

"Relax, man. It's me."

Weylin. It's just Weylin.

"What the fuck are you doing under Rafe's truck?" I ask, my voice edgy with adrenaline.

Weylin stands up, and it's then I see he's holding string and a bunch of empty soda cans. "It's a wedding, remember?" He shrugs, the cans rattling against each other. "We've gotta get the truck ready for their send off. Here," he says, dropping the string and pulling a can of silly string from his pants pocket. "Help me out, would you? Cover as much of the truck as you can."

He tosses me the can, but I toss it back to him. "Can't. I've got to get out of here."

Even in the dim of early nighttime, I can see the expression of pity on his face. It stirs something in me—not anger, I think. Determination. "It's not the wedding. Tala was here, just a couple minutes ago."

Weylin stares, his eyes wide. "What? Why?"

I shrug. "I don't know. She was hiding something though. I'm headed out to her place, to keep an eye on her."

"Keep an eye on her? You think she's in danger?"

"I don't know. All I know is that I need to make sure she's okay."

Weylin narrows his eyes at me, his jaw set in an expression I know well. He may be the youngest of us, but he's a mirror of our father and was born with an old soul.

"Be careful, Channing. I mean it."

"I will," I say, and I do mean it. I have a plan.
****

I drive to her house, hoping she hasn't moved to a different place since we broke up. But no, about a quarter mile away, I can make out her police cruiser in the driveway. I don't want her to know I'm here, so I pull over onto a rural side road and ease my truck between some pines, hiding it from view. If she shifts tonight, she'll know I'm here. I can't do anything about my scent. But it's worth a try.

I take off my jacket and the rest of the suit and shoes and the terrible tie, and everything else, until I'm standing naked in the darkness. I love this, this feeling of freedom. My coyote shift comes over me easily, my animal form rejoicing in the dark night and space in which to roam.

My heightened sense of smell helps me to home in on her immediately, and I have to push it aside so I can focus and do what I came here to do—to stake the place out and make sure she's safe and the only one here.

So far, so good.

I cross over the road and descend into the wooded ravine that surrounds her property. I haven't been here since I proposed to her and she immediately handed the ring back to me. We have a lot of memories here. Too many, maybe. I'm having a hard time concentrating on anything else.

It's this lack of concentration that almost costs me my life.

I'm prowling around the porch when the front door of her farmhouse opens, throwing a beam of yellow light out into the yard, illuminating me. I duck away, lowering myself into the shadows of a nearby tree. But it's too late. In the shaft of light I see her silhouette, aiming her handgun—directly at me.

"Stand up!" she shouts, her voice steady, strong, lethal. "Come out and let me see you!"

Okay. The jig is up. She's about to get what she asked for, an eyeful of it.

I step out into the light again and shift, making sure she can see me. One of the advantages of dating another shifter—you never have to explain why you've shown up to her house naked.

"Channing."

Her voice resonates with relief. Who did she

think it was?

"You'd better get in here."

She doesn't sound too happy about inviting me in. I try not to let it bother me. Right now I'm more worried about why she's so jumpy.

She watches me walk up the steps, her gaze staying on me as I pass her to enter the house. When I'm inside, she closes the door and deadbolts it.

Then she whirls on me. "What are you doing here?" She punches me in the shoulder. Hard. "What if I shot you, you idiot? Have you already forgotten what happened to your brother?"

I rub my shoulder. Damn, Tala can hit. "I didn't mean to get caught…" I say, flinching at the way my explanation sounds. "I mean—I'm not trying to break in or stalk you or any creepy shit, Tala. I'm sorry."

"Okay." She nods, but she's studying me like she's not sure what to believe. "Then why are you here?"

"I'm worried about you. You were acting kind of off at the wedding, and I don't think it was all because of me."

She puts her handgun down and crosses her arms, like she's officially interrogating me. "So you're skulking around my house because you thought I was acting weird?"

I scrub my hands over my face. "Damn it, Tala. If you would tell me the truth already about why you were at the wedding…"

"I told you. I was keeping an eye on things."

"What *things*?"

She sighs, a long, drawn-out sound I know well. For her, I think, it's the sound of resignation.

"I was on patrol, okay?"

She glares at me, clearly pissed I pushed her to tell me this much. But I don't give up easily. "What were you patrolling?"

She starts to walk away from me, but I catch her by the arm and hold her. "Tala, please. Tell me."

"Channing. It's work stuff. You remember how it is."

Yeah, I remember. But there's no way in hell I'm letting this go yet. And she's not going to like what I plan to do about it. Here goes.

"Well, you're not staying alone tonight, anyway," I tell her, using the belligerent tone she hates, but hey—whatever it takes.

She blinks, real slow. "What?"

"I said, you're not staying alone tonight. Let me hang out on your couch. I'll keep watch for you."

She blinks again, stunned, I think. I try not to let it sting. "Is the suggestion of my staying over so bad, Tala?"

"N—no." She shakes her head, and I think I believe her. "It's—well—I haven't *seen* you in a year and you show up at my house like this…"

She waves her hand over me. I guess my nudity does have some effect on her after all. I smile at her, my best half-cocked expression she used to love. I'm ready for her to fight me on this, with everything she's got, and I'm ready for it.

"Okay, Channing. You can crash on my couch."

Really? Why so easy?

"For tonight and tonight only. You got it?"

I nod, speechless. Is her secret so bad she actually wants me here to watch over her? Or is there another reason she doesn't mind me sleeping over? There's a nudge of hope rising in my chest, somewhere in the region of my heart.

Chapter Four

Tala

I hope Channing doesn't get the wrong idea. When he showed up, I was pissed—mostly because he knows better than to sneak up on me. I might've shot him. Not that he wouldn't have deserved it for prowling around my place uninvited.

But now—now I can keep watch over him without him having to know why I would need to in the first place. Apparently, he still hasn't found out about Bryce.

Channing must've left his phone in his truck with his clothes, or he'd know by now. I sent officers out to his parents' house and his brothers' houses too. The locals know who Bryce is, most know his reputation as a convicted killer—what the human locals will never know is that Bryce's victims are always shifters. No one knows how he sniffs them out, but if he's on the loose, one can't be too careful.

I'll tell Channing the truth tomorrow morning. At least this way I won't have to worry about him running around out there tonight, looking for a serial killer. Maybe by tomorrow morning the feds will have found him.

"Well, goodnight then," I say to him, avoiding eye contact as I make my way toward my bedroom. "You know where everything is. Help yourself to whatever you need."

I close my bedroom door behind me. I'm tempted to lock it—not because I'm afraid of Channing, but because I'm afraid of the temptation he is, sleeping twenty feet away from me.

I've missed him. In every way possible.

Take a cold shower, Tala.

I remove my uniform and do exactly that, the cold water reviving me. I slip on my nightgown and slide between the sheets, reaching under my pillow for the familiar comfort of my service weapon.

Damn. There's nothing there. Channing's arrival messed with my routine and I've forgotten it, left it on the table next to the living room couch—where Channing has probably fallen asleep by now.

Damn it. I can't sleep without it. Especially now, with Bryce out there somewhere. I'll have to risk waking him to retrieve it. I flip the lock and open the bedroom door, as slow as I can stand it. Then I slip through, my bare feet silent on the hardwood floor.

There's some light filtering through the windows from the moon and I can see his body, stretched out on the couch as much as a man of his build can stretch on a couch, anyway. He's covered, just barely, with the couch throw, and I suffer a stab of guilt for not taking the time to find him a better blanket. He is naked, after all.

I try not to stare at his smooth skin and bulging biceps as I creep closer to the end table. My weapon rests there, so close. Two more steps. One more step.

"I knew you couldn't resist, babe."

Damn.

His voice rumbles through the quiet room.

"I'm here for my gun, Channing. I left it on the table." I point to it. I need him to see I'm not lying. Otherwise, he will get the wrong idea, for sure.

He glances at the gun, then at me, then he stands, the small blanket falling to the floor.

"Come here," he says quietly, gesturing to the couch. "Sit with me. Let's talk for a minute. Then you can go to bed."

"Channing, I can't…" My unspoken words die on my tongue when he steps in front of me and lowers his lips to mine, so close his breath whispers against my skin.

"Channing." What was I going to say? His scent surrounds me, enveloping me in memories; beautiful, delicious memories.

Chapter Five

Channing

I watch her eyes. I want her to want what I'm about to do as much as I want it. Then I pull her into my arms, against my chest, and slide my hands down to her butt, holding her as tight as I can without hurting her.

"Come on, Tala. Don't you need some release?" Her eyes widen a little when I say 'release.' I'm encouraged. "I can make you feel so good. You remember." I say this and press into her a little harder until I know she can tell just how badly I need her. "Tala," I whisper into her ear, brushing her cheek with my lips—something she always loved. "Tala, *remember*."

Oh, she remembers, all right. I can feel her hardening nipples through her shirt. I grasp her tighter, grinding my hips into hers. She gasps, tilting her head back. *Yes.*

"Tala." Saying her name again, and like this. I swear I'd die for this. "*Tala*," I say her name again, whispering it over and over again in her ear while I brush my lips over her cheek, her, chin, her neck.

Her fingers skate across my naked back. *Yes,* this is happening. I knew it. She's never stopped wanting me.

I grind into her again, again. I need more. I'm desperate. Starving. My inner beast is raging under my skin and it's all I can do to tamp it down. "Tala," I moan, pleading.

I capture her lips with mine, kissing, kissing, devouring her top lip, then her bottom. When I pull away to catch my breath, she's panting breathily. Oh, fuck. She has no idea what she does to me.

"Tala, please," I beg. "Please."

Her hands move lower. God, yes. I pull away just enough to grant her access. Her fingertips slide over my hip bones, then graze over my swollen, aching cock.

"*Fuck*," I groan, thrusting into her hand. "I've dreamed about this. So many nights…"

I can't finish what I was going to say because she's massaging me now, with both hands, her grip strong and confident. *Fuck.* If she keeps this up, this'll be over way too fast.

But damn, I don't want her to stop. I close my eyes and thrust into her hands, trying to ease this terrible ache. And then, suddenly, she lets go. My eyelids are heavy with lust, but when I open them—oh God. She's taken me into her mouth. Her full, lush red lips are wrapped around my cock. *I'm dead,* I think. *I must be. There's no way this is really happening.* It's like all this time apart—it's like it never even happened.

She hums a little, creating a vibration I remember all too well. She's sucking, hard.

"*Tala,*" I'm practically whimpering as I say her name. She sucks harder, her hands wrapping around my balls, kneading them. Oh yeah, she knows what she does to me.

I nudge deeper into her hot wet mouth, my hips thrusting harder, faster.

I can't hold back. I want to. I planned to. But I can't. I can't … she's … oh, God.

"Tala, *wait.*"

She stops, staring at me with those dark eyes of hers, shining with lust.

I grab her hand, guiding her over to the sofa. I pick her up, lay her on the leather cushions, then fumble with her nightgown. I think, *no way I'm going to make it*, when my fingers find bare skin where her panties should be. *Yes*. I dip my fingertips inside her, teasing, rubbing. I want to do more to her, but there's no time.

"Now, *now*." She gasps.

She grabs my cock, guiding me into her. I push, push, all the way in. "*Channing*." She cries out my name, her inner walls closing tight around me. "Oh, damn. Oh damn. Oh—oh!"

Holy shit. *This*. Oh, God. I can't think. She's coming, hard. I thrust. And thrust. More. More. *More*. "Tala," I moan. "Tala, I'm—"

She wraps her legs around me, latching on, locking me against her. She cries out, finishing me. I release on a shout, and then another, as wave after wave of ecstasy swallows me. Fuck, I can't breathe. I'm seeing stars.

I come back to myself slowly, and find Tala staring up at me, studying me. Her fingers are brushing over my forehead in soft, comforting strokes.

Thank God, she's not looking at me with regret. No, there's a certain sadness in her eyes, I think. *Don't analyze it, Channing. Just enjoy the moment.* And that's exactly what I plan to do.

I stand, taking a second to catch my breath.

"Channing, what are you do—"

Before she can finish, I scoop her up into my arms and carry her into the bedroom.

Chapter Six

Tala

I awaken before Channing does. He's naked and on his back, his left arm flush against my body, his hand cradling mine, his fingers interlocked with mine. We've slept, for who knows how long, like this, hand-holding while we dreamed. The thought makes my heart flutter in my chest.

How could he ever think I stopped loving him?

Some slight movement catches my eye and I realize Channing must be having a very certain sort of dream. His cock is swelling, stiffening, as his grip on my hand tightens. A low groan rumbles from deep within his chest and his back bows, ever so slightly, off the mattress.

A powerful jolt of lust punches through me, stealing my breath. Instantaneous, searing heat sizzles through every cell in my body.

He groans in his sleep again. I start to rise to my knees, trying not to bounce the bed. His grip on my hand tightens. "Mmmm."

My gaze snaps to his face, still serene and sleeping, but there's a tightness to his jaw as he murmurs while he dreams.

That does it for me. I manage to slip my hand from his as I shift my body until I'm straddling him. His hips suddenly jerk a little, lifting, enough that the tip of his cock rubs against me. My skin burns and heat rages through my blood.

I move my hips. Hijacked by desire, I grind against his hard shaft, savoring the sensation of silk over hard steel.

Channing moans incoherently as he thrusts his pelvis upward, his tip nudging inside me. Damn. I'm dizzy with need. I lower myself an inch, then another, and when he thrusts up from the bed again, I'm partially impaled by him. A sharp intake of breath bursts from me before I can stop it.

His eyelashes flutter open, his gaze colliding with mine in the dawn-lit bedroom.

"*Tala*," he hisses, wrapping his hands around my hips, his fingers clutching me like a lifeline. "I thought I was dreaming."

"You were," I whisper. It's hard to speak, hard to find the breath for it. "But," I gasp as his hold tightens, pulling me down onto him even more. "You're not dreaming anymore."

His eyes widen and he smiles. "I want to wake up like this every day."

So do I. But I can't. *We* can't. This—this is just for fun, it can't mean anything, not anymore.

"Fuck," he wheezes, pulling me from my thoughts.

He pushes against my pelvis, then starts to withdraw, leaving me aching, empty. "Channing," I whimper, desperate.

"What's the matter?" he teases, his smile growing as he pulls away from me almost completely. "You want me?"

I lift a hand to his face, cradling his bristled jaw. "You know I do."

I press my lips to his to prove it. He devours my kiss, biting my lip and slipping his tongue inside my mouth. He thrusts his tongue against mine, again and again, until he breaks the kiss with an anguished groan. "Show me." His voice is rough, rumbling within his chest. "Show me how much you want me."

I grasp his cock as I straddle him, sitting back on my heels. I take my time, my limbs trembling, as I lower myself over him. He's hard and hot and throbbing as I start to slide down over him. It's not an easy thing. He's almost too big, really, and I'm only halfway down when I need to stop.

"Come on," he murmurs. "You've done this before, sweetheart."

Ah. How I've missed his voice, especially his impassioned sex voice. Heightened desire flares within me. I lower myself another inch, then another. His breathing is labored as he holds steady.

"I need," he rasps. "I—ah. *Tala.*"

He's thrusting, ever so gently, moving his hips up and down in an undulating rhythm.

He's so deep inside me, every tiny move he makes fills me, his tip teasing against my clit. There is no pain, only building heat and pleasure every time he thrusts.

His hands move from my hips to my breasts. He fondles them, squeezes them, his thrusts increasing in strength until he's pushing us both up off the bed. His fingertips brush over my nipples, then skim the undersides of each breast slowly, the sensation sending prickles of electric heat straight down between my legs.

I cry out a little, riding him harder, tightening my inner muscles around his pulsating cock.

"Fuck," he breathes. He lowers his hands until he's holding my hips again, slamming me down on him with an almost aggressive force.

That does it for me. "Channing," I whimper, still struggling for breath. "Channing." I'm unable to utter anything else.

He pumps harder, faster, impossibly deeper. I clench him tight as a climax crashes over me. I shout something incoherent, riding wave after wave of raw, burning pleasure. He keeps driving upward into me, his eyes closed and his lips parted. I want to make him come, hard, like he did me. I clasp him again, swiveling my hips, shoving him inside so deep it hurts.

"*Oh*, Oh shit," he moans, writhing beneath me. "Holy sh—"

He comes, and so do I—again, when his liquid heat bursts into me. We both keep moving against each other, rocking our bodies back and forth, riding the aftershocks, one right after the other.

"Tala," he whispers, wrapping his hands around my arms, guiding me off him and onto the mattress next to him. "Just marry me already."

Oh, Channing. No.

I sit up in bed, pulling the sheet to my chest. "Honey, I *told* you—"

"I know what you said." He rises off the bed, standing over me. Then he lowers himself to the floor on one knee. "But I don't care. Marry me, Tala."

I grip the sheet so hard my knuckles ache. Here we go. His heart is going to break all over again.

"No." I almost choke on the word, knowing what it will do to him.

"We aren't over, Tala. If last night and this morning have taught you anything…" He stands and strides across the room toward the door, then stops, turning to me. "You *can't* tell me we're not perfect for each other."

Damn it.

"I'm not saying that. But how perfect we are for each other is irrelevant."

"*Irrelevant*?" He runs his hands over his scalp, then smacks the doorframe with his hand. "*Fuck* relevant, Tala. Do you love me or not?"

This is it. My chance to break it off with him once and for all, my chance to protect him. Because I love him more than I can ever make him understand.

I'm a terrible liar, something he used to always tease me for. But now—now I have to lie better than I've ever lied before. His life may depend on it. I look him straight in those unearthly green eyes of his.

"No, Channing. I'm sorry. I did once, but—I don't love you anymore."

His gaze hardens, his jaw a rock-hard line. "You're lying."

Hold it together, remember what's at stake, I remind myself.

"No, I'm not, Channing. I. Don't. Love. You."

His eyes flash and he studies me, like he's committing my face to memory, like he's never going to see me again. Then he turns away and bolts out the door.

A sense of unease shivers down my spine.

God. What have I done?

Chapter Seven

Channing

I shift the second I'm out the front door. Goddamn, but she hurt me bad this time. Why did I expect one night with her would change her mind?

You're a fucking idiot, that's why.

I run, my four feet eating up the distance like it's nothing. I'm grateful for this animal skin, grateful it doesn't let me feel the burn of shame and humiliation and unbelievable pain my human body would.

I'll grieve over her all over again. What the hell was I thinking? Stupid. Stupid. Stupid. I run faster, hitting the ground in time with the beat of my thoughts.

Maybe I should stay in my shifted form, living in the endless acres of forests, avoiding Tala and other humans forever.

The thought is tempting. No more exposure to anyone who can hurt me. Just rise, eat, run, sleep. Tempting.

In the distance, I can see my truck parked, nestled in the trees. Once I get there I'll put my clothes back on, check my phone, get ready to head back into work tomorrow, and then go home to my silent, lonely house.

Or not.

I hesitate, standing at the edge of the road, switching my gaze between my truck and the stretch of forest behind me.

I'll go back to Tala's, I decide. I'm not giving up on us so easily. All I need to do is prove it to her.

I should've kept going, or turned back, or never left the warmth of Tala's bed in the first place. Because one second I'm paused by the roadside, contemplating this insane decision, and then—after it's already too late—a strange, dangerous smell hits me full on as the sound of bootsteps rushes up behind me. I hunch low and twist my head toward the source of the smell and the sound, but it's too late. All I catch is a glimpse of a man in an orange prison jumpsuit, with a huge mesh net in one hand, and a baseball bat in the other.

Shit! Run! My inner human voice screams.

But I don't get the chance to even begin to shift before the baseball bat comes down, bashing me full in the face.

****

Now

I close my eyes and open them again. Nothing but inky blackness as far as I can see.

God, my head. My *jaw*. It feels like something shattered it.

And fuck. Why can't I see?

"Wakey, wakey, you filthy dog."

Dog? I don't recognize the voice coming from somewhere behind me. I'm lying down on my side. I stretch out my hands, trying to push myself up, trying to remember how I ended up on the ground in the first place. There's a smell of dust beneath me, so much it's almost a soft layer under my body.

I remember the forest—I was in the forest—no, on the edge of it. And I was in my shifted form. But not anymore. I blink again and realize I can see my hands, bound together by links of chain.

Fuck. This.

The beast within me rolls under my skin, raging to escape. *Be calm, be calm.* The last thing I need to do is go full out coyote when I don't even know where I am.

I blink, trying to let my eyes adjust to the thick

darkness. *Focus.*

I can make out the shapes of some sort of barricade around me. I inhale, breathing in the scent of hay and old wood. A barn? A stall? I blink again, trying to see better, but I can't. Either it's simply dark as pitch in here or whoever attacked and kidnapped me hit me hard enough to damage my sight.

My stomach does a twisting sort of flip-flop at the thought. I don't feel good at all. And I don't remember shifting back into my human form, which makes me hard-core uneasy.

"Did you hear what I said, you fuckin' mutt?"

Every muscle in me tenses and goes still. If I'm in my human body, and this crazy-ass dude is calling me a dog and a mutt—*shit.*

I remember now. He hit me with a fucking baseball bat when I was still a coyote. He knows I'm a shifter. This psycho motherfucker knows what I am. And he's got me chained up so damn tight the metal links he's bound me with are biting deep into my wrists.

I try to loosen the chains enough to slip a hand free, but I stop when there's a warm gush of wetness sliding down each forearm.

"Don't bother," he says, moving closer, in front of me. He's a silhouette in the darkness I can barely see. "I locked those suckers on you so tight, you won't slip 'em, not even if you shift." He laughs. I strain my eyes, trying to see him.

"Who are you?" I ask, my voice raspy. It hurts to talk, to move, to breathe. I want to, *need* to try to get up, try to fight my way out of here.

"Bryce Holter. I've been looking for one of you fuckers for a *long*-ass time."

Bryce Holter? *Oh, shit. Fucking shit.* "You're the shifter-killer."

He laughs again. "Well, yeah, I guess I am."

All the locals have heard of Bryce Holter. We shifters know him as a bat-shit crazy psychopath who targets our kind. A few years ago he was finally put away with a life-term for murdering a couple a few towns away.

"But you're supposed to be in prison. You were convicted of murder."

"Broke out. Had unfinished business."

Oh, I can imagine what he means by that. "You broke out to keep hunting shifters." I've got to be careful about what I say, in case he doesn't know about my family. Or Tala.

Tala.

I can't let this asshole anywhere near her.

"Well, yeah. What else? All I've gotta do is prove to the world what you are, show 'em I was never lying in the first place. After I show everybody how I've saved them, hunting down you monsters—well, they'll clear me of all charges, make me a free man."

What a full-on nutjob. "You killed people, Holter. No one's going to clear your record." *You fucking moron.*

"*They will!*" He's suddenly in my face, screaming. "And you're gonna do every fucking thing I tell you, or I'm gonna cut you so bad, you're gonna beg for me to kill you, and when I'm done havin' fun with you, I'll find every last mutt you know and kill 'em."

He'll do what he says. I can hear it in his voice. Funny, of all the ways I've ever imagined I may die, getting kidnapped and tortured to death by a raving, homicidal lunatic was not one of them.

But Tala. And my family. If I die, who's going to warn them? I'll do anything to keep them safe.

I take a shaky breath, raising my head up to the shadowed figure standing over me. My decision is an easy one.

"Fine," I say. "You win. What do you want me to do?"

"I want my proof. No one believes me. You're going to do your thing and transform into a dog while I film you. That'll show 'em. They'll pin a medal on me after this. They won't call me a murderer anymore."

He leans in so close to me I can smell his breath, rancid and heavy with tobacco smoke. "They'll call me Bryce Holter—monster killer."

Chapter Eight

Tala

I call Channing. When he doesn't answer, I call again. And again. He's pissed at me, I get it. Beyond pissed, probably, since I crumbled his heart into tiny pieces this morning. I'd hate me too.

Apologizing wasn't the only reason I had in mind for calling him. I checked in with the station this morning, and Bryce Holter is still loose. I *need* to know where Channing is. There's a solid lump of unease sitting heavy in my chest.

By mid-afternoon, I give up. I'm off duty, but my instincts are screaming at me to take the cruiser out for a drive. I should stop by Channing's house too, see if he's really not answering his phone simply because he's furious with me.

I'm on my way out the door, keys in hand, when my phone buzzes in my pocket. *Finally.* I breathe a sigh of relief. *He's calling me back*, I think.

But no. I pull my phone out and look at it. Weylin, not Channing. Weylin never calls me, at least he hasn't since his brother and I broke up a year ago.

I swipe the screen, my hand a little unsteady. "Weylin?"

"Hey, Tala. I think something's wrong."

My breath catches. I pause for a second, fortifying myself. "What's happened? Are my officers still keeping an eye out at your place? Is it Bryce?" All the possible scenarios whirl through my mind, but I know, of course, what he's going to say before he says it.

"It's Channing. He's missing."
****

I find his truck alongside the road, not a mile from my house. Locked inside it are his clothes and cell phone. Wherever he is, he's either shifted or he's running around naked. It's possible he's chosen to remain in his coyote form all day.

But what if? What if something has happened?

I search the perimeter of the truck, then spread out, further and further, trying to cover any place he might've traversed. I imagine where Channing would walk, what paths he chose. It's not hard. I know him well—well enough that I should've known better than to upset him this morning, forcing him out and onto Bryce's radar.

Guilt. It stabs through me, making my chest hurt. If anything has happened to Channing— I pause at the edge of the road to catch my breath, imagining my life without him. This last year without him has been hell, if I'm honest. The only thing that carried me through was convincing myself I did the right thing by rejecting him.

But now…

I just need to find him. Immediately.

I press on, crossing the road, and that's when I see it. There are some long, wild grasses on the edge of the forest, swaying in the late afternoon breeze. Several blades are broken and bent, crushed by something heavy. I hunch down, investigating closer.

And that's when I notice the blood.

Chapter Nine

Channing

Holter knows nothing about shifters. God only knows how he ever found out about us. But one thing's for sure.

Despite what he thinks, these chains aren't going to hold me, not once I shift.

Which will be soon. And then … then I'm going to kick his ass. He's a murderer and these chains are goddamned tight, but there's no *way* in hell I'm not getting out of them and taking him down before he gets to Tala.

Footsteps shuffle through the hay and the dust. "Smile for the camera," he says, standing *right* next to me with a small video camera in his hand, the light from the camera illuminating the dark with harsh brightness.

Oh, I'll smile for you, all right. Right before I rip out your heart with my teeth.

"Okay. When I say shift, shift."

I force myself to raise my chin and look up so I can see him. It'll be more fun crushing that smug-ass grin from his face if I see what he looks like before I pulverize him.

He's smiling, all right. Looking down on me like he owns the world. "Why the hell do you hate us so much?" The words burst out of me.

His face twists, the smile disappears. "None of your goddamn business."

He's riled. Good. "Yeah, I think it is my business. You've got me chained up in a barn and you're threatening my people."

"Your people?" He laughs, a harsh croak coming

from his throat. "You ain't *people*."

And then, faster than I'd imagined possible, his booted foot comes up lightning-quick toward my face. I jerk out of the way, but he still skims the side of my sore head with his heel.

Big mistake, motherfucker.

"Now. Shift. *Now*." Holter spits out every word.

I'm keeping my face angled away from him, in case he decides to try again. My blood is boiling hot and the coyote within wants out so bad I don't think I could hold him back if I wanted to. The agony in my head beats a pulse of *rage, rage, rage.*

The fury strengthens me, white-hot adrenaline sizzling through me as I transform. My claws come out. My legs and arms narrow into canine limbs, and as I hoped—with some luck and a little more pain, I'm able to slip free of the chains.

****

Tala

It's the blood that helps me find him. There's something to be said for being both a shifter and a cop. With my heightened sense of smell, I detect the coppery scent miles away.

"Chief Akecheta," a voice crackles through my police radio and I turn the volume down. I pull over, slowing my car to a stop alongside an old dirt road. There's an abandoned-looking barn standing on the top of the hill and I don't want to be seen. I turn the car off and step out silently, inhaling the smells carried on the wind.

If my senses are as strong as I think they are, Channing is here.

"*Chief Akecheta*." The voice is more persistent, worried, probably. I should respond. But calling for backup when a shifter is involved in an incident is tricky—most of the other officers I work with are humans and they have no idea shifters exist. I plan to keep it that way.

But not telling anyone at dispatch where I am is sheer stupidity, so I quickly check in and add "potential lead on location of Bryce Holter" before giving my location. Hopefully this will give me enough time to get Channing out free and clear before the human officers and press swarm the scene.

"*No!*"

A scream pierces the air, shrill and violent. I pull my weapon free of its holster and start to run up the hill to the barn, where the cry seems to have come from. My feet whip through the grasses and my heart starts to beat a rapid rhythm.

"No! *No!*" The voice again. Definitely a man's voice. And definitely not Channing's. I'd know Channing's deep baritone anywhere.

Breathing hard, I race up the last leg of the hill and I see a door, warped and bent, partially open. I dig my fingers into the old wood and pull.

Hurry, Tala, Hurry. I have a sick feeling in my stomach, a squirming mass of unease so strong it takes my breath away. There's no more sound coming from in the barn as I slip inside, darkness instantly swallowing me.

And then—a growl. So long and so low it comes from the bottom of the earth. It's a rumble I feel all the way to my toes.

Channing.

"Fucking mutt!" A man shrieks, and then, by the sound of it, he falls to the ground.

Keeping my weapon in one hand, I reach for my flashlight with the other. My hands are shaking, ever so slightly. I've never had to come in shooting before and I've always hoped I'd never have to—especially when someone I know—someone I love—is involved.

Someone I love.

Keep it together, Tala. I take a breath, hold it. Then I flick the flashlight on and direct the beam of light toward the direction of the sounds of struggle. Instantly, white light washes over a man lying on the floor, covered in dust, grappling with a gigantic coyote.

Bryce Holter. And Channing.

Shit.

Don't think about it. Just stop them.

"Freeze! This is the police!" My voice resonates throughout the barn.

Bryce doesn't falter one bit. But Channing— Channing stops and lifts his head, his animal-yet-human eyes meeting mine.

Something flashes in the light—something metallic.

Shit. Bryce has a knife.

"Stop, Holter! Or I will shoot you!"

Channing has Holter pinned to the ground but I'm afraid it's not enough to hold him for long. Holter twists his head until he's facing me, his eyes glittering with pure craziness. "No you won't," he rasps. Channing is standing on his chest, his teeth bared and poised over Holter's throat. "You can't shoot me without putting a hole in this—this thing."

Channing is looking at me still, watching, I think—to see what I want him to do. I know what he wants. This ass-wipe Holter hurt him, took him, for God-only-knows what reason. Channing wants vengeance. But he's not a killer.

"Holter! I said—"

The blade catches in the light, rising high.

Channing lunges, but Holter's blade sinks into Channing's flesh.

"No!" The word rips from my throat. I slam the flashlight against the handle of my weapon, directing the beam at my target. Channing hasn't backed off at all, though I can see the glistening of blood spread wide across his flank. "*Move*, Channing!"

He listens to me, crouching low, but Holter raises the knife high again, reeling back for another attack.

I fire.

The blast dispels the darkness with a flash of white.

The recoil knocks the flashlight from my hand and it turns off, throwing the barn into thick blackness once again.

"Channing! *Channing*. Are you all right?"

I'm scrambling for the damn flashlight, my fingers suddenly trembling so much it's all I can do to fumble through the dust. "Channing!"

"Tala, relax. I'm fine."

There. I find the barrel of the flashlight and switch it on again. I shine the light ahead and see Channing, in human form, on his knees in the dust. Next to him is Bryce Holter, unmoving, with a bullet hole in his forehead.

"It's okay, honey. He's down. You got him."

"Shit." It's all I can say for a second. I wanted to take Holter to trial. I didn't get up this morning thinking I was going to kill someone.

But Channing—he's breathing hard, squinting into the bright flashlight beam. I holster my weapon and kneel next to him. A red smear of blood covers his right shoulder and darker, older blood has dried in rivulets over his head and face.

"You're so not fine," I mutter, not trusting my

427

voice. There's a lump in my throat, threatening to choke me.

"There's an emergency kit in my car," I say in a hoarse whisper. "Can you walk?"

I want to get us both out of here and away from Holter's dead, staring eyes. Channing nods. He leans on me as he stands, a testament, I think, to how shitty he's feeling.

I manage to get us to the door and then I kick it open, giving us more room to get through. My adrenaline is still running high and the door flies off the hinges. We step into the diminishing light and Channing starts shaking. I stop, alarmed. "Are you—" And then I realize— "Are you *laughing*?"

He is. The sonofabitch is laughing at me. "Remind me not to ever push you too far, Tala," Channing says, wincing.

"You're an ass," I say, but there's no anger edging my voice. I'm relieved he's well enough to laugh at me.

We stumble down the hill to my cruiser, slipping with awkward steps. The closer we get to the car, the more Channing leans on me. "Hold up," I say, trying not to sound as worried as I feel. "Here. Sit in the grass and rest against the wheel."

There's an emergency kit in the trunk with bandages, a blanket, and a few other things that might prove useful. I grab the bandages first and lower myself into the grass next to him. He's got a hand over his ribs where Holter stabbed him.

"Let me see."

Channing hesitates, blinking slow. "Leave it. It'll heal on its own. Give it time."

Stupid, stubborn man.

"I know how shifter healing works, Channing.

And it doesn't happen fast if the wound is deep. Let me see."

His lips are set in a tight line, his skin paler and clammier than it should be. Still, he doesn't move his hand. *Oh, come on.*

"Channing—"

"On one condition."

What? "What are you talking about? You're probably bleeding to death. Let. Me. See."

"I will. If you admit something to me."

Oh, Jesus Christ. "We don't have time to chat, Channing."

He flinches, going paler still. What if he really is bleeding to death? "Okay, goddamn it," I concede, my throat going dry with fear. "But hurry the hell up."

He smiles a shaky smile. "This whole thing with Holter." He pauses, catching a breath. I hold mine. "He got to me even though you and I aren't married. Aren't even together."

"Okay…"

"So, you see what I'm trying to say?"

Ah. I see. "And you're bringing this up *now*?"

"Why not?" His smile turns cocky, self-assured. "I've got your full attention, baby."

Then his face turns serious, and I put my hands over his hand that's covering his chest, trying to force it away so I can do something about the knife wound.

"Wait. Tala. Listen. Look at me."

I do, hoping his stubbornness doesn't kill him.

"The people you care about can get hurt whether they're with you or without you. I can get hurt, even though I'm not married to you."

I know what he says is true. I get it. "But my job—"

"Saved my life. If anything, I'm safer with you

than without you."

I don't have a response for that. I do want to marry him. It's just the fear—it's had a hold on me for so long now.

"You're a badass, Tala. I wouldn't change it for anything. But don't make me stay away. I need you."

He stares at me, expectantly, I suppose, waiting for me to tell him I need him too. I *miss* him. But...

"Give me time," I tell him, watching his hopeful expression crumble. "That's not a *no*, Channing."

I will marry him. When I'm ready.

"First you have to let me save your life. Move. Your. Hand."

He smiles again, gently, and then grimaces when I push one of the bandages into the hole in his flesh. "Not so cocky now, are you?"

"Don't enjoy this too much."

I'm not enjoying it at all. Watching Bryce Holter almost murder Channing has put me in anything but an enjoyable mood. His pallor worries me. "We've got to get you to one of our people at the hospital."

Our people—the local doctors and nurses who are shifters or know about shifters and won't freak out when something weird pops up on blood tests.

"Too late for that," Channing says, his attention focused on something behind me, coming down the road. And then I hear them. Sirens.

Shit. It's my backup. "I had to call them. I didn't know what I was going to find. And now, since I had to kill Holter..." My heart is racing, an erratic drumbeat against my ribs.

"Don't worry, Tala. I've got you," Channing says, reaching up to push my hair behind my ear. "I'll tell them the truth. Holter kidnapped me because he found me alone on the road. He took me here, beat me up, stabbed me, stole my clothes. He was going to murder me until you stopped him. Nothing about my story is a lie, baby."

He's right. The only part we'll leave out is *why* Holter took Channing. It's irrelevant anyway, now with Holter dead.

"I know people at the hospital. It's all good, sweetheart. I promise."

I lean into his touch, his words. I do need this, whatever *this* is. Love, I suppose.

Chapter Ten

Channing

My tie is choking me. Again. It's been almost a year since I stood here, almost in the exact same place, grappling with my tie while waiting for my brother's bride to walk down the aisle. But it's not Rafe's woman I'm waiting for this time.

It's mine.

The music starts up, the guests—family and friends, shifters and humans—settle in their seats. After the whole Bryce Holter thing settled down, and my wounds healed up, Tala finally agreed to marry me. I almost lost her again six months ago when I told her I wanted to join her on the local police force. It took a hell of a lot of convincing, but I kicked ass all the way through the academy, and I think she likes having me by her side. She's my boss now, instead of Rafe. And Rafe had to hire somebody new to replace me at the shop. I like him more, now that I don't have to take orders from him all the time.

I'd rather take orders from my woman.

"Look alive, bro," Rafe says, elbowing me. "Here she comes."

Sweet Jesus. A door opens from outside and there she is. She's walking toward me with the sunlight shining behind her, her white dress glowing and her beautiful dark hair shimmering.

Goddamn.

Her eyes are sparkling in the soft light of the church. I never thought this would happen. There's a tightness in my chest and in my throat. Weylin is standing on my other side and he reaches out and squeezes my arm, just for a second, reminding me to breathe, I think.

When I catch my breath, it comes out as an exhalation with her name on my lips.

"Tala."

She smiles, stepping up to stand next to me on the dais. I know there are other people here, watching, but I don't care. I stare at her, drinking in her beauty, basking in the reality that she's finally marrying me.

The ceremony starts and we exchange the vows, the rings, the kiss. The kiss. This is where I almost lose my cool for real. Her dress is insane. The neckline plunges low between her breasts and hugs her curves tight. She's a present wrapped in silk and I want to unwrap her.

So when it's time to kiss her, I go for it, really go for it. I only stop when she bites me, gently, on my bottom lip. "We have an audience, Channing. Remember?" I hear her words, but her voice is anything but angry. It's amused, I think. And aroused.

The music roars to life again. We step down from the dais, and I get high-fived and back-slapped all the way down the aisle. The second we're outside, I draw her to me, kissing her again.

"We're supposed to meet the photographer in the garden behind the church," she says, laughing when I let her pull away to catch her breath.

"We will," I promise her. "Soon."

I'll die if I don't have her now. Waiting for hours until the reception is over? No way.

I take her hand, leading her out to the parking lot by the reception tent, where I saw her more than a year ago, for the first time since she broke my heart.

"Where are we going?"

I smile. "We're coming full circle, baby."

She smiles back. Yes. She's game for this, then. I pull my car keys out of my pocket and open the back door. My car is hidden, surrounded by trees. I glance around. No one is watching.

"Get in," I command, not that I need to. She's already sliding into the back seat, tugging me behind her by my tie.

I slip inside, pulling the door shut. She's kissing me. Everywhere. My neck, my face, my lips. I take her lips in mine and she bites me again. *Damn.* "Tala," I moan.

She's unbuttoning my fly with one hand, massaging my cock with the other. I thrust into her hand, desperate for relief. "*Tala.* I want us to go at it hard, baby." I know she knows what I mean by this. I want us both to shift and then screw until we both end up scratched and bleeding.

"We can't." She laughs. "Not now, at least. We've still got photos and a reception to get through."

"Fuck," I gasp as she wraps her hand around me like a vise. Then she suddenly releases me, leaving me aching. Through a heavy-lidded haze, I realize she's reaching under her dress, slipping off her panties. "God, yes," I say, my words a hoarse growl.

I wrap both hands around her body, laying her flat on the seat. I want to rip this dress off her.

"Remember, Channing. Careful."

It's like she can read my mind. "Later then," I promise her. Just wait until later.

As carefully as I can, I push her skirt high, sliding my hands along the smooth, silky skin of her thighs. She lifts up, high enough to capture my mouth with hers, kissing me, kissing me. Her breath is soft and panting and the sound of it pushes me past my last threshold of self-control.

"Tala…" It's all I can manage. I cover her body with mine, lifting her hips up to mine, then I shove my cock into her, all at once.

She cries out, arching her spine, wrapping her legs around me. "*Channing.*"

I pause, catching my breath. "Goddamn, Tala. I will never get tired of hearing you say my name like that."

She smiles. "Anytime you want," she says, her voice husky.

Anytime and forever, now that she's married me. The thought sends another surge of sizzling heat through my cock. I thrust again. Deep. It's not enough. I plunge into her again, harder this time, going deeper still. Her breath catches on a sharp inhalation and I know I've hit right where she likes it. I do it again. And again. She starts squeezing me with her inner walls every time I push into her, setting me on fire.

"*Fuck*, Tala," I gasp. When she wraps her legs around me tighter, pulling me in impossibly closer, I lose my ability to talk. "I ... ah, God. I'm going to ... *Tala.*" I give up trying.

Suddenly, I notice her chin is tilted high, a low whimper escaping her lips. I know what this means. And not a minute too soon. I drive myself into her on one last, savage thrust. "*Channing!*" She screams my name, her hips crashing into mine as she works herself on my cock. "Husband," she whimpers. "Husband."

That does it for me. I come in a white-hot blaze, wave after wave of blinding pleasure crashing over me. A harsh cry rips from my throat. My hips keep thrusting, riding the aftershocks. *Husband*, she said.

"You're mine," I manage to whisper. "Forever, Tala."

Mine.

The End

MY VERY SOUL

Tesla Storm

Chapter One

If there was anything to be said about the house of Elliot Rochester, it was this: something about it was wrong. It was huge, yes—a mansion if ever I had seen one and breathtakingly beautiful. The sprawling building sat at the edge of a glassy lake, complete with swans. The west-side walls were blanketed in a thick carpet of ivy, and the garden on the east side was lush and meticulously cared for. Every bloom was perfect, and not a petal seemed out of place. Every brick was aligned with the next, and every shutter was hung perfectly level. But that was it—the place was too perfect, as if it would disappear in the night, taking all the inhabitants with it.

It also had exactly zero cell service.

It wasn't, strictly speaking, my idea to work for a billionaire recluse in rural New Hampshire. In fact, it was the complete opposite of what any freshly graduated journalist would want. But as it turned out, my mother had been right—there just wasn't much you can do with an English degree. At least live-in tutors made money.

The front door, in keeping with the rest of the home, had an old-fashioned and heavy brass knocker that I stared at for at least thirty seconds before actually using it. And just as I expected, the person who answered the door was not my boss.

"You must be Miss Edwards," she said, pushing a shock of curly red hair out of her green eyes. "Come in."

"Jessa," I corrected her with a small smile. "Please."

"Oh." She smiled back, revealing a little gap between her two front teeth. "Then you can call me Grace. Grace Peterson."

I offered my hand to her, but she reached for my bags instead.

"I'll get you settled in." She lifted my suitcase as if it weighed nothing. "Mr. Rochester will want to have dinner with you."

So formal. I shouldered my duffel bag and dragged my footlocker over the threshold.

The inside of the house was just as immaculate as the outside. The banister curling around the staircase was clearly hand-carved, and the walls were hung with paintings that must have cost a fortune. I tried not to stare.

"This is your room," Grace explained, depositing my suitcase in front of a massive mahogany door complete with wall sconces on either side. With a smooth movement, she unhooked a ring of keys from her hip and dislodged a long, antique-looking specimen. She slid it into the lock easily, and with a metallic clunk, the door swung open.

Inside, there was a four-post bed enclosed with heavy velvet curtains, a stone fireplace, and a floor-to-ceiling window overlooking the west wing of the house. From my window, I could see a candle lit in the downstairs west wing, the light nearly obscured but for one small sliver between curtains.

"You'll want to wash up," Grace advised, giving me a once-over. "And dress for dinner."

She gave another half-smile, pocketed the skeleton key, and slipped away.

I tried not to think about her judgmental stare at my t-shirt and jeans.

****

Taking a page from Grace's book, I wore a dress to dinner. It was the only one I brought, but judging by the attire of the rest of the dinner party, I would need to buy more. Addison, the little girl I'd be spending my days with soon, was dressed in her Sunday best, a pink cotton dress and matching hair ribbons in her pigtailed hair. She was the picture of good manners, waiting quietly to be served and only staring at me when she thought I wasn't looking

Grace wore a different dress—a black, low-cut number that highlighted her ample chest, freckles sprinkled above and below her collarbone. And at the head of the table, in a sleek black suit, sat Elliot Rochester. The shirt inside his suit jacket was unfastened at least two buttons down, and he had abandoned his tie to eat. The swell of his Adam's apple peeked through the gap in the shirt, leading to a square jaw covered in a faint shadow of dark stubble. From this side of the candles burning on the table, that was nearly all I could see. Well, that, and the dark eyes peering from beneath a head of dark curls.

"You graduated from where?" he asked me, savagely spearing a potato with his fork. "Some public university?"

"Michigan State," I answered, sawing a piece of steak in two.

"Mmph." Another bite of potato, just as violent as the first. "So you think you're overqualified. Too good for the job?"

He locked those dark eyes on me again, and the full force of them felt like a palpable thing, like a wall of inexplicable fury coming across the table at me.

"I'm not too good for the job," I replied carefully.

"But you do think you're overqualified," he pressed, a nasty smile twisting his features.

I met his gaze levelly. "Wouldn't you agree?"

Grace's fork clattered to her plate, earning a look from everyone at the table. I wondered absently whether it was intentional because in a second, she was clearing her throat and speaking.

"Why don't you tell Jessa your favorite subject, Addie?" she prompted the little girl.

"Oh, that's English." Addie smiled wide. "Just like you. I want to be a writer."

I returned her sweet smile. "That's wonderful! We'll have to work on that as soon as possible."

A snort of derision came from the end of the table.

"That is," I continued, against my better judgment, "unless your daddy doesn't approve."

I raised my gaze to Mr. Rochester, not shying away when those black eyes bored into mine. I didn't even blink.

"Uncle," he corrected me stiffly. "I'm her uncle."

I was still staring at him, my jaw set and my dinner forgotten, when Grace rose suddenly.

"Addie, time for bed," she announced. And with a twitch of her mouth, she took the little girl's hand and left the cavernous dining room.

"I think I'll join them." I rose from the table, nearly knocking over the empty wine glass by my place setting. And I nearly made it out the door before a soft, strangled sound came from him and halted me.

"For us to coexist, you'll need to understand," he managed with difficulty. "I can be … difficult at this time of night."

I shot him a glare. "And I am tired."

Without another look in his direction, I followed Grace and Addison up the stairs.

****

It was a few hours after dark, as I was in the hazy space between sleep and awake, when I heard the subtle *chunk* sound from across the room. Soft as it was, I nearly jumped out of my skin in the darkness. It could have been anything—old houses made plenty of night noises, didn't they?—but it wasn't *anything*. I recognized the mechanical sound from earlier in the day.

It was the lock.

To check test my hypothesis, I crept across the room and tried the door handle. It didn't budge. I swallowed hard, trying to ignore the fear snaking up my throat. I tried to tell myself that I was safe in here. After all, wouldn't I rather be locked in than out? Here, nothing could get to me. But that did little to ease my terror. If Grace Peterson were locking me in this room, she was trying to keep me away from something. The question was … what?

That settled my mind a bit. Questions, no matter how dangerous, were the territory of journalists everywhere. The more dangerous the question, the better the story. And that was what convinced me to climb back into bed, only succeeding in resting my eyes for an hour or so.

Sleeping in the eerie chamber at the top of the

stairs proved even more difficult when the moon rose—full and luminous—to flood through the space between the dense curtains. With intentions of dousing that light, I rose from the soft mattress and padded to the window. Taking hold of one velvet curtain, I yanked the heavy fabric to the side, but it hardly budged. The next violent pull moved it half an inch.

Maddening.

Digging my fingers deeper into the velvet, I gritted my teeth, planted my feet, and prepared for the end-all-be-all death match with the curtains that prevented me from my much-needed sleep. But then, a sound.

The echoes of furniture being jarred made me freeze, hands still buried in material for a moment. Something like a snarl followed, more thumping, and a short squeal. My curiosity got the better of me, and I dropped the curtains to press toward the window. Below, the only light to be seen was the candle still burning in the bottom window. And after a quick flash of movement, that too was extinguished.

In the oppressive blackness that followed, only one sound could be a heard. A soft, mournful howl echoed through the mansion, raising goosebumps on my flesh.

Chapter Two

For the rest of my first week, I was mostly spared any interaction with the master of the house, which was to my liking. My bedroom door was also unlocked, which made me feel as though the events of the first night were all part of an elaborate nightmare. My time was spent mostly with Addie, who obediently completed her grammar exercises, played the piano, and sat politely. It was not, by any stretch of the imagination, interesting work. But something about the household—something beyond the strange first night that I wasn't sure I remembered quite right—still kept my interest.

In Grace's small smiles and frequent disappearances, there was a secret. And in Elliot Rochester's black eyes, there was something far more dangerous. But it was something I liked looking at all the same.

The only interruptions of my time with Addison were the nightly dinners Mr. Rochester insisted upon, always consisting of multiple courses, a red and white wine, and other perfectly ridiculous luxuries. I would be lying if I said I didn't enjoy them though. They provided me with an opportunity to watch him, and in some deep part of me, I suspected he was watching me too. Taking stock. Making judgments.

Tonight, Addie had abandoned the adult dinner for something more kid-friendly in her room. I couldn't blame her. One of the courses was a cold soup, some kind of gazpacho with a blood-red shiraz to accompany it. It was not something that would have appetized me at her age, either. I was taking my first swallow of wine when he finally looked up from his own bowl and addressed me.

"Is the soup to your liking?" He rested his elbows lightly on the table, peering at me with sudden intensity. "If it isn't, we'll send it back."

"I haven't tried it," I admitted. "I'm sure it's just as delicious as everything else. I'm just not used to … this."

His head of raven curls cocked to one side, and the movement revealed a warm glint to his eyes. They weren't black after all— they were deep brown, flecks of gold showing under those dark lashes. A faint smile curled under the straight line of his nose.

"This being … the finer things?"

"I suppose." A smirk crossed my features. "I *am* a lowly journalist from the Midwest, after all."

His smile widened to show a flash of white teeth. "You'd better get used to the finer things, Jessa Edwards from the Midwest."

"Or what?" I countered. "You'll hors d'oeuvre me to death?"

"Or I'll have to give you lessons. The devil"—he ran one finger around the rim of his wine glass, never breaking our shared gaze—"is in the details."

Grace shifted in her seat, making a point of *not* looking at either of us. A faint flush was flowering across her cheekbones, one I was beginning to think might be mirrored on my own face. The banter was quick and familiar, nothing like our interaction before, and the exchange of wit was leaving me breathless. Who was this man and what had he done with Elliot Rochester, moody billionaire from the first night?

"I'm off to bed," Miss Peterson broke in, gathering herself up. "Goodnight."

"Goodnight." My and Mr. Rochester's voices spoke in tandem, and I felt an internal thrill at the synchronization.

Once she was gone, he sat back in his chair, tucking lean arms behind him to support his head as he observed me from the other end of the table. So much space between us, yet I still felt overheated and nervous at the conversation, like it was wrong somehow. It was that exquisite wrongness that made it so exciting. After a moment, he spoke.

"I don't apologize."

My eyes narrowed. "What makes you think I want an apology from you?"

"I—" To his credit, he looked baffled for a moment. "The first night, you—"

"The first night," I explained softly, "is long gone."

And to my immense pleasure, what came next was something of a miracle. He was speechless.

Blood coursing through me, I slowly stood, drained my wine glass, and licked my lips.

"I'm going to bed," I informed him, biting back my smile. The look on his face—something between bewilderment, irritation, and admiration—was utterly picturesque, and I hoped desperately that I could memorize it.

He didn't speak to me the whole walk to the doorframe, and on a whim, I stopped with my fingers resting lightly on the molding.

"And Mr. Rochester?" I called over my shoulder. "I don't apologize, either."

****

That night I didn't sleep for a very different reason. Though less light flooded the plank floor of my bedroom, I spent hours staring at the ceiling, the dinner conversation ringing in my ears. Sometime in the quietest part of the night, I finally decided to accept that sleep was not coming easily to me. After carefully sliding from the sheets, I crossed the room to the small writing desk and lamp atop its surface. It didn't illuminate the entire room, but it did provide a little light I could write by. But that was when I noticed the light from below. Another window was glowing with warm, yellow light, the same window I'd looked down on the first night I couldn't sleep. Only this time, there was a silhouette in the frame, looking up at me.

Elliot Rochester.

His features were half shrouded in shadow, but it was clearly him. And he was watching me. I followed his gaze to my shoulder, bared from where my robe had slipped on my journey across the room. A wicked smile curved at the edge of my lips as I shrugged, letting the robe slip off my other shoulder too. Underneath, I wore a black slip of a nightgown, trimmed in delicate lace. Half-hypnotized, I walked my fingers gently across my collarbone, nudging the dainty strap off my left shoulder. In the window frame below, I could see him strain closer to the glass almost imperceptibly. A fire started in my core, traveling deeper inside me until I felt not just powerful, but *hot*. Breathless. Ready. I wrapped one hand around the neck of the lamp to anchor myself. Hooking my finger through the other strap, I dragged it. Torturously slowly, the silk brushed across my skin, and finally, in a delicious release, the entire thing fell to the floor.

Then I turned out the light.

My chest was heaving, every fiber of me alive with the exhilaration of what just happened. In the darkness, I couldn't stop the smile that spread across my face.

Chapter Three

It is a truth universally acknowledged that when a single man is in possession of a good fortune, he must throw lavish and absurd parties. This was the case for Elliot Rochester, at any rate. He'd run the guest list by Grace Peterson dozens of times before he was satisfied and let her send out the cardstock invitations.

Her role in his house still confused me, but she was ever-present: a butler, nanny, secretary, and whatever else he needed, all in one ginger-headed package. And she was equally helpful to me, collecting my laundry for the maids who dashed in once a week to tidy up the already immaculate house. And when she spoke to anyone—whether it be me or the master of the house—she was efficient, professional, and always wore that thin smile.

Neither Mr. Rochester nor I spoke of the night at the window, but on the occasion that we made eye contact, there was a secret shared there that made me weak at the knees. Why had I done it? And why had it felt so good to keep him frozen there at that windowpane, slave to my every move? I didn't know, but I wasn't sure that mattered. My mundane life had been transformed, and I didn't want it to ever go back to the way things were before.

But things were about to change even further. Over the course of three days, guests turned up in groups, laughing over bottles of expensive wine in the parlor when we normally would have been eating dinner. I was expected to be in attendance—Grace saw to that, at Mr. Rochester's request—but never did anyone speak directly to me. I was as much a piece of décor in the room as a guest. Through the clouds of cigar smoke, I would sometimes catch him looking at me, those molten eyes piercing through the crowd no matter how many stood between us. But that was all.

When the remainder of the guests had arrived, the festivities lasted for days. The house was never quiet, and—as Addie had been banished into the west wing of the building—I was at a loss for anything to do besides watch the sophisticated masses transform into drunken messes. Mr. Rochester, despite always having a full glass of something or other, somehow avoided this intemperance. I wondered if it were possible for him to let loose at all.

The last night was so wild that I slipped away unseen even by the pair of gold-flecked eyes in the corner of the room. Once I was inside my bedroom, the thick wooden door muffling the antics of the party-goers downstairs, I breathed a sigh of relief. There was only so much cigar smoke and noise one person can take, and I had reached my limit. I would much rather have spent the night in the west wing with Addison, but it was late by then, and she was undoubtedly asleep. But that didn't mean I couldn't try to find a quieter place in the west wing to spend the rest of the night.

The sound of breaking glass and delighted laughter from below cemented the plan.

I shrugged into my robe, grabbed a book, and crept into the hallway with a little flashlight from my bag.

The walk to the west wing was long, but pleasant. The further I got from the raucous uproar, the better. And I would have agreed with that statement the whole night through, were it not for the scene I came upon when I rounded the corner.

An icy wind was whipping through the deserted

corridor from a smashed window. Broken glass littered the floor, and in the moonlight, each little shard glittered. There at the center of the mess was a meandering path of red droplets. Blood.

Cold fear gripped at my chest. This was no errant tree limb or hailstorm. Someone or some*thing* had come in through that window, and now it was in the house.

Addie.

I was running before I could think twice, and I leaped the expanse of broken glass as best I could to pass through the hallway. Her room and Mr. Rochester's were in the very end of the wing, Rochester's on the inside of the curve and Addie's opposite, overlooking the forest.

Skidding around another bend, I laid eyes on the end of the hallway and the two doors. They were both closed and locked, as they should have been.

A breath of relief escaped me. She was safe.

But the rest of the house was still in the east wing, drinking and laughing and completely unaware of the danger. Sprinting to the very end of the hallway, I reached the west staircase and descended so quickly it left me winded. But I couldn't stop. Tearing across the first floor to the parlor at top speed, I nearly careened headlong into a tall figure. He caught hold of me by the shoulders, cutting off the shrill scream threatening to break loose from me by stepping into the light.

It was Elliot.

"What on earth are you doing running around?" he asked, a faint smile playing at the corner of his mouth. "Did you get into the whiskey?"

"No." I gasped a frantic breath. "Something's wrong. There's a broken window in the west wing."

"The west wing?" His brow furrowed.

"Addie's fine," I hurried to tell him. "Her door was locked and it was quiet. But there's—there's blood."

His expression darkened, and the tumult behind his dark eyes was fierce.

"She's come back then," he growled under his breath.

"She?" I asked, still trying to catch my breath. He let go of my shoulders, stalking in the direction of the broken window. "Who?"

He opened his mouth to answer, probably to brush me off or to tell me to go to bed, but he was cut off by a strangled scream coming from upstairs. Impossibly quickly, he climbed the stairs and was well on his way down the corridor when a second cry went up.

"Wait!" I hissed, trailing at his heels. But I stopped dead when I looked up.

There on the Oriental rug, just outside the second-floor bathroom, was a slumped figure. And looming over it was the largest creature I had ever seen. I froze, blinking, unable to comprehend what was in front of me. The hulking beast had tawny fur, and under it, a well-muscled body and razor-sharp teeth. It threw one look in our direction and fled, completely silently, into the night.

"It's a *wolf*," I realized, eyes wide.

Elliot didn't lose a moment, rushing forward to the figure on the ground.

"Are you afraid of blood?" he asked.

I shook my head. "Is he alive?"

"Yes. Now help me get him up."

Between the two of us, we hoisted a moaning guest to his feet and dragged him to the closest place to hide him: my bedroom. While Mr. Rochester got him into bed, I turned on the lamp, and only then did I see the extent of the damage. On his left side, the whole of his white shirt sleeve was in ribbons and stained red with blood. Jagged bite-marks marred the flesh of his arm, and a steady stream of blood was oozing forth with no signs of stopping. The man was no longer moaning. He was no longer conscious.

"Apply pressure," Mr. Rochester instructed, shrugging out of his button-up and offering it to me as a compress. "I'll call the doctor."

"Doctor? What are you talking about? We have to call an ambulance. We have to call the police! That *thing* is loose somewhere, and it's dangerous!"

He fixed his gaze on me, and it sent me into a new level of terror. His irises were pure gold.

"Be brave," he demanded, reaching for my arm. Sharp fingernails bit into the soft flesh. "Jessa, I need you to be brave."

I nodded slowly, still staring into those yellowy eyes, and accepted the shirt. I pressed it as hard as I could to the man's wound, and when I looked up again, Mr. Rochester was gone.

Chapter Four

As soon as the doctor arrived, I was evicted from my own bedroom. Grace, under strict orders, was finessing the party guests and pumping them full of so much wine they wouldn't know what country they were in. I was given no more orders. I sat on the chaise outside the bedroom door, covered in a stranger's blood and listening to the hushed conversation between the doctor and a man whose eyes I'd just seen *change.* It was more than just their color. It was something deeper, more complex. And what did I want? Nothing more than to see those eyes again.

Just before sunrise, the last of the remaining party-goers stumbled back to their respective bedrooms uneventfully, and the house was finally quiet. Grace vanished, and still, I was alone. And it wasn't until the pink glow of sunrise that the doctor and Mr. Rochester finally opened the great wooden door. Elliot looked at me, alarm coloring his already exhausted features.

"You're still awake?"

"I thought you might need me." I blinked. I didn't like the way that came out. I was tired, physically and emotionally, and I didn't like the idea of him knowing he had any pull over me.

He knelt before me, taking my hands, dried blood and all, in his. "No, you've done more than necessary," he murmured. "You've earned your rest. Now come. You'll sleep in my bed."

A little thrill ran through me at that, and if I had more energy, I'm sure a wise crack would have slipped from my mouth as easily as exhaling. But I was tired, and when I stood up, I realized something was wrong with my foot. As I faltered, I looked down and noticed a smear of blood on the polished wood floor, just under my heel.

"The glass..." I realized absently. "I must've stepped on it."

A low growl rumbled in his chest. "You're hurt."

"It's a sliver of glass, Rochester, I think I'll survive." And I was about to make another attempt at standing when he offered his arm to me. My fingers found his forearm, bracing only for a moment before he swept me up, cradling me against his chest. The movement, the lack of sleep, and the scent rolling off his neck dizzied me.

"You've got some kind of hero complex," I mumbled, my head falling back against his shoulder to get a better view of his face.

"Something like that," he muttered, his voice reverberating against my side.

"Well, I'm not so easily won," I pointed out peevishly, though all I could think of was how good it felt to be in his arms. "I'm not some damsel in distress for you to save."

"No..." He sighed. "Evidently, you are not."

Turning the corner into the second-floor bathroom, next to the conspicuously stained rug, Elliot loosened his grip around my shoulders. He set me gently on the edge of the claw-foot bathtub. Wordlessly, he dropped to his knees and turned on the water, testing it with the inside of his wrist. When it suited him, he took hold of my ankle, his touch feather-light despite the evident power in those muscled arms and wide palms.

"I'll try not to hurt you," he murmured, not looking at my face. I wanted to crack a joke about the irony of the situation—Elliot Rochester, billionaire, washing the feet of "the help"—but something in the softness of his voice, the softness of his touch … it was making it difficult to be funny.

The rest of the early morning seemed to unfold in slow motion. His hands moving over my skin to dislodge the piece of glass, the bandage he wrapped my heel in once he was certain it was clean. By the time the sun rose, he was tucking me into his own bed, and I could almost forget the events of the night.

"Mr. Rochester," I managed as he turned his back to the bed, heading for the door.

"Yes?" He didn't turn.

"Last night … we're never going to talk about it, are we?"

"No, Miss Edwards. I don't think we will."

Though he couldn't see me, I nodded into the pillow.

I thought so.

****

The cover story was a simple one. Mr. Bradley Hildebrant had—in his drunkenness—gone through the large window in the west wing and had to be taken home to recover. All in all, not a bad night. To be expected, some even argued, from someone as wild as Mr. Hildebrant. And so the night was forgotten by all but the three adults of the Rochester household. Addie didn't seem to know, and as far as I was concerned, that was the most important thing.

Why a giant blonde wolf had mauled a guest and no one was admitting to it, I didn't know. But I could see that Grace did. Every time she met my eyes, it was only for a moment before she had to look away. She knew what happened that night, and from what I could tell, she had an idea why, too.

"Grace," I began one day after Addison had gone to bed and her uncle was missing from dinner. "It must be lonely out here, in the middle of nowhere with no one but Mr. Rochester for company."

Grace considered this for a moment. "I have you and Addie."

"We hardly see each other," I pointed out. "Except at dinners. What do you do all day, anyway?"

"Oh, you know that." She smiled. "Whatever he tells me to."

I rolled my eyes. "Of course. Always sending you on errands. Don't you get sick of it, being at his beck and call?"

She bit her lower lip, speaking carefully. "Mr. Rochester is a complicated man. You've seen his moods. But he's a good man, and he is good to me. I always do as he asks."

She met my eyes then, and it made her words even clearer. She knew I was digging, and she wasn't going to give up the information.

"Of course." I stiffly returned her smile. "I'm going to go read before bed."

On my climb up the stairs back to my old bedroom—now that the ruined bedclothes had been disposed of, and the memory of the gray-faced man in my bed had almost been erased—I realized faintly that I should have been afraid. I was in a house with a man full of secrets and his secret keeper. And I was not one to leave secrets alone. It was the same cat-killing curiosity that bred hungry journalists.

Inside my room, I couldn't stop my head from spinning in circles, trying to figure out every possible way I could extract the truth. Grace was a vault, and Mr. Rochester ... well, he was a puzzle of his own. And yet I felt I understood him completely. He was arrogant and charming, cruel and kind, fiery and cold. He was whatever you gave to him forged with whatever you wouldn't expect.

I was filled with a new curiosity. Though it had been weeks since the night at the window, I couldn't stop myself from crossing the room and parting the curtain slightly. My heart leaped. In the window across the courtyard, I could see the glow of a candle. He was awake.

It was such a simple thing. Anyone could have been awake then. It was early in the night, and there was no reason for me to feel the strange connection I felt. But it was there, all the same. It felt … destined. As if tonight we were meant to be awake at the same time, both missing sleep by way of dark thoughts. A shadow crossed the pane, and despite the brief urge I felt to shrug away, I kept still, not bothering to hide my stare.

This time, I didn't take a flashlight. I knew this place inside and out now. I could've walked it in my sleep, and in a way, I felt like that was what I was doing. Sleepwalking, dragged forward by some internal force stronger than my willpower. And it felt *good.*

Soon, my bare feet padded across the tiled hallway to the Rochester suites. Through my hazy, hypnotized awareness, I made a resolution. This time, I wouldn't undress myself. I'd let him slide the silk of my nightgown over my skin. I'd let him release my hair from its band. And then … I'd let him do whatever else he wanted with me.

With anticipation aching in my chest, I reached for the door handle. Before I could wrap my fingers around it, the brass turned itself, and the door swung open in the darkness. I nearly fell forward, ready to let Elliot Rochester take me in his arms again, until I saw who was standing before me.

"Oh!"

Grace let out a little cry, shying back from me in

the dim light that spilled from the room. She was flushed, her red hair mussed a bit and her eyes wide.

A sick feeling slithered into the pit of my stomach. Over Grace's shoulder, Elliot was rising from the bedclothes, bare-chested and wearing a similar expression to Grace's: guilt.

I felt my face contort before I stumbled backward, muttering some excuse about being lost.

"Miss Edwards!" I heard him call down the hallway.

It didn't matter. I was already gone.

Chapter Five

In the days following my discovery, I ignored every invitation to dinner, no matter how many times Grace delicately reminded me that they were "mandatory." What would he do, fire me? It wouldn't matter. My bags were already packed.

It was Saturday mornings that I usually got to myself, as Mr. Rochester took coffee in his study, Addie slept in, and Grace was off doing whatever the hell she always did. This made it the perfect day for me to call my cab, load my things into the trunk, and disappear.

So I did.

From the back of the cab, with tears in my eyes, I pulled my cell phone from my bag and waited for the bars to grow. When they did, I dialed the only number I could think of. He picked up on the third ring.

"Hello?"

"Jon?" I pulled the receiver closer to my mouth. "I—I'm in New Hampshire and I need someplace to stay."

The silence at the other end of the line was almost worse than everything leading up to it. It had taken all I had in me to dial the numbers to call my ex, and it pained me even more to consider the possibility that he might turn me away.

"I screwed up," I told the static. "And it'll only be for a day or so until I can get a plane ticket back home."

"Of course, Jessa," he said softly. "What kind of person would I be to turn you away?"

I didn't answer that question. I just breathed a sigh of relief, told him I was on my way to the train station, and hung up. Then I slept.

When I woke up, we were just pulling into the station. Stretching, I gathered my things and withdrew a wad of cash from my purse. I placed the bills on the center console, not looking up as I reached for the door handle. But just as my fingertips brushed the handle, the peg of the locking mechanism clicked into place audibly.

I blinked, frozen for a moment before I looked up at the cabby's face in the rearview mirror.

"Staying at the Rochester place, huh?" asked the blonde woman casually. Her green eyes were piercing, even through the barrier of the mirror.

"Yes," I answered carefully. "But not anymore."

"A dark old place, isn't it?" She was still looking at me intently, and I was mentally shuffling through the possibilities. More likely than not, she was a paparazzo with a strange interest in rich recluses, but something about her face struck me as familiar.

"Yes. Too dark for me," I muttered, slowly reaching for the lock.

"He's fucking the redhead, isn't he?" She spun in the seat abruptly, long red fingernails biting into the vinyl on the backside as she finally faced me.

"Grace?" I bit back all the questions I wanted to ask, including how she knew anything about the Rochester household. Then I realized this was my shot, and though it was a low blow, I took it. "Grace Peterson, you mean. And yes. He's fucking her."

I allowed the dark satisfaction at selling him out settle into me. It felt mean, but it felt *good*. I hoped it would be plastered all over whatever trashy magazine this woman wrote for. I hoped he'd see it and know it was me. To my relief, the locks unclicked then, and I propped the door open just as she asked her next question.

"And you too, I suppose?" She kept those jade

eyes boring into mine.

"No." I swallowed hard. "Not me."

"You're joking." A perplexed look furrowed her brow. "I can smell him all over you. You have to be fucking him."

She leaned forward then, took a whiff of me, and returned to her confused stare. And it was only then that I realized two things in turn.

She wasn't a reporter.

Her eyes were familiar because I had seen them before, just not since that night when a golden wolf locked its gaze with me before disappearing into the darkness.

****

No matter how hard I tried to shake the images of the woman and the wolf from my mind, I couldn't seem to do it for the entire train ride. That was the trouble with the truth: you can't un-know it. Even when it was impossible.

I tried to tell myself that even if I were right, even if by some miracle I'd stumbled across something legitimate, I could just chalk it up to the fever dream that was my time in Elliot Rochester's house of horrors. If the word *werewolf* —I could hardly think it without hysterical laughter bubbling out of me—were something more than fodder for cheesy eighties movies, I couldn't afford to care. I had nothing to do with it now. And Elliot? She could tear out his throat for all I cared.

Jon picked me up at the train station right on time, wearing a pair of oversized headphones and a stupid hipster mustache. He was smiling too, but like he was posing for a photo. I fought the urge to board the train again and hide under the seats.

"Jessa!" He waved, like I couldn't see him twenty feet in front of me.

"Jon." I raised my hand in the best approximation of a wave I could muster.

He didn't offer to carry my bags and instead opted to chat about his latest photography exhibit in Manchester and how I should "def check it out" while I was in town. I nodded, and he kept talking the whole way back to his apartment. It wasn't until I was sweating and breathless from dragging my luggage up three flights of stairs to his place that he finally asked about me.

"So, what happened, Jessa? How'd you get stranded in New Hampshire?"

I sighed, wondering how much of the truth I was willing to give him.

"You know Elliot Rochester?" I asked finally.

Jon wrinkled his nose. "Obviously. He's evil. Capitalist slime."

I inhaled, trying to pacify my violent urge to roll my eyes. "Yes, that's the one. I was his niece's tutor. Turns out he is … slime. Like you said."

"Well, I could've told you that."

And in typical fashion, the conversation was over, reminding me not for the first time how absolutely terrible college boyfriends are. Pissing off your mother by dating a starving artist just isn't worth the aggravation of dating someone like Jon.

"Right, well, I'm going to try and get a plane ticket home by Tuesday or so," I told him. "So thanks for this. I won't overstay my welcome."

"No prob." He crossed to the small galley kitchen. "There's green juice in the fridge and some quinoa in the cupboard. I'm vegan, you remember."

"Jesus Christ," I muttered under my breath. "How could I forget?"

But soon, I was spared the insufferable presence of my host as he had a drum circle or some equally obscure thing to attend for the evening. That suited me just fine. I was happy to curl into a ball on the couch and go straight to sleep.

****

I resisted the very real temptation to devour a steak in Jon's presence for the remainder of the weekend, sticking to his "greens and grains" diet out of the minimal respect I still harbored for him. Between varyingly revolting mealtimes, I scrolled through flights to Michigan with dread. It wasn't that they were badly priced. I could fly out easily with the money I'd saved. But going home would mean admitting that I failed not at just my plan A or even plan B—I'd failed at my last resort. In a rare moment of insight, Jon must've guessed my reluctance, because he sat beside me on the couch and draped a blanket over my shoulders.

"I get it," he said softly. "And you can stay longer if you want. I mean, the way things ended between us … it was amicable. Who's to say we can't … pick up where we left off?"

I looked up from my phone screen and into his clear blue eyes. He wasn't unattractive—a lean build and big blue eyes worked in his favor—and if he shaved that damn hipster mustache off his face, he would be genuinely handsome. Aside from being obliviously self-centered, he wasn't a bad person. It was abundantly clear what he was offering me: an option that didn't involve admitting failure.

It just required settling.

It would be easy enough to do, just accept that this is the life that I chose and get some day job. Maybe I could write for the local paper, though that was about as close to journalism as a cat to a jaguar. It wasn't perfect, but it was a life. Did I have that waiting for me back in Michigan?

"I don't know, Jon…" I cast my eyes back down to the list of flights, the same ones I'd been watching for days while they took off and landed without me.

"Then we'll take it slow," he suggested, taking my hand in his. "You can meet my friends. Tim and Stacey have a brewery we could visit. I swear to God, their IPAs are to die for."

He smiled excitedly, and I did my best to return it despite the fact that I had told him dozens of times that I hated beer. Unbidden, a memory sprang into my head of the Spanish red from *that* night. I was a wine girl. Jon should've known that.

But it didn't matter anymore. I had an alternative to failure, and I had already made up my mind to take it.

"Sure," I managed weakly. "We'll have to do that."

****

We were a week into our new arrangement when Jon suggested brunch at his favorite bistro in town, and three mimosas in, I wasn't regretting the decision to go. Jon didn't seem to notice much beyond the newspaper he'd found on one of the other wire tables.

"I love print media," he was saying, flipping through it. "I normally get my news from podcasts, but there's something really authentic about *reading* it, you know?"

"Mmm." I swallowed the bottom of the orange juice-champagne mixture that I was convinced had been sent directly from God.

"Hey." Suddenly Jon was leaning forward, interested in something. "Isn't this the place you were working?"

He flipped the paper to face me, and on the front page, I saw the image he was referring to. And yes, at one point in time, that might have been the Rochester mansion. But in this picture, where the west wing once stood, there was nothing but ash. Above the image, the headline read, *Rochester home burns, woman dead.*

"Oh, my God." The words left my lips in a breathy whisper.

"Early this morning, the body of a woman was discovered in the aftermath of a fire at the home of Elliot Rochester," Jon read aloud from the article. "Authorities have identified the body as Miss Caroline Finch, a former lover of Mr. Rochester. It remains to be seen how the blaze began, but sources report that Rochester was granted a restraining order against Finch after the attempted kidnapping of his niece and ward in the fall of last year."

"What?" I snatched the paper from Jon's fingers, no longer content to hear the story secondhand. "The other inhabitants of the home are reportedly unharmed," I read slowly.

And then I caught sight of the other photo. It was a portrait of a strikingly beautiful woman, blonde and smiling with piercing green eyes.

The dead woman.

The woman from the cab.

Chapter Six

Scrambling out of the bistro and leaving Jon dumbfounded was the easiest and fastest decision I had ever made. I didn't even consider the consequences it would bring until a brief moment as the train rolled into the station. And even then, the moment was fleeting. Nothing mattered but the news I'd just heard.

Though the pictures in the newspaper made my blood run cold, nothing could have prepared me for the sight of the destruction in person. When the cab rolled to a stop in front of what was left of the mansion, my mouth went dry.

Reporters were clustered around the yellow police tape that separated the Rochester property from the rest of the world. Two cruisers sat in the long driveway, and even from the road, I could see the officers struggling to keep the gawkers under control.

I picked my way up the driveway to join them and casually ducked under the tape to the flagstone sidewalk.

"Hey, you!" an officer called, pointing a finger in my direction. "This is private property, not a tourist attraction! Have you no decency?"

"I live here!" I bellowed over a shoulder, taking off at a jog for the east wing entrance. The door was, of course, locked, but I hammered the brass knocker into its plate over and over until Grace finally wrenched the door open.

"What do you—?" Her expression of frustration melted into one of recognition a second before she folded me into a hug. I stiffened, remembering the last time we saw each other, then wrapped my arms around her awkwardly.

"We had no idea where you were," she said, pulling me inside. "I wondered if Caroline had—" She broke off, looking uncomfortable. "I'm glad you're back."

"And Addie?" I asked, looking over her shoulder into the hallway. From this part of the house, it was difficult to tell that anything was wrong at all.

"She's fine," Grace explained, leading me to the east living room. "I can let her know you're here. And Mr. Rochester…" She gave me a look that asked permission, asked if I *wanted* him to know I was home.

"I can't wait to see her." I hoped that was clear enough an answer for her.

Grace nodded and ducked up the east staircase. I found a seat on the couch, fiddling with my fingers and wondering what on earth I was doing back here. I'd left. I'd started a new life. So why had I jumped into a cab this morning without looking back?

Footsteps on the stairs outside the living room echoed off the walls, but they were too heavy to be Addison's. Too late, I rose from my seat and made for the door to the dining room. Suddenly, there he stood, his curls disheveled and his eyes cupped by purple shadows. He looked like he was seeing a ghost.

"Miss Edwards," was all he could manage. And then he was crossing the room, drawing me to him without restraint. I braced my palms against his chest, forming a barrier to the embrace.

"What are you doing?" I demanded, stepping back from him.

"I was—" He looked confused, then irritated. "How dare you leave this house? How *dare* you abandon that little girl?" He jabbed a finger in the direction of the wreckage. "You left without so much as a goodbye. We didn't know if you were living or dead."

"Oh, and not knowing the truth bothered you?" I shot back at him. "That must be upsetting. Being lied to, I mean."

His face darkened. "Miss Edwards…"

"I know," I interrupted him hotly. "You don't apologize. And I'm still not asking for one. I'm *telling* you. I met Caroline Finch before she lit your house on fire. And I think you and I both know there's more to her than you told the goddamn newspapers."

At his sides, he clenched his fists. "Yes," he spat through gritted teeth.

"Honesty," I mused, laughing humorlessly. "Refreshing from you, I have to admit."

"I didn't lie to you because I wanted to," he began, reaching for me again.

"No!" I jerked out of his reach. "You don't touch me. Not ever again, Elliot Rochester. Not after you've touched her."

"Caroline?" The muscle in his jaw worked manically. "She was a psychopath, you saw that!"

"Not *Caroline*," I hissed. "Grace."

"Grace Peterson?" To my complete shock, he threw back his head and barked out a laugh. "I've never so much as laid a finger on Grace Peterson. You have no idea what you're talking about."

"Don't I?" I snapped, rolling onto my tiptoes to get in his face. "I know I saw her coming from your bedroom in the middle of the night. I know you are both keeping secrets. And"—I dropped my voice—"I know there is much more going on under this roof than you two sharing beds."

With that, I was done. The fuse of my anger was nearly burned out, and I could feel the imminent crisis the end would bring.

"By the way," I muttered offhandedly, "I'd like to sleep tonight. Don't keep me up howling."

Ignoring his slack-jawed expression, I climbed the stairs to my old bedroom, slammed the door, and burst into tears.

Chapter Seven

For obvious reasons, I didn't receive an invitation to dinner. That was good. Any person in my room would've been greeted by obscenities at best and a flying lamp at worst. Besides, I wasn't dressed. The one garment left in the wardrobe was the silk nightgown, and I wore it out of necessity. It wasn't what I wanted—I *wanted* to mope around in sweats—but it would have to do.

Elliot's reaction to my words had told me the truth, which—contrary to everything I'd ever believed—made me feel much worse than I had when I was only guessing. The prospect of not one but two people who could *change,* could shift from something human to something else, was mindboggling, to say the least. And the idea that I might have fallen for one? That was unfathomable.

I'd never been so confused in my life.

As evening morphed to night, I stayed firmly in between the bedcovers, vacillating between short bursts of rage and long stretches of hopelessness. If I thought I'd hit rock bottom when I was sleeping on the couch in Jon's apartment, this was somewhere below the rock. Worse, I had no one to blame but myself. I'd taken my new life, and I'd cast it aside in favor of the insanity that had sent me running to begin with. Now I really was out of options. Failure wasn't just inevitable, it had already happened.

I just needed to admit it now.

And that was what kept me awake for the last of so many sleepless nights under the roof of Elliot Rochester.

I had every intention of embracing the insomnia, accepting the self-deprecating night thoughts that sounded eerily like my mother. But the soft knock on my bedroom door put an end to that. And because it may have been Addie—though some part of me knew it was not—I answered.

"I'll never touch you again as long as I live," Elliot explained, standing in my doorway. "Not if you don't want me to. But I owe you the whole story. From the beginning."

In his eyes, there was a foreign look of uncertainty. Silent, I stepped to one side, admitting him into the room. He waited for me to find my way to the bed before he sat beside me, a platonic distance between us.

"Caroline Finch is—*was*—my Maker." He swallowed hard, as if just saying it aloud was difficult. "She was the one to turn me. She tried to introduce me to her pack, and it didn't go well. There are roles in a shifter pack, same as a regular wolf pack. So when they realized I was an Alpha … things got violent." He looked at me to gauge my reaction. I nodded, carefully keeping my face impassive.

"I refused to fight for control of a pack I didn't want to lead, and she couldn't handle that. She wanted me to make her some kind of queen and I … I just wanted to go back to my old life. I tried."

He gestured around him. "Obviously that didn't work. She was so vindictive after I left the pack that she would do anything to lure me back in. When she tried to take Addie, her intention was…" He trailed off, looking ill.

"To turn her," I realized. "So you'd go back."

"Yes." He sighed. "That's when I hired Grace. She could be another set of eyes around the house that didn't look like security. She knew my secret within two months, but it didn't scare her away. And Jessa? Grace is my cousin." He laughed softly. "Didn't you ever wonder where Addie's green eyes come from? That side of the family. That night, she was in my bedroom to make arrangements for my next shift. I was worried I would come to you in the night without knowing what I was doing. I was worried I'd hurt you, or worse."

He looked down at his fists, clenched in his lap.

"The night she broke in, she was sending me a message. She could have killed every person in that room, easily, but she didn't want to. She wanted to play games."

"What do you mean?" I asked carefully.

He inhaled audibly. "She was hoping the stress of it all, on top of the full moon, would send me into a shift. I'd have killed you all. Then I'd have to join a pack. For protection."

"And the fire?"

"Must be she finally she had enough and figured if she couldn't convince me to come back to the tribe, she could at least put an end to it all." He shuddered. "She locked herself in my bedroom. She thought we would all go down in some blaze of glory together. Addie woke up, smelled the smoke, and woke Grace. I wasn't even in the house."

"I see," I murmured, letting all the pieces fall into place.

"When you left," he began, softly trailing a fingertip over a wrinkle in the down comforter, "I wanted to go after you. I wanted to tell you everything, and then—"

"Then what?" I asked, my heartrate picking up.

"I think you already know," he said huskily. A flash of gold glinted in his eyes, and I felt my insides clench at the sight. God, how I'd missed those eyes.

"Tell me anyway," I whispered.

"Well, first I was going to tear that damn nightgown off of you."

I glanced down at my chest, rising and falling beneath the silky black nightdress.

"And then?"

"Then I was going to lay you down on this bed, and I was going to kiss your neck, your collarbone—" His eyes traveled down my throat, and the force of them there was almost palpable. "Down your chest, the curve of your hip, between your thighs…"

"How long are you going to torture me?" I gasped.

"Until you ask me to touch you," he said, leaning so close to me that his breath tickled my lower lip. With a will of its own, my chin tilted upward, trying to catch his lips with mine. He pulled away by a fraction. "Until you beg."

"In that case," I told him, leaning forward, "pretty, *pretty* please."

His mouth, soft and warm and desperate, found mine about the time I locked my hand around the back of his neck. With the gentlest of movements, his tongue played across the curve of my lip and coaxed me closer. With one arm around my hips and the other anchoring my face to his, Elliot laid me down on the bed and made good on his promise to undress me. Breaking the kiss for only seconds, he peeled the silk off me, nearly tearing it in half in the process. With impossible grace, he slid his pants off. My bare skin tingled with electricity, and when he lowered himself on top of me, the lean planes of his skin pressed against the slope of my stomach, I wanted nothing more than to feel him inside of me. But Elliot had other plans. Agonizingly slowly, he planted a kiss on my mouth, my cheek, the edge of my jaw.

"You have no idea how long I've been wanting to do that," he whispered into my ear, nipping at the lobe.

My mind was spinning.

"More," I managed hoarsely.

"Don't worry." He unleashed a wicked laugh against the skin of my collarbone. "I'm not even close to finished with you."

With his left hand, he lifted me and deposited his hips between my thighs as his other hand took hold of my right breast, squeezing in time with the wet kisses he planted on my collarbone. The rigid flesh of his cock pressed into me, and I arched my back despite the thin fabric of his underwear between us. I reached for the waistband, desperate to tear them off him like he'd disrobed me, but he caught hold of my wrist. The restraint in his tensed muscles sent another wave of want over me.

"Patience, Miss Edwards," he instructed. And then the underwear was gone too, leaving nothing between us but space. "I still need to finish those kisses."

He gave me a wide smile, teeth glinting white before he bowed low and dragged his tongue over the crease of my hip. And then, in a shower of sparks, he buried his mouth between my thighs. A low moan escaped my lips as my hands found purchase in his hair, pulling him closer if that were even possible. Lips and tongue and the edges of teeth became a dizzying triad of pleasure as I rocked back and forth, begging him for more, always more. And when my moans climbed toward a crescendo, rising in pitch, he drew away. Only then did he lay himself down on top of me again, his face inches from mine and drunk with desire.

And with one torturously slow thrust, he was inside me. Deep in his chest, a primal growl rumbled forth, and using one hand to support himself, he pumped into me again and again. My fingernails dug into his back as I tried desperately to hold on.

"Elliot," I whimpered, matching his rhythm stroke for stroke. Of all the words in the English language, his name was the only one I cared to remember.

"Oh, fuck, Jessa," he groaned, cutting off my gasps with another deep kiss.

The sound of my name on his lips sent me over the edge, igniting a tremor in my chest that radiated out all my limbs. While my every cell quaked, Elliot was shaking too, fisting his hands in the sheets as he bucked into me, hard. That was all it took. Arching my back and screaming his name, aflame down to my very soul, I exploded into a thousand pieces of light.

Epilogue

Six Months Later

It's funny how success works. Just when I thought I'd made the biggest mistake of my life, I was taking the first step up from rock bottom. When I woke up after that night, tangled in Elliot's arms, I finally knew it.

I never went back to Jon's apartment for my things. Those were relics of an old life, something I no longer needed. And I didn't want to set foot in that kale-scented apartment ever again.

What I did do was get on the train the next day and go to New York City. And after scouring the city for job offerings and finding none, I didn't quit. I went back to the Rochester mansion—which was in a state of rebuild for months—and I pitched article ideas to every editor who would listen.

And eventually, one of them said yes.

I don't write for the *New York Times* … at least not yet. And I don't have a perfect life. But I am not a failure, and at the end of every day, I get to come home to a new family who loves me.

Sometimes, I even think of them as my pack.

The End

BEARLY CAUGHT

Sarah Marsh

Chapter One

The exit sign reading *Hillion Falls* was a welcome sight after a two-day drive up North from Dani's hometown. Well, what *had* been her hometown until her control-freak ex-boyfriend made it clear he wasn't about to let Dani move on with her life. When she'd gotten the call from her Aunt Bess's lawyer a week ago, informing her that her aunt had passed away, she'd been devastated to lose the last of her family. But the news that Bess had left her estate to her only niece gave her the perfect opportunity to get out of Dawson and away from Andy trying to ruin her life so she'd be forced to run straight back to him to fix it.

Asshole. Like I'd ever go back to that pathetic excuse for a man. If he loses his shit when I go out with some friends for dinner after dating for ten months, his control issues will only get worse. I can fix up the house before I sell it. By that time, Andy will have moved on as well, and I can get back to my life.

She was tired, hungry, and her ass was pretty much asleep. Hillion Falls seemed like a quaint little town—if you can call a place with only one streetlight a town. This certainly wasn't the city life she was used to. Dani made her way down the main street and decided to stop for some dinner before heading out to her aunt's, as there was no way she was eating one more bologna sandwich out of the cooler. The neon sign flashing the words *Burgers and Brews* was calling her name something fierce. She pulled into the parking lot of the Blue Moon Pub and was surprised at the number of cars there. One could only assume that meant the food was good, right?

Dani hoped it was since it was unlikely the grocery store in a town this small was still open at seven PM. She'd instructed Bess's lawyer to keep the power and water on at the property so at least she knew the fridge would be working and ready for a load of groceries—that would be her first chore tomorrow morning.

There were two men walking toward the entrance in front of her and she was surprised when the second one waited and held the door open for her. She hadn't thought they'd seen her at all.

"Thank you." She nodded politely.

"Anytime, darlin'." His smile grew larger as he looked her up and down. "I'm good with holding a lot of things if you need a hand tonight."

His blatant innuendo left her speechless.

Wow, the men around here sure aren't shy, are they?

"Uh, good for you?" She felt like an idiot as soon as the words left her mouth, but how in the hell was she supposed to respond to that?

His deep laughter echoed through the doorway as his smile turned from flirty to genuinely amused. "You are a riot, Red."

She blushed as he gave her a mock bow and ushered her up to the bar.

"Enjoy your evening, darlin'." He smiled once again at her and walked toward the other side of the room to a large table of people who greeted him enthusiastically.

"Can I get you a menu?"

The deep voice sent a shiver down her spine and as Dani turned to face the speaker, her eyes went wide at the virile specimen of a male who stood behind the bar, his lips quirked up on one side as if he knew exactly how devastating he was to the female species.

Dani cleared her throat and hopped up onto the empty stool. "Yes, please, and whatever wheat ale you have on tap."

"A beer drinker." He winked as he slid over the small menu and the pint. "My kinda girl. Be right back to take your order, love."

She watched him as he moved down the dark wooden bar top, gathering drinks for the patrons lined up on the other side. He had to be over six feet tall and built like a predator—all muscles but not bulky gym-borne ones. These muscles were probably from doing ridiculously manly endeavors such as felling trees with only a tiny ax, and then hollowing out a canoe from said tree to save orphans from drowning or something.

Yeesh, this bartender just might be the hottest man I've ever seen.

His curly, deep-brown hair fell almost to his collar, and he had the most delicious soulful brown eyes, but it was his mouth that kept drawing her attention. The full lips looked like they were made to do all sorts of dirty things.

Eyes up and mind your business, woman! There's no time to get distracted by seductive eyes and a smile that could melt the panties off a nun. Remember, you're here avoiding a man, not looking for a new one.

Dani's scowl, which was aimed more at herself than the handsome stranger, only seemed to amuse him as he walked back toward her.

"Not pleased with the menu selection?"

"No, it's fine." She managed a smile. "Can I please just get a cheeseburger and fries?"

"You got it." He turned and spoke to the man in the kitchen and then began wiping down the counter next to her. "Are you just passing through? These roads aren't great after dark, but there's a small inn right at the edge of town if you want to wait until daylight."

"No, I inherited some property in town and I'm just here to fix it up before I sell it."

He looked up and paused for a moment, then a smile grew on his face.

"Are you Bess's niece Daniella, then?"

Dani was speechless as she stared at him, and then she blinked. "How in the hell do you know that?"

He chuckled. "First, we don't get a lot of visitors around here … you may have noticed we're a bit out of the way."

She didn't want to be charmed by his teasing, but dammit, there must have been something wrong with her hormones.

"Second, because it's a small town, word gets around about most things, and we were all very fond of Bess. Her lawyer, Jeffery, told the town council that you'd be arriving soon to finish up with the estate."

"First, no one calls me Daniella, it's Dani, and *you're* on the town council?" She thought it seemed odd since he couldn't be much older than thirty.

"Mayor Emmett Greyson, at your service, Miss Holt."

She assumed he wanted to shake her hand as he offered his own, but she realized too late he was raising it to his lips and she'd only make a scene if she yanked it out of his grasp.

Yeah, tell yourself that all you like, sweetheart.

Chapter Two

Emmett inhaled the scent coming off Dani's wrist as he gently kissed her hand. What was it about this woman that had his bear nudging awake? Sure, she was cute enough; there was no doubting that. Curves a man could get lost in, long, dark-red hair that made him picture it spread out on his pure-white sheets, and vibrant green eyes that conveyed quite succinctly that she took no bullshit.

... and they're narrowing on me as we speak. Yup, she's definitely Bess's niece, all right.

"So." She pulled her hand out of his grasp and settled it around her beer. "Mayor *and* a bartender? That's an interesting mix."

He laughed at her raised eyebrow. Damn, this woman sure wasn't afraid to bust some balls. Emmett took another deep breath of her scent. It was a shame that she was only human.

"I'm just covering the bar for a friend," he explained, "but, as mayor of this humble town, I am a Jack of all trades. If you're going to be staying for a while, you'll run into me quite a bit around these parts."

"Thanks for the warning," she whispered back at him.

This time his head was thrown back as his laughter boomed, so much so that many of his pack in the bar turned to see what was afoot. When some of the males' attention turned to Dani beside him, his bear rumbled its irritation inside. Huh. Emmett's animal side didn't seem to like that one bit.

"Are you always this feisty?"

She laughed along with him. "I swear, I'm not

normally."

Dani shook her head. "There's just something about you that seems to, I don't know? Rile me? Do you have this effect on a lot of women?"

"Not that I know of."

"Huh." Her cheeky smile was adorable.

"Huh." He smiled back at her until someone called his name from the other end of the bar. Emmett winked and left to ponder what exactly it was about Dani that was so intriguing.

The bar started to get busy, so he didn't have another opportunity to chat with her aside from dropping off her food, and he was getting antsy for Callen to get back so he could concentrate more on Dani. Luck wasn't on his side, but when he saw her drop cash on the bar for her tab, he couldn't stop himself.

"Bess's place can be tough to find in the dark if you don't know your way around town." He set down her change. "I could show you to the house if you'd like?"

Whatever he was expecting her answer to be, the loud snort followed by a chuckle wasn't it.

"I appreciate that, but I have this crazy new invention called GPS that can show me the way."

He put on his most shocked expression and whispered, "Sorcery..."

It received the laugh he'd been aiming for, and she was shaking her head at him once again.

"You're an odd duck, Mr. Mayor."

"I've always preferred 'curious bear' over 'odd duck,' myself."

That made her laugh out loud. "That one must be a local saying. I've never heard it before."

"We have a lot of those around here."

"Well, I look forward to hearing all of them before I leave." She hopped off the stool and nodded a little too cordially for his taste, as if their bantering and attraction was something that happened every day. "See you around town, Mr. Greyson."

"No need to be so formal—you can call me Sir." He winked again before tossing a towel over his shoulder. "But seriously, if you need anything at all, don't hesitate to ask anyone in town, they'll get in touch with me."

"I'm not anticipating getting into any kind of trouble that would be 'mayor-worthy,' but I appreciate the sentiment … *Sir*."

Emmett watched her snort another laugh and then turn to walk toward the exit, her sweetly rounded hips swaying hypnotically as she went. Never had the word *sir* sounded more mocking and damned if it didn't put a smile on his face.

He was still watching her leave when he sensed Boone's presence beside him. "That one's feisty. Who is she?"

"That, my friend, is Bess's niece, Daniella."

Boone's whistle of appreciation followed Dani's delectable backside out the door, causing Emmett to turn abruptly, his silly smile quickly morphing into a snarl before he even realized it. Every shifter in the bar stopped what they were doing to look his way, ready to attack whatever had displeased their Alpha, and Emmett had to breathe deep to get his emotions back under control. Good thing his enforcer was more ballsy than bright, as the other male just smiled and raised one eyebrow in question.

"So, it's like that, is it?" Boone asked.

"Apparently it is," Emmett grumbled, running a hand through his unruly hair. "There's just something about her that my bear doesn't seem to want to let go."

"Is she human?" Boone's head tilted. "Bess

wasn't able to turn when Philip tried to change her, even with the recessive genes. She smells human."

"I know, I wasn't getting anything from her except for human." Emmett couldn't help but be disappointed. While others in the pack were able to mate humans, even if they would never be able to shift, as Alpha of this mixed pack, he was expected to mate another shifter to keep his line strong.

"Too bad." Boone shrugged. "But that doesn't mean you can't have some fun while she's in town though, does it?"

Emmett just grunted in return, thinking back to the fact that she'd actually rebuffed his advances rather easily.

"Huh." Boone's eyes had a mischievous glint to them that Emmett didn't care for at all right at this moment. "Don't tell me she turned you down?"

"I'm a stranger. She's a smart woman, that's all," he snapped out a little too forcefully.

He racked his brain for the last time a female had actually turned him down and came up with nothing. As a matter of fact, due to his Alpha status, women usually came on to him quite frequently. His frown grew deeper. Why did it bother him so much that this one woman seemed immune to his charms?

"I'm sure she'll come around. They all do, right?" Boone winked and gave him a nudge.

For some reason, Emmett's bear wasn't appreciating Boone talking about Dani like that and another growl slipped out of his mouth. It was another embarrassing slip of control and he didn't like it one bit.

"Callen should be here any minute. Want to go for a run when he gets back?" Boone suggested casually, but his expression noted a little bit of concern. "Sounds like you need to blow off some steam."

"That sounds like a plan. Let's take the trail that goes past Bess's place so I can be sure Dani made it to the house okay."

"You got it, Mamma Bear." Boone laughed and ducked as Emmett chucked a bottle cap at his head.

"You're such an asshole."

The idiot just shrugged again. "I know."

Chapter Three

Dani held her breath as she drove up the short driveway to her aunt's A-frame home, not knowing what exactly to expect. She was relieved to see the porch light was on. She'd asked the lawyer if her aunt had put in motion detector lights for the outside of the house, but he'd said with all the wildlife in the area, it would be turning on all hours of the night, which made sense, she supposed.

She parked and got out of the car, finding the spare keys exactly where Jeffery had told her they would be. The house itself was actually very cute when she opened the door and turned on the main lights. Sure, it needed some work, but overall, Dani just knew it would be fantastic with some light renos. The main floor was all open, leading back to the large kitchen that seemed to have been the last thing Bess had updated. Dani flipped on the light for the deck and peered out the patio door, impressed with the outdoor space. She imagined her nature-loving aunt spent more time outdoors than inside with a patio like that, not to mention the vast garden that led right to the edge of the thick forest.

She continued the tour. There was a small laundry room off the kitchen that wouldn't need much work, aside from the spackle and paint the whole place needed. The staircase was finished with what appeared to be reclaimed wood and Dani admired it as she wandered upstairs. There was a loft bedroom and an office up the stairs, with an en-suite bathroom that was delightfully spacious. Bess certainly had splurged on the Jacuzzi tub and Dani was practically rubbing her hands together in anticipation of enjoying that while she was here.

Back down on the main level, a cute little half-bath was on the far side of the stairwell, then her focus moved back to the living room. It wasn't bad, but what it was missing was a proper fireplace mantle. She hoped there might be a carpenter in town who would take on the job of making one. All in all, it was pretty darn cute, and when Dani was done with it, this house would be amazing.

She smiled as she walked back out to the car and grabbed her suitcase and the cooler. The rest could wait to be unpacked until tomorrow.

Don't get too attached to this place, girl. It's only a vacation until things go back to normal at home.

She finally got the bed made and fell into it around midnight, her mind already making a list of things she would need to do tomorrow to get started. But the last picture in her mind before sleep took her was of the irritatingly handsome mayor and his cheeky smile.

I have a feeling he's going to be nothing but trouble. Best to avoid him completely while I'm in town ... but you know what they say about best-laid plans.

****

"You know, Bernie, for such a small town, you certainly do have a banging paint selection." Dani winked at the ancient man mixing her choice of paint. She swore he blushed but it was hard to tell with the beard taking up three-quarters of his face.

"Now you behave, Miss Dani." He looked up and winked at her. "My Martha can be a jealous one."

"In your dreams, you old coot!" Martha hollered and then giggled from the other side of the store, making Dani hope that her hearing was half that good if she ever made it to their age.

The couple had been amazing as soon as she stepped into the hardware store, helping her find everything on her list and then some. It turned out that Bess and Martha had been good friends. The older woman had already promised she was going to stop by the next couple days and drop off some dinner, since 'poor Dani would be working so hard all day.' No matter how much Dani insisted it wasn't necessary, Martha wouldn't take no for an answer.

"I'd really love to get a fireplace mantle done for the house. Is there a carpenter or contractor in town who might be interested in doing it?"

"Oh, yes." Martha seemed excited at the prospect. "A mantle would look so nice, now that you mention it. I'll call around and send someone on over to the house this afternoon for you, hon."

"Thanks so much. You two have been wonderful."

"Nonsense, dear, you're practically family, after all." Martha came around to give her a big hug while Bernie hauled the bags out to her car. "If you get lonely out there, just give me a call anytime."

Dani couldn't help the moisture that gathered in her eyes. It'd been a long time since she'd felt welcome somewhere. Almost every single person she'd run into since arriving in town this morning had been ridiculously nice, but then again, she imagined that must be a small-town thing. Next stop was the grocery store.

She was just reaching for the ice cream when the most delicious, low voice came from behind her.

"You know, they say that geniuses choose mint chocolate chip." Emmett smirked as he held up his very own pint that was the same she had her hand on.

"I would have pegged you for a butter pecan man, Mr. Mayor."

He looked surprised for a second, then his charm slipped back into place. "Have you been peeking in my freezer, Miss Holt? That's my number two flavor."

She laughed. "Just a lucky guess, I suppose."

"Have you been over to Pete's confectionary yet? They do happen to have the best milkshakes in town… I could walk you over and introduce you if you'd like." He winked. "You may even get the town council discount if you play your cards right."

Dani was almost tempted. Emmett certainly was a tough man to turn down, but she also knew she had a ton of work waiting for her back at the house—not to mention, ice cream that was getting warmer by the second.

"That's nice of you to offer." She was trying to be quiet now, as the teenaged check-out girl seemed extremely interested in their conversation as she ran through Dani's groceries. "But I've got a long day ahead of me."

Chapter Four

Emmett couldn't believe it. She was shooting him down again? No, 'maybe another time' or 'I can't but I'm free tomorrow.' One thing could certainly be said for Dani—she knew how to check a male's ego. Poor little Katie who was running the cash register, the expression on her face looked like she was wanting to crawl under the counter, probably expecting him to lose his temper. Her mom had brought her here less than a year ago. They'd been fleeing an abusive Alpha and Emmett didn't blame the two females for being slow to trust.

"No problem." He tipped the brim of his ball cap. "Have a great day, Dani."

Was that a flicker of disappointment I saw in her eyes? No worries, sweetheart. I'm not even close to giving up.

Two hours later, Emmett pulled up to Bess's house and ambled up to the front door with a smile. When Martha had called to tell him about some woodwork Dani had asked about, of course, he'd jumped on the opportunity to assist. The way his bear was insistent on spending time with Dani, Emmett was beginning to wonder if the little spitfire *was* actually his mate—human or not. He'd never really considered taking a non-shifter on as a mate before he'd met her, but it seemed fate was determined to make it happen regardless, and to tell the truth, stepping down to let another lead his people seemed a small price to pay for spending the rest of his life with the woman meant just for him.

He could hear the music from outside and he grinned as he knocked, wondering if she'd even hear it over the noise. After waiting a few minutes with no answer, he tried the doorknob and carefully opened the door a crack, not wanting to startle her.

"Hello?" he yelled out. "Dani?"

When she didn't appear, he inched further into the house and he grinned when he finally saw her in the kitchen, back to him, dancing up a storm while singing along to No Doubt's "Just a Girl," while she filled holes in the wall. Dammit if she wasn't the most adorable picture he'd ever seen.

"Dani?" he tried again as he reached over to her iPod dock and turned the music down a bit.

"Ahhh!" She jumped, flinging a large dollop of putty from the knife right into her hair. "Jesus, Emmett! You scared the hell out of me!"

He tried not to laugh at the picture she presented. Hair in a disastrous ponytail with wild pieces flying all over the place … except for the bit now plastered to her forehead by drywall filler. She wore a plain white tank top with a *Star Wars* logo on it and a pair of delightfully short jean cut-offs that showed off her tanned legs to perfection. He tried like hell to not stare at the generous cleavage that teased his animal side—but it was easier said than done.

"Sorry, darlin', I knocked, but I guess you didn't hear me over the music."

"Oh, of course," she answered, looking confused. "Why are you here?"

"Martha called and said you needed some woodwork done?"

Oh, there go those eyes again, narrowing with suspicion. Who knew that would make my dick hard?

And it did. Good thing he was wearing some loose canvas pants today so she wouldn't notice his reaction.

"And let me guess, you're the guy who can build me a mantle for the fireplace?" She crossed her arms, most likely not realizing it only pushed those delectable breasts up further to make his mouth water.

"Guilty as charged." Emmett winked at her and didn't even try to hide his grin.

"Fine, whatever." She sighed, but he could see the slight flush creeping up her cheeks. "I'd like to try and mimic the style of the staircase. Is there anywhere around here that we can find some reclaimed wood?"

He looked toward the stairs, taking in the texture and color of the pale-gray wood, and agreed it would be a fantastic feature piece. His gal had a great eye.

"As a matter of fact, there are some old cabins in the woods that would match up with what you had in mind."

His bear rumbled with happiness when her face lit up with excitement.

"Really? That's awesome. When can we go check them out?"

"I've got some office work to do this afternoon. How does tomorrow sound?" He gave her his most charming smile. "Say around noon?"

Dani might be a tough nut to crack, but the only way he was going to do it was by spending more time with her ... any way he could manage it.

****

"Perfect, I'll see you then." She smiled politely, even though on the inside she was grinning like a smug fool at the look on his face in the wake of her dismissal. His eyes narrowed for a moment and it seemed that he was going to say something, but then he grinned and shook his head.

"See you tomorrow." Emmett turned to walk back out the door and Dani couldn't seem to stop from watching his ass as he went. In all fairness, it was a *really* nice ass.

The rest of the day flew by as she moved and covered up furniture and pulled stuff off the walls, getting ready to prep for new paint. Dani hadn't even realized it was so late until Martha's yoo-hoo reached her ears over the music in the background.

"My, you've been hard at work, my dear!" Martha set down a box that smelled delicious on the kitchen island.

"I have, I just really get in a zone when I'm doing stuff like this. I love it." She edged closer to the food. "Oh, man, that smells amazing!"

"I brought you a casserole and some salad. I don't know if you had a chance to peek in the garden, but there should be plenty of veggies to sustain you while you're here. Jeffery mentioned that you wanted to sell once the renovations are done. Who knows, though. Maybe you'll fall in love with our little slice of paradise and end up staying." Martha winked at her with a beaming smile before she hugged her and went back home to her husband.

Dani had a feeling that Martha was on the recruitment committee, and from the smell of that casserole, the elder woman might just be the perfect person for the job.

Chapter Five

Dani was having a fantastic morning, sitting on the deck with a steaming cup of coffee, listening to the birds enjoying the small pond on the other side of the yard. After working late last night, she'd indulged herself with a luxurious bath and then fell into bed.

She felt her phone vibrate just like it had been all last night, and Dani took a deep breath, knowing that if she didn't answer Andy's call, he'd just keep calling and leaving more pissy messages.

"Why are you calling me, Andy?" Dani tried to keep her tone neutral, but she had a sneaking suspicion she wasn't succeeding.

"Dani, why haven't you been answering my calls?" His winey voice immediately grated on her nerves. "Where are you? You haven't been back to your house in days."

"Jesus, Andy. Have you been watching my house? That's not creepy at all." Dani took another deep breath, trying to keep calm. "We broke up, and I'm sorry that you're having a tough time moving on, but you just aren't the man for me. It's a simple as that."

The quiet on the other side of the phone actually made her even more nervous, because she knew a quiet Andy was much worse than a yelling one.

"Listen, bitch." His tone was scathing. "You're mine because I want you. I don't give a damn what you want. Tell me where you are right now, or you'll be sorry."

Her heart beat a mile a minute and she had to set her coffee cup down before she spilled all over herself.

"Don't call me again, or I'm going to the police,

Andy."

His laugh sent chills down her spine. "Try that, Daniella, and you'll find out right quick who's more important in this town."

She hung up immediately and turned off her phone, hating that she had answered at all. How could she have thought he was such a nice guy? When she'd first met him, he seemed like a normal, charming guy, maybe a bit high-strung, but nothing that had set off any red flags. It wasn't until a few months into dating that he seemed to try to control more and more aspects of her life, and by the time Dani had gotten fed up and broke it off with him, she'd been worried his verbal attacks would turn physical. After weeks of trying to avoid him around town, which was difficult when he and his friends pretty much stalked her every move, Jeffery's call about Bess's house seemed like just the break she needed to get away from the creep. It just proved that you never really knew someone.

Now that her good mood was officially ruined, she sighed and took her coffee back into the house. She may as well get to work.

She was just coming back downstairs, happy to have distracted herself and gotten the bedroom walls painted, when a knock at the door startled her.

Shit, that must be Emmett.

As much as she hated to admit it, Dani was looking forward to seeing him. There was something about him that intrigued her, aside from his handsome face.

"Hi." She smiled as she opened the door and grabbed her keys.

"Hi." His grin was enough to knock any woman off her game, but then it slipped a little as his head tilted and he looked closer at her. "Are you okay?"

Dani didn't want to know how this man, who was practically a stranger, could see that she was still upset from Andy's call, but nonetheless, it warmed her that he would even care enough to inquire.

"I am, just wasn't feeling great this morning." She shrugged it off as she locked up the door behind them.

"Are you sure you want to come? I can go myself and bring the wood back if you'd like to stay and rest?"

"Nope, I'm fine." She could tell he didn't really believe her answer, but he was a smart man and let it go before holding the truck door open for her.

Dani watched him out of the side of her vision as he drove them deeper into the woods. She had to admit there was something about Emmett that seemed to fascinate her—and that just pissed her off. He was a figure of authority and had a presence that felt like it filled up the entire room, and she was barely just out of a dysfunctional relationship with a controlling asshole. It would be extremely stupid to get entangled with another alpha male.

He's not even that charming, is he?

The lie fell flat in her head, but it was all she had at the moment. He turned onto a narrow road that was barely cleared enough for the truck to get down and soon a run-down cabin came into view as he pulled up and parked.

"I'm going to go see what we've got that might work. Why don't you stay put? I think it's going to rain by the looks of those clouds."

"I can help, you know." She rolled her eyes. "I'm no carpenter but I can manage to pull off some old wood."

"Just let me see if there's even anything here that will match what you already have, all right?"

"Okay," Dani relented, but only because he was doing her a favor in the first place. She watched him as he grabbed a few tools from the bed of his truck and walked into the cabin, noting the way his jeans hugged his ass, despite herself. A few minutes later, she got bored and got out of the truck to investigate the surrounding yard. Dani could hear him doing something inside so she popped her head around the corner to see him prying boards out of the corner of the room.

"This stuff looks like it will match great!" She crouched down to get a closer look at the small pile of wood that was forming. "I'll start hauling it out to the truck."

"I can do it in a bit. The wood is pretty rough," he answered back. "I thought you were waiting in the truck?"

"I'm not a pet, Mr. Mayor ... I don't just wait where you put me." She gave him a pointed look before grabbing a piece of wood in each hand and turning to leave.

Dani heard him curse before he was following her. He gently took the wood from her hands and put it into the bed of the pickup, and then he turned grabbed her hands to examine the palms.

"Did you hurt your hands?"

She could see the actual concern on his face and it sent a little thrill through her, not to mention what the feel of his rough, warm hands against her own skin was doing to her.

"I'm fine, really, Emmett."

His gaze met hers and he seemed to realize he was still holding her hands. He let her go and sighed before stepping back.

"If you're going to insist on helping then at least wear some gloves. You've already got a few splinters in your skin. Unless I can convince you to get back into the truck?"

"Nope, I insist." She snatched up the gloves he offered and immediately went back for another load of wood.

"You don't follow directions well, do you?" He chuckled from behind her.

Dani paused for a moment before looking back over her shoulder at him. "Nah, I'm much better at giving them." She was smiling when she continued on toward the cabin, and she could have sworn she heard him mutter, "I'll just bet you are."

Chapter Six

The sky opened up just as they were hauling the last of the wood back to the truck, and in the matter of seconds it took to put a tarp over the contents of the truck bed, they were both soaked through. Emmett tried his best not to stare at the way Dani's white tank top clung to her curves, teasing with a bright-blue lace bra underneath—but he was only a man, and *damn*.

"Is the hardware store still open?" She broke the slightly awkward silence in the cab. "I could use some more putty … if you don't mind stopping."

He quickly checked the time. "I don't mind. We should just make it."

Five minutes later, they pulled up to stop in front of the store. "Let me just run in and grab what you—"

"No need," she interrupted him with an impish smile, "my house, my putty."

Emmett had a hard time pretending not to be amused. This little gal was confounding his bear at every turn. He realized now his instincts were driving him to take care of her, more so it seemed than the rest of his pack, but Dani seemed to have some serious control issues and he wondered what that was all about. What he thought was being polite and gentlemanly, she certainly took in another way.

Her eyes locked onto him as she jumped back into the truck, putty in hand.

"So, Martha tells me she sent my dinner with you?"

He shrugged as he put the truck into gear and headed back to her place.

"I thought perhaps we could eat and then I can

help you with the walls. Looks like you have a fair amount of work on your hands."

Emmett suspected her first instinct was to decline, but by the grace of the Goddess, she nodded slightly instead.

"Okay, thank you. That's really nice of you."

It wasn't the most enthusiastic acceptance to a date he'd ever had—and though she may not know it yet, it *was* a date, but he'd take it.

Emmett was more than happy to let her pick the music as they worked. His belly was full of Martha's fried chicken and Dani's sweet scent filling the room had his other half rumbling with contentment. It was tough to keep his mind and eyes on his work, however, with her bouncing and singing along in those tiny shorts. The humidity after the rain was almost stifling, even with leaving all the doors and windows open. Her dark auburn hair was curling every which way it could escape her ponytail, and there were smears of white putty on pretty much every inch of her body. In all honesty, she was a hot mess. And he fucking loved it.

He grabbed a couple of ice-cold bottles of water out of the cooler and went over to her, quite simply because for the life of him he could no longer stay away.

"Thirsty?" He offered her one of the bottles.

"Thanks." She accepted with a shy smile, and he inched even closer, his bear in full stalk mode.

****

Dani watched the muscles in his neck contract as he took a long drink of water. The more time she spent with Emmett, the more he seemed to weasel his way past her guard. She didn't know if it was the heat or the humidity, but something was definitely getting to her. Her body thrummed with an energy she'd never felt before.

Suddenly, his gaze captured hers and no matter how she tried, Dani couldn't manage to pull herself away from those intense brown eyes. She could feel him moving closer and closer, and something in her responded as she slowly backed up until she felt the cool wall against her shoulders. He groaned when she licked her lips, and then in a sudden move, he lunged, his mouth diving at her own, claiming it in a savage kiss that she was helpless not to return with the passion that surged up inside of her.

"Wait!" Her panting was loud even to her own ears as she struggled to push him away, not because he wouldn't cooperate, but because her own legs refused to unwrap from around his waist and relinquish their prize. "We shouldn't be doing this … we don't even like each other."

"Well now, love." He continued to trail kisses along her collarbone in the most distracting way. "It should be fairly obvious I like you just fine."

He punctuated the statement with a roll of his hips that had his deliciously hard shaft rubbing against her in all the right places.

"In fact, I more than like you, Dani."

"But we fight like cats and dogs…"

He chuckled. She must have missed the joke.

"Nah, that's not right at all."

"Since you've been here, you've mentioned my 'sharp tongue' at least three times." She groaned as his huge hands cupped both her breasts, kneading to perfection.

"That's because I find myself thinking about your sharp tongue all fucking day … I think about you running it all over my body, one spot in particular." He looked up with a cheeky wink.

Dani managed an eye roll, and that had him

pausing for a moment.

"You're a strong woman, Daniella. But I don't want you to think for even one second that I don't like that about you. I fucking *love* that about you. You've been busting my balls since the moment you strolled into town, and it makes me harder than anything ever has."

He moved against her again, causing a whimper of need to escape her throat.

"You are glorious in your ferocity. Don't let *anyone* ever try to tell you different."

The only thing Dani could do was blink at his words. The warmth that bloomed inside her as he stared directly into her eyes was nothing short of life-changing.

Chapter Seven

Emmett finally must have said something right because he saw the moment that she made up her mind to let go and let this fire between them rage as it will. She threaded her fingers through his hair and pulled his head back up to meet her mouth as her legs wrapped tighter around him. He could feel the heat of her sweet folds against his aching cock and his hips moved against her as he explored her mouth with his own.

Goddess, she tastes perfect.

Like honey and sunshine, and his bear wanted to roll around in her scent until it was permanently combined with his own and became a part of him. Her small hands tugged at the bottom of his shirt, and he eased back just long enough for her to pull it over his head and let it drop to the ground.

"Are you sure about this?" he growled out in between kisses.

"No, but right now, my body doesn't care one bit." She drove her point home by biting the side of his neck, causing him to grip the luscious curves of her ass even harder. "Take me upstairs, Emmett."

She didn't have to ask him twice. Emmett lifted her fully and turned to make his way up the stairs while Dani continued to kiss and nibble along his neck and ears. He pried her arms from around his shoulders and laid her down on the edge of the bed before stepping back to take a look at her.

Sweet Goddess, she was glorious. Her lips were swollen and wet from his kisses, and that wild mane of red hair now loose from its binding was spread around her head in a halo of fire. Her breasts heaved as she watched him right back, and the desire coming off her in waves was almost palpable, making any thought aside from satisfying this woman inconceivable.

"Mmm, let me see you," she whispered before she bit her lip, her hands coming up to tease at her breasts.

Emmett couldn't tear his gaze away as he unsnapped his jeans and let them fall to the floor, his cock throbbing with desire as she looked her fill. He wrapped one hand around his aching flesh, using the moisture gathering at the tip to ease the way as he slowly stroked himself, letting Dani see exactly how much he needed her.

"Fuck," she groaned, "that's so sexy. I want you, Emmett."

He watched as she quickly shimmied out of her top and shorts. The evidence of her desire soaking through the bright-blue cloth of her panties broke his control and he pushed her up the bed so that he could settle himself between her splayed thighs.

"Yes," she moaned, her hands gripping his hair as he nuzzled against the wetness before trailing the flat of his tongue along her covered folds.

"You smell so fucking good, Dani," he murmured in between licks until finally he gripped the sides of her panties and ripped them free of the flesh that was taunting him. "I'm going to feast on you until you come all over my tongue."

"Oh, God." Her breathless answer spurned him on as he watched her undo the clasp on her bra and toss the material away, revealing her perfect breasts tipped with rosy little nipples that made his mouth water even more.

"Pinch those nipples while I eat at this juicy little cunt." Emmett ran his thumbs along the now exposed folds of flesh, slick with her honey. "Show me what you like."

****

Dani followed his commands, trailing her hands up to her sensitive breasts. She pinched her nipples between thumb and forefinger, starting off firm, imagining it was Emmett's rough hands on her flesh instead. She gasped as a bite of pain made her realize she was squeezing harder than she'd ever done before, but when a bolt of pleasure followed immediately on its heels, she smiled. Knowing that Emmett would be the kind of lover to push her beyond anything she'd experienced before.

He lowered his head and the tip of his tongue ran circles around her aching clit while he gently pushed two thick fingers into her wet channel, twisting and twirling as he forged in and out. She closed her eyes and imagined how incredible that thick, long cock was going to feel as he worked himself inside of her, gasping as he suckled and licked at her most sensitive flesh.

"Faster, harder, please, Emmett."

He answered her pleas with a groan of his own before he stroked into her at a furious pace, but it was the bite of pain as he sucked hard on her clit that brought her screaming around his fingers. Dani's hands reached out for him, nails digging into his shoulders as the pleasure moved through her in a rush.

She felt him place one last kiss against her swollen flesh before slowly moving up her body, kissing and nibbling as he went, his talented hands caressing every inch of her skin like a prayer. The look in his eyes as he leaned in to kiss her was so intense, it felt like he was staring into her very soul. But despite his raging need, when his lips met hers, it was gentle and soft. The salty tang of her own flavor only heightened her renewing desire, and she wrapped one leg over his thick thigh in an effort to pull him closer to her.

They both groaned when the heat of his rigid shaft slipped through her soaked cleft, and he stroked himself along her flesh several times before slipping a hand down to notch the thick head of his cock against her opening.

"Open your eyes, baby," he whispered, "watch me as I fill you up."

Dani stared up at Emmett, not really understanding what this was that was happening between them. She barely knew him—and yet, something about his body joining to hers felt like … coming home. Even Dani knew that was ridiculous, but just for this one moment, she let the fantasy and whimsy overtake her. For just one moment, she imagined what life would be like if this beautiful man belonged to her, and she, in turn, belonged to him. In those seconds, as he moved inside of her inch by inch, Dani felt as if a bright light was blossoming deep in her chest. As if the very sun itself were rising inside of her soul. As if, after a lifetime of darkness and loneliness, she'd suddenly found her place.

Chapter Eight

Dani gasped as he finally slid all the way home. The warmth of her body rippling around his cock was the most intensely pleasurable sensation Emmett had ever experienced. Not only that, but he was now more than ever convinced this incredible woman was his fated mate. It was simply not possible to feel as connected to her as he felt in this moment, and not have it be a gift sent straight from the Goddess herself.

He began to move inside her, long, slow strokes in and out, never looking away from her beautiful face. Emmett wanted to catalog every single expression of pleasure and longing, and he tried to remember every move that had her gasping for breath or moaning low. He wondered if even a lifetime with this woman would ever be enough. Perhaps, if he spent the remainder of his existence trying to please the Goddess, she might grant him a chance to reunite with his beloved in the next life as well? It was a worthy goal to strive for.

Neither of them spoke as the passion grew more insistent and their bodies strode toward bliss. Faster and harder, they clung to one another, desperate to find their release.

"Emmett!"

Finally, Dani called out to him as her body contracted and tightened around him, sending him tumbling straight into an orgasm after her. The rush of pleasure moved out from his groin to reach every extremity, leaving him blind in the moment of pure ecstasy.

Their breathing was loud and harsh as he fell to the bed on his side, taking her with him in his arms.

Emmett never wanted to let go of this woman, for even a moment.

"Wow," she whispered, still panting, "That was … incredible."

"It was." He gently leaned in to kiss her lips, "*You* are incredible."

He felt her smile against his mouth, and he wondered what he was going to do next. If she were a shifter, she would know immediately how blessed they were to have found one another, but humans were different.

"I'm just going to close my eyes for a minute," Dani whispered, and seconds later, her breathing told him she was already asleep.

He watched her for as long as his own eyes would stay open, imagining their life together, and he prayed to the Goddess that she would help him convince Dani to stay here in Hillion Falls. Emmett simply had to have faith that fate would find a way.

****

Dani woke up with a smile on her face, her body was aching in all the best places, and she felt more at peace than she ever had.

Huh, who knew mind-blowing sex could make you feel like this? Ha! And who knew every man before Emmett had been doing it wrong?

She opened her eyes and noticed the empty spot in the bed next to her. It was disappointment she felt, surprisingly enough. Most mornings after, even in long-term relationships, Dani had always been annoyed to wake up to a man invading her space.

So why am I irritated that Emmett isn't here next to me?

Then she saw the note.

Baby, I woke up early to get a jump on the mantle. You looked so peaceful I didn't want to wake you. I should be back with something for you later this afternoon. I'll bring lunch. XOXO

Dani wasn't usually one for pet names. Andy The Asshole had always called her *doll* when he was trying to distract her from something, and it only pissed her off more. But it was beginning to feel like—aside from his bossy tendencies, Emmett couldn't do much wrong.

She was humming as she grabbed a plain cotton slip dress and threw it on before heading downstairs to start a pot of coffee. Dani opened both patio doors and sighed as the smell of fresh morning dew and sun-drenched forest drifted into the house. It was so incredibly beautiful here, being surrounded by raw, unspoiled nature. Dani understood why her aunt hadn't left often.

Wandering out into the backyard, steaming cup of coffee in hand, she enjoyed the refreshing feel of the soft, damp grass against her bare feet. Someone must have been watering and tending to Bess's vegetable garden since she had passed, as it was green and loaded with delicious things. Dani would have to ask Martha who'd been looking after it so she could thank them.

A small noise drew her attention to the woods to the left of her. It was almost like a whimper, or the cry of a small child. When the sound came again, Dani immediately followed it, hoping the animal was okay. The call had pulled on her heartstrings and she could never leave an animal that was hurt.

After picking her way through the bushes, she came to a small clearing. On the other side of it was a brown ball of fluff, and it cried out again when branches broke beneath her feet.

"Oh no, are you hurt, little one?" she cooed, trying not to startle what she now realized was a bear cub.

The cub stilled when it heard her speak, and then, suddenly all that brown fur seemed to melt down until a small, filthy toddler sat in the very spot the cub had been.

"What the fuck?" she yelled out, startling the small boy just as much as herself as his lip wavered and he began to cry.

She was just stepping forward to reach for him when a huge blur of dark brown came barreling at her from the side, an ear-piercing roar along with it. Dani felt the burn of something sharp along her arm and torso before she hit the ground and everything began to slowly fade.

"Oh poop, what have I done?" A woman's voice sounded far away and faint. "Billy, you'd better run and fetch the Alpha, right away!"

That was all she heard before she slipped into darkness.

Chapter Nine

"How did this happen, Patty?" Emmett tried not to growl as he looked down at Dani lying in his bed, being tended by their healer. The angry, bleeding claw marks running down her shoulder and torso made him see red.

"Ben wandered off on his own and got lost. We were out looking for him when I heard him cry out and my sow just took over. She must have heard and come to investigate the same time I found him." Patty wrung her hands nervously. "You know, sows and their cubs and all that. I didn't mean to hurt her, Alpha."

Emmett sighed and pulled Patty in for a hug to reassure her. "I know, Patty, I just hope Dani's going to be all right."

"Alpha?" Derek, who'd been their pack healer now for ten years, sounded surprised as he looked up from the stitches he was currently placing in Dani's pale skin, "Take a look at this. It looks like the wounds are trying to close."

Emmett released Patty and took a closer look. "How is this possible?"

"Well"—Derek shrugged—"just because Bess wasn't able to turn doesn't mean that Dani doesn't have the ability. Though, without some kind of catalyst to begin the change, even a traumatic injury shouldn't be enough to start it. Did you have any open wounds, Patty? Did she get your blood in her?"

Patti shook her head, and then it dawned on Emmett. He hadn't used protection when they'd been together last night, so it was his semen that would have been the catalyst to cause Dani to begin turning. He breathed a sigh of relief. These kinds of wounds would heal quickly for a shifter, and they wouldn't have to worry about infection or complications. The only thing to worry about now would be how Daniella was going to take the news that she was now going to be much more than human.

****

When Dani woke this time, it was with none of the warm fuzzy feelings she'd had this morning. In fact, her entire body felt like it had been hit by a train. Before she even managed to open her eyes, however, the most incredible scent came to her nose, and it was one that she knew.

Mine.

Whoa. What the ever-living hell was that growly voice in her head? Had she fallen down and knocked something loose up there? Dani cracked open one eye to see she was in a room she'd never seen before. Not only that, but there had to be about ten people in the room with her, none of whom she recognized except for Martha and Emmett, who was standing by the door talking with a tall, blonde woman. The woman reached out and placed her hand on Emmett's chest and something inside Dani just snapped.

Before she even registered what her body was doing, she had leaped out of the bed and grabbed the blonde by the offending wrist. She felt satisfaction when the tips of her claws dug into the soft flesh beneath her grip.

"Mine." She snarled, her teeth only inches away from the other woman's neck, who was now down on her knees. "How dare you touch what's *mine.*"

Besides her own heavy breathing and the slight whimpering from the woman in her clutches who had turned her head away in submission, you could have heard a pin drop in the room.

"Shhh, it's okay, Dani."

She heard Emmett's voice from beside her and turned toward him only to see a fine dusting of brown fur along both her arms. Dani screamed, holding up her hands to see not only the fur but the long dark tips of claws at the ends of her fingers. She felt her ass hit the floor as she scrambled back away from everyone.

"Everyone out." Emmett's voice was firm and had a tone that almost insisted she stand and follow the procession out the door. Then his palm was cupping her cheek and she couldn't help but lean into his touch.

"Hey, I know this must seem insane." His voice was gentle. "But it really is going to be okay."

"What's happening to me?"

"Well, it's a combination of two things that started your transition. First, it was having sex with me, then when you stumbled upon Ben and Patty accidentally attacked you, that put your body into survival mode and it activated the dormant shifter genes that run in your family."

She just stared at him for a few seconds, waiting for the 'just kidding' to follow his explanation, but he simply stared back.

"Are you *kidding* me?" she screamed at him. "You're telling me you gave me some hinky-ass STD, I was attacked by a bear-lady … and now *I* change into an animal?"

Emmett's lip quirked up at the corner, and so help her God, if he laughed, she was going to punch him right in the balls. Apparently, her expression said it all because he cleared his throat and continued.

"First off, it's not an STD. If you hadn't had dormant shifter genes, then sleeping with me wouldn't have made a difference. But lucky for you, you did. I don't want to scare you any more than you already are, Dani, but you were mauled by a female grizzly bear protecting her cub." He finally sat down on the floor beside her. "With the wounds you had, and the blood loss? Let's say a regular human most likely would have died."

"I think I'm freaking out." She looked up into his soft brown eyes and hoped this was all in her imagination. "This has to be a dream. Emmett, tell me I'm just sleeping right now."

"I'm afraid not, baby." He stood and picked her up, gently placing her back in bed. "But I'll be right here to help you get through this."

When he let go to sit further down the bed, she grabbed his hand, almost desperate for contact with him. "Will you just please hold me for a little while? I feel … calmer when I'm touching you for some reason."

Chapter Ten

Emmett debated telling her anything further just right that moment, but what would be worse: telling a scared woman she'd inadvertently joined herself to him for life while her shift was unstable? Or telling a woman that had *control* over her shift into a huge, dangerous predator, that you may have omitted the fact that for all intents and purposes, they were now married?

Nah, with how many members of the pack that were present when she claimed him out loud, there was no way they'd be able to keep that quiet.

"About that…"

Dani had snuggled into his arms, and Emmett tensed, hoping her reaction wouldn't be too bad as she looked up at him.

"About *what*?" Her eyes narrowed in suspicion.

"Why you feel comforted by my touch and my presence. You'll also heal faster with me here, because, well … I'm your mate, and you are mine."

Dani's eyes went wide with surprise as that information sank in. Then he felt the ripple of muscles under her skin and he released her just in time to watch her first full shift into a lovely grizzly sow with dark auburn fur. A loud yip sounded from her as she realized she was no longer bipedal and just as suddenly, the pale softness of her skin came flowing back until she was a panting, naked heap in the middle of the bed.

Emmett's heart ached to see the tears that trailed from the corners of her eyes and he gathered her close once again, kissing her head as he gently rocked her back and forth as she grieved for the world she thought she knew. He hoped she realized, from now on, she'd never be alone in anything, ever again. Dani would have him and an entire community to support her for the rest of her life.

"How is this even possible?" Dani looked at her hands like she was searching for any clue that there were now deadly claws hiding just under the surface.

"Love, it's in your genetics," Emmett softly explained. "Your mother's family were shifters. That's why Bess lived here with us."

"Oh, my God, Aunt Bess was a bear too?" she screeched.

"No, Bess's shifter gene was dormant. So she could never change. But her husband was one of my pack and a wolf shifter."

She just sat there staring for a moment.

"My grandmother," she finally whispered. "She always swore my mother's family had the devil in them. That's why she kept me from my aunt after my parents died. Do you think she knew?"

"I doubt it, but some full humans naturally can sense the predator in us, and it makes them uncomfortable. It's one of the reasons we tend to live in isolation."

"This just can't be happening."

"It is happening, baby, and once it has time to sink in, I swear you're going to love it."

She looked at him like he'd grown another head. "Love it?" she choked out. "Why would I love turning into an animal?"

"Dani, your sow has always been inside of you. She's been a part of you from birth," he explained. "With your change triggered, you will be stronger. You'll finally be whole and exactly who you were meant to be."

"Just close your eyes and sleep for a bit, love." He pulled the blankets up over them both and lay back.

"That was really fast for a first shift, and your body needs time to re-settle."

Emmett was still contently watching her rest when the bedroom door cracked open and Boone popped his head in. "Everything okay in here, Boss?"

"Yes." Emmett gently removed himself from her grip and joined him in the hall. "She's just sleeping off her first full shift. What's up?"

Boone's eyes went wide. "She did a full shift already? Damn."

"Her mother's line is very strong." Emmett could tell from his friend's body language that something was up. "Now tell me."

"They got an alert at the cop shop on Dani's name. Someone's looking for her … and he isn't being too subtle about it."

"Is it a warrant?"

"Nope, that's what raises the red flags. All it says is that she's a person of interest and to notify Dawson PD if she's spotted, but not to engage."

Emmett couldn't stop the growl from his chest at the idea that someone was looking for his mate. Jeffery had mentioned in passing that he'd gotten the impression one of the reasons she'd been so keen to come and do the renos herself was that she was looking to get away from something—or someone, perhaps?

"Notify the pack. If anyone we don't know sets foot in town, I want to know about it."

"Yes, Alpha." Boone nodded before he paused and added, "Also, Keith may have gotten himself arrested in Cutler."

Shit. "For Goddess's sake, again?" Emmett ran his fingers through his hair in frustration.

"I tried to speak to the Alpha to get him released, but you know that ornery son of a bitch. He won't do anything until *you* go see him in person."

It was an hour drive there and back to get to Cutler, and Emmett really didn't want to leave Dani at the moment, but since Keith lost his brother in an accident a few months ago, the wolf had been getting into all sorts of trouble. Emmett worried that he'd eventually pick a fight he couldn't win. His pack member needed him.

"I want someone with Dani at all times. Make sure she has anything she needs." With luck, Dani would still be sleeping off her first shift by the time he got back, a sad wolf in tow.

Chapter Eleven

Dani woke with a stretch and this time, she felt pretty good.

Pretty good? Damn, I can't remember the last time I've felt this amazing.

And then her brain caught up with her body and she sighed.

"This trip has really gone down the rabbit hole," she mumbled, pulling the covers higher until high-pitched giggles sounded out from across the room.

"Now, you boys be quiet and let our Alpha sleep," a matronly voice whispered right after, but it was too late. Whatever this new entity was inside her seemed to be the curious sort, because she couldn't resist cracking one eye open. The huge brown eyes and adorable mussed mops of brown curls were peering from the edge of the bed, but from the tops of their heads, she could tell the boys were about four or five years old.

"Boo!" She popped up from the blankets, smiling, and a riot of giggles and baby squeals followed, making her laugh in return.

"Oh! Alpha, you're awake."

Dani recognized the woman's voice as the same one who she stumbled into in the clearing that started all this mess. The poor woman looked incredibly nervous and meek—which seemed odd for a woman who could change into a giant bear.

"Patty?"

"Yes, Alpha," she replied and came closer. "Is there anything I can get for you? I'm so very sorry about what happened."

Dani looked at the small children who were now

staring up at her with possible adoration, and she may not have babies of her own, but of course, she could understand the instincts Patty had been dealing with.

"It's okay, I know it was an accident." She took a brief peek under the covers and cringed. "Could you get me something to wear?"

"Of course." Patty smiled and seemed relieved to have something to do. "Boys, you stay right here and don't cause a fuss, I'll be right back."

They just stared at her, shy smiles on their faces, until their mother returned with an armful of clothes.

"Where's Emmett?" Dani asked once she was dressed.

"The Alpha had to go into Cutler to take care of one of our pack, he should be back in a few hours. We were given instructions to make sure you have everything you need while he is away. Your wounds have all healed. Your bear is exceptionally strong."

"Honestly, Patty, what I really need is some alone time. Can someone give me a ride back to my place?"

"You want to leave?" The crestfallen look on Patty's face hit her harder than it should have, but for some weird reason, it pained Dani to have her upset. Before she realized she'd even moved, she had pulled the relative stranger into a hug.

"I just need some space to collect my thoughts. This has been a lot to take in is all, Patty." Dani stepped back, nodding in satisfaction as the other woman seemed to have calmed.

"Of course, it has, forgive me Alpha—"

Why did she keep calling her that? Deep inside, something rumbled that it was appropriate, but Dani was getting a sneaking suspicion that there was more to the job of being Emmett's 'mate' than anyone had told her as of yet … and it was just one more thing that was beginning to freak her out.

"Dani," she interrupted, "you can just call me Dani."

"Oh." Patty paused. "Okay, Dani. I will ask Boone to escort you to Bess's house."

An hour later, she had half of the living room painted in a soft warm taupe but Dani just couldn't concentrate for a second more. It had taken quite a while to convince Boone to drop her off and leave. He said she shouldn't be alone this early after her transition, but when Dani lost her temper and outright told him to leave, he seemed to be unable to argue with her and left mumbling something about stubborn females and Emmett dealing with her when he got back.

Something inside of her felt like it was trying to take over, telling her to go back to Patty and the children, back to the house where her mate would soon return. It was like having a complete stranger trying to take over her brain, and Dani didn't like it one bit. She needed space to absorb all of this, and the only place she could think to go was home.

So, she did. Dani hopped into the car and headed back to Dawson, where hopefully things would be normal.

****

"This is you looking after your new Alpha female?" Emmett growled at Boone as they sped down the highway. He was pissed as hell that he'd been gone for four hours and his pack had managed to lose his brand-new mate.

"She ordered me to go! Your mate is really stubborn … and sneaky … and *hot*."

"Watch it…" Emmett was fairly certain she was headed home from the direction she left town, according to Bob, who ran the only gas station in town, but he was concerned that she was heading back into a populated city so soon after her first shift. Any threat or surprise could have her bear making an abrupt appearance, and Goddess only knew how much trouble could follow if that happened and she was all alone. The two-day trip to Dawson was going to be torture not knowing if she was okay. At least with both him and Boone taking turns driving, they would catch up on the head start she had on them. His stubborn mate refused to answer any of his calls and his bear was telling him that Dani needed them.

Chapter Twelve

Dani was exhausted by the time she arrived back in Dawson—so tired that she almost didn't notice the cop car that started following when she stopped for gas just outside of town. A few butterflies tumbled around in her stomach as Andy had been having his buddies in the police force keeping tabs on her before she'd left town. But when it veered off in the opposite direction once she got halfway home, she decided it was just a coincidence and kept driving before she fell asleep at the wheel.

She was already missing Emmett, and that just made her grumpy. She'd never been the clingy type before … in fact, most of her previous boyfriends complained about her being too aloof and not paying them enough attention.

Barf. What a bunch of sissies they had been—not like my Emmett. Dammit, Dani!

This new voice inside of her head was really getting bent out of shape that Dani had gone anywhere without their mate at all, that she could feel quite clearly. She was also not enjoying how noisy and crowded Dawson seemed to be after spending time in Hillion Falls. Dani begrudgingly agreed with the fuzz-bucket on that score. Being back in the city felt like a million attacks on her senses, constantly surrounding her, and it almost made her claustrophobic.

So many changes were happening, whether she wanted them to or not, and all Dani craved was to crawl into her own bed in her own home and try to ignore the lot of it. At least until she could make some decisions on her own terms … preferably while in her 'thinking' pajamas and eating ice cream on her couch. After all, that was how important decisions were supposed to be made.

Tomorrow. Tomorrow, I'll figure all of this freaky shit out like a champ.

Her cool sheets felt like heaven against her bare skin as Dani slid into bed. One loud sigh and a fleeting picture of Emmett's face went through her mind until it was soon overtaken in some long overdue sleep.

She had no idea how long she'd been sleeping for, but it was long enough to scare the bejesus out of her when the bedroom door slammed open against her wall with a crash. Dani was awake and enraged in an instant, and before she could even realize what was happening, fur flowed over her entire body as it grew and grew into her grizzly form, the bed creaking under her increased weight.

Instincts had her on the intruder in seconds. A loud bang sounded and she felt something burn across her shoulder, making her roar out in pain. A high-pitched screaming noise was now hurting her sensitive ears and she swiped one massive paw in the direction it was coming from to try to get it to stop. A grunt was followed by sobbing immediately after that, and then finally she looked down to see who was in her house.

Huh. Why is Andy sitting on my bedroom floor, crying like a little girl?

Dani heard another roar from downstairs, and as much as she wanted to seek out the person it belonged to, it irked her to have Andy in her bedroom. She didn't want him here.

We told him not to come back. We told him we didn't want him. He's weak. Make him stop making those noises.

Dani agreed with the voice wholeheartedly. Things seemed much simpler in this form. Didn't want this asshole here? *Make* him go away. Easy peasy.

Just as Dani's furry arm was raised up once again to get rid of the pest that was her ex-boyfriend, a giant bear ran into the room and bellowed at her.

She knew it was Emmett, even without Boone poking his head around the corner and swearing when he saw what was happening. Just like that, the other half of her receded and she was suddenly standing there, very naked in her room. With a sobbing ex-douchebag, a giant grizzly bear, and another man she barely knew, all staring at her.

"Kinda rude to just barge into my house, don't you think?" She scrambled for her robe as Emmett turned back into his delicious two-legged alter-ego, but then Andy's muttering drew her attention and she felt her rage increasing all over again. It was like a living thing building up inside of her.

"And *you*," she yelled at Andy, "why the fuck are you in my house, you sniveling waste of skin? Not so tough now, are you? It must suck getting beat down by a woman, huh?"

"I heard a gunshot and then you roared!" Emmett grabbed the gun that had been sitting beside Andy, who was now rocking back and forth, mumbling about bears and boobies. "What the hell is going on? Who is this guy?"

Dani shrugged and looked back down at the man she'd actually grown to fear before she'd left town. Apparently, he was more bark than bite. "This is Andy, my asshole ex."

****

Emmett was barely able to think, he was so enraged. When they'd pulled up into the driveway and heard a gunshot, he'd imagined the worst. Lucky they had arrived when they did, as it looked like Dani's bear had had enough of the pathetic male sitting sobbing on the ground. He was certain she would have killed him if they hadn't interrupted, even though it would have been due to her new instincts. When she'd changed back and the adrenaline had worn off, Emmett was certain that would have scarred Dani emotionally.

He could smell the scent of blood coming from her and he pulled her further away from the male, pushing the neck of her robe aside to reveal a bleeding gouge from a bullet.

"He shot you!" The growl that came from him had Andy's cries turn frantic.

"He … did." She looked shocked as that sank in and her anger from before seemed to slip away as she sat on the edge of the bed while Emmett looked in the en-suite bathroom for a first aid kit.

"I called the cops. They're on their way." Boone frowned, looking at Andy. "Should I tie him up or something? At least we don't have to worry about the cops believing his story over yours. The guy has completely lost his mind."

The sounds of sirens getting closer must have had reality slamming into Dani. Her breathing started to increase as Emmett held a compress against her wound to stop the bleeding.

"Boone, go grab my clothes, would you? And then wait for the cops." Emmett stroked Dani's face with his other hand. "Baby, just breathe. All you have to do is tell them what happened … without the bear stuff, of course, and they'll take him away for good."

"I can do that." She nodded up at him, but her hands dug into his arms as if she was scared he would leave.

"Bears … naked bears," Andy muttered. "I had sex with a bear…"

"Shut up!" Emmett hissed in the rocking man's

direction. "Or we'll finish what we started."

That made the sobbing come back, but at least he wasn't babbling about naked bears anymore.

Boone threw his clothes at him and Emmett quickly dressed before he heard the footsteps down the hall. Two officers came into the room, weapons drawn, with Boone close on their heels.

"The gun he tried to shoot my fiancée with is on top of the dresser, officers." Emmett didn't move from Dani's side. "I only touched the butt when I came in and saw it on the floor. Did you call the ambulance as well?"

"Paramedics are on their way. What happened here?" The female officer took in the scene with a much calmer eye than her male partner.

"Jesus, Andy! What the hell did you do?" The other officer, who obviously knew Dani's ex, knelt down in front of him, trying to get him to talk to them.

"I woke up when the door slammed against the wall. He must have broken in when he found out I was back in town. Before I even realized it was Andy, he came in and shot at me." Dani's voice was quiet. "I honestly thought he'd be over our breakup by now. After the gun went off, he kind of just crumpled and started talking gibberish."

"Boobies and bears!" the man in question yelled out, his eyes wildly looking around the room.

Well, the asshole got his timing just perfect—at least the timing was perfect to convince the cops he'd had a psychotic break and tried to kill the woman who'd left him for another man, and that was all that Emmett could ask for.

Chapter Thirteen

By the time the paramedics arrived, Dani's wound had started healing, looking more like a scratch than a graze. They'd wanted to take her to the hospital, but Dani fought until they relented and bandaged her up with instructions to go see her regular doctor if she had any problems. They filed out behind the cops dragging a nonsensical Andy between them and Dani waited until she heard the cars pull away before she turned back to Emmett.

"Why did you tell them I was your fiancée?"

"*That's* what's bothering you in all of this?"

The words were out of Boone's mouth with a laugh before Emmett could answer her question, and she threw a glare at him, hoping he would mind his own business. These shifters were a nosy bunch; there was no doubt about that.

Her eye daggers must have been epic because he quickly threw his hands up in surrender and winked before opening his mouth again. "I'm going to run out and get some food for us. I'm starving."

"Thanks, Boone." Emmett waited until the other man left before he pulled Dani over to the couch and onto his lap. "I told them that because it makes more sense that your ex would be in a jealous rage to find out you'd moved on. And … because we *are* mates, you know."

"I know what you've told me, but, Emmett, you saw Andy. I had to leave town to get rid of one insane, controlling man. I'm not interested in being with another one."

Dani was surprised at the expression of

confusion, and then the hurt she saw on his face as he took in her words.

"You think I'm controlling? That I'm like that *asshole*?"

"No, I know you're not like Andy." She quickly tried to explain what she was feeling, "But you have to admit that you're used to being in control ... of pretty much everything."

"I'm Alpha, that's my job." He shrugged. "That's what my people need from me. That's what they would need from you as well."

That made her stop in her tracks. "What?"

"As my mate, you're Alpha female of the pack, Dani." He cupped her cheek so that he could look into her eyes. "I'm hoping that you will come home with me and stand by my side, be my equal. We can make our choices together, Daniella. That's what I want from you. And if you think I'm being too bossy, or overbearing, I'm one hundred percent certain that your sow will let me know it, one way or another."

That made her smile, despite herself, but it also reminded her of what could have happened if Emmett and Boone hadn't arrived when they did and her smile crumbled under the grim knowledge.

"I think I would have done something horrible to Andy if you hadn't stopped me, Emmett." Her eyes closed as she whispered the words and confessed her fear, and she felt Emmett's arms tighten around her in comfort.

"It wasn't your fault, Dani. Startling and attacking a shifter like that would have any of us defending ourselves, but the two halves of your soul are still finding a balance. You have remarkable control for someone who's only shifted twice so far. Instincts were responsible for your reactions, and *Andy* would have been the one responsible if anything else had happened. This is why new shifters don't usually leave the safety of the pack until they've been mentored and are in complete control."

Her nose scrunched up as she realized what a mess she'd made of things.

"I'm sorry. I was just freaking out and thought a little space would calm me down."

"Do you feel calmer here?" he asked, his hands moving in soothing strokes along her arms and back.

"I feel calmer"—she exhaled a big breath and looked up into his eyes—"now that you're here."

It was the truth. Now that she was in Emmett's arms, she felt safer than she ever had, but she also felt strong.

"Me too," was his perfect response as he seemed content to simply sit and hold her.

****

The sun was starting to lighten the sky as Boone arrived back at the house, his arms filled with grocery bags. Emmett could tell that Dani was exhausted now that the adrenaline had worn off. She could barely keep her eyes open.

"Do you have a guest room we can stay in? he asked as he stood, still cradling her in his arms. "Neither one of us will get any rest with Andy's scent in your room."

"Yeah, up the stairs on the left," she murmured, burrowing closer to him.

Emmett locked eyes with his enforcer. "You have the first watch. We're going to get some rest. Tomorrow we'll have to figure out where to go from here."

He found the guest room and laid Dani on the bed before peeling her out of the robe and pulling the covers over her. She reached for him when he released her.

"Stay," she whispered.

"I am, love, I'm just getting naked." He stifled a grin as those words had her cracking open one eyelid so she could watch.

"Good, I *like* you naked." She waggled her eyebrows and it made him laugh. Even dead-tired and with all that had happened, Dani's vibrancy couldn't be denied. He silently thanked the Goddess for sending him such a treasure.

Emmett's body reacted to the proximity of his mate as she watched him, even though he intended for them only to rest. He slid under the covers next to Dani and pulled her back until she was flush up against him, the warm skin of her back against his chest. They both sighed as the comfort of being safe with their mate soothed the stress of the night away and sleep soon overtook them.

When he woke hours later, it was to the sensation of incredible, wet warmth closing over the head of his quickly hardening shaft. He groaned out his mate's name as she slid further down to take the length of him inside of her mouth, his fingers tangling through her soft hair.

She released him and slid up his body, the hard tips of her nipples teasing his skin until her lips finally met his own. Emmett's hands came up to help her settle as she straddled his hips. The feel of her slick sex gliding along his cock was a perfect kind of torture. He pulled her down more firmly, making sure to catch her swollen clit on each movement until Dani pulled her mouth away with a growl.

"No more teasing. I need you." She snarled before sitting up enough to wrap one hand around his length and fitting the tip against her opening.

"Take what you need, love," he groaned as she slowly sank down, taking him in to the hilt. "It's all yours … only yours."

Chapter Fourteen

Something in those words made everything snap into place for Dani. This man inside of her right now, he *was* hers. Just as she belonged to him and no other. She could feel the animal inside of her convey its relief that she finally understood. Their place was beside Emmett, now and forever.

Dani slowly began to move atop him, lifting up until she almost released him, then slowly coming down once again. All the while her hands caressed every inch of skin she could reach, she wanted to learn her new mate and every touch and stroke that drove him wild.

"Fuck, Dani, babe." Emmett's fingers tightened on her hips. "You're killing me here. You feel so good around me. But I need you to move faster."

She dropped down on him hard, kissing him before whispering in his ear, "You do it. Take me like you want me, Emmett."

Dani didn't have to ask him twice. Before she could even blink, he had her on her back, his lean hips still in between her thighs, cock buried deep inside of her. He thrust into her powerfully, every lunge hitting her aching clit, pushing her one step closer to the bliss she was looking for.

"Yes, harder." Dani felt her nails digging into the skin of his back. She wanted everything this man could give her.

"Goddess, Dani, I can feel your pussy pulling me in." Emmett's voice was a low growl now, and he hooked her knees over his arms so that she was completely open to him. "I can't wait to feel you come all over my cock. To feel that sweet heat milking every single drop of cum from my body."

"Yes, Emmett! Oh, God, I'm coming!" Dani didn't know why those particular words pushed her over the edge into orgasm, but who cared about the why when the reward was sheer bliss running through every single muscle in her body.

"Dani!" Emmett thrust in deep as he reached his own release. She felt his lips against her neck and shoulder. The sharp pain of his bite quickly turned into something else, and it was as if a shockwave started all over again in her clit and worked its way outward until she felt it out to her fingertips.

Her hands idly stroked up and down the length of his back as they both tried to catch their breath. Dani knew without a shadow of a doubt at that moment that she was done here in Dawson. All she wanted was to go back to Hillion Falls with this man and start an entirely new chapter of her life.

Emmett's stomach chose that moment to make its plight known, causing her to giggle as she felt him slip from her body.

"Time for breakfast, baby." He dropped a quick kiss against her lips before getting up and tossing her robe toward her. "Boone is probably waiting to get some sleep … but if we ask really nice, he might just make us one of his famous omelets."

"Mmm, get me an omelet and this might just be the best morning ever." Her own tummy joined in when she thought about oozing cheese and crisp, salty bacon.

Before they left the room, Emmett tugged aside the neck of her robe to check on his bite mark and Dani shivered when he gently kissed the spot.

"My mark looks so fucking hot on you," he whispered, his hands gripping her ass and pulling her to him so she could feel him hardening against her.

"Do I get to mark you too?" She arched one eyebrow at him before she leaned in closer to nibble on his earlobe.

"Fuck," he hissed out when she lightly bit down. "I fucking hope so."

****

Emmett's dick was still rock-hard as he watched his mate moan over another man's fluffy eggs. Dani liked to tease, he could tell, but in the end, he knew they'd both always get what they needed, so who was he to argue?

"So, after my nap, should I go grab some boxes and a U-Haul and get started on packing you up, Dani?" Boone was just finishing up the last of the dishes and his question clearly caught Dani off guard, as she stopped with her fork halfway to her mouth.

Emmett held his breath to see what she would say.

"Thanks, Boone, that would be great." She shrugged. "I have some boxes in the garage. We can start while you rest."

He must have had a goofy grin on his face because when she looked back at him, she rolled her eyes and threw a piece of sausage at him.

"Sheesh, I may be a bit slow on the uptake, but I get it now." She laughed at him when he shrugged back and popped the sausage into his mouth. "Besides, have you guys noticed how loud and crowded it is around here? There are people, like … *everywhere*."

Boone burst into laughter and Emmett couldn't help but join in.

"That's your bear, love," he explained, taking her hand and turning it over to place a soft kiss in her palm. "Bears like their solitude, but other shifters like wolves are much more social. Still, with our enhanced senses, city life can get overwhelming. Most shifter groups you'll find in isolated areas. It makes it much safer for us to let loose our other sides as well.

"Oh, that makes sense."

"And on that note, I'm taking my social ass to get some sleep." Boone surprised her by leaning down to place a chaste kiss on Dani's lips. "Welcome, Alpha."

She looked back to Emmett. "Umm, is that normal?"

"It wasn't sexual." He shrugged before standing and offering her his hand. "Most shifters crave touch and contact for comfort, especially from those pack members who are higher up in the hierarchy than they are. It shows their submission and reassures them at the same time."

"I see, and what if it *was* sexual? Hypothetically, that is."

He laughed and gave her a wink. "Well, your bear would have taken care of it pretty swiftly ... then mine most likely would have taken issue with whatever bits were left over after you were done with him."

Emmett pulled her into his arms and kissed her, loving the feel of her surrender under his touch.

"Now are you ready to get your old life packed up so we can go home?"

"I am ... Sir." The teasing light in her eyes didn't stop his body from reacting to certain scenarios his brain conjured up at her calling him that, but at least Emmett knew that his life would never be boring with this woman in it.

Chapter Fifteen

Dani looked around at the faces that surrounded them and smiled as Patty and Martha wiped the happy tears from their eyes as Jeffery wrapped up their bonding ceremony. She had been back in Hillion Falls for two months now, and no place had ever felt so much like home to her. There were children playing and laughing all around them and for the first time in her life, she looked forward to holding her own little boy or girl, one that hopefully looked just like their daddy. All that was left now was to get to making that baby…

"Are you ready to go for a run, love?" Emmett drew her attention back as he squeezed her hands in his own.

"I am," she answered, moving her hands up his bare arms and shoulders, loving the soothing heat of his skin under her fingertips. This would be her first run with the pack as officially their Alpha female, and after two months of shifting to her bear, nudity around her pack members wasn't even a blip on her radar anymore. Dani enjoyed how Emmett's muscles tensed as she trailed fingers down his chest and then stomach to loosen the pants he was wearing until they dropped to the ground, leaving him clad only in his gloriously bronzed skin.

He, in turn, slipped his hands up the V of her silk robe and gently pushed the material from her shoulders until it slid down her skin, sending shivers of awareness through her entire body. The rest of the crowd followed suit and began to shift and lope off into the forest around them.

Emmett wrapped his arms around her in a warm hug and kissed her.

"I can't wait to get inside of you, my love," he whispered before nipping the side of her neck. "And then I can't wait to spend the rest of my life with you."

"You've got to catch me first." She kissed him quickly and stepped back, shifting into her other form before she ran off into the trees, but not before she heard him answer back.

"Always."

The End

DENYING THE ALPHA

EVERNIGHT PUBLISHING ®

www.evernightpublishing.com

47726934R00328

Made in the USA
Lexington, KY
11 August 2019